Countermeasure

LINDSAY MCKENNA

Blue Turtle Publishing

Countermeasure
First edition 2024
Original Copyright © 2015, R. Eileen Nauman
ISBN Print Edition: 978-1-951236-57-1

This is a work of fiction. Names, characters, places, and incidents are either the product of the author's imagination or are used fictitiously, and any resemblance to actual persons, living or dead, business establishments, events or locales is entirely coincidental.

This edition is published by arrangement with Blue Turtle Publishing Company.

Dear Readers,

Welcome to Jessica Courtland's world. Jessica was chosen to lead a Navy Seabee well-drilling team in a small valley in Afghanistan after a Taliban raid killed her boss. Two Navy SEALs, snipers, were sent to help keep the Taliban from attacking them again with the intent of wiping out the Seabee's unit. Logan Randall, a SEAL with ten years of warfighting in Afghanistan, doesn't expect to see a woman directing the well-drilling team. Logan doesn't expect to fall deeply for Jessica. And, nor does she. They can't reveal how they feel about one another to anyone under these dangerous circumstances.

It was up to this team to dig five wells to help the people in villages that sit on a scrub brush desert floor below the mighty Hindu Kush mountains. The Seabees are not a fighting force but a force for good between people of different countries and languages. As a peaceful mission and forging goodwill, they never expected to be seen as the hated enemy and had an honorable record of being the good neighbor next door. Afghan farmers were dying of disease because they had no fresh water supply. Without a good water source, their crops would fail, and children would die.

In a bold move, the Taliban want to capture the only woman on their team. The leader has been paid a million dollars to capture her and then take her over the border to Pakistan. Some warlords want to buy her and parade her, an American military woman, across videos of her capture and later, behead her while broadcasting it around the world. Logan finds Jessica gone one dawn morning and captured by a local Taliban group. He's ordered to locate Jessica and return her to the American side. It's more than the orders that drive Logan to find her—he's fallen deeply in love with Jessica. Can he find her? Will she still be alive? Nothing is more important to him than finding her and bringing her home.

Warmly,
Lindsay McKenna aka Eileen Nauman

Dedication

To all the readers who love romantic military suspense!

CHAPTER 1

September 2020, Germany

JESSICA COURTLAND SWALLOWED hard. She couldn't cry. She didn't dare. Sitting in the empty surgery lounge at Landstuhl Medical Center in Germany was the last place she thought she'd ever be. Jess slowly rubbed her dirty face with hands that, until a few hours ago, had been covered with blood. The blood of Navy Chief Dan Callahan, her boss. She wanted to forget what had happened, but the firefight between the Taliban and the Seabee crew, paired with the A-Team of Special Forces, raged behind her tightly shut, green eyes. Tears leaked out anyway.

She felt the grit of the fine sand of Afghanistan still on her face, clinging there because of the sweat from the terror and adrenaline rush she'd gone through as she'd tightened a tourniquet on Dan's left thigh. A Taliban bullet had found him, cracking his femur, cutting the main artery, blood spurting out in an almost hypnotic rhythm from the open fracture. Jess had been closest, firing her M4 rifle at the horsemen charging like wild men toward their position near that village on the slopes of the Hindu Kush Mountains. They'd been there two days, bringing in a well-drilling truck and other necessary equipment via crane helicopters, all to provide the suspectedly pro-Taliban village with fresh water. Their only source of water was dirty, full of worms and other parasites. It killed babies, young children and the elderly.

She was sitting on a green plastic couch in the small surgery's lobby area. Outside, she could hear nurses talking in low voices at their nearby desk. Was Dan going to make it? She'd sat, numb and in a daze, on that C-17 medical jet that had taken off from Bagram Army – Air Base and flown them to Landstuhl. It was the place badly wounded, or dying, military personnel were taken for the most advanced medical treatment available in this part of the world. Jess was grateful to have been able to accompany Dan, who'd been unconscious all the way in. She felt fiercely that he shouldn't be alone. Not through this.

Her hands draped tiredly across her thighs. *Three hours.* For three hours they'd been in surgery with Dan. On board the specially modified C-17, Dan had been one of eight wounded men and women on their way to the American hospital in Germany. The physician on board, a woman doctor, had sat with Jess at one time, giving her an update on Dan's status. She'd said it didn't look good. Jess had felt her eyes burn with tears but had gulped them back down. She'd hoarsely thanked the doctor, leaning back against the bulkhead in her nylon seat, uncomfortable physically and hurting emotionally.

Jess sat up, bringing herself back to the present, realizing she had to get cleaned up. There was blood on her desert-colored blouse and cammie trousers. The coppery smell made her nauseous. It struck her all over again that it was Dan's blood: His life that had been spilling out onto the sands of Afghanistan. Her black hair had come undone from its ponytail, and was dirty and dusty, laying limply around her shoulders. Torn, Jess didn't want to leave the lounge. It was as close as she could get to the operating theater where Dan had been taken. It was crazy, but she felt if she left, he'd die. He *had* to live. She prayed so hard for just that one thing. He had a wife and three beautiful children. Dan had been attached to the Port Hueneme Naval Mobile Construction Battalion with her for five years. They'd dug wells in Iraq and now, Afghanistan, helping improve people's lives. This hurt so much. She worried about Dan's wife, Sophie. They had been married when they were eighteen and he was now thirty-five. *Oh, God....* Jess knew Sophie had been told that Dan had been wounded. She was waiting at home, not knowing, either...

Jess was so internalized over Dan and Sophie that she almost failed to realize someone had silently entered the surgery lounge. It wasn't a noise that alerted her. She'd been in the Navy Seabees since she was eighteen and, over the decade since then, had developed a strong survival intuition. And it red-flagged her, even though she had tipped her head back against the wall, eyes closed. Sitting up, she opened them and saw a tall, lean Navy SEAL walk past her. She saw the hard look on his square face with its three-day growth of beard. His hair was dark brown, longish, his cammies also bloodstained, dirty, and his boots, the same. He wore a drop holster, holding what Jess was sure was the signature SEAL Sig Sauer P226 pistol, riding low on his right thigh. There was nothing weak about this man, his hands covered with dried blood and, like hers, mud. He sat down opposite her, never meeting her eyes.

Her heart tugged as he wearily slumped into the seat, his long-fingered hands slowly rubbing his dirty face. He'd just come out of combat, no question. They shared bloodied uniforms. Jess didn't have the emotional resilience to say even a simple greeting to him, much less start up a conversation. The SEAL looked as internalized as she felt. Neither of them had any strength left within them to push into the outside world now and be social. Grief made everyone withdraw deeply into themselves. Shock was funny, Jess thought sluggishly, having gone now forty-eight hours without sleep, only reacting, not even thinking once to clean her hands and face. It numbed her out emotionally, made her feel like a robot. But she knew there was a deep well of emotions writhing like a tempest, somewhere yet unrevealed within her. She could feel it in her knotted stomach that ached with a phantom pain all its own. Her eyes would burn from time to time, and she'd force the tears back that wanted to fall. But even though she didn't know this SEAL, his presence still gave her a sense of camaraderie, if nothing else.

Logan Randall felt himself falling apart internally as he took the elevator up to the surgery floor at Landstuhl Medical Center. His swim buddy and fellow SEAL shooter, Steve Dorsey, had been shot in the head during a firefight with the Taliban. In his dual role as combat medic, Logan had had the responsibility to do what he could for his friend, who'd had a bullet pass laterally through the rear of his skull and then exit out of it. Their Master Chief, Ken Carter, had ordered him to go with Steve to Germany. Logan had been more than grateful to fly with his best friend to Landstuhl. They did everything together. *Even this.*

He'd been a combat medic too long. By age twenty-nine, he'd tended all kinds of wounds among his platoon mates. This one was the worst. Brain wounds were rarely survivable, and he tried to, somehow, gird himself for that eventuality. Even if Steve survived surgery, he'd almost certainly be a vegetable, and that cut into Logan's gut, tears burning in his eyes as he choked them back down deep inside himself. He hadn't expected to see a woman in blood-soaked combat cammies sitting alone in the lounge. She had her head tipped back against the wall; eyes closed. His heart somersaulted out of grief into… something else… something he couldn't even begin to define. Even sitting down, she looked tall, maybe five foot ten inches or so, her black hair dust covered, loose around her shoulders, framing her oval, blood-and-dirt-covered face. Her black lashes were long on her high cheekbones, her skin washed out from stress and, more than likely, shock. His sharpened gaze missed nothing: There was blood all over her legs, too, and on her right sleeve. The desert cammies she wore, dirty. As well as the dust in her hair, there were thick smudges of it on one cheek. It was the way she held those full lips in a compressed line that reached deeply into him. She was struggling with trauma, no question.

Like me.

And when she suddenly sensed him, her head snapped up and her green eyes opened. Logan saw the cloudiness in them, saw tears that hadn't fallen. *Yet.* He wanted to cry but had struggled throughout the flight to hold it all in his kill box. Her hair had flowed forward, framing her attractive face even more so. She wore no makeup, but Logan enjoyed the naturalness of her. He wanted to stop to find out who she was, but his own grief pushed him past her and he headed toward a dark green chair in the opposite corner. Who was she waiting for? Praying for? Running the firefight, she'd just survived hours, or an eternity, earlier through her head again? Looking at her actions and decisions? Wondering if she couldn't have done more for her buddy in the field? Like *he* was doing? Guilt weighed heavily on Logan's shoulders as he sat down and rubbed his gritty-feeling face.

A doctor in blue scrubs entered the room. He looked around, his gaze settling on Jess.

"Petty Officer Courtland?"

Jess sat up, suddenly tense, trying to read the doctor's face. "Yes, sir?"

"Chief Callahan didn't make it. I'm sorry," and he gave her a kind look of sympathy.

It felt as if someone had punched her in the center of her chest. She let out a little gasp. Maybe a cry of denial. "But—," Jess stammered, slowly standing.

"I'm sorry," the doctor said more firmly. "We did everything we could for him. It was a very bad wound. His heart never recovered from the initial loss of blood. He died of cardiac arrest on the table. We worked nearly forty-five minutes afterward trying to resuscitate him. Now, if you'll excuse me, I have to call his commanding officer. His family back in the States needs to be informed."

Jess stood, feeling numb. She wavered a little, as if she were going to lose her balance. For whatever reason, she turned toward the SEAL. He was sitting tensely, his hands in fists resting on his thighs. He was staring hard at her. And she saw raw care burning in his eyes for her. Something... Jess didn't know what or why, pushed her in his direction. She gave him a wobbly smile and reached out, briefly touching his broad shoulder. "I hope your friend makes it...."

Tears burned in her eyes and, this time, Jess didn't try to stop them, feeling the warm trails moving swiftly down her face. She saw sudden emotion in the SEAL's previously grim expression. His game face dissolved. There was such agony in his blue eyes that it totaled her emotionally. His chiseled mouth thinned into a tight line, as if he were battling against his own feelings. And then, she saw tears in his eyes which he struggled with and pushed away.

"Thanks," he muttered gruffly, looking up at her. "I'm sorry you lost your friend... Take care of yourself, will you?"

Nodding, Jess allowed her hand to drop back to her side. Her throat closed and a huge lump started forming in it. Turning away, she moved as if in an unfolding nightmare, putting one foot woodenly in front of the other. Dan was dead! She touched her wrinkling brow, trying to think. Trying to do something… anything… but she felt frozen in time. Frozen with pain. Grief, so sharp and serrating, ripped up through Jess. And then she began to shake. First it was an inward quivering. And then, as she raised her hand to wipe the tears from her eyes, her fingers were trembling, too. Feeling as if she were falling apart, Jess numbly stumbled out of the lounge. She headed for the elevators opposite the nurses' desk. For a split second, Jess wanted to turn around, run into that SEAL's arms and be held. She needed somewhere to hide, to let down, to cry. But, somehow, Jess knew the SEAL would hold her, sooth her, and give her that sense of protection she so desperately needed right now.

It was a crazy thought. Completely off the wall. And yet, she felt so much around the SEAL, as if spilling out of him. His focus on her had made her heart fly open. Her emotions started tumbling out of her like a dam letting out thousands of gallons of tears. Even more, she felt the cloak of his protection wrapping around her, as if from afar. Imagination? There were so many impressions hitting her in the midst of the grief that was tearing her wide open. Jess wasn't sure what she was making up, what she was projecting on him in her present emotional state, or what was honestly real. But there was something to that man, the SEAL, and Jess was drawn so powerfully to him that it had shocked her out of her grief for a moment. Probably because they had both experienced the horrific physical trauma of someone they cared for very much. Misery *did* love company, she sourly reminded herself.

This was Jess's first time to the sprawling medical center on the hill. They had given her a room on the hospital grounds. She made her way downstairs, in a daze. The early-evening sunlight was striking through the huge windows in the lobby. It looked beautiful out there. Hopeful. But, as she walked toward the visitors' desk, she was haunted by the knowledge that Sophie Callahan would be getting a visit from two Navy officers bearing the bad news. Jess knew Dan and Sophie's children, ages 15, 10 and 6. When they'd all been back at the base, Port Hueneme, she'd babysat for the couple whenever they'd gone out on their monthly date night. Her tears wouldn't stop.

At the desk, a fifty-something woman in a bright pink suit gave her a map of the medical center grounds and directed her to the small apartment that was hers to use, all the while rattling off some of the local flavor. Jess had a clean set of cammies and even some civilian clothes in her ruck, and was grateful to hear there was a shower, towels, and clean sheets on a real bed waiting for her. Thanking the staff lady, Jess left the building, trying to think through her grief and find the place on the hill where she was to stay. As she walked out into the low-slanting sunshine, warm against her wet face, the birds singing, the hardwood trees stately and tall, it all looked so pastoral. Peaceful. But Jess felt anything but peaceful. What she wanted was a hot shower to wash off forty-eight hours of adrenaline-charged terror, Dan's blood, and Afghan grit. And wash her hair like a human being. She should get something to eat, but she didn't feel like eating anything. The only other thing that appealed to her was trying to get some sleep. And, although she rarely drank, right now a shot of whiskey seemed like a damned good idea. Quietly, the SEAL entered her mind, and she wondered if his friend was going to be all right. She hoped so.

It was 1900, military time, when the neurosurgeon appeared at the door of the surgery lounge. Logan had been dozing, head against the wall, exhausted, but when the doctor entered, he instantly snapped awake, tense, on full alert. His gaze shot to the doctor who wore a green cap on his head, his face mask hanging around his neck, his green scrubs meticulously pressed and neat. He gave Logan a frown. And Logan knew: Steve had died.

He slowly unwound out of the chair, every joint in his body aching like hell. Stiffness had set in and the tension thrumming through him added to his discomfort. "Steve?" he demanded; his voice hoarse.

The doctor shook his head and approached him. "I'm sorry. We couldn't save him, Petty Officer Randall. Just too much damage to his brain. We did everything we could… and it just wasn't enough."

Giving a jerky nod, Logan whispered, "Thanks, Doc," and he offered his hand to the sad-looking surgeon, and then walked past him, heading out of the hospital. There was nothing else Logan could do. Not a friggin' thing! And rage boiled up inside him, eating at his gut. He fought tears as he blindly made his way outside and headed to the barracks for military personnel nearby. Right now, all he wanted to do was get a shower, shave, put on some civilian clothes and go get friggin' drunk in the town of Landstuhl, about fifteen minutes away, down at the bottom of the hill.

The dusk was deepening. Logan dragged the clean, fragrant smell of fresh air deep into his lungs. For whatever reason, he thought about the Navy woman in the lounge. How was she handling her grief? Logan felt such a powerful lurch in his chest for her, and it completely caught him off guard. He didn't even know her full name or where she was stationed. Afghanistan would be a safe bet, given the desert cammies. But where? Suddenly, he wanted to see her again. As mad as it seemed, even to him, she felt like the only positive in his world now. Something living. But she was gone, and the best way he could think of to perhaps calm that nest of snakes in his gut was a drink of whiskey. He'd buy two drinks. One for himself. One for Steve.

Pulling his phone out of his cargo-pants pocket, Logan dialed Master Chief Ken Carter who ran his platoon stationed at FOB Bravo. He had to let his SEAL mates know what had happened. They were all worried. Upset. And he didn't like placing the call, but Logan wanted it to come from him, not some

Navy pogue who didn't even know Steve, or that he had been the best friend a guy could ever have. His heart clenched as he thought of the two SEAL officers who would show up at Annie's house. Steve had been married for seven years with one child, a little boy, Sean. It was going to devastate Annie. Logan had never seen a love so powerful, so good, as the love between those two people. He'd always kidded Steve that their love was the kind found in a romance novel: a happy ending. But, hell, this was anything *but* a happy ending. Rubbing his face, Logan slowed his pace along the empty sidewalk bracketed with neatly cut green lawn on either side. It hit him all over again: Steve was dead.

JESS COULDN'T SLEEP. She'd gotten a hot shower that had helped the tension she'd carried in her shoulders. And, *finally*, had been able to wash her hair. She had crashed on the bunk in her temporary quarters, but sleep evaded her. Staring wide eyed up at the light green ceiling, was all that happened. Too wired, too grief-stricken. She even found, to her chagrin, that she couldn't even cry after the initial tears had rolled down her face in the surgery lounge. Her mind wouldn't shut off. So many incidents and experiences she'd had with Chief Callahan in Iraq and then Afghanistan, sinking wells for so many villages, kept replaying in her numbed mind. His jokes. His laughter. Him showing the latest photos of his kids that Sophia had sent him via email. Worse, Dan was like the big brother she'd always wished she'd had. As an only child, she'd often wished for a sibling. A playmate. Someone to confide in. Laugh with. Go exploring together with and get into all kinds of kid trouble. He would have been her lifelong playmate and dearest friend, but it was not to be.

Rolling over in her bunk, Jess got up, disgusted with herself. She'd tried to eat earlier and promptly threw it up. Not her idea of how to grieve. Her stomach had finally settled down, but her head was going ninety miles an hour or maybe more like a gerbil running on a wheel, unable to stop.

At 1900, she decided to hell with it. Climbing into a pair of well-worn jeans, a dark blue tee and her old, favorite Levi jacket that had kicked around with her since she joined the Navy, this was going to be her civilian uniform for the night. Slipping into a pair of worn Nike tennis shoes, Jess combed her hair until it shone like a raven's wing. The strands curled slightly at the ends, brushing her shoulders, and she never had to do anything with it except the basics, thank goodness. Her job as a construction Seabee meant her hair was in a ponytail ninety-nine percent of the time, but not tonight. She picked up her small ruck that was more like a day pack and hitched it across her shoulders.

The woman at the visitors' center had given her the bus schedule for the medical area and a map of where the bus stopped in the town of Landstuhl down below the hill.

There was the popular bar located in the town of Landstuhl, fifteen minutes south of the airbase. The woman at the visitors' desk had said if she liked American atmosphere, good beer and Nashville music, that was the place to go. Right now, Jess wanted those sad Nashville songs that made the heart ache. The bar was owned by an American who had been an Army Ranger at one time, a native of Ft. Worth, Texas. It seems he'd married a German girl and settled down but missed his home state and decided to create an American bar for the many soldiers who made Ramstein Air Base their home away from home. It sounded good to Jess.

She caught the bus, which was right on time. She could see a storm was coming their way, the western sky dark and swallowing the sun. In twenty minutes, the bus made a stop right in front of the bar. As Jess got off, she saw it was a nice bus stop with intact, graffiti-free glass on all three sides and a good roof to protect those waiting from inclement weather. The streets were clean. The bar was right in the center of downtown Landstuhl. Many of the buildings were painted white with red-tiled roofs. She saw two steeples of two different churches nearby. There were single-story homes, mixed among those with two stories or more and, looking further down the main strip, there were many smaller, narrow asphalt roads branching off, lined with houses squeezed together. They reminded Jess of row houses she'd seen in Pittsburgh, Pennsylvania. Some were painted white, pale green or yellow, and the sidewalks were paved in red brick. There were masses of ivy climbing on some of the sides of the homes. Towering, mature trees were everywhere, giving the town more of a country feel to Jess. The storefronts had oval or square signs hanging outside, proclaiming who and what they were. Cars were all parked on one side of the street.

It was easy to spot the Texas Bar. It had a big cowboy hat on an oval sign out in front of the red-brick entrance. When she entered the bar, she saw it was huge, crowded with men and women younger than her. Jess would guess all of them were either Army, Air Force and a few, like her, from another branch of service. A sad honkytonk song was playing and the square, wooden dancefloor was filled with at least twenty-five couples. She stood to one side of the two brass-and-glass doors, simply absorbing the festive, noisy atmosphere. There were plenty of square tables with white linen tablecloths and fresh flowers in vases, and waitresses in tasteful black dresses and white aprons were bringing food to the customers seated at them. Off to the left, she spotted a darkly lit bar. Just what she was looking for: somewhere to hide, to be alone, to nurse a whiskey and hope like hell it shut off her mind.

Jess made a guess that sixty percent of those in the bar were male. The rest were female. That was good. The odds of being hit on were tremendously less than if it had been a complete bratwurst-fest, she thought with an unexpected inward grin. She felt old in this crowd of young people. Most looked to be in their late teens or very early twenties. She was twenty-eight and felt somewhat like a trespasser in this hangout of the youth. Jess had learned long ago to not make eye contact with interested males. It was an invitation to them and she had no wish to talk to anyone tonight.

The shadows were deep at the small, out-of-the-way bar, nestled in one shadowy corner. It was much quieter there. The bar looked like it came out of a John Wayne cowboy movie, with its long, L-shaped mahogany top with brass around the edge. The stools were four-legged, padded with black leather, and there was nothing but men on them. These were older men, late twenties, early thirties. Hopefully barflies, as interested in private indulgence as she was. The shadows were so deep that Jess couldn't really tell much about the faces along the bar as she walked down to its far end. The L portion of the bar was where the two women waitresses, both in the same black dresses and white aprons, had their station right next to an empty stool. Jess didn't want to sit between two men. That could be a buzzkill. She could already feel heat on her back; men looking at her, sizing her up. She hated the feeling. Dammit, not harmless barflies, then! Regardless, doggedly, Jess headed for the seclusion of the single barstool next to the waitresses' station where they picked up bar drinks for their patrons.

The bartender, in his fifties, dressed in cowboy duds and a Stetson, wandered down toward her.

"What'll it be, little lady?" he rumbled, wiping the countertop off with a damp cloth.

"Boilermaker," Jess said. She saw the bartender, with his long, black handlebar mustache, raise one eyebrow and then he nodded. Yeah, it was a helluva drink combo, Jess knew. Whiskey chased with beer.

He brought a bottle of whiskey and put down a draft beer in a cold glass frosted with beads of water in front of her. Taking a shot glass, he filled it with the amber liquid.

Jess laid out a U.S. twenty-dollar bill. He picked it up and left.

"I want change," she said.

"Yes, ma'am," he rumbled back over his shoulder.

Jess took a deep breath, tipped her head back, and slugged down the whiskey. She set the glass down, teeth clenched, sucking air in between them as she reached for the ice-cold beer with its good head of foam. The burning sensation of the spirits was like a red-hot snake slithering down her gullet and then hitting her stomach with a fiery explosion. It was like a bomb going off, the warmth radiating outward in tentacles, and already, Jess could feel the tendrils of heated relaxation beginning to chase her inner tension away. Sipping the beer, she closed her eyes, focused on the whiskey unwrapping her like a ball of too-tightly-wound yarn. She was vaguely aware of more sad, soulful honkytonk music being played. It felt depressing and heartbreaking. Just like she felt. Sad songs with sad endings.

Jess had just finished the cold beer, and had closed her eyes, starting to feel the shock being deluged by the alcohol. It was also making her feel the exhaustion of forty-eight hours without sleep.

"Hey," a male voice murmured near her ear, "that's a serious combo. What you need is a man like me around to make it all feel better."

Jess opened her eyes. The dude was tall. Over six feet. Muscled. Her nostrils flared as she smelled the sour odor of alcohol on him. He was dressed in civilian clothes, cocksure of himself, a grin on his face that told her he was an arrogant asshole. "Trust me," Jess growled, "there's NOTHING I want from you. Take off."

She watched his black brows draw downward, the set of his mouth becoming an inverted crescent. "Unhappy" would be the word to describe the bastard in dark blue chinos and a crisp, white college shirt, sleeves rolled up to just below the elbows. Jess just bet he was a Ranger. She'd seen his type before. Not all Rangers were like this dude, but some really strutted their stuff, and it turned her completely off.

"Hey, sweet thing," he growled, "no need to get so hostile."

Gritting her teeth, Jess hated the look he gave her, undressing her with his eyes. "Go hit on someone else. I'm not interested." She saw him glare at her and then turn away; his male pride hurt.

"Another Boilermaker, ma'am?"

"Yes," Jess muttered to the bartender. She hated going into bars, but where the hell else, in a foreign country, was she going to get drunk enough to forget the last two days of her life? Maybe this had been a bad idea. But Jess LIKED the fact she was finally getting off the precipice of that cliff inside her. The grief had finally been muted, and she was eternally grateful for that. She didn't feel like crying, either. *Amazing.* Relief tunneled quietly through her. One more boilermaker and then she'd get the hell out of this bar and grab a bus back to the medical center. Then, she knew she would be able to fall asleep.

CHAPTER 2

LOGAN WASN'T SURE why, when he saw the Navy woman walking toward the bus stop, that he decided to follow her. He'd cleaned up, shaved, put on a pair of Levi's, a red t-shirt and his old leather bomber jacket that had seen better days. Being a SEAL, his life depended upon noticing details. And it was a pleasure to look at this black-haired woman with those amazing green eyes of hers. She wore a frayed Levi jacket. The elbows were almost threadbare and the exposed threads whitish looking. As quirkily trivial as he knew it was in his shock-fogged mind, he couldn't help but feel more kinship with her because she wore Levi's jeans too, and they were well worn, even a little baggy on her. He wondered if her job entailed certain duties that had caused her to lose weight. His mind hopped around, and he finally settled on the theory that she might be in a combat slot. Humping sixty-pound rucks for six to ten hours on a patrol was one hell of a way to lean down in a hurry. Best diet in the world.

When he'd come down another sidewalk and spotted her on the main path leading to the bus stand, Logan slowed down. He'd been in a black funk since talking to the surgeon, but just SEEING her lifted that suffocative darkness. It did something amazing to his grieving heart. He actually felt *hope*. This word was not in his vocabulary or reality, generally speaking. He recalled seeing her desert-camouflage jacket at the hospital and, above the left breast pocket, the last name of Courtland. Yeah, she was tall, but she was built lush, with nice, large breasts, ample hips and such long, long legs. A model she wasn't, but he wasn't drawn to stick women, anyway. Give him some warm, soft, velvet flesh he could mold between his hands. He'd always liked "Venus de Milo" women ever since when, on the cusp of adolescence, he'd first seen the statue on his computer. She wasn't overweight at all; just solid. Really nicely built.

Logan was a realist, so he wondered if she was married. Maybe had a couple of kids already? That really put out his fire for her, and he scowled. He wanted her single. She was hot. Really hot. And she seemed completely clueless as to how she might affect a man. He wondered why she didn't wear any makeup. Her hair was loose and free. Even from this distance, he could see it shining like an ebony lake at night with moonlight skipping across it here and

there. His eyesight was great, and when she lifted her left hand to pull the small
ruck up on her shoulders, he saw no wedding ring. But that didn't mean a
thing. Military people in combat didn't wear jewelry of any kind because they
were around machinery or flights, or in war slots, where it could accidentally
take off a finger or interfere with vital equipment usage. And that habit often
carried over into downtime, but Logan really wanted her to be single and
available.

She was in her late twenties; more or less around his age, although her face
looked teenage fresh and scrubbed, a slight tinge of pink to her cheeks. There
was an ease she had with herself, confidence and a lack of self-consciousness.
He wondered how she'd achieved that. Most women never got there, always
worried what others thought about them and living their lives in hiding, based
upon that. Logan didn't think this woman cared what anyone thought of her,
and one corner of his mouth lifted into a grin. Her eyes were wide spaced, a
broad forehead above them with soft strands of black hair dipping across half
of it. She would often take her fingers and push the hair back off her face.
Logan wondered if she had ever trained in ballet because her movements were
like a graceful dance. Either that, he told himself, or she was indeed in a
combat role, and had that kind of grace as a result. In any case, she was in top
shape, athletically speaking. His curiosity burned brighter about who she was.

Logan had been to Ramstein too many times to count. He knew the place
like the back of his hand. The medical center and airbase sat on a huge hill. The
village of Landstuhl was a fifteen-minute walk down that steep hill. Drunk
personnel who thought they could just stroll on up, back to their barracks, had
coined a name for that climb: Heart-Attack Hill. And it was no challenge to *get*
drunk, if that's what one was after; the town was packed with bars for all the
military types wanting a beer, or stronger alcohol, after a hard day at work.
Landstuhl rocked at night and had its share of full-on bar fights and minor
skirmishes out on its cobblestone sidewalks. The German police were always
on the prowl. And so were the MPs, military police, as well as the Air Police.

The bus would come shortly. He saw Petty Officer Courtland at the stop.
She went over to a nearby fruit tree, lifted her hand, and cupped a red, ripe
apple hanging within her reach. She stood on tiptoes to smell it. A country girl,
he'd bet. City people never seemed to notice things like that. He continued to
walk silently and stay out of her line of sight. He spotted two busses approaching, each going to different places. The first bus went to Landstuhl. The second
bus went elsewhere. Her posture convinced his perceptive eye that she had
hers fixed on the first bus. Logan was confident she wasn't going far. He could
get on the second bus, which would take the same route for a bit, remain
unseen, and follow her once she got off hers.

Logan continued to hang back until she did, indeed, board the first bus, and soon he was on the second, following hers as they wove slowly down through the streets of the town. He got off after she stepped off the lead bus in the center of busy Landstuhl. Did she have a destination in mind? She had to be feeling rough emotionally, like him. They'd both lost good friends today. Straight to a bar was where he wanted to go initially, but he was intrigued with her and decided to table that need for now. If anything, he'd like to introduce himself to her. But, for all he knew, she could be meeting her husband! Logan sincerely hoped not.

And when she turned and went into the Texas Bar, Logan groaned softly to himself. That was the biggest pick-up joint in town. WHAT was she doing in there? Was this her first time here? A newbie? He couldn't leave her unprotected. A lot of Rangers from the 10th Mountain Division, especially the young bucks with something to prove, mingled there. It was a real Army hangout, and thus, often rough. Navy and Air Force personnel rarely frequented it. They had other favorite hangouts for their branches of service. Mouth tightening, Logan waited until he saw her inside through the large picture window facing on the sidewalk. She was moving toward the bar at the rear of the place. Another mistake. Prostitutes hung out back there, big time. Granted, she wasn't dressed like one, but to the men hanging around in there, eyeballing every female who walked in like she was meat on the hoof, she was open game. She was walking into trouble. *Damn.*

Eyes adjusting quickly to the dimly lit interior, Logan wanted to remain out of her sight. She had taken about the most obviously isolated stool at the bar that silently said: *leave me alone.* He moved to the other end of the bar, to an open stool next to the wall. It was a perfect location to stay hidden by the darkness that enveloped this den of Army iniquity. She would never catch sight of him there, unless he wanted her to see him. Ordering a beer, Logan sat with his back to the wall, the quickly delivered stein in his left hand. He was deliberately positioned so that he had a clear view not only of who came into the bar, but also of who went in and out the back door behind the woman, too. As he sipped his beer, he saw her knock back a shot of whiskey, her cheeks turning from their fresh-scrubbed pink to red. He grinned to himself because it was obvious she was not a drinker. But maybe… just maybe… she was so overwhelmed with the death of her friend that this was one way to bury it for a while? Logan had to plead guilty to that route, too. The hangovers that came from refilling drained bottles with trauma were a sonofabitch, though. Still, the cold beer tasted damn good after swallowing what felt like half the sandbox of Afghanistan.

Logan kept a casual eye on the bar and the men in it. He could tell a Ranger from a Delta Force operator or a Special Forces A-team guy by sight alone. They all had their own, unique swagger: their walks, each with its own particular brand of ballsy confidence. This was a Ranger hangout. They didn't like SEALs. It was an Army-Navy thing. Sipping his beer, he saw four Rangers at his end of the bar, looking in their late twenties, dressed in civilian clothes, eyeballing Courtland. Never once did she look up or around as if to invite a man's attention. Her eyes were on her hands surrounding her beer stein. Scowling, he saw clearly that she was really grieving hard. He could see it in her darkened eyes. There was a burden of pain in them, and he felt his heart wrench in his chest. What she needed was to be held, so she could cry and get it out of her system. Women liked to cry. It was a release for them. Logan hated crying, but he'd done his fair share of it. And he'd cry for the loss of Steve, too. But not here. In private. When he was alone. The ache in his chest widened as he watched this woman wrestle with the emotions that showed clearly on the surface of her very readable face. She'd never make it as an operator. But Logan didn't want her to. There was something so damn refreshing about her that he felt mesmerized. She wasn't a flirt. She didn't want any company. She sat as close to the wall at her end of the bar as he did at his.

But then, one of those four rowdy young-buck Rangers swaggered over to where she sat. Logan almost came off his stool as the Ranger leaned his big body over hers like a friggin' vulture and whispered something in her ear. He could see it startled her, lost in her own thoughts as she was. She was clearly locked into memories of her dead friend. And then, he grinned to himself. Her face got hard looking, and those green eyes of hers flashed lightning at the sloppy, slobbering dude. Whatever she'd said to him, it had him blushing to the roots of his crewcut hair. And he wasn't a happy camper about the second curt reply she snapped off, either. Ranger One gave her a glare and marched off in a huff, his hard jaw set, pissed off and angry.

Logan relaxed. But when her second Boilermaker arrived, he got worried. That was a helluva lot of alcohol in a short amount of time. And women's bodies simply did not process the stuff that fast. She could get seriously drunk. And, judging by the four Rangers still talking among themselves, occasionally lifting their heads, staring at her from across the room, these dudes were just waiting to pick her bones. They knew what he knew: she'd get drunk as hell and then they'd launch a frontal assault on her. She wouldn't stand a chance. But then, maybe she would. If she was in a combat slot, she'd been trained to stand her ground. Granted, she probably didn't know close quarters combat, CQC, like he did, but she should be able to handle herself. However, the odds of four against one weren't good, either. He sipped his beer, keeping tabs on the Rangers. They were drinking whiskey now, not beer. Probably getting their balls up to go over there and hit on her again, thinking that, in her soon-to-be-drunken state, she'd be more amenable toward them. More welcoming of their vaunted attention, he thought wryly.

Logan didn't think she'd be friendly at all. She wanted to be left alone to drown her sorrow in her cups. But this was the wrong damn place to choose to do it. He flexed his fist, watching the Ranger foursome. They were indeed getting their courage up, laughing and slapping shoulders. He wondered if it would be two of them to accost her this time. Or, all four of them trying to threaten and intimidate her with their presence?

Jess was beginning to feel absolutely no pain after gulping down her second whiskey. God, it burned awful in her stomach! But then, that warmth, like magical, invisible fingers, spread out through her chest and gut, removing the heaviness, making her feel better, burning the grief away. At least for a while. Jess didn't fool herself; she was a lightweight. She knew she'd have one helluva hangover. Eyeing the beer in her hand, she'd saw she'd barely touched it. But, lifting her hand and pushing hair away from her face, she decided she'd done enough damage to herself for one night. Leaning down, she grabbed her ruck from the floor and pulled it up over her shoulders. And then, as she stood, she felt more than saw, male energy returning her way.

"Now, sweet thing," Ranger One, the same one who'd tried before, said, giving her his best come-on smile. "Me and my friends really think you're too lonely over here by yourself."

Jess smelled his sour breath and wanted to gag. She looked up to her left where he was hanging over her, leering at her, no guesswork needed about what he wanted. The other man, probably his friend, just as tall, helped bracket her stool. She couldn't get out around it to go anywhere. Anger surged through her.

"Get the hell out of my way," she snarled at Ranger One.

Ranger One's smile dropped and twisted into a smirk. He put his hand on her left shoulder.

Jess pushed him away with all her strength. No one touched her, dammit! Ranger one stumbled and staggered back, not at all prepared to be pushed by this woman. She was breathing hard, her chest rising and falling, well aware of Ranger two on her right. Was the bastard seriously going to try and touch her as well? She twisted her head, glaring up at him, a silent warning to back off.

Ranger one growled, hands moving into fists as he caught his balance and charged forward.

Logan appeared from one side and stood between him and the woman.

"Now, friends," he said in a calm but growling tone, keeping his eye on Ranger one as he jerked to a halt, "why don't you give the lady the breathing space she asked for?" Logan was six foot three inches tall and two hundred and twenty pounds. Ranger one was about an inch less than him. Ranger two was three inches less.

Jess gasped as she saw who it was. The SEAL! She blinked, her mind spinning from the whiskey. He was standing casually but she could sense the tension in him. And he was smiling but it sure as hell wasn't reaching his eyes. His entire demeanor felt like a magnificent male lion issuing a warning growl to these jerks who were acting like half-grown cubs. Just as she was about to speak up, to stand up for herself, Ranger Two's hand clamped down on her right shoulder. Jess took a swing at him with her left fist, connecting solidly with the side of his face.

Logan saw her give the Ranger a roundhouse slug to his jaw, sending him crashing to the floor. Ranger One snarled a curse and came at him. Logan moved easily inside the lumbering, drunken charge and opened the flat of his palm, smashing it into the man's hawk-like nose. Logan felt the crunch of bone, heard the Ranger scream. He was staggering back, blood pouring out of his nostrils. Logan turned and gripped the woman by her arm.

"Let's get out of here," he told her firmly, holding her angry, unsettled look. "*Now.* Or I'm going to have about thirty Rangers wanting to hang my hide. Do you want that to happen?" and he grinned mirthlessly at her.

"No," Jess growled, slipping past the stool. She allowed him to propel her to the back door and down the four concrete steps outside. It was raining hard. She felt the SEAL's hand on her arm, guiding, monitoring but not hurting. Before she could speak, as he hurried her down the darkened cobblestone alley toward a streetlight in the distance, Jess heard the door open behind them. There was a roar of male curses. Jerking her head over her shoulder, she saw four men barreling out of the bar. Heading straight for them. She gasped, her heart taking off at a pound. Tensing, she didn't know what to do.

"It's all right," Logan told her calmly. He guided her over beneath the eaves of a roof and said, "Stay here. I'll be back in a minute." And then he pinned her with a firm look. "*Don't move....*"

Jess gave a jerky node and watched him turn, the huge drops of rain streaking down his old leather bomber jacket. He walked with a casualness that belied his SEAL authority toward the four charging Rangers running to meet him. Oh, my God! What had she caused? Jess's left hand hurt like hell, her knuckles scraped, bloody and bruised. Hand going to her mouth, eyes widening, she watched the SEAL wade into the four Rangers. In less than a minute, he had taken all of them down and they were moaning and groaning on the rain-glistening street, all the fight gone out of them. And then, he turned with that fluid male grace of his, walking toward her as if nothing had happened. He was flexing his right hand and, even in the dark, between bars of shadow and light, Jess could see blood across his knuckles. Who WAS this man? She'd didn't know any SEALs, but knew of their hard-won reputation, of their prowess in a myriad of combat disciplines. One simply never messed with them.

Shivering, having gotten instantly soaked upon leaving the bar, Jess wrapped her arms around herself. As the SEAL approached, she heard police sirens wailing in the distance, coming their way. *Oh, no….*

"My name is Logan," he said in way of greeting, sliding his hand around her upper arm. "What's yours?"

"Jess Courtland," she whispered, cold, wet and terrified. What would happen now? It was all she needed to be busted in a bar fight like this. The man she hit could press charges against her. This wasn't good. And she was drunk, barely able to think. She searched Logan's glittering eyes. His hair was longer than military regulations. Water was running down the hard line of his jaw.

"Okay, Jess, we need to get the hell out of here right now, unless you want MPs crawling all over us, hauling us to the brig, and spending the rest of our night being interrogated."

Gulping, Jess shook her head, feeling as if she were beginning to unravel on a deep level within herself. The rain was pouring down in front of them like a waterfall from the eaves above. She heard thunder and saw part of the sky flare up with lightning. Her hair was damp, and she pushed it away from her face, looking over her shoulder at the Rangers who were slowly sitting up, holding their heads or trying to stop their noses from bleeding so badly. "I-I don't know where to go… I've never been here before," and she gave Logan a panicked look. His hand was firm around her arm, as if he knew she needed support. His narrowed blue eyes intently assessed her.

"You're going to have to trust me, then. I've been here one too damn many times. You're drunk. And with this bar fight, they're going to card and stop everyone going back to the base. The MPs will have a description on both of us because those Rangers are going to provide all the details." His mouth thinned. "When's your flight out of Ramstein?"

"T-tomorrow at 1100. Why?" She saw him thinking. He was urging her out from beneath the eaves of the house, back into the pouring rain, hurrying her down the dark, wet alley.

"We're going to lay up for the night."

Her eyes widened. "What?" Jess nearly came to a halt, but her feet weren't working well and she almost tripped. She was drunk. Embarrassed, she looked up at his rugged profile. "Logan? Are we in trouble?"

He cut her a glance, his mouth curving. "Yes. We are the victims, but the

MPs are going to hold us here for God knows how many days until the interrogations, the stories, are all sorted out. The Rangers are going to lie and tell the MPs I started it."

"But... it's not the truth!" Jess leaned heavily into him, suddenly dizzy from the whiskey. "God, I shouldn't have drunk so much so fast. I'm so sorry...."

"Don't be," Logan rasped. He wanted to wrap her lush body against his. Bad idea. He pulled her out of the alley and found another overhang to get them out of the rain. Placing her against the wall of the closed store, his hands on her upper arms, he studied her closely. "Look, you've been through a lot today. How long has it been since you slept?" Because she had dark smudges beneath those glorious-looking green eyes of hers. Logan groaned. He felt responsible for her. She was a lamb being led to slaughter here, and he wasn't about to let her be sacrificed to the Rangers or the MPs. There was no doubt in his mind that she was not only drunk, but far past the onset of sleep deprivation, disoriented, grief-stricken and still in shock over her loss.

Pushing her wet hair off her cheek, Jess whispered unsteadily, "At least two days... more now... I think," and she searched his gleaming face, his eyes slits as he considered her admission. "Look, I've really screwed up. I don't want to be stopped at the gate and then taken to the MPs for questioning. How can I avoid this? Do you know Ramstein?" Because he looked like he did... Wait! He'd even said so... *hadn't he?* Damn the drink! She saw his mouth lift into a wry position. Maybe a grimace.

"Stop blaming yourself," he told her gruffly, looking around. Logan could hear the police sirens drawing nearer to the bar. Pretty soon, he knew the MPs would be trawling these back streets, hunting for them. "I've been here more than I ever wanted to be," he told her. "If we don't get out of this weather, hide, those MPs are eventually going to find us tonight." He could feel her shivering, the Levi jacket too thin for early-Autumn weather in Germany. It was getting cold, the temperature dropping with the line of storms coming across the region. He searched her eyes that were clearly showing how drunk she was. "There's a small inn about a block from here. We can get rooms there, dry off and sleep."

Nodding, Jess whispered, "Great. Let's go."

Only, as Logan led her into the alpine-styled inn, the clerk who grumpily came out of the other room, looking as if they had awakened him, told them the bad news. There was only one room available. Jess gulped. Logan paid the man and took the key. Her heart started to pound as Logan walked her up the stairs to the second floor. Once up on the landing, Jess halted.

"I-I can't do this. I don't know you..."

"I don't bite," Logan soothed, keeping his voice low at this time of night. "You're shaking with cold, you're wet and you don't know where you're at, Jess. I want the same thing you do; get out of the rain, get warm, get a shower and hit the rack." He saw her considering his gruff reply. She was so exhausted. Shock, from whatever the full story was of what had happened to her, was taking her down the rest of the way. "Listen, this isn't a trap I set for you. *You're* the one who went into that Army Ranger bar."

The problem was, Jess was drawn to the SEAL. She licked her lips and nodded. "You're right: I got myself into this mess. I'm sorry I'm questioning you. I should be grateful you're helping me out of this jam."

"We've both had a rough day," Logan admitted wearily, leading her down the carpeted hall. He stopped, unlocked the door, and pushed it open for her.

Jess saw one large bed, a chair, a desk and a bathroom. *One bed.* She didn't have time to think about it. Logan shut the door, turned her around and eased the soaked knapsack and then the wet Levi jacket off her shoulders. He hung them both over a chair and then guided her to a very large, clean, tiled bathroom.

"Look, get into the shower, get it hot and get warmed up. I'll be out here if you need anything. Towels and washcloths will be sitting on the counter."

Searching his face, Jess saw several small scars. One was on the right side of his clean jaw. Two more on his neck. He was handsome in a rugged kind of way. Tall, well built and, she was so drunk she wasn't thinking straight. "Okay," was all she managed, still feeling like she was going to fall apart. He nodded and then quietly shut the door. There was a small, cushioned chair in the bathroom, and she trudged over in her wet tennis shoes, and sat down on it. Her fingers shook as she got undressed, turned on the shower and then stepped into its steamy confines. Jess felt torn, upset, and felt herself continue to unravel. She was so exhausted that she put her hands on the shower wall, just allowing the water to fall on her head and shoulders. Tears started coming them. And then sobs. She couldn't stop crying, her entire body shaking. A distant part of her hoped that Logan couldn't hear her crying over the noise of the shower.

After ten minutes, Jess felt more cleaned out because she'd finally been able to cry. Even if the whiskey didn't do anything else other than get that horrible heaviness out of her gut, she'd gladly deal with the hangover. Her heart turned to Logan. He cared. She'd felt his protection envelop her as they'd walked the rainy streets of Landstuhl. He was like a guardian angel of sorts. A badass SEAL for sure. As she soaped and washed up, Jess knew he'd done a lot for her. They were complete strangers. The only thing they shared was the surgery lounge. She wondered if his friend had survived. She hoped so.

Washing her hair, she rinsed it and then turned off the faucet, wanting to save some of the hot water for Logan.

Climbing out, her movements sluggish and awkward, Jess knew she was crashing. Whatever worries she'd had about sharing a bed with Logan were gone. Her mind was mush and thinking hurt. She took one of the two fleecy white terrycloth bathrobes and pulled it on. It hung on her and she thought it was probably a man's robe. No matter. She opened the door, steam escaping into the room. Barefoot, she saw Logan sitting in a chair. He looked exhausted now, his game face no longer in place.

"I left you hot water," she said sluggishly, pointing toward the bathroom. "Your turn."

Logan stood, thinking how vulnerable Jess looked right now. "You're crashing."

Nodding, she said, "Yeah, I am. I've got to sleep."

"Go ahead," and he turned down the bed for her. The exhaustion was clearly shadowing her eyes. Logan wanted to hold her because that's what she really needed. A little human care. From her red-rimmed eyes, he knew Jess had cried a helluva lot in there. He'd heard her sobs, and it had torn through him. Logan had got up twice to go in there and do... what? She would be naked. It would embarrass her. Scare her. And he didn't want to do that. It was a helluva uncomfortable position to be trapped in. Yes, he wanted Jess. He wanted to bury himself in her warm, wet depths, feel her arms come around him. They could hold one another. Comfort one another. Love one another. He reluctantly squashed all those ideas. "Climb in. I'll turn off the light."

Nodding, Jess almost asked where he was going to sleep, but was simply too fried, too weary and gutted, to worry about it. So far, Logan had conducted himself like a friend, not a sexual predator. There was an honor to him and, as tired as Jess was, she could feel it and see it in him. "Okay," she whispered, "thanks... thanks for everything. I've got to sleep...."

Even as her head hit the pillow, she had already made good on her word.

CHAPTER 3

T HE LIGHT FROM the bathroom flooded out through the steam-filled doorway as Logan padded quietly out into the bedroom. He halted, feeling heat purl into his lower body. Jess had laid down on the bed, oblivious to the blankets, the oversized terrycloth robe bulky around her as she slept deeply. Her hair was partly dry, not even combed, she'd been that exhausted. His heart bloomed in his chest as he stood there, a towel wrapped around his hips; the woman's robe that, in her daze, she had left for him having proved impossibly and comically small, unable to wear it. Pushing his fingers through his damp hair, he couldn't avoid the fact that, sometime while Jess was sleeping, the robe had slipped off, revealing nearly the full length of her left leg, from mid-thigh all the way down to her delicate foot. She had amazingly beautiful legs. Logan's gaze moved slowly, appreciatively, down her exposed limb. This woman was in top shape; no flab on her, just lean, tightly muscled, with a sculptured thigh that damn near made him salivate. He could feel his reaction. *Not good.* He wasn't about to take advantage of her.

The low light moved softly across her face. He saw the tension in it, knowing that shock had its way with a person for days, weeks, even months after a death. There were some recent pink scars on her calf that reminded him of shrapnel wounds. Her left hand was laying out across the pillow, and he saw how swollen and bruised-looking her knuckles were. That was the fist she'd hit the Ranger with, and he smiled a little. Jess might have been drunk and exhausted, but the woman knew how to land a mean uppercut. She hadn't been just messing around with the Ranger who'd thought he could reach out and touch her without her permission.

Her hair was drying, lying like a black cloak across her shoulder, hair he wanted to slide his fingers through, feel how clean and silky it was. More than anything, Logan wanted to kiss those soft, parted lips of hers. Jess had a wide mouth, lips full, beautifully shaped. Groaning to himself, Logan shook his head and walked over, pulling the sheet up and across her shoulders. It was best if he couldn't see her partly undressed. Damn, if his teammates knew he was sharing a room with such a gorgeous woman and not laying a hand on her, they'd never let him live it down. Shaking his head, Logan took a second towel, dried off his hair, then ran his fingers through it, taming it into place.

Tonight, whether Logan wanted to or not, he was going to have to sleep in the room's overstuffed chair. Logan didn't trust himself to sleep in the same bed with Jess. He didn't even know if she was married or not. Or where she was based. Sitting down, the second towel wrapped around his shoulders, he closed his eyes. It was midnight and he was exhausted. In moments, having trained his body to go to sleep on command, Logan spiraled into blackness. He'd have given anything to lay down on that bed next to Jess, ease her into his arms, hold her, and sleep with her. He'd been six months without a woman. He missed their warmth, their softness, and their quiet, healing strength. And there was a woman less than eight feet away from him, sleeping. Beautiful. Sexy. *Off limits.*

THE FLASHBACK STARTED insidiously for Jess. She was at the well-drilling truck, listening to the jackhammering going on ceaselessly as the equipment pounded another forty-foot casing into the sandy earth, hunting for the water table. Her men knew what they were doing. It was her job, as supervisor of her crew, to walk about, check the equipment, make sure there were no breaks in any lines, and that everything was working. She'd checked the fuel gauge and made sure enough gasoline was in the tanks to keep those casings going into the ground they'd just drilled. Jess spotted Dan's short blond hair and saw all six feet of him on hands and knees, peering at something. The thirty-five-year-old Navy chief knew a drill truck and rigging like few others ever would. Jess had learned a lot from him over the five years they'd been together on the same Seabee team.

She ambled his way, the Afghan dust rising up in puffs with every step of her leather combat boots on the gray-tan sand. They were in a pro-Taliban valley, on the slopes of the mighty Hindu Kush mountains, and everyone wore their sixty-five-pound Kevlar vests and sweated like pigs. The May temperature was hitting a hundred degrees Fahrenheit, already. Lifting off her tan baseball cap, and wiping off her brow, she came around the front end of the drill truck.

"Find something?" she called, leaning down, hands on knees, peering beneath the rig where Dan was.

"Yeah," he grunted, backing out from beneath the hood area and slowly straightening to his full height. "Got an oil leak."

"Crap," Jess muttered. She watched as Dan rocked back on the heels of his desert-colored boots. Even though they were in the Navy, they were land based and wore desert cammos, not the "blueberries" uniform of shipboard personnel.

Dan lifted his own cap off his head, grazing his short blond hair with one dusty hand. "Yeah." He grinned, flashing her a smile. "Not like we can hop in a truck and drive down the block, find a gas station, and buy a hose, right?"

Jess grinned back, always looking around. The Taliban were active in this area. She wore a .45 pistol at her waist. Everyone did. And then, she saw a white Toyota Hilux barreling down the dirt road toward them. Squinting, she saw at least four men in the bed of the truck, with rifles.

"Dan, we got company, and it doesn't look good," she warned swiftly, grabbing the radio from her pocket. Instantly, she called the ODA, a Special Forces A-team that was stationed with this and four other villages in the area. Captain Sean Anderson answered.

Jess called in what she saw, as well as the direction they were coming from. She heard the captain's voice go flat.

"Take cover, Jess. We'll be there as soon as we can."

"Oh, hell," Jess muttered, and she told Dan.

Instantly, Dan was bellowing at the crew to shut everything down. He was striding forward, Jess right on his heels. She'd pulled the .45 pistol out, her heart hammering, adrenaline flooding her bloodstream. The Toyota truck was racing at high speed toward them, a rooster tail of yellow dust rising a hundred feet high into the hot air behind it.

And then, she heard the shots being fired at them. Some of the bullets struck the truck. Others hit the drilling-equipment crane on the back of it. Sparks flew. She ducked. *This is going to be bad....*

Jess screamed. She jerked upright in the bed, her arms flying outward, caught up in the nightmare.

Instantly, Logan snapped awake at the terror in her voice. Launching himself out of the chair, he saw her sitting up, her face tight with terror, sobbing. He saw her eyes fly open, tears streaming down her face. He knelt on the bed, reaching out for her shoulder.

"Jess!" he growled, giving her a little shake. "Wake up. Wake up, you're having a bad dream..." Logan saw the glazed look come to her eyes, the tears streaming down her taut cheeks. The robe had pulled open, revealing the swell of her breasts. Groaning, Logan sat down next to her, leaned against the headboard and hauled her into his arms. She whimpered, resting her head against his chest, trembling. *Oh, hell....*

"Jess," Logan murmured soothingly, running his hand lightly across her dried hair, "it's all right. You're safe, safe... I won't let anything hurt you..." and he kissed her hair, inhaling the flowery fragrance in the strands. She sobbed, her fingers pressed against his chest, trying to hide. Logan knew she was still caught up in the flashback of whatever had happened to her. His chest became wet with her tears. Her sobs filled the room, tearing out of her, every one of them shaking her body. Logan held her more tightly. She was almost in a fetal position against him, still trying to hide. "Shhhh," he whispered, his voice hoarse, low, "it's all right, Jess. You're safe... no one is going to hurt you..." Logan knew the only way to get someone out of the clutches of a crippling flashback like this was keep talking in a low, calm voice to them. Sooner or later, they would hear the person's voice and start orienting toward it, instead of the battle web they were caught within. And Logan had no doubt that Jess had been in one helluva firefight.

It hurt him that she was trembling like a frightened rabbit in his arms, hunkered down against him, her face pressed against his chest, gasping and sobbing. He placed small kisses across her hair, grazing her tearstained cheek with his fingers, trying to calm her. Gradually, Jess stopped crying, and he could feel her beginning to relax. "That's better," he rasped against her ear, "you're doing fine, Jess. Just keep listening to me. Come back to now. Let that flashback dissolve..."

She felt so damn good in his arms. One of her legs was across his. Logan stared at that beautifully curved thigh, felt the warmth and velvety texture of her skin against his darker, hairy leg. It was like looking at beauty and the beast. He felt her shift, and he allowed her to sit up, his arms falling away, but keeping one hand against the small of her back. The robe had parted, and he could see the full swell of one of her breasts, shadowed, and softly curved. He wanted to run his fingers around that luscious curve, find and capture that hidden nipple beneath the robe. Cursing himself, Logan forced his mind back to Jess, the person. She sat up, wiping tears away with trembling fingers, realizing her robe was open. Logan eased it closed. Okay, he had this. He caught her marred gaze.

"Better?"

Sniffing, Jess saw the warmth and concern in Logan's blue eyes. She felt his hand resting gently against her lower back. Absorbing it all, she gave a jerky nod. "I-I-I'm sorry...."

"I'm not." Logan reached out, pushing some of her thick, black hair gently back across her hunched shoulder. "Want to talk about it?" He saw her lips glistening with tears, saw the lower one tremble. Yeah, she was crashing. Hitting that brick wall everyone hits after a firefight. Logan knew different people handled it differently. Women cried. Jess was excruciatingly vulnerable, raw even. Logan couldn't help himself, wanting to touch her. NEEDING to touch her because it was helping him with his own grief he'd savagely suppressed deep inside.

Jess felt the powerful protection Logan was feeding her wash across her once more. She closed her eyes, so badly needing every small, light touch he'd give her. When his calloused fingers grazed her damp cheek, she wanted so much more from this man. It vaguely hit her that he was dressed only in a towel wrapped around his hips. His chest was broad and deep, a sprinkling of dark brown hair across it. There was such powerful masculinity oozing out of him. It was nothing overt; it was just THERE, and it was affecting her as a woman. His scent lingered in her nostrils, part soap, part male. She felt her lower body react. Logan was affecting her just as powerfully as the grief that paralleled that feeling right now within her. She felt so vulnerable. In all her years in the Navy, she'd never been in a firefight before. And it shook her in ways she could never have anticipated.

"I-uh... I was in a firefight with my team," Jess whispered brokenly, holding his empathetic blue gaze. She felt his arm come up and over her shoulder, his fingers moving gently against her upper arm, as if to comfort her. Logan's touch felt so good. When he eased her toward him, Jess went. Because she hungered for human contact, desperate for a safe place right now, from feeling so raw and unsafe. The fight in the bar had stripped open an already festering wound.

"Where?"

"On the slope of the Hindu Kush, a... a valley." Instantly, she saw Logan's eyes narrow. Felt a shift of energy around him. Felt his arm tighten around her as she rested her head on his shoulder, her brow against his jaw. Closing her eyes, Jess started rambling, words tumbling out, sometimes out of order, sometimes in such a rush she felt like if she didn't get it all out, she'd die. It was that visceral. "I'm a Seabee. I work with well-drilling teams. We're in that valley to drill a well in each of five villages. We knew it was pro-Taliban. We knew it was dangerous." She choked, feeling his other hand move slowly up and down her left arm. He must have sensed how needy she was for his touch. "T-they hit us from a Toyota truck. Six of them. Dan... my chief... he was like a brother to me... took a bullet in the thigh. I saw the bullet tear into his leg, saw the bone break and saw the artery torn... oh, God... Logan, it was horrible," and she pressed her hand against her face, more tears flooding her eyes.

"I know it is, Jess, I know it is," and he threaded his fingers through her hair, feeling the strength and silkiness of the strands. He held her tightly as she sobbed. When she quieted, he asked, "Was that who was in surgery yesterday afternoon when I came into the lounge?"

"Y-yes."

She felt so damned fragile in his arms. Logan's mouth flexed and he slid his arm around her waist, tucking her tight against him, feeling her utterly trust him, nuzzling his neck and shoulder. He was no stranger to firefights. He lived for them. But most people, when trapped in one, wouldn't't feel or react like he did. As a warrior, he lived for the conflict. He wanted to take down the bad guys, and it didn't bother him that he was the instrument of their destruction.

Leaning down, he kissed her hair again, breathing in the floral scent, closing his eyes. "I'm sorry," he muttered against her ear. "I really am." Because she'd lost someone she loved like a brother. "You have to hold him in your heart's memory now, Jess. Dan won't ever die in there." He felt her nod once, her fingers splayed out across his upper chest, her warmth and softness meeting the tough, tinseled firmness of his sunburned flesh. His muscles responded to her innocent caress. Logan didn't know how to interpret what was happening between them. His erection was full, pushing against the towel, obvious. But he wasn't sure Jess was even aware of it, as wrapped up in her own shock and grief as she was right now. Never had he felt so damn protective toward a woman before. Jess was different. Beautiful. Courageous. Hauntingly vulnerable. And trusting him to do the right thing. Although Logan was worried he might be losing perspective on what that meant in this moment with Jess in his arms. He could feel the lush swell of her breasts through the robe, pressing against his chest, teasing him. Making him want forbidden fruit. He would not initiate anything with Jess. That would be taking unfair advantage of her. And Logan might be horny as hell, throbbing with a bitch of an ache, but he wasn't going to use her. *No way.*

Logan's low, gruff words, *Dan won't ever die in there,* shattered through Jess. She wasn't even aware she was moving her hand in exploration across his broad chest. The male scent of him was stirring her lower body to bright, throbbing life. Jess didn't understand how she could feel so grief stricken and yet be longing, aching, to have Logan inside her. Jess felt dampness collecting between her thighs, feeling like if she didn't make love with this man, she was going to die. The emotion was so vivid, so visceral, that she felt pushed along by invisible hands toward Logan. Her mind wasn't working coherently. Jess felt utterly exhausted and yet never more vibrantly alive than right at this moment. In Logan's arms. She could feel his lean, hard body against hers, feel the palpable electricity between them. Wanted more. Wanted HIM. How could that be, under these terrible, heart-wrenching circumstances? Dan had just died. *She* had nearly died in that attack.

Logan stilled as Jess leaned up, her mouth seeking his. It stunned him. He hadn't anticipated it. And yet, as her mouth, soft and searching, brushed against his, as if to ask him if he wanted to return the kiss, a groan began deep in his chest. He took her mouth gently, testing, asking without language whether she really wanted this or not. Wanted him now. It was survivor sex. Did she realize this? Her mouth opened like a lush bloom against his, and Logan dragged in the scent of her skin, her fragrance filling him, making him ache even more, if that were possible. Logan turned toward Jess, sliding his hand upward, cupping her cheek, angling her mouth so he could take her deeper, his hunger on a leash, but a leash that was shredding in a helluva hurry. He heard her moan as he slowly moved his tongue across her full lower lip, felt her respond by pressing her breasts wantonly against his chest. He had to think for both of them, and *think* was the last thing Logan wanted to do.

He eased from her mouth, watching her glazed eyes slowly open, their green depths filled with arousal. It wasn't his imagination. It was as real as it got between a man and a woman. His lips hovered just above hers, his eyes locked with hers. "Jess," he rasped thickly, "is this what you really want? People do weird things after a trauma like you have just gone through. I don't want to take advantage of you or have you be sorry tomorrow morning."

The urgency was overwhelming. It just kept on feeling like if she didn't love Logan with the fierceness that was driving her, she *would* die. She saw his blue eyes narrow, thoughtful, aroused, just like her. Jess knew he wanted her, but she felt him pulling away. It almost felt as if he were trying to protect her in this crazy, upside-down circumstance. She looked deep into his eyes, saw he wanted her and, at the same time, him trying to do the right thing. Whatever that was. She'd felt a connection with this SEAL from the moment he'd stepped into that surgery lounge. It was there, strung silently, teasingly between them again… right now… Aching. Wanting. Needy. Her throat burned with so many shed tears. "I need you, Logan…"

The sweetest words he'd ever heard.

"Are you protected?" he asked and saw her shake her head. "Okay," he murmured, releasing her. "I need to get a condom out of my wallet. Stay put."

Jess felt like someone else. She would never have loved a stranger in this kind of situation. But now, as she saw Logan walk over to his Levi's, she felt like a mare in heat and him a stallion; driven by primal instincts, erasing her common-sensed mind, who she was, until there was nothing left except the want to have this man bury himself deep within her. Jess felt the pulverizing need to seek relief. Focus on something that was beautiful, powerful and life affirming. When Logan turned back, moonlight caressed his tall, powerful body. The towel had dipped lower, his erection obvious.

Logan stood before her, watching Jess, gauging her. Jess's gaze was on his erection. He pulled the towel free, rolling on the condom. Her gaze didn't waver. There was no fear in her eyes. Just—need. Placing a knee on the mattress, he eased Jess onto her back, lying down beside her. The milky light of the moon spilled into the room, accentuating the soft curvature of her face and her parted lips. He eased his hand around her jaw, tipping her chin a little, their eyes meeting. "Look," he said in a rasp, "you're experiencing something that I'm familiar with, Jess. When a person's in a firefight, or any kind of life-and-death trauma, they reach a point in the process where they want to prove they're alive." His voice lowered and he eased his fingers along the slope of her velvet cheek, watching her eyes partly close, telling him it gave her pleasure. Logan wanted to give her so much more. It had been a driving power pushing him since he'd first laid eyes on her. "It's called survivor sex, Baby. And I really want you to think it and us—through before we do this. "One other small matter: Are you married?" he asked.

"No…," she saw some relief in his eyes. At least he had honor just by asking this very important question.

"Engaged?"

"No…"

"Anyone waiting for you where you work or back home in the states?"

She shook her head, becoming more solemn because he was taking responsibility in this moment for her and himself.

He rasped, "Seriously though, I don't want you having regrets tomorrow morning. Feeling guilty?" and he waited. This was not a one-way street. And he didn't want any guilt that she might be feeling, either. "Okay?"

"No guilt," Jess whispered, her voice strained. "All I know, Logan, is that I need YOU. It's you. From the very first time… when I saw you in the surgery lounge." Jess licked her lips, giving him a confused look. "I don't know what it is that's pushing me to wanting to love you…"

"We'll probably never see one another again," he told her, frowning. That hurt to even say it, dammit. Because Logan wanted to drown in her eyes, find life and heat in her lush, curvy body. He wanted to know what she thought, wanted her on every level. And that was a first for him. Women, to him, were made for sex. That was all Logan had wanted from them since… no, he didn't want to think about his past. But now… with Jess… it was frighteningly different and he felt like she did: he didn't have a damned clue as to what was going on between them or why. He couldn't untangle his need of her and contain it within his steel-trap mind. It was as if both of them were offline somehow; prey to their primal animal instincts and that was it. His body ached for her. His heart was going through wild shifts and he couldn't explain the bubbling happiness radiating throughout his chest like heated rays of sunlight.

Closing her eyes for a moment, Jess nodded. She opened them, staring fearlessly into his troubled, narrowing gaze. "I-I know…." Her heart felt as if it had been torn out of her chest at the mere thought of never seeing him again.

"I just feel so broken inside, Logan," Jess said, in a low, anguished voice. "I just need... you... what you can give me... it will help me heal. I know it will..."

Logan understood only too well. "We're both in the same place," he told her, kissing her cheek, her brow, inhaling her fragrance. "I want you just as badly as you want me, Jess. We can give each another something good, something important tonight between us... healing... life... not death..."

Logan had the words she couldn't articulate. A little hitch in her throat made her unable to speak, but she held his gaze, focusing on his every tender, hesitant touch. She slid her fingers around the nape of his neck, pulling him down upon her, wanting his mouth against hers, to take her someplace away from the fierce, serrating pain cutting deep within her. This time, his mouth was not tentative as he curved and imprisoned her lips beneath his. She got a taste of his power as a man, the sleek steel of his corded arms bracketing her. His hand slid down to the sash of her robe, pulling it free, and her skin danced in anticipation as he pulled the garment open, baring her breasts to him. Jess felt no shame. His fingers followed the swell of one and she moaned into his mouth, arching upward, wanting desperately for him to touch her hardened nipple screaming for his skillful attention.

Logan's mouth left her lips and gave her what she so desperately wanted. He suckled her gently and Jess started coming apart in his arms, feeling her lower body turning hot, hungry and melting. Her mind dissolved beneath the fiery shocks radiating from her breast, jolting hotly into her wet channel. Twisting, she pushed hungrily against his hips, feeling him groan and tense. Jess wanted nothing more than to drown in every stroke of his fingers, his mouth teasing her, his lean, taut thigh sliding across hers, opening her. Opening her to him. Her breath grew uneven, her pulse leaping as he moved to her other breast, capturing the nipple, giving it lavish attention as well. The pleasure was incredible! It was as if she were burning up, aching, starved for his touch. Logan knew how to please a woman, there was no doubt of that in her barely functioning mind. He was strong, but he monitored his strength as he moved his mouth down the center of her torso. She squirmed as his tongue moved slowly into her belly button, heat erupting between her thighs, a whimper tearing out of her mouth. Her fingers opened and closed against his thick, broad shoulders, his masculine scent filling her flared nostrils.

As he kissed the curve of her taut thigh, Logan slid his hand over her other thigh, feeling her tense. Jess felt his hips move hungrily upward and wanted him to touch her in her secret place of pleasure. Please her. Oh yeah, he sure as hell was going to do that and so much more. There was a wildness glimmering in her half-closed eyes, her lips parted, still wet from his last kiss. More than anything, Logan wanted her to orgasm first. His pride, his desire, was to always please his woman first, last and best. It wasn't just about sex. It was about teamwork; something SEALs valued above all else. Logan wanted to see Jess melt into his arms, hear her cry out in gratification. Moving his finger up the inside of her thigh, close to her entrance, he found she was so wet it made him want her even more. The sex scent of her was an aphrodisiac to Logan as he teased her moist folds, feeling Jess whimper and then sob. Her hips pressed toward him, and he smiled, leaning down, kissing the silky curls of her mound as he slid a finger slowly into her entrance.

The combination made her gasp, her hands frantic, dancing across his shoulders, her body tense, hips thrusting. Finding that sweet, swollen knot of nerves, he stroked her while sliding his other hand beneath her restless hips. Angles created pressure, but also gifts, and they were everything, and Logan moved her, finding out just where it gave her the most intense pleasure, hearing the soft moans, the whimpers rolling out of her exposed throat. As Logan moved his fingers deeper, he discovered just how tight and small she was. His mind locked on that discovery as he teased her, feeling her walls begin to contract. How long had it been since Jess had had sex? *A long time.* This warned Logan to go slow. He couldn't just pump into her, taking her hard and deep. There was no way she was prepared for it. And then, he felt her walls contract, heard her cry out, felt her hot fluids flowing across his finger, her spine a taut arch as she orgasmed. Logan felt powerful, felt good about giving her that very needed release she so desperately hungered for and deserved. He absorbed her softening cries, her fingers digging deep into his muscles. She was hot. So hot. And wild. There was no inhibition in Jess at all and he gloried in that. She was untamed, ravenous and as he milked every bit of that first orgasm from her, prolonging her pleasure, gifting her. Logan smiled. Yeah, this woman was special, no doubt. She was comfortable with her body, liked sex one helluva lot, and celebrated it with her sweet moans and cries. He felt an incredible release of the heaviness that had inhabited him since the firefight. Just watching her full lips curve into a satisfied smile made him feel it even more intensely. And he'd barely touched her. She was like a finely strung instrument, the lightest touch rippling deep and wide within her body.

The heated waves just kept flowing throughout Jess's lower body. She had closed her eyes, drifting, floating, absorbing every intense, pleasurable moment Logan gifted her with. She felt him move, felt his long, hard body lay next to hers. She barely opened her eyes, smiling up at him, seeing the glint in his own narrowed eyes. "That was… wonderful… thank you, Logan…."

He smiled a little, caressing her flushed cheek. "There's more to come," he growled. "How long has it been since you had sex?"

Jess laughed softly. "I'm a little rusty."

Logan met her smile. "I like a woman who goes wild in my arms. You're more animal than human. I like that," and he kissed her mouth, luxuriating in the softness of her. Easing his mouth away, he held her lustrous gaze. "How long, Baby?"

She wrinkled her nose. "Over a year." Jess saw him shake his head and focused on his hand trailing slowly down her left arm, his calloused fingers eliciting more fires of pleasure across her skin.

"You felt really tight and small."

"My job doesn't work well with having a steady relationship," she murmured wryly.

"I'm not in a relationship, either," he rasped. "Nor am I married or engaged. We're free to be who we are, Jess."

Logan moved his mouth against her lips, feeling her instant reaction, her own mouth opening eagerly to his, pulling him in, her tongue as bold as his was. Logan knew he'd met his match. Her utter feminine fearlessness was the biggest turn on of all for him. As he licked Jess's full lower lip again, and heard that same moan vibrate in her throat, he said, "We're more alike than I could ever have guessed. But I sure as hell couldn't hold out for a whole year." He heard Jess give a throaty laugh, her eyes sparkling with gold in their depths. She was truly sated and happy, Logan realized. There was such an artlessness to her.

It made Jess feel better knowing that Logan wasn't married. She'd made a point to never make love to a man who was, because of the morals of the situation. Yes, it was lucky he was single because, just being with Logan, all her morals were gone anyway; burned up in the heat of his mouth, his talented hands and hard male body. She watched his eyes change, a feral look coming to them as he eased up on his knees, put one across her leg and pulled her open. She burned and ached to have him inside her. She craved Logan. All of him. Any way she could have him. As he settled between her legs, she sighed.

"Hurry," she whispered. "I want you in me so badly…."

Logan leaned forward, gliding his torso up across her belly, chest hair tangling in her tight nipples, hearing her sigh, her hips moving to meet his in invitation. As he planted his elbows at her shoulders, he framed her face with his hands, moving his erection to her wet entrance. "I want to see your face when I enter you," he rasped, his voice thick with hunger. Her answering smile tore at his senses. *So fearless. Bring it on.* He moved slowly into her, watching her eyes, watching her expression closely. But *he* was the one who gritted his teeth, dragged in a deep breath, feeling her warmth wrap around him so tightly it pulled a groan out of him. He rested his brow against hers. Felt her hands move like feathers across his back, the caresses light, meaningful. And, as her fingers slid down his long, tense body, settling on his hips, Logan felt her lift hers. She'd read correctly that he was afraid of hurting her. She was small. And she sucked him deeper into her, hearing her own sigh, but it wasn't a sound of pain. It was relief, maybe.

Logan moved slowly, in and out, getting her lower body to accept him. Each time he moved more deeply, her fingers tensed against his hips, and he heard that hum of pleasure vibrating in her throat. Maybe he was the one being prudish here? Jess was asking him bluntly, hands on his hips, urging him forward, to come fully within her. Logan lifted his head, his gaze pinned to her half-opened, sultry-looking eyes. This time, he surged into her. The moment was shocking to both of them. He felt as if a fist had just grabbed him, damn near painful. Jess had gasped, her eyes flying open, her lips parting. Logan cursed to himself, realizing he'd screwed up.

She had to be in all kinds of pain because he sure as hell was close to it himself. But then, he felt her body relax, adjust to him, and she was moving her hips rhythmically against his, the sounds bubbling up her throat telling him she enjoyed their rocking motion. Okay, so, he really *had* been being conservative with her, but Logan didn't care. Her gaze was blinding, green eyes filled with dappled gold, speaking directly to him, letting him know just how much pleasure he was giving her. Logan couldn't ever recall feeling this good about sex, about loving a woman, in his memory. And he had a damned good memory. There was just something so natural and honest about Jess that she made every stroke feel like a hot rush of lava melting pleasurably between them.

Her eyes began to close, and he felt her body getting ready for another orgasm. Logan brought her right to that precipice by angling her with his hand beneath her hips. Jess's breath caught, and he felt that swift tightness contract around him and then that sweet, hot flood of fluid drowning him. It was then, only then, that he took her hard and pumped a few strokes into her before he felt the bolt of heat roar down his spine, spilling out of him. He gripped the covers on either side of her head, teeth clenched, head down, paralyzed with the visceral, scalding pleasure burning through him. Her cries matched his groans. His whole body quivered uncontrollably as his own release surged and throbbed out of him. As Logan weakened, he fell against Jess, their skin damp, sliding against one another. He felt like he'd just died and gone to heaven.

CHAPTER 4

LOGAN LAY AWAKE for a while afterward. He'd tucked Jess next to him as he lay on his back, saturated in her warmth and soft curves against him. It was the best feeling in the world and he drank in the moment like a man who hadn't drank for days after being stranded in a desert. She fit him in every possible way. Tall, curvy, feminine and wild. A slight smile tugged at his mouth as he closed his eyes, inhaling the scent of her hair. Where had Jess been all his life? His body felt a depth of satiation he'd never experienced before. Was it due to Survivor Sex? That he hadn't had sex in six months, which was a damned long time for him? Or was it HER? Logan felt her breath go shallow and slow, indicating she was sleeping deeply. He held her, wanting to give her the protection she needed. Jess wore her vulnerability out on her sleeve. She didn't play tough woman, nor did she have a game face to put in place. What had made her so natural? So confident in herself that she didn't have to behave like other women? There was honesty in her at every turn, as he'd discovered tonight.

Moonlight filtered silently into their room. The storm had passed. They'd both been through their own ones, too: stormy, emotional hells. Now, in this calm afterward, it felt like a gift from the cosmos had been given to Logan for surviving it all. His mind moved to a thousand questions he had for Jess. But first, he had to get some decent sleep, or else.

JESS AWOKE SLOWLY, feeling a languorous satisfaction thrumming quietly through her satiated body. As she turned over, she saw the morning sunlight made the room bright and cheery. She heard the birds singing out in trees nearby and rolled slowly onto her back. The covers had been drawn up over her, but she noticed the lack of Logan's warmth. Opening her eyes, she saw he was gone. Swallowing, Jess sat up, her hair tumbling around her shoulders. He'd placed a robe, the women's-sized one this time, at the end of the bed where she could easily pull it toward her. Rubbing her eyes, she saw a note on his pillow. Reaching for it, she saw, in a scrawl, *"Out to get our breakfast. Be back soon. L"*

Looking at the clock on the dresser, Jess saw it was 0700. She had a flight to catch at 1100. Moving slowly, feeling achy in all the right places from their lovemaking last night, she picked up the robe and walked to the bathroom to take a shower.

By the time Jess left the bathroom, wrapped in the now-fitting robe, the door opened. She looked up, seeing Logan enter with two sacks in his hand. He hadn't shaved yet and the shadow of stubble accentuated his strong face. She smiled as she sat on the bed, legs crossed beneath the robe. He wore his Levi's, the same red t-shirt that outlined that magnificent chest of his, and his old leather bomber jacket, that appeared to have dried now from its soaking in last night's pouring rain.

"Hungry?" he asked, smiling hello to her as he shut the door. How did Jess get to look even more beautiful than before? Her cheeks were a soft pink below her flawless, green eyes with gold in their depths. Her black hair had been brushed and tamed, shining in the light from the window.

Jess grinned. "That's a double-edged question if I ever heard one," she murmured, taking the offered sack from him. She saw the glint come to his eyes and felt like she was being hunted by Logan's primal side. It was a delicious feeling. Even her lower body, tired and achy as it was, flexed over the burning look he gave her.

"True," he murmured, setting the other sack on the dresser. "I took a chance you like good, strong black coffee in the morning?" He handed her a paper cup and then shrugged out of his leather jacket.

"Mmmm, thank you," Jess whispered, holding it with both hands. "How did you know?" She watched as he took his own coffee out of the sack on the dresser. No matter what the man did, it was sensual. The corded muscles in his forearms and biceps were hard.

"A wild woman who is as natural as you are, would like her coffee straight up." He grabbed a wooden chair and brought it over to the bed. Jess had taken the paper plates, four croissants, and jam and butter from the paper sack he'd given her and spread them out on the mattress. That was a European continental breakfast.

She gave him a grateful look. Before Logan sat down, he came over and placed a warm kiss on her mouth. Her heart swelled with unexpected happiness. "You look better this morning," she observed softly, taking the lid off her coffee.

"You look beautiful," Logan countered, gratefully sipping his own coffee. "How long have you been up?"

"About forty minutes." Jess pulled open the croissant. It was still warm and smelled wonderfully fragrant to her. She opened the strawberry jam, working some out onto the pastry with a plastic knife. He was watching her and she didn't mind the attention. It struck her that he was mentally photographing her. Looking up, she said, "Tell me about yourself?"

"I was born in Cheyenne, Wyoming. How about you?"

"I've led a twisted life."

"Try me?" Logan liked the warmth in her eyes as she regarded him. The woman's mouth was certifiable as she nibbled on the croissant. She made it look sexual. And yeah, he was getting hard all over again.

Shrugging, Jess said, "I was born in Cape Town, South Africa, but I'm a U.S. citizen. My mother and father were Navy Seabees for twenty years. She's a civil engineer and my father is a geologist. They met in the Middle East, got married and they were transferred to Africa, where, ta-daaa, I was then born."

"So, that's where you got your wild-woman genes?"

Laughing, Jess said, "Is that how you see me?"

"Absolutely." Logan kept his smokey tone. "Last night, you were wild, free and it was great for both of us." He saw some shyness come to her eyes, a stain of pink flooding across her cheeks. For all her brazenness while making love, in the daylight, she was softer. Approachable. The confidence, however, was always there. "That was a compliment," he added, becoming serious.

"Thanks," Jess murmured, "you were wonderful, too." She saw the pleasure in his expression as he absorbed her return compliment. Logan was utterly and truly confident, she thought. Not swaggering like those Army Rangers at the bar last night. Rather, he held a quiet self-assurance that broadcasted out to everyone who met him. Logan was a man among men. The type she silently thought of as a matriarchal male, not the toxically masculine kind of man she'd punched at that bar last night.

"We're good together," Logan agreed, wishing they had at least a week to share. One night was not enough.

"Yes," she sighed. "I'll never forget it." *Or you.* Too soon, Jess knew they would separate and go their different ways. She didn't want it to happen, but reality told her otherwise. Logan's male smile warmed her. Her body remembered, and a deep glow beginning to throb in her once again.

"So, you were a military brat? Traveled the world?" Logan prodded.

"Yes. I grew up on just about every continent. My mom built bridges and highways. My dad did soil analysis, geology, and they worked as a team."

"You were a wild, barefoot and carefree child. Weren't you?" Logan swore he could see her as a child being just like that.

"I wasn't brought up in the States," she said wryly. "I know smatterings of a lot of languages because my parents were overseas most of the time. I always had a nanny and a teacher. I think I grew up lucky." Jess licked off her fingers that still had jam on them.

Logan's erection ached as he watched her tongue slide over her fingers. The woman didn't even realize what it did to him. So natural. So unaware. Just HERSELF. His curiosity ate at him. "So, you spoke of that valley you and your team were working in…"

"We were up on the slopes of the Hindu Kush, near the villages I mentioned. We arrived a week ago. There's five of them in the area and we're doing some nation building by digging a well for each one."

Logan shook his head. "That's damned Taliban country. Big time. Who in their right mind sent you there?"

Shrugging, Jess said, "I don't know. I just get told where to take my well-drilling team. We were briefed and informed it was a hotbed of tribal warfare, and the Taliban and Hill bands had a strong foothold in the mountains above us, as well."

"A lot of American men and UN soldiers have poured their blood into the sand of that valley," Logan warned, now worried for her. "Are you the only woman on your team?"

"Yes. I'm a Petty Officer First Class. I'm the boss, so to speak. I've got nine years in the Seabees and my claim to fame is well digging."

"Do you have military protection, Jess?"

Nodding, she said, "We have a Special Forces A-team with us."

"That's a twelve-man unit. Is that all?"

"Yes." She saw he was concerned. It wasn't in his expression, but she could feel it. His eyes were dark looking. Last night, in the moonlight, his eyes had been stormy, like a thunderstorm moving across a valley.

"Do you have any snipers on overwatch?"

"No. We've never needed them before."

"You've never been in that area, either," Logan said grimly, finishing off one croissant and starting on the second one.

"With Dan dying in an attack," she said softly, frowning, "I don't know what kind of protection they're going to give us now. We each wear a .45 pistol, but our job is drilling wells, not keeping watch for the Taliban."

"I hope your superiors do something," Logan said, scowling. It bothered the hell out of him. A twelve-man A-team wasn't enough in that hotbed of enemy activity, but he didn't say that to Jess.

"Where are you stationed, Logan?"

"Camp Bravo. It's an FOB about thirty miles from the Pak-Afghan border." He lifted his hand making and down motion. "We're located almost exactly opposite of one another except for that mountain. It's roughly fifty miles from Bravo to where you are doing the well drilling."

"FOB Bravo isn't far from where we're drilling, then. How long have you been deployed there?"

"Six months. We got three more to go and then we'll swing Stateside for eighteen months," Logan said, then paused and asked, "What about you?"

"We spend a month more there, and then we're heading down to the Kandahar area. There're six villages there that are desperate need of a clean water source."

"But," he muttered, "don't you get leave? Or do you get deployed Stateside?"

"We're three months into a year-long deployment. Then, we go back to Port Hueneme Battalion, back in California. We're a part of the 74th Water Well Detachment."

"Then, you remain stateside for a year?"

"No. Six months, usually. This is a long deployment because the Pentagon wants as many wells as possible dug before the US pulls out completely someday. There's no date on when, yet. It's all political, of course. We both know there's going to be at least a few black ops teams in the country even after the regular troops leave."

"Yeah," Logan said. "I'm with Seal Team 3 and, I can guarantee you, I'll be going back there long after this whole war is forgotten by the media and the American public." He gave her a sour smile. She brightened. He liked the luminous quality in her eyes, that keen intelligence of hers showing through. In Logan's mind, Jess was the whole package. "Is that why you aren't married? Or engaged?" he teased.

Jess laughed a little. "My job sends me around the world. There aren't many men who are willing to follow."

"Look at your mother and father, though," he pointed out.

"Yes, they are a great love story." She sighed and gave him a shy look. "I've never seen two people more in love than them. I grew up thinking I'd find a man like my father, marry, and be happy like them."

"Didn't work out that way?"

"No. I married a man called Mark at twenty-four. He was a Seabee, too. I guess, in my romantic blindness, I didn't really see HIM. For two years, he tried to control me. I grew up with parents who were equals, who respected one another. Mark wanted me under his thumb. I divorced him."

Logan heard the pain in her voice. "Don't lose your idealism, Jess. I like it." He saw her respond with a small smile. "I married at twenty-three. But SEAL life isn't for most women. Maryann divorced me three years later because I was never home."

"I'm sorry," Jess said, meaning it. "Any children?"

Logan shook his head. "No. We both agreed to wait on that. I'd never be around to be a father. It would all fall on my wife. That wouldn't be right."

"When you went out earlier this morning? Were there still MPs crawling around looking for us?"

Logan grinned. "Nah. The village is quiet this morning."

"Do you think we can get on base without causing a riot? A fight? Or having Rangers coming after us again?"

"We'll take the bus back to Larmsee."

"Larmsee?"

"Sorry, like I said, been here too many times. Where we were at yesterday was the Landstuhl Regional Medical Center or LRMC. You know how the military makes sounds out of acronyms? We call it Larmsee."

"Good to know," Jess said. "I NEVER want to be here again. Once is enough."

"I hear you," Logan said. He'd didn't want to tell her he'd been flown here five years ago, badly wounded, and then sent off Stateside to recover. Or about coming here twice to be with a badly wounded team member. *Too much, too soon.*

Jess looked delicious in that white robe, a bare hint of her breast visible. He'd touched those breasts last night. And already, he wanted Jess again. But time wasn't on their side. "I made a call to a friend of mine who mans the Operations desk at Ramstein. You and I are catching the same C-17 Globemaster flight back to Bagram. Our names are on the manifest."

Sure, they'd fly back together, but what were the chances they'd ever get to meet in-country again? And their deployment schedule didn't match up at all. Now, he felt a new kind of sadness. Like a knife slicing his heart open. *Sonofabitch.*

"Look," he said, "I'd like to stay in touch with you, Jess. I want to give you my email address?" He wasn't sure she wanted to continue any kind of on-again-off-again relationship with him. Logan had his answer when he saw her tear up. *Oh, hell.*

"I'm sorry," Jess whispered, quickly wiping her tears away.

"Was my offer that bad?" he asked warily.

"No," and she managed a watery smile. Taking a deep breath, Jess said, "You have no idea how much you helped me last night… this morning. I was so torn up inside, Logan. You were so steady. Quiet. Caring." She held his dark gaze. "I can't EVER thank you for what you did for me, how you loved me. It's as if you realized how fragile I really was." Jess reached out, touching his arm. "I would love to have your email address. But I don't see how we'll ever get together again…," and she swallowed against her tightening throat.

"I'm a SEAL, Baby. No one knows black ops better than we do." Logan gave her a confident smile. "You just hold onto that. Okay? We know how to work the system." And he was thinking of Master Chief Ken Carter. He ruled a wide swathe of the military world and could pull strings no one else could. Logan slid his small notebook out from his Levi pocket and grabbed a pen, writing down his email address. Tearing the paper off, he folded it and handed it to Jess. "Your turn."

Jess took the notebook and wrote down her address. She tore it off more daintily than he had and handed both back to Logan. "I've never been around SEALs," she admitted. She saw the challenge in his dark blue eyes and the careless smile that came to his face. Was there really any hope for them? Even though she grew up reading all the classics, all of Aesop's fables, all the fairy tales of Europe and America, which fed her dreamy and romantic side, Jess knew, in their line of work, hard, gritty reality ruled. "I don't even know your last name," she admitted lamely, giving him an apologetic look.

"Logan Randall, Petty Officer First Class. I'm a sniper with my platoon." He saw her eyes widen over that statement.

"A sniper?"

"Yes, among other things." He rose, taking the paper food sacks, wadding them up and tossing them into the wastebasket. He placed her address in his wallet for safekeeping. "If I can find a workaround to drop in sometime and see you, maybe meet you at Bagram for a day or two, I'll do it," and Logan gave her a serious look. Jess had to know he meant it. Because he *did*.

"I sometimes go to Bagram. But I know I'll never be at FOB Bravo."

"Let me worry about the logistics of us getting together again," Logan said, seeing the worry, the sadness in her eyes. If they just had a little more time together, but it was already 0800. "We need to get going," he said, hating to say it.

"Yes," Jess whispered, uncrossing her legs, smoothing out the robe and standing up. Her heart ached. Did he feel as miserable as she did right now? As if to answer that unspoken question, Logan stepped forward, sliding his arms around her shoulders. She lifted her head, drowning in his stormy blue eyes. That was the way they'd looked last night as they'd made love with one another. He moved his thumb across her lower lip.

"You're an incredible woman, Jessica Courtland. And if you think I'm letting you go, you've got another *think* coming…" He leaned down, gently taking her mouth. She tasted of strawberries, coffee and her own, sweet inner taste. One that he already craved. Her mouth opened, eagerly kissing him in return. He felt her arms slide around his shoulders, pressing herself wantonly up against him, her breasts against his chest, her hips moving seductively against his erection.

Jess broke the kiss, her voice uneven. "We've got maybe an hour, Logan, if we cut it closer. I don't want to waste it. I want to love you again…"

He groaned, but a smile shadowed his mouth as he tucked some errant strands of hair behind her ear. "You're reading my mind, Baby…" and he slid his hands beneath her robe, opening it, her naked body so lush and gorgeous in the morning light, her breasts full; those nipples begging to be touched and suckled once more. He ran his hands lightly across her shoulders, curving down around her breasts. She gasped softly, her eyes shuttering closed, leaning into his large palms.

"You are so incredibly beautiful," he growled, leaning down, capturing a nipple between his lips.

Jess moaned, gripping his shoulder, her knees weakening. "Oh… Logan…," she moaned straining forward into his hands.

He felt her tremble. Releasing the taut, pink nipple he lifted his head, kissing her swiftly, with the hunger he had inside for her. Picking her up, he placed Jess on the bed. And then he got out of his clothes. He rolled on the condom in record time. They had fifty minutes and, dammit, he was going to make every minute count.

The C-17 Globemaster took a spiraling, evasive pattern to land at Bagram air base. Logan was used to it, but Jess was not. They now sat in two of the nylon-webbed seats ranging along the sides of the fuselage, as they had since awakening.

Earlier, Logan had shown Jess how SEALs slept on long flights, bringing out two hammocks and stringing them between some of the huge metal containers strapped to the deck of the transport plane. It was a way to catch up on badly needed sleep, and they were both still owed payback for a deficit in that regard. She'd slept in hammocks many times as a child, but they got a lot of laughs out of her having to remember how to get into one without flipping out of the netting. Then, hijinks over, they had grabbed as much shuteye as possible.

Logan had awakened first, about an hour out from Bagram. He'd threaded between the two containers where Jess was sleeping deeply, despite the shaking and shivering of the aircraft, and the continual vibration and noise of the engines. Everyone wore helmets with ear protection built in on these flights, making sleep just barely possible.

Luckily, the transport crew hadn't been around, and he'd been able to wake her up with a long, deep kiss. The radiance in her eyes as she'd awakened beneath his mouth had taken his breath away. He'd ached to love her again.

Logan didn't know what was going on between them. They shared an unshakable, inexplicable link. It made her one hell of a lover, that was for sure.

Back in the here and now, Jess gripped his hand, her knuckles white, as the C-17 groaned, the pitch of the engines changing as the plane spiraled in for landing. Such evasive maneuvers when approaching one of the many runways at Bagram kept the enemy guessing and stopped them from taking down an aircraft.

Logan glanced over at Jess. She was attempting a smile, but it was more a grimace, and her eyes were wide with fear. It was just one more thing to add to his growing mental list; He liked discovering small things about Jess, committing them all to memory and into his heart. She'd been friendly with the crew, he'd discovered; A warm smile for all, something kind to say to each of them, and meant with sincerity. She was an attentive listener, never interrupting the other person. The captain of the flight, a woman, was thrilled to see another female on board. It was like Old Home Week, a military reunion tradition, for them in a way, Logan thought with a grin.

In another thirty minutes, they'd be parting company. Logan scowled, his mind racing for a fix, but finding no purchase. It was no use. He had never worked with Seabees before and so he was going to rely on Master Chief Carter to see what could be done. Just holding Jess's long, spare hand, remembering her fingers trailing over his body, he longed for her, and his body was being honest. Good thing he wore bulky cammies. They hid everything. Plus, it was dark. Landing in the dark had its advantages, it seemed. Speaking of which, Logan thought, his last change to take full advantage of the situation was rapidly approaching: He wasn't going to let Jess escape without one last kiss.

Jess took a long, deep breath, feeling the tires of the C-17 screeching and hitting the runway. They were down! Her stomach was flipping nervously. That damned spiraling approach was like riding a roller coaster at Six Flags. All through the plunge, Logan's large hand had been warm and comforting on her sweaty, damp one. She drilled wells for a living, her roots firmly in the earth. Flying wasn't on her top ten list of favorite things to do. Still, Logan's solid, quiet presence filtered into her and Jess had become calmer as a result.

Yes, thankfully, they were down and the taxiing was over. The rear ramp on the C-17 finally started grinding open. The noise was earsplitting even with the helmets on. There were no lights on anywhere because at night the Taliban would love to have a brightly lit target to shoot at. Jess relied on Logan's experience as to when to get up and walk out of the rear of the huge plane. He also had a set of NVGs, night vision goggles, and she didn't. When the ramp stopped grinding, Logan squeezed her hand and kept a hold on it. The military frowned on such things, but he could care less. He was in his SEAL gear, and

everyone knew you left SEALs alone. They wrote their own rules. Jess probably was aware that romances were officially discouraged throughout the
military, no matter which branch it was. Holding hands was a definite no-no,
but he shrugged it off.

Logan led her off the ramp and, once they were on the tarmac, off loaders
began to gather to remove the large containers still strapped down on board.
Logan threaded her through the gathering men and machines, heading for
Operations. He was due to fly out in just an hour on a medevac Black Hawk
which was based at FOB Bravo. The wind was blowing warm and there was
plenty of grit in the air, along with the smell of jet fuel everywhere. Jess held on
to his hand and he shortened his stride for her sake.

Once inside the busy Ops building, he released her hand. Jess gawked
around. Logan knew she hadn't been here before and it was a big place with
lots of pilots coming and going, everyone busy. He led her over to the briefing-
room area. Checking the rooms out, he spotted one that wasn't being used.
Opening the door, Logan guided her in, shut and locked it behind them, and
put up the sign that said the room was taken.

Jess turned and smiled. "You're in stealth mode, I can tell." She saw him
grin and she opened her arms as Logan walked over to her. It was so easy to be
wrapped into his powerful arms and swept, literally, off her feet for a moment
as he plastered her against his body. Jess could feel his erection pressing against
her belly. His mouth came down on hers, swift and hard. As he eased Jess's
feet back to the ground, Logan's tender and welcoming kiss deepened, and he
framed her face with his hands. She purred beneath his incredible male
gentleness. Jess was sure few ever saw this side to Logan. Her body went hot
with longing, and she felt achy just from his mouth softening hers, licking her
lower lip, kissing the corners of her mouth, teasing her tongue. The man was
so damned sensual! Jess had to give both of them some leeway; Logan hadn't
had sex in six months and she, in over a year. They were both a little needy and
hungry.

Slowly, their lips separated. They were both breathing unevenly, their gazes
locked. "Listen to me," Logan rasped, "you HAVE to be alert out at your
drilling site now, Jess. If the Taliban or anyone of those Hill chieftains got that
close to you before, they're going to try again to kill you." Frustration lined his
voice. "Can you talk to the A-team Special Forces captain? See what he can do
to give you a better safety perimeter? I need you to be proactive about this,
Baby."

Jess compressed her lips and nodded. "I promise I will, Logan. I'll go to
him first thing tomorrow morning. Before I left, Captain Anderson said
something was going to be done about it. I'll find out what he's decided."

Logan eased his hands around her shoulders, feeling how strong and proud she was. "I want to take a photo of you with my phone."

Startled, she smiled. "Okay. I'll bet, as a SEAL, you don't let anyone take *your* picture?" She saw Logan nod and pull out his cell. Jess sat on the edge of the briefing table while he backed up with his iPhone and snapped the photo.

"Something to remember you with until we can work things out to get together again," he told her.

Jess felt her heart fall. Her smile disappeared as he pushed the iPhone back into his cargo-pants pocket. "Logan, you seem so sure, but I don't see how we'll be able to get back together." Jess saw him give her a sly smile.

"You never tell a SEAL he can't do something, Baby," he murmured, sliding his fingers though her soft, black hair. Her eyes were the richest green Logan had ever seen. Their shade reminded him of the lush grass in the Grand Tetons of Wyoming in July.

Closing her eyes, Jess placed her hands on his biceps, feeling the muscles respond beneath her fingertips. "Thank you, Logan… for everything…" and she gazed up, studying him. His mouth was set, his eyes carried a determined look.

"This is NOT goodbye, Jess." His voice was firm. Stubborn.

She frowned a little. "You operate in a world I know practically nothing about, Logan. I'm a worker of the earth. Not black ops." Her throat tightened as she searched his deep blue eyes. "I don't want to say goodbye to you either."

"I know you don't," Logan rasped, kissing her gently. "But I'm going to make this work. That's a promise."

Her lips tingled in the wake of his tender kiss. She could feel how badly he wanted her to stay with him. It was mutual. "I feel like a lovesick teenage girl…" His smile at that sent sunshine pouring through her.

Logan smoothed some strands away from her face, drowning in her green gaze glimmering with tears. "Don't cry, Jess," he whispered. "It's not goodbye. You'll see…"

"You've done so much for me already, Logan. I arrived at Ramstein broken into so many emotional pieces." Jess touched his jaw, near where the scar on it was, her voice trembling. "You've healed me on so many levels, Logan. I-I just can't explain it. I don't know how, but you have," and she gave him a sad smile. "In my world of rock and dirt, I have to be practical. I'm grounded. I don't see how we'll see one another again for a long, long time." *If then…*

"Baby, you just stay focused on staying safe out there." His voice dropped and became a growl. "I need you, Jess. More than I can tell you right now. We just need a little patience… And I'm going to see what I can do for us." Logan dug into his pocket. Inside a small plastic zip-lock bag was a four-leaf clover.

"Here, I want you to promise me you'll wear this on you every day. You don't NOT wear it, Jess."

She frowned, slowly turning over the small plastic bag and examining it. The dried green four-leaf clover was backed with some cardboard. "What is this?"

"My good luck charm," he said, resting his hands on his hips. "Most SEALs have one they always carry with them. We are never without it on an op or mission. We really do believe it keeps us safe. Keeps us alive. And I want you to have mine."

Deeply touched, Jess gave him an anguished look. "But… you need it, Logan. This thing looks so old and worn… like it's been doing a good job for a long time. And you believe in it! I want *you* safe, too."

"I'll be fine." *Because I've found you. I've got something to live for as never before.* He wasn't about to tell Jess that. If she only knew how much she held his heart, it would probably frighten her off. Logan needed time to woo her, to get to know her, and vice-versa. They had to have *time.* He just had to figure out a way to carve it out of their schedules. He closed his hands over hers. "Promise me you'll keep it in a pocket of your uniform every day, Jess?" and he dug into her widening eyes.

"Okay… I will." She was so touched by his care. Jess could feel that protection radiating off Logan, wrapping around her, giving her such a strong sense of safety. She tucked the clover into her blouse pocket and Velcroed it shut. "I won't leave home without it," she promised him solemnly. Logan looked relieved. He must really believe in his lucky charm, she thought, and that was, after all, exactly *why* it kept him safe.

Glancing at his watch, Logan muttered respectfully, "I have to go, Jess. To get the bus over to the women's barracks here on base, just walk straight out the main doors. There's a bus stop to the right. You can't miss it."

Jess smiled tenderly, lifting her hand, smoothing his blouse across his chest. "Stay safe out there, Logan?"

"Count on it," he growled, sliding his arms around her, drawing her against him, taking her mouth one last time. He poured every bit of emotion he held in his heart into this remarkable woman who had stunned him with her nurturing warmth. Her mouth was inviting, opening to him. Jess trusted him with her life. Logan could feel it. Reluctantly, he withdrew, memorizing the look in her druzy eyes, the love shining in them. Love? Yeah, love. And on his end, too. How the hell could this have happened to him? This quick? Logan's head spun, but he didn't try to explain away the unspoken look in Jess's eyes. "I'll see you sooner than you think," he said, giving her a wink.

Jess stood in the briefing room, feeling the loss of Logan's vital heat, the protectiveness he always embraced her with. She stood at the door, watching him trot across the shining floor, pushing open the doors that led back out to the tarmac. And then… he was gone. *Gone.*

Jess felt like she'd been hit by a Mack truck, stunned. She'd met Logan by accident less than two days ago. Now, as she absently touched her lower, tingling lip, still tasting him, she couldn't live without him. Her heart felt like it was breaking.

CHAPTER 5

September, 2020, Afghanistan

WHEN JESS EMBARKED from the Chinook helicopter that had brought both her and supplies for the well drillers in, she was met by Lieutenant Brad Parker, the man in charge of the drilling unit. She had her protective eye goggles in place, but was still left almost sightless by the dust the twin blades spinning above her were picking up into the air. The rotor wash was so powerful, it almost knocked her over, would have, in fact, if she hadn't known to be braced for it. Never mind the small to large pebbles and gritty dust that rose around her. She spotted several of her men, with their own eye goggles in place, running toward the ramp of the helo to help unload the supplies so the bird could get back into the air as soon as possible. A helo on the ground was a sitting target for bullet rounds and, worse, RPGs. The village where they were presently drilling was on the sloping hills leading up to the Hindu Kush Mountain Range that rose to fourteen thousand feet above them, with two different enemy groups hidden but watching them.

She hurried toward the Navy officer waiting in his desert cammos. Finally, she was out of the blast zone of the rotors where dust, gravel, brush, and even rocks were being kicked up by the blades. Brad gripped her arm, leading her toward the opened gate of the village standing at the end of its valley. Jess pushed her dust-coated goggles down to now hang around her neck, and she saw a large crowd of villagers standing and watching what was going on.

"Welcome back, Jess."

"Thanks, Brad." She wiped the dust on her face away, sliding her dirty hands down her cammo pants. She looked over at the Navy officer. He had red hair, cropped short, and his blue eyes were trained on what was going on with the helo. It was always threat time whenever the helo was on the ground. He wore his side pistol, a .45 in a holster, but also had an M4 in its sling harness over his shoulder, barrel pointed to the ground, just in case. Jess had all her equipment, rifle and ruck stored away in a currently vacant stone village hut. As a woman, she got quarters to herself, which was nice. The rest of the men were two or three to each mud-and-rock house within the village that was not otherwise occupied.

"How are you doing?" Brad asked, looking back from his threat scanning, and into her eyes.

Jess shrugged. "Okay." She turned, watching her men helping the two hard-working loadmasters quickly moving off forty-foot sections of casing. The casing would be used to sink the well down to a depth where water could be found. "How is everyone?"

Brad grimaced. "We've been pretty down since you called and told us about Dan, which is to be expected. But... you were *there*. It had to be tough on you?"

She nodded. "Yes, it was. It's going to take all of us time to get over his passing."

Brad stood, watching the offloading of the pipe as it was being stacked. Soon, the men of the unit would have to get the front-end loader with its bucket to carry the pipe to where it was needed. "While you were gone, we found we needed a lot more casing."

"Haven't struck water yet?" Brad was thirty years old, stood five foot ten inches tall, her height. He was a civil engineer by trade and a damned good one. Jess felt lucky to have someone of his experience in her Seabee unit.

"No. But plenty has been going on since Dan was... shot."

Jess watched the last of the sixty casings being stacked by the men who'd busted their humps getting them all off the helo in record time. She could see them sweating even in the frigid early-morning air. The shadow of the mighty and beautiful Hindu Kush blotted out the rising sun's rays over the valley and left the area near freezing. But as soon as the sun peeked over the rugged peaks, it would feel like someone had suddenly turned on a boiler. Jess knew the desert climate would jump up to near one-hundred degrees Fahrenheit. She had an Afghan *shemagh*: a scarf woven in the Shinwari tribe's colors of yellow on green checks that she'd be putting on soon enough. It soaked up the sweat, stopping the collar of her uniform chafing her neck raw, and helped ward off the constant sand and grit around this place.

As soon as the Chinook pulled up its ramp, it took off, raising huge, towering clouds of yellow-gray dust hundreds of feet into the air once again. Brad gripped her arm and said, "Come on...." and they hurried away from the helo's LZ. As they walked through the village, the children quickly surrounded Jess. She stopped, pulling out wrapped hard candy from her pockets. The boys would always push the little girls away to get it first, so Jess made them stand apart. She would then hand the candy out on a girl-boy-girl-boy basis, to each group in turn. Jess had found that if she gave all the little girls their portion first, the boys would attack them, punching and hitting them, to grab the candy and then run away. The Afghan and Muslim way of treating women, even little girls, made her angry. They were considered less important than a cow, goat or sheep. It sickened Jess, but there was little she could do about it except enforce her little candy rule and hope it taught them something.

When her pocket was emptied of the candy, and every child in the village had a piece, they all ran off, scattering like a flock of wild birds in all directions. She saw Brad smile.

"You're such a softy pushover, Courtland."

Grinning, she said, "Yeah, I know it. Hey, I'm the only woman around. What do you expect? I draw kids like a magnet. They see 'mom' written all over me." She saw Brad nod, take off his utility cap, and run his fingers through his short hair, wiping the sweat off his brow with his palms.

"At least these kids SEE a woman doing something other than being a broodmare and being treated like a piece of shit."

"No kidding," Jess muttered, falling into step with the officer. Some houses were made of mud, some of stone, some a combination of both. They were all one story, except for the chieftain's, who was the heritage- and lineage-based leader of the village. He and his wife had a two-story stone home that stood like a castle above the hovels below it. Brad's "office", as he ruefully called it, was a mud home that had been abandoned. They ducked into it, the door only about five foot six inches tall. The Afghans were not a tall people, compared to the average American. Jess had more than once banged her head on a doorframe while distracted. She saw Brad's wooden table, with a map spread across it, and its two accompanying stools. No electronics. He always wore two clipped-on radios on the shoulders of his uniform, not leaving anything worth *anything* in the house. People stole habitually around here, and the radios were lifelines for their team members.

He went over and turned on the gas-canister hotplate with its beat-up copper kettle. They were the fifth replacements just this month, but he had a small crate of them stowed away and wasn't about to start lugging kitchen appliances around as well.

"Tea?"

She snorted. "I wish it were coffee, but yes, I won't turn it down," Jess said, taking off her Kevlar vest and helmet, setting them aside on the table, next to the map. She and Brad regularly spent hours on end poring over hydrology, geology and terrain maps of the area. Not that there was much information on the hydrology of this valley. This was the Third World and tribespeople were not aware of water tables below the ground or aquifers; underground lakes. They were uneducated and Jess couldn't fault them on that. But to drill a well, trying to strike water without proper data, had become a real issue in this valley.

"I sent an email off to Dan's wife, Sophia, while you were gone," he said, bringing out two aluminum cups and setting them nearby. His mouth turned down. "It's a shit job, Jess." and he turned to her as she sat down on one of the two wooden stools at the map table.

"I know," she whispered, suddenly choked up. "I was waiting to hear from you that the Navy officers had told Sophia of Dan's death before I sent her an email myself."

Shaking his head, Brad muttered, "This sucks. When we were in Iraq, every village we ever drove into welcomed us with open arms." He poured the tea leaves from a container into two strainers and then dropped them into the tops of the cups. "Here, in this valley, they don't trust us. Go figure. Their babies, children and old-folk are dying all the time from parasite-infested water. We're bringing them safe, clean water to drink. You'd think the Taliban would leave us alone to do the well drilling for these people."

Jess felt Parker's frustration as he puttered around his office. Her heart swelled with warmth as she saw him pull out another tin, this one full of his favorite Oreo cookies, sent to him by his wife, Olivia.

"This must be a real occasion for you to pull out your Oreos at 0700," Jess teased, grinning over at him. The hut was coolish right now, but once the sun rose over the mountains, it would become a sweat box. There was one window, which couldn't be opened, and the heat built inside these huts to the point where no one wanted to be in any of them during daylight hours. And, of course, no electricity meant no air conditioning. Brad, engineer that he was, kept a small gasoline generator on hand to create enough electricity to charge their radios, cell phones, and computer Toughbooks, but running an air conditioning unit, twelve or more hours a day off of one, was out of the question.

"Well," Brad said, setting the cookies down in front of her, "it sort of *is* just that: a special occasion."

"Oh?" She watched him pour boiling water from the kettle into the awaiting cups.

"Yeah, things have been hopping here, ever since Dan was shot," he muttered. Brad handed her a cup. He sat down opposite her at the table, grabbing one of the vaunted, sacred Oreos. "The admiral back at Bagram has authorized us a sniper team. We have no idea who they are, which branch of service they're from, or when they'll arrive. The admiral said he was going to talk to a Marine Force Recon commander at the base and see if he couldn't get a team out here to stand overwatch. In other words, protect our asses while we work. Keep an eye on who's comin' down into the valley to kill us. Most likely, the two snipers will each stand twelve-hour watches, one on, one off."

"That will help a lot."

"No shit," Brad muttered, chewing on the Oreo.

"What about our A-team?" Jess asked, dipping the strainer in and out of her steaming cup. "What does Captain Anderson suggest?"

"He was the one who came to me and suggested getting the two-man sniper team in place." Brad gestured on the map toward the higher hills less than a half a mile from the village. "Sean said those snipers will take the high ground. He said he was trying to get a couple of Army Delta Force guys in here, but I doubt that will happen. Those guys are the blackest ops groups around, and they want action. They don't want to sit around a village and play watchdog. Then, there's the other matter...."

Nodding, Jess thought about Logan being a SEAL sniper, but she kept that to herself, and replied, "Another rivet's popped loose?"

Smiling a little at her turn of phrase, Brad said, "Yeah. We just got a Marine dog-handler in here by the name of Sergeant Andy Stapleton. He and his bomb-sniffing dog arrived here the day you left. His dog, a Black Lab named Ace, has already helped us out. Yesterday morning, your number two, Ben Gilbert, had the Marine handler and his dog sniff around the drilling truck. Damned if he didn't find an IED buried right smack-dab in the ground near the vehicle."

Gasping, Jess's eyes widened. "Really?" Her heart pounded in fear to underscore this awful new development.

"Yeah," Brad said grimly as he sipped his tea. "So, new orders went out from me: whoever is on morning shift with the drill rig, gets Sergeant Stapleton and Ace to FIRST clear the area where they're going to be working. That includes the truck, and the casings, too, Jess. *Anywhere* the team's working, I want it all cleared first by them or you don't go near the area. No exceptions."

"Right," she murmured. "Who'd have thought we'd have to watch for IEDs around our equipment?"

He gave her a dark look. "Sean had warned us that, among the Pashtun, there were pro-Taliban villagers within the population. I'm sure the bomb maker came from one of their villages. Sick, isn't it? Dumb bastards don't even understand the importance of a well with clean water in it. But whoever it is, they are more than willing to kill us for trying to help them. Sick."

"So? Apart from all that, it's business as usual, Brad? Are we going to be assigned a new chief?" It hurt to ask. She saw pain in the officer's eyes. It wasn't a topic she wanted to talk about, but it was necessary. The chief became the fulcrum point between what Brad needed the drilling team to do and the team in the field, a vital link along the chain of command. In this case, the final link at the end of that chain was *her*, the person in charge of the whole drilling team.

"Yeah," he muttered. "That admiral at Bagram put in that request as well. I haven't heard anything yet." He struggled with his emotions, shrugged, and then gave her a warm look. "Until then, you get to play chief. You okay with that? You've got more experience at well drilling than anyone here, other than what Dan had."

Wincing, Jess whispered, "Yeah, no problem. I can do it."

"Sean is going through the village with his sergeants. They're trying to catch our friendly neighborhood bomber red-handed, or at least find someone who might be able to point them out. The Pashtun people are pro-American, as a whole, but they're afraid of some of the people who come to their village, and I'm pretty sure those people are undercover Hill tribe members or Taliban." Shrugging, Brad went on, "Probably a hopeless task because these people are just as afraid of Taliban reprisal as we are. We know there are Taliban insurgents hiding and living among the villagers, but they aren't going to rat them out just like that, for fear those bastards will kill their whole family if the father comes to us with intel."

"These people," Jess sighed," are caught between a rock and hard place. Most of them just want to be left alone to survive. They've got the Taliban wanting to tell them how to run their lives on one side. And then they have us on the other. There're so many fine lines for them to walk. I feel sorry for them."

"Chief Behzaad Sahar, leader of the village, told me yesterday, after he found out an IED had been planted near our truck, that he was sorry it happened."

"That was nice. I always took him for being Taliban."

"He could be. But even if he isn't, he almost certainly damn well knows who the bomb maker is, but he's not talkin'."

"And if he did," Jess said, finishing off her tea and standing, "then it's the same story, even for him: he'd get a Death Letter from the local Taliban warlord telling him he and his family were going to be killed for consorting with the Americans."

"Yeah," Brad sighed. "Helluva situation, you know?"

She pulled on her Kevlar-4 vest, hating the weight of the ceramic plates in it. Before, they hadn't worn them. But, just before Dan was shot, Brad had put out the order that everyone had to wear the forty-pound vests, based off intercepted Taliban chatter. She put on her dark green baseball cap and picked up her helmet. "I'm going to my hut and then I'll go out and join the team. I also want to meet Sergeant Stapleton, thank him and Ace for saving more of us from getting killed. I love having a dog around." The grimness of her task weighed her down. Normally, well-drilling teams were seen as protectors in less-developed countries. Village people would invite them into their homes, the chief and his wife would hold a celebratory feast in honor of the fact that the team was there to bring them fresh water. But not here. The ungrateful Taliban utilized rat lines; trails up and over passes in the tall, craggy mountains curving around the villages. They could hit-and-run as they pleased, disappearing into the scrub trees that ranged upward to the snowline, already in place at this time of year.

"Later," Brad said. "Make sure your radio battery is charged? I want to stay in close touch with you at all times when you're on your shift."

"Roger that," She finished off the now-luke-warm tea, sat the cup on his map table and raised her hand to Brad as she ducked out beneath the doorframe. It seemed as if she'd been in both a nightmare and a dream over the last two days. Losing Dan and finding Logan. Her heart felt heavy about both of them. Looking around as she walked the two blocks down to her mud home, Jess remained alert. She saw one of the A-team sergeants, and raised her hand in silent hello to him. He was dressed in full combat gear; a sign of the heightened defenses put in place since the Taliban attack. It didn't make her feel any safer. There was no such thing as safety out here. But Jess did feel the sniper team would be a step in the right direction. They had long-range scopes on their rifles and could see an attack coming from a long way off. They could sound a warning, allowing enough time to get her people to safety instead of being shot at like sitting ducks.

Inside her stone-and-mud hut, she pulled out her *shemagh* of green and yellow checks, wrapping it around her neck, with a triangle of its bright cloth left hanging down the front of her uniform. Apart from just protecting her exposed skin, it would also stop grit from sifting down inside her shirt and chafing the sensitive skin beneath her breasts and armpits. The Kevlar vest was an extra forty pounds of weight she had to carry for eight-hour shifts. They drilled only during daylight hours. At night, everyone slept like logs because of the brutal physicality of their work demands. Tucking her radio into a nylon belt around her waist, she picked up her .45, making sure there was a round in the chamber, and then safed it before sliding it into its dark green nylon holster. She grabbed her constant companion: her Swiss Army knife, which she slid into her right cargo pants' pocket. It was one of the handiest tools she had, able to get in through gaps and deal with many breakdowns on the drilling equipment that regular-issue tools couldn't even hope to reach.

For a moment, Jess allowed herself to think of Logan, of how he'd made love to her in that small German inn. It seemed like some delicious dream now.

Not reality. Her heart swung darkly between grief over Dan's death and the conviction that she'd probably never see Logan again. Mouth tightening, Jess tucked all those feeling deep down inside. They had a well to dig, and her men were waiting for her to show up, be a leader, and get the day's drilling underway.

It was a blistering hundred degrees at noon when Jess gave her crew the order to stop drilling and take an hour to rest and have lunch. Where had the time gone? She'd been back to work for two weeks. She trudged back through the village, sweating heavily, hating the weight of the vest. Before she went to see Brad, she detoured to her house. Hauling the damned-heavy Kevlar vest off her shoulders, she opened it up and pulled out every last ceramic plate, hiding them beneath another *shemagh*. Jess couldn't handle the combination of the desert heat *on top* of the Kevlar holding in her body heat as well, creating a sauna-like condition inside the vest. She'd drank over a gallon of water already. And she was on her crew to keep hydrated. They hated the order to wear the heavy vests, too. Jess was willing to take her own chances without the armor. Hauling the blessedly plate-less vest onto her shoulders, she closed its Velcro and shook out the dusty *shemagh* over the front of her chest. She suspected her entire crew would go back to their huts and get rid of their plates, too. If so, she hoped that Parker wouldn't discover what they'd done. She wasn't about to rat them out.

Just then, Brad radioed her to come to his command center, that he had good news for her. She dipped into Brad's hovel. He looked up from studying his maps. There was a light in his blue eyes and she thought he looked happy. "What's up?" she asked, taking her cap off and wiping her sweaty brow with the ends of her *shemagh*.

"Good news," he said, grinning. "Just got a call from the admiral at Bagram. We're getting a replacement Seabee chief in two weeks." His grin widened. "Even BETTER news?"

"Yeah? I don't think I can take *too* many doses of good news in a row," Jess said wryly, sitting down opposite him. She opened up a protein bar, chewing on it and sucking water from the CamelBak tube across her shoulder. "Tell me you found the bomb maker in the village?"

Brad shook his head. "No, but we got two snipers assigned to us. They're coming in on a Chinook that will arrive shortly."

"Wow, that was fast," Jess murmured. "I think they'll be as important as Ace is to us."

"The Admiral said they'd be assigned to us as long as we're here in this godforsaken, Taliban and Hill infested valley."

"Good," Jess murmured, seeing the relief in Parker's eyes. She knew he bore a heavy burden of responsibility for all of them. That's what a good officer did: take care of his or her people.

"How's it going wearing those damned Kevlar vests?"

"Hot; sweating gallons, drinking gallons of water. Really, can't we just have them sitting nearby and put them on when a sniper sees a Taliban crew galloping toward us? It's really hampering our work efforts, Brad," and she gave him a pleading look. She saw him mulling it over.

"Not yet," he hedged, worried. "Let's see if this sniper team can give us the credible-threat signal in time to be able to haul those vests on if the occasion arises."

Making a face, Jess said nothing. Brad had been around, and probably knew she and her crew had dumped, or were going to dump, those plates. If he did, he said nothing.

"How's it going out there?" he asked.

"We're at eighty feet and nada."

"That's what I thought. Is the soil standing up or not?"

"No," Jess said flatly. "Nothing but sand. We're having to spend a lot of time drilling until we can get a metal casing beat into the ground to hold what we've drilled. That sand is a bitch. It caves in all the time. We're spending extra time supporting the soil, because of it." And then she added grumpily, "Wished to hell it was clay." Because clay was the thickest and least porous of all soils. When the drill bit churned and ground an opening, the clay would move and hold everything else that could move remaining in place. They didn't have to put in a casing every hour like they did with the damn quixotic sand.

Brad's radio took off. He pulled it out, answering it.

Jess listened to the scratchy conversation. It was the Chinook co-pilot, saying they were arriving in fifteen minutes with the two snipers. Could they clear a landing area with a green smoke cannister in that timeframe? She quickly ate the rest of her protein bar, washed it down with huge gulps of water, and stood. She saw Brad's eyes light up with excitement as he said he'd have the LZ, the landing zone, ready for them. This was a first: a well-drilling team having to have two snipers assigned to protect their asses. She smiled a little and followed Brad out of the hut. Jess felt excitement, too, but even more than that: relief.

The double-rotor Chinook came in quickly and landed, sending up clouds, hundreds of feet high, of rolling yellow dust in all directions. Jess stood back with Brad, watching the unfolding ramp appear and disappear within the swirling brown-out dust. She noticed several villagers, mostly women and children, watching with interest. It wasn't every day a military helicopter landed here. The dust was so thick that she couldn't see anyone on the mostly-obscured LZ it had landed on. This was going to be a fast off load of personnel and then an even swifter takeoff because the pilot at the controls was keeping the blades turning at well over two hundred RPM, revolutions per minute. That was near-takeoff speed. The noise pummeled her ears, the invisible rippling effect of the rotors whipping around, like fists punching into her body. At the drill site, she normally wore earplugs, but they were hanging around her neck at the moment.

"There they are," Brad said, pointing to two figures appearing out of the cloud of thick, roiling dust columns.

Squinting, Jess could barely make out two men, each carrying a heavy duffle over their right shoulder and a cased rifle over their left. Their heads were down, and they were running to escape the choking, blinding dust raised by the noisy Chinook.

"I'll be damned," Parker muttered, surprise in his voice.

"What?" Jess asked, watching the snipers appear and disappear in the swirling dust as they approached.

"I think," he muttered, lifting his hat off his head and wiping sweat from his brow, "I don't think they're Marines....I thought they said back at HQ at Bagram they were going to give us Army snipers…"

"What do you mean?" Both snipers appeared out of the last cloud. Jess felt her heart leap into her throat. Her eyes narrowed. No! *It couldn't be!* Her mouth dropped open as she saw Logan Randall, along with another SEAL, trotting toward them in full combat gear.

"They're Navy SEALs!" Parker exclaimed, excited. "I'll be damned! This is great! They're the best! When I talked to the admiral, I requested SEALs on the off chance, but I never thought in a million years I'd ever get a pair of 'em. Damn, our luck's changing, Jess. Let's go meet them!"

Jess gulped. The SEALs were slowing to a walk, hefting their huge, heavy duffle bags, probably weighing a hundred pounds or more each, on their broad shoulders. And, as they drew closer, Logan's gaze turned her way. She felt her stomach flutter. And then her heart pounded with silent joy. And then, she worried. If Parker suspected anything, it could spell bad news. She eagerly searched Logan's dusty, sweaty face, his game face, for any sign of his feelings, but his expression remained set and alert. The other SEAL, who was about an inch shorter than Logan, had the same stolid look on his face. These were the best of the best! Professional warriors. Jess could barely still her happiness. How had Logan managed this? She remembered his gruff promise to see her sooner, not later. What were the odds? The chances?

LOGAN KEPT HIS face carefully arranged as he and his partner, Chris Lowery, approached Jess and the officer standing next to her. He saw the shock and disbelief in her green eyes, saw her wrestling between happiness at seeing him again and trying not to let it show. The gold flecks in her eyes sparkled, even at a distance, telling him how glad she was to see him. She looked so different out here; hair in a ponytail, coated with the ever-present dust and grit, her baseball cap in place, shading her wide, intelligent eyes. The cammies all but hid her delicious body from the world, but Logan knew that body intimately and he could feel himself stir. No one would see it, but from the look in Jess's dancing gaze, she knew.

He dropped his weapons bag and did not salute Parker because the Taliban and Hill soldiers targeted officers. Instead, he thrust his hand forward in the normal, but strong, manner for a handshake.

"Petty Officer First Class Logan Randall, reporting as ordered, sir. This is my partner, Petty Officer First Class Chris Lowery. We're here to provide you security for the duration in this bitch of a valley," Logan said and grinned.

Brad grinned back and shook his hand. "You're a sight for sore eyes, Randall. We're glad to see you, and you too, Lowrey." He shook the other SEAL's hand and then turned to Jess, where he introduced her to them. "Why don't you take them to that empty house diagonal from yours? You know which one. They can stay there."

Nodding, Jess said, "Will do." She stretched out her hand to Logan and pretended to introduce herself. When his hand enclosed hers, she felt his heat, felt his desire, even though there was absolutely nothing in his face to suggest he even knew her. He was protecting her and Jess breathed in relief. Chris Lowery was a lanky Texan, with a thick drawl that made her smile. She liked this bearded SEAL with his long, red shaggy hair.

"Come with me," she told the SEALs, gesturing for them to follow her.

Logan checked out the people standing nearby. SEALs dressed dramatically different to other black ops groups and, unless he missed his guess, the elders, who had come out of the village as a group, had surprised looks on their deeply weathered, tanned faces because of that. Maybe, as word sped like wildfire through the village that there were SEALs here, the attacks might stop. He could hope. He lengthened his stride to catch up to Jess. He saw her face was flushed. Right now, he couldn't do or say anything. Chris, his swim buddy, knew about their relationship, but he'd have Logan's back and keep their relationship secret. The crew would never know a thing. First and foremost, though, Chris was here to protect this woman who had stolen Logan's heart, which he would do at all costs.

"Is Lieutenant Parker going to give us a briefing?" Logan asked Jess, meeting her eyes. He saw her nod.

"Yes, as soon as I get you guys set up in that abandoned house, I'll take you to his office."

Chris caught up and walked on her other side. Jess thought it was such a SEAL thing to do; to be protective of women, and she smiled to herself. Both men were looking around and she could feel them on guard, watching, evaluating the people and the area. "Ma'am? Are you the only woman here on the well-drilling team?"

"Call me Jess," she told the SEAL. "Yes, I am." She knew she was an anomaly.

"And could you point out where you stay at night?"

Surprised, Jess pointed to the right. "I'm here. Why?"

Lowery shrugged. "You're an American woman. That makes you an automatic target of the Taliban and Hill Chieftains. We need to know where you're located, is all."

Some of her excitement bled off. Chris was right. He was doing his job, figuring out all the angles and the players, so he, as a sniper, could properly grasp the lay of the land. "Well," she said, gesturing ahead, "your hut is catty-corner from mine. I'm about twenty feet, diagonally speaking, away from you guys. I think I'll feel safe enough," and she gave Chris a grin. He smiled back, nodded, but maintained his seriousness.

"If you have coffee at your hut," Logan warned, "you're liable to see both of us over there every morning with our mugs, begging for some."

Jess laughed. "Yes, I have coffee. And yes, I'll be happy to share with you guys." She liked the deviltry dancing in Logan's eyes. His mouth made her lower body go hot and achy. The man's smile made her melt.

"Thank you," Chris said, lightening up a bit. "We brought coffee grounds in the hope someone here in the drilling unit would have a coffee maker."

"I'm the only game in town," Jess said, raising her hand, again enjoying the drawl of the easy-going Texan. He was leaner than Logan, and he had a rolling gait that belied the fact he was a deadly sniper.

"Woman after my own heart," Logan murmured, giving her a wink.

She felt heat rush to her face. Jess could hardly wait to get Logan alone. No one would think anything of him being in her mud-and-stone home. Word would get out the SEALs liked coffee, and she was the only one in the village with a pot and a generator hooked up to create electricity to make the brew. It wouldn't raise eyebrows. Jess could barely think straight and had to force herself to focus. Logan was here! And, judging from the sly 'I-told-you-so' smile he gave only to her, he was as happy about it as she was.

CHAPTER 6

I T WAS DUSK. The mountains cast long shadows across the valley as Jess made sure everything was shut down for the night. She walked slowly around the truck on her own, notepad and pen out. Because she was the supervisor on the project, it was her job to ensure everything was stowed away and locked up. She heard a lot of men's voices, Americans, in the distance, laughing. Most evenings, the Special Forces soldiers and the well drillers met at a hut, sitting down and shooting the shit while they ate the MREs that made up their dinner. Jess usually didn't join them. Men had their thing, and she was fine allowing them that time. When a woman was around, men tended to lowkey it. She wondered where Logan and Chris were. Off and on throughout the afternoon, she'd seen the two SEALs walking the area, M4 rifles in harnesses across their chests, dressed in full combat gear. Both wore the Shinwari tribal scarves around their necks to keep the sand and grit from getting past the neck region where the thick hand-woven cloth wrapped around. She smiled a little. They were definitely sending a not-so-subtle message to those who were pro-Taliban or Hill soldiers in the village that they were around and watching. That don't-fuck-with-me attitude was well on display.

"Jess?"

She gasped, spinning around. Logan stood casually by the hood of the truck.

"You scared the piss out of me, Logan!" she whispered, her hand going to her throat, her heart banging away with a spurt of adrenaline.

"Sorry," he murmured, giving her an apologetic look, standing, his gaze sweeping her from head to toe. "Lieutenant Parker said I'd find you out here finishing off the duty for the day."

She closed her eyes, dragged in a ragged breath and then stared at him. He was wearing his black baseball cap, and had his H-gear on, the H-vest pockets loaded with magazines of bullets. His M4 was across his chest, and his black shooting gloves on.

"I always make a last check on our equipment before dark," she said, feeling his gaze follow her. At this hour, Logan didn't have his sunglasses on. They were perched on the bill of his cap. She saw the burning quality in his blue eyes, could feel him wanting her. Looking around, Jess wanted to make sure no one was within earshot.

"Don't worry," Logan assured her, a slight smile tipping one corner of his mouth, "no one is nearby. They're all chowing down right now."

"Good," and she pointed her chin toward the stacks of casing pipe. "Gotta go over there and count them."

Logan followed, cutting his stride to match hers. He gave her a glance. "Your surprised I'm here?"

Jess laughed a little, her heart fluttering. "You know I am." And then she sobered. "I never expected," and she choked up, "...to see you again."

Logan kept his distance, always looking around. Jess was a certifiable distraction, but he wanted to protect her, and that made it easier to keep a stranglehold on his emotions and his desire for her. "Well," he admitted wryly, as he watched her stop and begin counting the huge stacks of pipe, "I got a helluva surprise, too, when the opportunity came up, the master chief assigned me to this mission." He waited until Jess was done counting, watching the way she moved, the way she leaned over, thinking she had the finest ass he'd ever seen. And cammies couldn't even hide it. This woman was sensual as hell and didn't even realize it. He watched as Jess dutifully wrote down the amount of pipe stacked before them.

"Why do you count this?" he asked, pointing to the pipe.

"Villagers steal them," she said with a shrug. "I don't know why. Taking it out to irrigate their fields, maybe?"

"These people are always on the edge of starvation," Logan agreed, walking up to her. "Are you done here?" He saw her eyes grow warm and he had a hell of a time not staring at her lips.

"Yes. Why?"

"Walk with me? And don't give me that look. Your LT would expect you to be working with us. You're the supervisor on this project."

Jess nodded. "You're right. I'm just jumpy, Logan."

"I've got your back, Babe."

His low growl moved through her as if he'd sensually stroked her with his hand. "We'll have to be careful..." Logan gave her a feral grin as they walked along the outer perimeter of the village, heading south.

"I'll invoke SEAL stealth. We're black ops. No one will ever see me at your hut. Guaranteed."

"But," she worried, "what about Chris? He'll know, won't he?"

"He already knows." Logan saw her eyes widen with anxiety. He wanted to kiss her, caress her cheek, but he could do neither. "Chris is my swim buddy," he told her in a low voice. "That means he's like my brother. He knows about us and he has our backs."

"Is that why he also came to my side earlier today after you off loaded from the Chinook? I felt like I was bracketed by protection, like I had two SEAL bookends." Jess saw a slow grin crawl across Logan's mouth. She wanted to kiss him so badly she could taste it. And yet, even in the dusk, people could see them. They both had to play adult here, not give in to their intense emotions for one another.

"Yeah, he knows you're my lady. He'd take a bullet for you, if he had to." And then Logan added somberly, holding her gaze, "So would I."

Groaning, Jess muttered, "Don't talk like that! I don't want anyone else hurt." *Especially you*, but the words caught in her tightening throat. Jess gestured ahead to a tall stand of green bushes. "The kids play out here during the day a lot, Logan. Hide 'n seek. You can always hear them laughing and squealing, so don't think it's Taliban or Hill soldiers hiding there. Okay?" and she slanted him an amused look. She saw him studying the grove of high, lush foliage. It was over twenty feet tall and about ten feet wide.

"It's still a prime hiding place for them," he warned, walking toward one end of it, wanting to scope it out more closely. "If they wanted to ambush this place, they'd come in at night, wait until dawn and then attack. It would catch the southern end of the village by surprise. People would die."

Jess followed him, feeling safe, simply because he was near her. Logan was all business as he scouted out the entire grove. At the other end, the light failing, he said, "Follow me…"

Jess turned, going back to the center of the grove. Logan moved the rifle to his right shoulder. He turned smoothly, catching her off guard, his gloved hand sliding behind the nape of her neck, drawing her lightly up against all his gear, pulling Jess as close as he could, leaning down, taking her mouth gently, tasting her, feeling her tense and then suddenly sag against him. He knew the kiss had to be quick. Hell, he wanted it to last all night. But that wouldn't be smart or wise. Lifting his mouth from hers, Logan saw the aroused look in her green, half-closed eyes, felt her hands on his shoulders.

"I needed to kiss you," Logan rasped, easing her away from him, holding on to her arm until he was sure she had her balance back. When Jess touched her wet lower lip, he felt intense longing, and almost groaned. Even though she wore clothing that hid her magnificent body from him, he itched to open that blouse of hers, see how her full breasts made that green t-shirt she wore stretch and curve. He reached out, caressing her hair, watching her eyes soften with longing for him.

"I needed that too," Jess admitted huskily. "You are so damned stealthy, Logan," and she smiled a little.

"Come on, let's mosey out of this here stand of brush," he suggested in a put-on cowboy drawl, dropping his hand. "It's going to be stealthy like that from now on," he warned her. "If you hear three soft knocks in a row at your door?"

"Yes?"

"It's me. Let me in?"

"But... what if someone sees you?"

"What? At midnight? When everyone's sleeping? The only people on watch will be the A-team. I'll get their routine down and be sure to come to your hut when they can't possibly see me."

"I sleep on the floor, Logan." Jess saw him grin. Saw the challenge in his eyes.

"Not a problem for me, Babe. Will it be for you?"

"No, but it's not that German inn."

"You're a woman that's flexible," he said with assuredness, a gleam in his eyes.

Chewing on her lower lip as they rounded the brush, darkness beginning to fall over the village, Jess said, "We'll have to be quiet..." She saw his grin deepen. "That's not funny, Logan."

"No, but we'll deal with it, Jess. Okay?" More than anything, he wanted her to realize he had her back. He would always protect her. He would never let her down on that front. Nor would he ever tarnish her reputation. "We'll work it out," he promised, giving her a serious look. Jess looked more convinced, not so worried as before. They walked back to the drilling site and then moved down one of the wide, dusty streets toward their part of the village.

"Okay," she admitted, making sure there was the right amount of space between him and her. "I'm just jumpy, I guess."

"I understand," he said. "Trust me?"

She gave him a fervent look. "With my life...."

"Come join Chris and me for dinner? Our hut? We'll eat outside where everyone can see us. And it will be cooler outside, rather than inside those huts."

Jess smiled a little. Logan's face was deeply shadowed, bringing out the strength of it. "That would be nice."

"And maybe later, we can amble over for a cup of your coffee before we hit the rack?"

"Sounds like a plan, Randall. You're quite the plotter." She saw amusement in his eyes, but he said nothing as they walked deeper into the village proper.

It took Jess a few minutes before she got over to the SEALs' hut. They were both sitting outside the hut on the large, flat rocks someone had placed there long ago. The perfect natural stools. Jess saw a third rock nearby. It was almost dark. She didn't need NVGs, though, because she knew the way fairly well. There were no lights anywhere. Electricity did not exist here except for their one dedicated generator. Just kerosene lamps and candles. Both SEALs immediately stood when she appeared. Flustered, Jess said, "Sit down, please?"

They only sat after she had. SEALs were throwbacks to another era to a time when being a gentleman counted. Jess found it heartwarming that they continued that tradition. Yes, *warriors from another era.* It fit. She pulled open her MRE packets. "Have you two gotten a feel for the village yet?" she asked them.

Chris spoke up. "Well," he drawled, "this village is pretty much like all the rest: laid out in a rectangle. There're no walls around it, which means Taliban could come and go as they pleased."

"It's not a very defensible position," Logan agreed.

"And how will you guys work around that, as snipers?" she wondered.

"The highest place in the vill is the chief's house. It's a decent enough place to set up an overwatch. Not the best but, other than climbing into a tree, it's all that's available," Chris said.

"The chief wasn't too happy to hear we'd chosen his roof," Logan said, amusement in his low voice. "What we'll do, Jess, is set up a tent. Nothing large or obvious, but just enough to shade us from the overhead sun. We have to lay up there for hours at a time."

"That sounds like torture," she said, giving them both a worried look.

"Better than rocks cutting into you for hours or days at a time," Chris deadpanned.

"What kind of schedule will you have?"

Logan finished his MRE, dropping the empty pouches at his feet for now. "We'll spell each other every three hours from the time you start your day until you quit. The fact you have a military-trained dog and he's close to where we are? At night, we don't need to stand watch. Anything that dog hears? He'll be barking and wake everyone up. The daylight hours have been assigned to us. Our job is to be on the lookout for enemy coming our way, whether it's on a motorcycle, the bed of a truck, horseback or on foot."

"And if we see anything," Chris assured her, "we'll be on the radio simultaneously not only to you, but to your LT and the A-team."

"We spent late afternoon with the Special Forces guys," Logan told her. "We wanted a combined QRF, quick reaction force, if Chris or I spot Taliban or we THINK it's a threat coming our way, they will immediately group with whatever we need to do. We'll be a force to contend with that way and most

Taliban and Hill tribes don't like meeting head on with us. They'd rather sneak up, attack, and run and disappear into the trees or the night."

"Sounds like a good plan, but really intense," Jess murmured. "I'm sorry you guys have to bake up on that roof, though. That sounds horrible ever for three-hour stretches."

"We're used to it, Jess. Don't worry about us, okay? We've been sent here to keep you and your crew safe," Chris assured her.

Jess wanted to reach out and grip Logan's hand. He was about two feet away. "Well, just know I'm indebted to both of you."

Chris chuckled. "You can pay us back in coffee."

She smiled in the darkness, liking his soft drawl more and more every time she heard it. "It's the least I can do," she told him, meaning it.

Logan became serious. "Listen, we wanted to talk to you in private, anyway. Your LT and the Spec Force boys know about this area. We didn't necessarily want your crew to be concerned."

"About what?"

Logan rubbed his jaw. "There's a Hill Tribe warlord by the name of Qader Khogani. He's the twenty-nine-year-old leader of the tribe up in the Hindu Kush mountains. He's Taliban all the way. Satellite intel has been following him and his men for the last three years. He's got about two-hundred soldiers on horseback and they're well equipped and have good weapons. Intelligence believes it was one of his groups that swept down and attacked your crew."

Grimacing, Jess said, "Where are they now?"

"Khogani has broken up his main force into roving bands of about twenty men each on horseback, now," Logan told her. "Those steeper hills a mile away from here?"

"Yes?"

"His men; satellite intel says he gathers them higher up in the mountains, above those hills, hiding between the forest and snow line at nine-thousand feet of elevation."

"And," Chris added, "they'd probably like to attack any of these five villages if they could. The Hill people have had a thousand-year-old feud with these Pashtun valley tribes. There's no love loss between them at all."

"So," Jesse said, finishing off her MRE, "they could be here to attack because of the feud?"

Logan settled his elbows on his thighs, hands clasped. "The last time they hit, Jess, they hit your crew. Not the villagers."

His words sent a chill down her spine. "But… why us? Because we're Americans? Don't they realize fresh water saves lives?"

"You're a woman," Chris reminded her. "They could have you targeted.

We just don't know their reasons yet."

"You're getting daily satellite intel, Logan?" Jess asked, feeling more and more like a target.

"Yes. I've got a laptop with me, and I receive a twenty-four-hour feed. It will help us keep tabs on them. But they hide in the hundreds of limestone caves up there near the snowline, too, starting at eight thousand feet, all the way up to twelve thousand. We lose sight and track of them for days at a time. They know those cave systems and we don't. Some caves are linked together by tunnels, or some are like a string of pearls. They could ride for a day or more in one of those systems and they'd never show up on our satellite photos feed."

"I see," Jess said in a low tone.

"I'm glad we're here," Logan told her. "We're another layer of protection for you, Jess. Plus, we're snipers and trackers. If anyone is going to see that Hill group up in the area, it will probably be us, and not a satellite." He reached out, squeezing her arm to reassure her. "Come on, I think Chris and I would like to take you up on that fresh coffee right about now."

She tucked the empty MRE pouches into her cammo pocket and stood. "Sure, come on over.

"You two go ahead," Chris drawled. "So long as you promise to bring me back a hot cup of coffee, Randall?"

Jess felt her face go hot. She was grateful for the dark.

"You've got it, Bro," Logan promised. "Stay put for a moment, Jess. I need to collect my gear and the cups for our coffee."

"That was nice of Chris," Jess murmured as she shut the door to her hut behind Logan. She lit a small candle on the wobbly table where her coffee pot sat. Walking across the small, hard-packed dirt floor, she pushed one of the two cushions she had into the small window nook to block any light from showing outside.

Logan put his gear in the corner, watching the candlelight caress her shadowed face. He saw Jess was exhausted. Taking off his Kevlar vest, he placed it next to his rifle, leaned down to untuck his work shirt made from wicking fabric, with long sleeves to protect his arms. He came over, walking up behind her, settling his hands on her shoulders.

"The coffee can wait," he murmured, pressing a kiss against her neck, feeling her gasp a little, her hands stilling over the pot.

"Really?"

Logan moved her ponytail aside, then kissed her again on the sensitive nape of her neck. He felt her tremble and slowly lean back against him, trusting him, as had quickly and mysteriously become the norm for her. Holding her weight, Logan laid his head against her shoulder and jaw, his arms going around her waist, gently holding her. "You smell so damn good... like flowers," he growled, nuzzling her jaw, feeling her react, hearing that soft intake of her breath. Her fingers came around his arms, moving across his hands.

"My shampoo," she said, her voice unsteady, feeling heat pooling in her belly. Her nipples going hard. Wanting. This man was so sensual, all he had to do was barely touch her and she was feeling her knees starting to go weak. His breath was warm and moist against her neck. She closed her eyes, absorbing his strength, his hands across her belly, his lips wreaking havoc on her neck, her flesh skittering with heat and pleasure.

"You just smell good," Logan told her, taking her, cupping her breasts. "You feel good, Jess, I missed you so damn much..."

Jess moaned as his large palms cupped her breasts. Even with her thick cammos and her cotton bra on, she felt his warmth, the way his thumbs caressed the hidden nipples that sizzled with shocks of fire as he languidly teased them. Wet between her thighs, she sagged against Logan, her head resting against his shoulder. "That... feels so good, Logan," and she quivered as he slowly released her breasts. Her breath was growing uneven and she was beginning to ache. She felt the thick hardness of his erection against her lower back. He was wanting her as badly as she wanted him.

"I've got to stop," he muttered, apologetic. "It's not fair to you, either, if I can't please you all the way." He eased her away from him and then turned her around, seeing the arousal in her slumberous green eyes. Groaning, Logan took her mouth tenderly, appreciating its softness, the way it moved in concert with his own. Framing her face, he inhaled her scent; a mix of shampoo, sweat, dust and her own sweet fragrance which drove him crazy. He was aching and it was killing him. "I can't stay tonight. I'm sorry, Babe. I really am..."

She held him close, savoring the strength of his mouth against her own. "It's all right... I know we're in a dangerous situation... this is enough... just getting to kiss you," and Jess leaned up, breasts against his chest, devouring his mouth, making no apologies for how she felt about him. It made Logan groan, and his hands slid to her hips, holding her hard against his erection. She was starting to melt in his hands, beneath his hungry, primal mouth, the sweep of his tongue making her shudder with hunger for more of him. Their breaths came ragged and rough, their mouths clashing against one another, hearts pounding.

Logan tore his mouth from hers, breathing heavily, his hands tight on her arms, staring down into her softly candlelit face. If there was EVER a time when he'd wanted to make love to this woman, it was right friggin' now. He caressed her face, saw the burning desire in her shadowed eyes. "We have to stop." He watched her swollen, wet lips pull faintly into a smile as she held his gaze.

"I'm aching. You have to be, too."

"Yeah," he muttered. Shaking his head, Logan said, "When we get together, fireworks start between us."

"Wild women are like that," Jess teased throatily. She tried to still her body, stop her hips rubbing against his erection. The agony in Logan's eyes was real. "Are you sure? You can't stay for just a little bit? Time enough to... well... love each other?" She saw Logan hesitate, his dark brows moving downward, his hands automatically smoothing the fabric along her shoulders.

"I planned on being able to come over late and staying the night with you, Jess. Leaving near dawn." Torn, Logan searched her eyes. "I don't want you thinking I'm here just to get sex from you. What we have is a helluva lot more than that. I was hoping... hell, hoping against hope, that we could have nights together at least once or twice a week. Time to lay with you, talk with you, find out everything about you."

Jess felt her heart swell with warmth for Logan. "I don't see you as the kind of man who has sex and then leaves afterward. Remember?" and she slid her fingers across his stubbled jaw, "I was with you that night? And in the morning, you came back with breakfast? You're not a runner, Logan. It's not your style. I KNOW that," and she held his narrowed gaze. "You're a man of honor. And what we have... well... I'm open to an hour as much as twenty-four hours with you." Jess licked her lips, holding his gaze, feeling his indecision. "When is Chris expecting you back?"

Grimacing, he muttered, "Probably an hour. We have to clean our weapons still. And I've got to make a final check-in with Bagram."

She smiled and slid her hands over his shoulders. "Okay, we have forty minutes. I want you, Logan. ALL of you." She saw the moment he made his decision, a feral look coming to his eyes. Jess smiled, drowning in that heated look that made her even wetter between her thighs. "Come on," she whispered, grazing his cheek with her fingers, "my bed is over there... on the floor..."

CHAPTER 7

C HRIS AND LOGAN came over, knocking on her door at five a.m. the next morning, coffee cups in hands. The look Logan gave her, one of intense longing, made her heart swell with such happiness that Jess felt as if she were walking on air. Whatever lay between them was good, solid and incredible. Jess had called out for them to come back in thirty minutes, gotten up, and used a pail of water to clean herself up. Then she threw on her green T-shirt and cammos along with her boots. By the time the two SEALs returned, the smell of fresh coffee filled the small mud house. The look of gratefulness on Chris's face made it all worth it. He poured his coffee and then made an excuse and left.

"Stay," she whispered, pouring Logan his coffee.

"I got about twenty minutes," he said. Setting the cup down, he went over and shut and locked the door. Turning back, he walked over to her, wisping his fingers through her black hair, tipping her head up just enough to slide his mouth across hers. Logan felt Jess sigh and lean languidly against him, her arms sliding around his shoulders. She tasted of coffee and that particular inner sweetness of hers that drove him wild.

"Did you sleep?" he demanded; his voice rough as he watched her eyes slowly close while he massaged her scalp.

"Mmmm, I did. Like a baby." Jess forced her eyes open, searching his. "And you?"

"I missed you. I sleep better if you're beside me."

The male growl in his voice made her quiver inwardly. Already, she was feeling her body flex in memory of what his hands and mouth could do to pleasure her. "We have to be patient, Logan."

"I know." He gave her a raw look. "But after last night…"

Jess picked up her cup. Her hand shook a little as she poured the coffee into it. "I wonder if this will last, Logan? Us? The intensity of how we feel around one another, how we make love, I-I've never experienced anything like his before." She cast a glance up at him. Logan wore only his work shirt, which clung like a second skin across his broad shoulders and deep chest. He was so male. Alpha male. He was territorial, protective of her, and Jess found herself feeling a sense of safety she'd never before felt. Why? Was it love? Or lust? She almost asked, but bit the question back, knowing it was the wrong time and place. Geez, it had all happened so fast! "In some ways," Jess admitted, her voice a bit breathless, "I feel like I've been spun around a bunch times fast. I've not gotten my balance back yet. I feel… out of kilter."

Logan slid his fingers beneath her hair, slowly moving them across her sensitive nape, watching her expression soften, her eyes go half closed. There was nothing but honesty in Jess. "I feel the same way," he admitted.

"Does it bother you?" She watched Logan's well-shaped mouth draw into a wry grin.

"What? That I'm attracted to you? That you are so damned hot I can't believe it? That I can't get enough of you? No, I'm not worried, Jess. I like every second of it. I like being with you." Logan moved her hair aside, lightly biting her nape, feeling her shiver and gasp, and then moved his tongue across her velvety skin and kissed the damp spot.

"You are half-man, half-animal, Logan. I swear, you are."

"But you like it," he growled, nibbling her earlobe, finding that sweet spot just behind it, licking there, hearing her sigh, feeling her starting to melt in his hands.

"Maybe I'm just a nymphomaniac and never knew it?" Jess asked, laughing softly, seeing amusement glimmer in his blue eyes.

"You hadn't had sex for a year," he reminded her. "That's enough to make you ravenous for a while. Don't you think?"

"Mmm, I don't know," Jess said honestly, searching his amused expression. "I've had three serious relationships in my life and that's not much to go on. You SEALs have a real reputation with the women. I'm going to rely on *your* ample knowledge of sex," she teased, sliding her fingers across his stubble.

Setting his cup down next to hers, Logan took her into his arms, maintaining a meaningful eye contact with her. "In all modesty: it's true," he admitted, "so that's why you really need to believe me when I tell you that no woman has ever tangled me up like you have. All I have to do is picture your face in my mind, Jess, or replay your voice in my head, and I'm growing hard. I'd been going around with a perpetual ache since we parted ways at Bagram, and it's your fault." Logan saw her eyes glimmer with laughter. "No woman has ever done that to me. Does that tell you something? That you're special to me? That what we have is so damned unique? I'm still reeling from it. I can't explain it, either. But I'm not going to run away from it either, just because I don't understand it completely. Are you?"

Jess relaxed in his strong arms, her hands resting on his biceps that flexed as she smoothed the fabric of his sleeves. "I'm not running. I've never felt like I feel about you, Logan. Sometimes, it scares me. I'm scared because I could lose you. We could be torn apart because of our military careers…"

"All you see is walls and hurdles," Logan teased, kissing the tip of her nose. "And all I see are workarounds."

"I like the way you think."

"I got here, didn't I?" When her lips moved into a warm smile, his heart opened so damned wide Logan felt like he might die of a heart attack. But what a way to die.

"You did."

He brushed her mouth. "Duty calls, Babe. I need to saddle up. I'll see you when I can. Have MREs with us again? Tonight, outside our hut?"

"Love to," Jess murmured, releasing him. She watched Logan pick up his gear and cup of coffee. Her throat tightened as he slipped out the door, silent like a shadow. As she sipped from her own cup, feeling the warmth of it between her hands, she heard the village waking up outside. Roosters were crowing. Goats were bleating to be let out of their corrals to go eat. It was nearly 0600. Time to get saddled up herself. At 0630, her crew would be waiting for her at the drill site.

LOGAN SAT WITH Chris up on the roof of the chieftain's house. The high, noontime sun was brutal in the light blue sky. This was their first day as snipers on overwatch and there was a lot to check out. They had rigged a desert camouflage tarp, stringing it up with ropes so that it hung stretched out overhead, shading them from the aggressive sun. It was still hotter than hell, despite their best efforts, but it was something at least. Logan sat with the terrain maps he'd brought along, and, on them, they considered the route of the only dirt road that led from here to the other four villages strung miles apart from one another to the north. The valley was not a large one, enclosed by the tall, rugged Hindu Kush mountains on either side. Throughout the morning, they had spotted men on foot leading a donkey laden with a huge bundle of cut wood, two men on motorbikes, and several on foot. There was plenty of trade between the villages, it seemed, and each time one of the scattered groups approached the village, the two snipers took long-lens photos of them. Right now, it was all about gathering the necessary intel to better understand the normal rhythm of this village. The photos were also being simultaneously transmitted from the laptop sitting between the two men up to a satellite and, from there, onward to SEAL HQ in Bagram.

Then, it was a waiting game to see if Bagram came back with hits on the men's faces, to find out if any of them had Taliban allegiance. Even with the full beards each man sported, the system could not be fooled. Over the years, the weblike network of black ops groups taking photos of anyone potentially suspect had paid off. More than anything, Logan wanted to try and get a fix on Qader Khogani. Sweat ran down his temples. His whole damn uniform was damp. Chris had just hauled up another two gallons of clean water for them. They'd already shot through the first two in just half a day up on this roof.

Taking his binoculars, Logan slowly scanned the open desert land between the village and the hills to the east. They were soft, rounded dirt hills with scrub trees and large sprawls of bushes dotting them. He saw several other men with ladened donkeys crossing the area. The only fuel any of these villages had was firewood. The flatland and foothills, over the years, had been stripped bare. So, now, these men, who made a living selling firewood to the village wives for their cooking, were busy finding it on the already partially skinned slopes. It was an environmental disaster in his eyes: leaving the hills vulnerable to devastating erosion. When rain came, huge gullies, *wadi* in the local parlance, were carved out of the sand and rockiness of the area.

Logan could hear the rhythmic clang from the well-drilling site of casing being struck and driven into the ground. He swung his binoculars that way, hoping to catch sight of Jess. From their vantage point on the chieftain's roof, only a part of the truck that did the heavy-duty work could be seen. The Navy Seabees were a damned hard-working group. He spotted LT Parker walking down the street that led directly to where the truck was located. By luck, he spotted Jess walking out to meet him. They stopped in view of his binoculars. Logan saw the dark splotches beneath the armpits of Jess's work uniform: a long-sleeved light blue shirt, the cuffs rolled up to just below her elbows. Her black hair was in that perennial ponytail of hers between her shoulder blades. She wore a Kevlar vest, but Logan bet the chicken plate, the ceramic armored plates, were not in it. Hell, even SEALs took their Kevlar vests off when they were in sniper mode. They were just too damned heavy and hot to wear.

He smiled a little, watching her open a map between her and Parker. There was no doubt about her gestures toward the drill rig; she was in complete command. Logan smiled a little, feeling his heart swell with unfamiliar emotions. Parker seemed completely taken with her. Or, perhaps they had worked as a team for so long the officer/enlisted wall no longer stood between them. There was so much Logan wanted to know about her. He ached for some downtime to simply sit and talk with her, search her past, understand what made her the incredible woman she was. Maybe tonight…

It was dusk, and Jess had gone back to her mud home after having MREs with Chris and Logan. Leaving the door open, the only in-and-out flow of air, she took her pail of water that she'd put purification tablets in earlier, to wash her face, neck and arms. Desperate to get the grit off, she didn't notice Logan's approach until she saw him out through the hut's door, standing right in front of her.

"Spit bath," she told him with a grin, wiping her face dry with a small towel she had sitting next to the large metal bowl filled with water. It was the first time they had been alone today. He was in his work shirt, the sleeves pushed up to his elbows, and his cammies and combat boots. Logan always wore a drop holster on his right thigh, his Sig Sauer pistol in it.

"Know them well," he murmured. He took a seat on a huge rock nearby. Just about everyone in the village used the big, smooth stones as stools outside their homes. He watched her wipe off her wet, gleaming arms. "Wish there was a shower around here." He saw her lips twitch.

She replied, "I always think I'll get used to this kind of living, but I never do. When I can get to Bagram, I run screaming to the women's TDY, temporary duty, barracks, get assigned a room and then stand under a cold shower on a hot day and think I've died and gone to heaven."

Nodding, Logan watched her graceful movements. Jess was tall, her limbs clean. He could see the muscles that had been developed by the nature of her hard work. "Chris and I are going to stay up on the roof tonight, so I'm not going to be around."

"You're getting a feel for the area," Jess said, understanding. She saw Logan nod, his gaze on her. It felt good. "Just getting a few minutes with you now is a gift," she murmured, hanging her towel on a nail she'd put into the edge of the wooden table. It had to dry somewhere.

"Come sit?" and Logan gestured to the rock about two feet from where he sat.

Jess came outside and sat down, absorbing his serious expression. "You said you were born in Cheyenne, Wyoming?"

"Yes."

Logan savored her nearness. He inhaled her natural scent. The soap they used on duty was odorless so that the fragrance didn't give their position away in close quarters.

Jess asked, "Tell me about your growing-up years?" and she met and held his shadowed gaze. The sunset in the west had turned from pink to orange under the clouds hanging over the peaks. Now, dusk was beginning in earnest.

"My dad worked as a wrangler on a big cattle ranch outside of Cheyenne. My mother is a CPA, certified public accountant. She keeps the books for the ranch."

"*You* grew up wild, too?" she teased, smiling a little, watching his own mouth move upward as well. Her lower body clenched. It was a mouth she wanted to kiss again.

"I did. One of my clearest childhood memories is of my dad sitting me on the back of his saddle, my arms around his waist. Riding with him when I was six."

"You have cowboy genes."

Logan shrugged, resting his elbows on his thighs, hands draped between his legs. "I guess I do. I learned how to repair fences, vaccinate cattle, rope, tie, and brand them. I learned to fish and hunt with my dad when I was eight. I grew up on venison, elk and trout."

"Do you think that kind of a background helped you become a SEAL?"

He marveled yet again at Jess's insightfulness. Her hair was loose, falling across her shoulders as she crossed her legs, arms resting on one knee as she observed him. "Yes, I do. My dad taught me tracking early on and that's something I use, to this day, as a SEAL."

"Are your parents still working on that ranch?"

"Yes. They own a small house near the main ranch complex."

"And you got to grow up in one place," she said, almost wistfully.

"Because your life is the exact opposite of mine? You were the tumble-weed?"

She smiled, drowning in his dark gaze. Jess swore she could feel his protection surrounding her. It was invisible, but it was there. She ached to kiss Logan, and she could see the same desire burning in his eyes as well. Anyone passing by would see them chatting outdoors; something that happened all the time between the Americans, and no one would think anything of it. Which was the way Jess wanted it. "You already know I was born in Cape Town, South Africa. From there, the Navy sent my parents to South America, Bolivia. The Seabees were taking part in a village well-drilling initiative. I don't remember much about that. I remember much more clearly when I was six or so, being back in Africa, running around, playing, picking up the local dialects." She smiled fondly. "I really did have a wild, free upbringing."

"Do you regret it?"

"Never." Jess sighed and straightened, gesturing to the surrounding village. "I've seen so many places on this earth, Logan, that are so desperate for fresh well water. My parents instilled in me that those who have much, should share with those who have so little."

"Is that why I saw you earlier today handing out candy to the kids?" He saw her blush, her mouth softening. He wanted to kiss her, hold her, feel her soft, firm strength against him once more.

"The kids have me well trained," Jess laughed. "They know I always have a stash of candy in my house. I learned early on to meet them in the center of the village at a specific time. The boys are nasty to the little girls because it's just such a damn patriarchal culture. If I gave the girls all their candy first, the boys would attack them, grab it out of their hands. If the little girls fought back, the boys would beat them up, even bloody their noses. It was awful."

"Yeah, it sucks," Logan agreed quietly, seeing the sadness in her eyes. "I watched how you dealt with it today: girl, boy, by turn."

She sighed. "It's the only way. My heart aches for these girls and women, Logan. They're so repressed by the Muslim religion in Afghanistan. They don't even live half a life."

"You're doing what you can," he told her, holding her pained gaze. "You're a role model out here to them. You do realize that? A woman working beside men? An equal? Respected?"

"Yeah," Jess muttered. "On some days, good days, I see that. On others, I come here at night, shut the door and cry for them."

Logan felt her pain. "It has to be especially hard on you, Jess. You've always been treated as an equal in the service. I don't think anyone ever told you that you couldn't do something if you set your mind to it?" He saw a faint smile cross her mouth.

"My parents gave me the freedom to learn who I was. I owe them so much for that. When I see how a lot of little girls around the world are treated, it makes my heart ache for them. I was lucky. Really lucky."

"I think you're a prototype for generations of women to come," Logan said. Jess shrugged, giving him an embarrassed look.

"Oh, I don't think so. I grew up with two parents who had the earth in their hands. I grew up loving the land, seeing it differently, seeing how it could work in concert with the people who lived on top of it. How to take care of it."

Logan studied her as the dusk grew deeper. He heard the bleat of the goats now being crowded into their main corral of rocks and mud for the night. At least the damned roosters were quiet, already asleep in the near darkness. "What are your dreams, Jess?" He watched her expression carefully, almost holding his breath. He so wanted to be a part of her life. She might not fully know that, at least not yet. Her mouth moved into a wry position.

"You'll laugh."

"No, I'd never laugh at you."

She rubbed her hands slowly up and down her thighs. "My answer is coming from my dreamer and romantic, idealistic side," she warned him, giving him an amused glance. "Maybe because I never really had a home, an anchor in my life, I've always wished for a home of my own. Some place I wouldn't have to move from. A place where I could plant flowers, like colorful poppies, some Iris in the spring to come up and bloom. And, believe it or not, I love to cook." She held up her long, spare hands. "I have this thing about spices. I've collected jars of them all over the globe. I love the different fragrances of each of them. I got lost in this spice bar in Egypt once. I've spent half a day in another spice bar in Istanbul."

"Where do you want to build that dream house of yours?"

"Oh, you're going to feed my fantasies?" Jess teased, grinning, falling into his warm gaze, feeling he genuinely cared about her dreams.

"Why not? It's about getting to know the different sides of you." Logan was absorbing her quiet husky voice, absorbing her dreams, fascinated to find out more about her.

"I love the ocean," she admitted. "If I could choose anywhere, it would be San Diego, California. Maybe near La Jolla, north of the city. There's a seal colony there, pelicans, fur seals… lots of wildlife…"

"And your house? What would it look like?"

"I would buy a piece of land not far from the Pacific. I know how expensive it is, Logan, and I certainly don't have the money for it, but since we're talking of dreams," and she smiled over at him, "it would be made of silvered cedar because I love the touch of wood. And huge glass windows that overlook the ocean so I could see the sunset every night, see the colors…"

"And what would you do for a living if you weren't in the Navy, then?"

"My parents have a small construction company and live in San Diego. They've often urged me to quit and not put in my twenty years with the Navy. They worry about me being over here in the Middle East. When they were in the Navy, being a Seabee, doing good deeds for the poor, was a much safer job." Her brows fell. "It's not safe anymore and my parents know that. I don't like them to worry about me and I know they do. I'm torn."

"But, if you quit," Logan pressed, "you'd work with them?"

Nodding, she said, "My parents own a very profitable company. They want me to, someday, take it over so they can retire."

"Is that your dream or theirs?"

Jess glanced at his serious demeanor, her skin riffling beneath Logan's roughened tone, almost a low, animal growl. "She opened her hands, "I could live in ONE PLACE, Logan. I know it doesn't sound very important to you, but it is to me. I guess," and her voice fell and Jess shook her head, "I dream of settling down. Finding someone who will love me, warts and all…."

"Children?" Logan wondered, seeing the longing in her face, hearing it in her voice.

"Yes. Two or three kids. I grew up as an only child. I remember being jealous of the large families in Bolivia, and in Africa, and I wondered what it would be like to have sisters and brothers."

"You want family." Logan felt his heart swell in his chest. He could envision Jess as a mother. She would give her children the freedom she'd had growing up. Smiling to himself, he knew she'd be a fantastic parent. Just watching her with the children today, had made him ache for her. Jess was unselfish, sensitive to the plight of others, wanting to make this planet a better place to live for everyone. There was nothing but admiration and respect for her in his heart. Never mind she was drop dead gorgeous, and had one of the most sensitive, hot bodies he'd ever encountered. Yeah, she was an earth goddess, no question and Logan liked that idea: A woman of the earth: sensual, real, honest and unafraid to be who she was.

"Family? Yeah, I do," Jess admitted. "But I'm twenty-eight. I won't marry and have children and leave them behind if I have to go on a deployment overseas. It just leaves me cold, Logan. I want to be there with my husband, with my children. I want to see them grow up, celebrate the important moments in their lives." She laughed softly, giving him a wry glance. "See? I warned you that I was a soppy romantic idealist."

"And don't you dare ever stop being one," Logan said. Because he saw himself as that man in her idealistic life. Saw her carrying his children in that soft, rounded belly of hers. There was such a powerful, primal response in his heart and soul that it left Logan stunned. He'd never thought about a second marriage. Many of his SEAL friends had gotten married, only to see their lives torn apart like his had been. Being a SEAL wasn't conducive to making a marriage work. He'd tried his level best to make it work with Maryann, but she couldn't handle his long deployments, his time away from her. In the end, Logan had never blamed her. He understood. And, as he absorbed Jess's profile, the need for her in his heart grew. He wasn't a romantic. Logan knew, even though he was falling in love with Jess, that in the long term, it would never work. And that hurt worst of all. A SEAL life was an anti-marriage machine, no question.

CHAPTER 8

Q ADER KHOGANI TRAINED his binoculars on the village sitting on the slope below him. Beside him, his thirty-year-old captain, Afir Wazir, lay quietly, eyes squinted. It was early morning, fog pooling just above the valley floor and clinging to the slopes of the Hindu Kush. Below the hill, he heard the snort of some of the horses. He had five of his best men with him on this planned attack.

"There she is," he grated. The woman they had tried, and failed, to kidnap before. It hadn't been a total loss as far as Qader was concerned. At least they'd killed one of the men on the well-drilling team. His full mouth puckered as he kept the glasses trained on the tall American woman. He smiled a little. "She will make a nice profit, and a fine slave to the warlord in Pakistan," and he chuckled.

Afir rubbed his black beard and scowled. "Sell her for money? Why not give her to the Taliban, instead? They could have her beheaded on video and it could be put up on the net? Think of the power of that? How it would draw new recruits to them? Swell their depleted ranks?"

Snorting, Qader muttered, "She's far more valuable to us as merchandise." He lifted the binoculars from his eyes, studying his second-in-command. Afir was a member of the Hill Tribe as all Qader's men were. He had fought the Americans since he was sixteen years old and had the battle scars to prove it. His father had fought the Russians. Above all others, Qader relied on the wily Afghan to plan their strategies and attacks, but often grew impatient with his prattle. "We need the money, Afir. You know that."

Afir's thin mouth flexed. "My lord, I realize you have two hundred soldiers to feed. Not to mention grass for their horses and bullets for their weapons. It's no easy task. But this woman, if we can capture her, would help the Taliban's efforts greatly."

"They," Qader ground out, "have not offered me money, Afir. They think we OWE them. I owe them nothing," he spat. "The Pakistani warlord has promised me a million US dollars if I bring her to him. He has already put one fourth of the amount as a deposit into my bank in Pakistan. She will disappear through the cracks of his country, never to be found again. He will be happy, and I will be happy. That's all that matters." Plus, Qader was being pressured to bring the American for sale within the next two weeks. If he didn't, the deal was off, but he'd said nothing to anyone about that. Not even to Afir.

Afir frowned. He was a strategist at heart, and still had nagging reservations about the whole matter. It was time to bite the bullet and voice them. "My lord, you must consider the reaction of the Americans if we kidnap her. They will not sit idly by. They will throw their Apache helicopters into the sky. They will use electronic surveillance of all kinds: satellites, drones, cell-phone eavesdropping."

"Let them. I have a plan." Qader handed Afir the binoculars so he could watch the woman's morning routine himself.

Afir nodded, realizing with a sinking feeling his lord was going through with his plan. It was always about money. Apart from the expenses he had just mentioned, there were also costly medical supplies, the restocking of weapons, and pay for the soldiers. They didn't work for free. Although they owed Qader allegiance, he was still expected to pay them for being taken from their crop-raising duties on their farms. Families had to be fed, too. It was a lot of responsibility on the twenty-nine-year-old's shoulders. Afir wished he had a simpler answer than kidnapping the American woman. She would cause trouble of the worst kind. His stomach knotted.

"My lord," he rasped, binoculars still pressed firmly to his eyes, "did you see this? There are SEALs there now since our last raid. On top of the twelve-man Army Special Forces team they already had." Afir handed the binoculars back to his boss, dread filling him. Qader scowled, rubbing his beard in thought. He had ridden his men in from the northern part of the valley two days ago. This was their first opportunity to observe the village since their attack on it weeks ago. SEALs. He hated and feared them. They were the most dangerous of all the American black ops groups.

Qader scowled, watching the two SEALs. "They're snipers," he hissed.

"Brought in because we attacked the village," Afir muttered, shaking his head. He'd been against the attack, but Qader had been certain his band of men could pull it off. They hadn't expected the Navy Seabees to fight back as well as they had. Qader had said they were only well drillers. What did those men and that woman know about fighting, he'd scoffed. Much more than Qader assumed, Afir thought. He could never bring it up to his lord, or he could have a bullet put through his head. No, best to remain silent. But with the SEALs there? This was a major complication.

"We must find out where they are going to be," Afir said. "What is their routine?" Because there was no way Afir wanted to fight with SEALs. Qader's men were poor riflemen anyway. They often fired their AK-47s on full automatic, tearing through a magazine of bullets in seconds. *Stupid.* A complete waste of good and expensive ammunition. But the SEALs... well, they fired slowly and only after acquiring their target. They wasted no bullets and when they pulled the trigger, they killed. This was a very bad situation to put them in, and it put Afir on edge.

"Bah! They are human! They bleed too, Afir. I do not fear them!" lied Qader.

Afir did. "My lord, let us stay here today and tomorrow? Watch them? Time the Special Forces who guard the Americans in the southern end of this village? There will be an opening, an opportunity, to snatch her out from beneath them. It is simply a matter of timing."

Qader growled but said nothing, watching the two SEALs walk into the village. One had a sniper rifle, a Winchester .300 magnum. He knew the weapon well and hated it. The other SEAL carried an M4. "They must be a sniper team. They always work in pairs."

"Not always," Afir cautioned. "We must see where they go. They have a hide, somewhere. The only question, is it in the village or not?"

Qader watched them disappear. He wished he was at a higher elevation, to better keep eyes on the SEALs' movements. "Most likely," he said, "they are going to take the highest point in that village. It would be Behzaad Sahar's home. It is the tallest building." He swung his binoculars to the two-story rock house dotted with small glass windows here and there. The roof was topped with a four-foot-high wall of rock and concrete all around. And it could very well be where the SEALs had chosen to set up their hide. They would be well protected by the one-foot-thick wall and still have a full visual on the entire village from that location.

"The real question is this, Afir: Are the SEALs on sniper duty night and day? Or only night? Only day?"

"We do not know, my lord. And we must find out. Otherwise, we are opening ourselves up to many casualties very quickly." He heard Qader grunt. But he didn't dispute his experience and wisdom. SEALs were to be avoided at all costs. Especially on something like a kidnapping. It was a delicate operation. It relied on precise timing.

Qader handed him the binoculars. "You watch. I am hungry. We'll eat." He slowly slid backward, making sure his head would not be seen over the rise of the hill.

Afir felt trepidation. Qader's approach to getting what he wanted was charging in on horseback, guns blazing. He felt his leader's restlessness, his need to get this kidnapping done. Everything felt pressured, but Afir didn't know why. It was a gut feeling, something he always paid close attention to. Surely, his leader would not do the same thing he'd already done? Not this time, with SEALs in the vicinity? Shaking his head, he swallowed his worry.

Jess wearily wiped the sweat off her brow with the end of her *shemagh*. The scarf would be wet and dirty by the end of the day. The sun's rays were slanting in the west. It was over a hundred degrees, and she could feel the grit rubbing her skin raw here and there. She climbed into the blue Toyota pickup and set her hardhat on the seat. A trouble-shooting call had come in from Max, who was on their backhoe. He was digging a ditch alongside a new field the villagers were creating so they could plant more crops and have more food between them. It was a mile away. Pulling out her CamelBak tube, she sucked more water down, her throat parched. Through her sunglasses, pulling her baseball cap down and shielding her eyes to cut the glare even more, she saw the backhoe stopped in the distance, its bucket down on the ground. Eli Gardner, their mechanic, hopped in the truck with her. The radio on her shoulder came to life.

"Jess? Where you going?"

It was Chris, on sniper watch on top of the roof. "Got a problem with the backhoe. I'm driving out to the area where our mechanic will check it out."

"Okay. I'll be watching you through the scope."

"Thanks," Jess said, clicking off the radio. She knew the .300 win/mag sniper rifle was good for a thousand yards. Logan had gone out earlier with the A-team and were on the other side of the village, checking the area. She was driving out beyond the rifle's range, out to the fields. But, it was still comforting that Chris could watch for enemy activity through his scope. Driving the truck down the bumpy dirt road, Jess saw nothing but flat desert in all directions. Hot air flowed in through both truck's open windows, its air conditioner on the fritz as usual. She braked on the closest part of the road to where the backhoe was and climbed out of the truck cab.

"Wish'd this hadn't happened so late in the day," Eli said with a rueful grin, wiping his mouth, having just drank from his canteen.

"Yeah," Jess agreed. They'd worked hard right through today in the unrelenting heat. All she wanted was to clean the grit off her sweaty skin, then go over and have her meal with the SEALs. Maybe tonight, Jess hoped, Logan could stay the night.

Jess studied the ground carefully as she walked with Eli, checking the soil. IEDs had been planted along the road here before. She wished that Sergeant Stapleton and his dog, Ace, were here. The dog could sniff out a bomb in a millisecond. They were away on the southern end of the village, though, working the area She walked slowly, her gaze skimming the ground for any disruptions of soil. Eli followed in her footsteps. They made it to the ditch where the backhoe was stopped. Max was standing next to where its dropped bucket rested on the ground.

"What's up?" Jess called as she approached. Max looked unhappy. He was digging a ditch from one end of the long field to the other. It was part of the irrigation project they were working on along with the digging of the well for the village.

"Crapped out on me again," Max said unhappily. "Bucket dropped. Broke a hydraulic line, I guess."

Groaning, Jess moved around to the other side of the backhoe, getting down on her hands and knees, twisting her head upward to study the underside of the engine.

"Yeah," Eli called, stretching out a long arm and pulling out a broken line, "you sure did. Busted an oil hose to the bucket, Max."

"Shit."

Eli pulled it down and out, showing it to Jess. "Bad news, boss. We don't have a spare."

"Bummer," Jess muttered. "Can't we find something in our boneyard supplies for a workaround?" They were very good at making do with other hoses. It wasn't like she could just drive to a town and buy what they needed.

Eli studied it. "Not this one. I got lines back at the supply truck, boss, but this is a high-pressure variety. One of the main lines." His face glistened with sweat, his teeth white against his darkly tanned face. "Looks like you get to go to Bagram, to Navy Supply, and pick us up a few. Lucky, lucky," and he chuckled.

Mouth curving down, Jess muttered, "That's going to slow our schedule down, dammit."

Suddenly, her radio crackled to life. Chris came over the channel, sounding calm but urgent.

"Jess, tangos at two o'clock from the direction you're facing right now. I'm alerting Lieutenant Anderson. We'll get reinforcements out to you ASAP. Over."

Jess damn near hit her head on the undercarriage of the engine block as she jerked out from beneath it. "Hold," she gasped, leaping to her feet, straining to look beyond the bucket. There, in the distance, she saw six or seven riders galloping hard toward them. They had rifles, waving them in the air. Her heart flooded with terror. "Roger, get out here *now*. We'll try and hold them off."

Max and Eli overheard the conversation, both turning simultaneously toward the threat.

"Get under the backhoe!" Jess ordered them, pulling her .45. She unsafed it, moving around the equipment, glaring at the stunned, frozen Max. "Jarman! Get your ass under this backhoe. Now!"

Max jumped, dug in his toes, and ran toward the engine block. Eli was already under there, on his belly, his own .45 drawn, ready to fire.

Eyes widening, Jess saw the hard looks on the riders' faces. Their horses were galloping swiftly toward them, rapidly closing the distance. She hurried around the bucket, sliding into the left of Max. What the hell? Were they attacking to kill them? She jerked a glance over her right shoulder, peering down the road. There was a desert-colored Humvee speeding toward them, a huge rooster tail of dust rising in its wake, telling her they were driving fast and hard to reach them in time. She turned, holding both hands on the .45 to steady it.

"Don't shoot until they do," she ground out to her men. "Rules of Engagement. You have to wait." Sweat was running down her temples. The sandy soil was hot beneath her belly. Her breath was uneven. Jess was scared as hell, but she couldn't show it. None of them, until a couple of weeks ago, had faced attacks from an enemy. It was a jolting experience, and she felt the thunder of the horses' hooves through her body as they approached.

"ETA two minutes," Chris said calmly over the radio. "Maintain your position."

SEALs sounded so friggin' casual about something like this! Jess felt anything *but*. She compressed her lips. "Get ready," she warned her men. "Slow fire. We don't have that much ammo on us. You have to make every shot count." Jess had never shot and killed a person in her life. Now that she could see the bearded faces of the riders even closer, their turbans and their rolled hats, their earth-colored garments flying around them like ragged wings, she saw the hatred in their eyes. That scared her even more.

The first bullets snapped and struck the metal around them.

"Fire!" Jess ordered, taking a bead on a man riding a gray horse. Her hand bucked hard as she fired. The .45 was known for its wicked recoil, but she was familiar with it. The first shot missed. She sighted and fired again. The man went flying backward off his horse, his hands and arms flailing like windmills.

More bullets tore into their position. Dirt spat up, blinding them temporarily. Jess cursed, wiping her eyes, unable to see. The horses galloped at a distance around the equipment. More bullets poured into where they lay, hugging the earth, flattened against it. The harsh explosions of the .45s all going off hurt her ears. She lost part of her hearing as horses reared and moved frantically around the backhoe. They were surrounded. And the Taliban were firing from their horses, down at them. The bullets thudded into the dirt, close to their faces and feet. Dust rose from the horses dancing around, blinding all three of them. They were like fish in a barrel, pinned down as they were.

Jess felt a sting in her left upper arm. It suddenly went numb. She ignored it, twisting onto her side, raising her .45 and shooting at one of the riders firing toward them. Her pistol roared and bucked. The man screamed and jerked backward off his frantic horse. Jess heard other rifles firing, a very different sound. The horses running around the backhoe suddenly left. She looked up, dirt and sweat on her face, seeing the Humvee approaching. The throaty sound of M4s filled the air. All-American-sounding weapons! Sharp relief tore through Jess. She watched what was left of the raiders, galloping at high speed for the hills due east of their position.

She shakily pushed out backwards from under the backhoe, getting to one knee, looking around the area, .45 at the ready to fire. The Humvee skidded to a halt, Special Forces men with weapons bailing out. The first person she saw rushing around the backhoe was Logan. His eyes were slitted and focused. She gasped. He was in complete combat mode, his M4 up, ready to fire. Max and Eli joined her side, holstering their pistols and wiping their faces. They looked at one another in disbelief.

"Jess?" Logan knelt down next to her. "You're wounded."

"What?" She frowned. Logan reached out, gripping her lower left arm. She looked down and saw that the upper arm of her cammies on that side was soaked with blood. Shock rolled through her. Logan slid his M4 across his chest as he searched her face. No wonder her arm felt numb.

"I'm okay," Jess said, meeting Logan's gaze, her voice sounding hollow to her. "I didn't even know I'd gotten hit."

Mouth thinning, Logan called into his shoulder-mounted radio to Sergeant Tony Cutter, the 18 Delta Corpsman from the Special Forces.

"Hey Cutter," he said, speaking into his mic, "can you get over here ASAP? Got a GSW," GSW was military shorthand for gunshot wound.

"Roger."

Jess sat back on her heels, worried. "Are they all gone?" she asked, unable to see much with the backhoe in the way.

"Yeah, they hightailed it," Logan reassured her. "They're checking out the two guys you three shot. How are you feeling?" Terror moved through him. He could see where the bullet had ripped through the sleeve of her upper arm. Logan knew it wasn't fatal, but he could see the shock setting in in Jess's green eyes. She was covered with dust, streaks of sweat through it.

"Why did they hit us?" Jess demanded, putting her pistol into its holster.

Cutter came trotting around the backhoe, his medical ruck on his back. He zeroed in on Jess and knelt on her left side as Logan moved away and stood above them, pulling his M4 off his chest, at the ready once again.

"Hey, Jess, what did you go and do? Play target?" Cutter teased, taking a pair of scissors and making a cut in the sleeve, gently pulling the edges open.

"Thanks," Jess said, "now I'll have to buy another blouse, Cutter."

Chuckling, he took a dressing, wiping away the blood purling where the bullet had gone through the flesh of her upper arm. "Oh, I think this will earn you a medevac flight, Jess. And a Purple Heart."

Making a face, Jess said, "I didn't even know I'd been hit, Tony. It's nothing," and she watched the blond-haired medic grin a little. His face was glistening with sweat as he opened his ruck at his feet and pulled on a pair of gloves.

"Well," he murmured placatingly, "let me noodle around here, and see? Just stay where you are?" and he took the scissors, fully separating the lower half of the sleeve from the upper.

She made a muffled sound. "You're kidding me? Right?" and she looked down at the cleaned-off area. A neat little hole had gone straight through the lower part of her arm and missed the bone and the main artery. She saw Cutter check the other side of her arm.

"Yep, it's a through-and-through," Cutter said, pleased. He looked up. "Do me a favor? Hold out your arm? Wriggle all your fingers?"

The moment she lifted her arm, there was real pain and she grunted, scowling. She wriggled her fingers through it. "Satisfied?"

"Yep," Cutter murmured. He quickly went to work, pulling out a syringe. "No nerve damage. That's good news. Now, I'm going to put some Lidocaine around the bullet-wound areas and deaden it so you don't feel any pain. I have to clean this sucker out and it's going to hurt like a bitch if I don't do this. You ready?"

Mouth quirking, Jess muttered, "Yes, go ahead." She'd been shot. In all her time in the Navy, she'd never had to lift a weapon to defend herself, now she had done so twice, bare weeks apart. Today, she might have even killed two men. And then gotten wounded herself. She felt the pricks of the needle, looking away. Max and Eli had left her side and she could see everything going down on the other side of backhoe.

"What are they doing?" she asked Cutter.

"Checking the dead bodies for identification, maps and anything else they might have that will help us know who attacked you guys."

She felt her stomach churn. "T-they're dead?"

"Yeah. Yours then, huh? Good shooting. Okay, I'm giving this Lidocaine five minutes for it to take hold before I go to work." Cutter took his stethoscope and listened to her heart and lungs. Then, he got up and came around, putting a blood pressure cuff on her upper right arm. Jess felt better just from Cutter's presence and professionalism.

"Hmmm, you feeling a little dizzy?" he asked, writing down her blood pressure in a notebook he carried.

"Yes, a little. Why?" Even Jess heard the alarm in her own voice.

"It's a little low. But that's to be expected. It's the effects of the shock." He gave her a slight smile meant to make her feel better. It did. "Blood pressure usually drops after getting hit. No big deal." He unwrapped the cuff and stuffed it back into his ruck. "You're going to be fine."

Jess closed her eyes as he settled at her left side, her stomach starting to roll.

"Okay, I gotta get to work here, Jess. You won't feel anything...."

He scrubbed the hell out of the area. Cutter was right; she didn't feel anything. The next thing Jess knew, when she opened her eyes, he'd already put a compress wrap around it, neatly covering the wound. "Thanks, Tony. You're good at what you do." She saw the twenty-seven-year-old sergeant smile, his gray eyes amused as he glanced up at her.

"Hey, 18 Delta Corpsman are the angels on the battlefield. Didn't you know that?" he teased, closing up his ruck and hauling it back onto his broad shoulders. "Feel like standing? Or are you still feeling lightheaded?

Jess wasn't about to not walk. It was only a bullet wound in her arm! She gripped Tony's outstretched, gloved hand and pushed up onto her knees. And as she did so, she saw black dots dancing before her eyes. Her knees suddenly felt squishy. And then it was as if a black veil fell over Jess's vision. It was the last thing she remembered.

CHAPTER 9

LOGAN WATCHED JESS slowly become conscious. He had carried her to her hut and laid her down on her sleeping bag. She looked waxen, and he knew that was from the shock of being wounded. He sat near her hip, legs crossed, catching her wandering gaze that was cloudy and confused. As she lifted her right hand, he caught it, giving it a squeeze, getting her a point of attention to focus on and follow back to lucidity.

Licking her lips, Jess squinted and looked up at him. The light within the hut was grayish and she frowned. "W-what happened?" She felt the warm roughness of Logan's hand around hers.

"You fainted," he told her quietly, watching her closely. "Remember? The Taliban attacking you? Max and Eli at the backhoe in the field?" Logan knew that trauma made the brain flood with shock. His heart contracted. Jess could have been killed in that attack. He couldn't tell her how torn up he'd been when the call from Chris had come through while Logan was with the A-team. All he'd been able to think about was Jess being killed. He saw her brow wrinkle as she tried to remember. Often, that could take quite a while.

"Oh, crap," Jess muttered, closing her eyes, rubbing her brow. And then her hand tightened around his. She opened her eyes and said, "Help me sit up?"

Logan slowly eased her into a sitting position. Her hair was dusty and strands had come loose from its ponytail. She looked exhausted. "Don't do too much just yet," he cautioned. "You went into shock after being shot in the arm. It's a common reaction." He saw Jess look over at her left arm with the tan bandage around the bicep. "Are you in pain?"

"I'm okay," she managed, drawing her legs up to sit cross-legged. The door to her hut stood open, allowing a little fresh air in, but it was still almost as hot as an oven in there. "I'm so thirsty…"

"Here." Logan offered her the line from his CamelBak. "Suck away." He smiled a little into her dark green eyes. Logan could tell the weight of what had happened to her earlier was starting to land on her shoulders. Jess took the tube and drank deeply, which was good. She handed it back to him, wiping her mouth off.

"Thanks…"

"The medevac is on its way here," he told her. "Should arrive in about twenty minutes."

"I don't need to go," Jess uttered, scowling.

"Yes, you do," Logan said patiently. He smiled a little. "LT Parker ordered me to go with you." He picked up the broken hydraulic hose sitting nearby. "After you get checked out at the hospital, he'd like you to rest up overnight, then go over to Navy supply tomorrow and get a couple of these high-pressure hoses for the backhoe." He saw her brighten. Jess was a workhorse. Devoted to what she loved to do.

"Oh," she murmured. "Then… I don't have to stay at the hospital at Bagram?"

"No. Just get checked out by a doc, is all. I'm sure they'll put you on an antibiotics course for ten days or so. They may want to see how your wound is healing, so you might have to go back one more time."

"That's not so bad then," Jess murmured. She brightened more. "And you get to go with me?" She saw how serious Logan looked, his eyes holding worry for her.

"Yeah, I'll be you're big, bad guard dog," he teased, smiling a little. "We'll fly out shortly and come back tomorrow night."

Jess started to lift her left arm. Pain instantly attacked her. Groaning, she held her wounded arm against her body. "Wow, that hurts."

He nodded. "It's better than the bullet getting lodged in your body. Through-and-throughs go through a lot of muscle, though. You're going to feel pain for at least six weeks. And you won't have full use of that arm, either, until then."

"Good thing I'm right-handed," Jess said, shaking her head. "Is everyone else okay, Logan?"

"Yeah, you were the only one injured."

"Why did they attack us?" and she searched his face, seeing the hard line of his mouth thin even more.

"The two Taliban you shot, are dead. We wanted to ask them the same thing. We frisked them for papers, maps and identification. LT Anderson is handling that. It appears that these men are part of Qader Khogani's Hill tribe army, but he's got to get confirmation from Bagram. We took photos of the corpses, and he sent them into Special Forces HQ there and we're waiting to hear back from them." Jess became grim. She'd been shot and she had killed two men. Logan wondered if she'd ever had to do that before. If she hadn't, then he knew a strong reaction in Jess would be coming, and he was glad he'd be the one who was at hand in case she had a meltdown. First-time kills were hard on everyone. And she was in the business of doing good things for poor people, not going into combat situations. *Until now.*

"What does it mean?" she asked hollowly.

"It means Khogani's in the area." Which wasn't good. "But we have daily fly-by satellite intel, so don't worry too much."

Snorting, Jess said, "Well, fat lot of good the satellite did. They didn't spot them in time to see this latest attack coming."

"I know, Chris found them first, and that's the importance of a sniper team in a hot area," Logan soothed. "LT Anderson is requesting a drone, but they're harder than hell to get. I don't know what will happen. I hope we get one. It will be a lot more reliable an eye-in-the-sky than a satellite passing over the area once a day."

"High-tech war," Jess agreed, weary. "I need to pack my go bag with some clothes, Logan."

He slowly got up. "Let me help you pack? You aren't going to be able to use that arm right now."

He was right, Jess discovered. Logan put her civilian clothes, a night gown and a fresh set of cammies and dry, clean socks into her bag. He already had the set of orders from LT Parker on him, so they were good to go. She continued to wear her dusty set of cammies for now, making sure she had her .45 pistol safed before boarding any helo. He insisted on taking off her Kevlar vest and putting the chicken plate in it. As he helped her back on with the heavy vest, Jess didn't argue. As unarmored as she'd been when the Taliban had attacked, had that bullet hit her body mass instead of her arm, she might not be alive. The thought sobered the hell out of her. Logan slipped his hand beneath her right elbow and led her out into the dusk.

"I guess everyone knows I fainted," Jess groused, embarrassed. She found herself a little wobbly, and glad for Logan's steadying hand.

"Yeah, but don't worry about it. They understand. Men faint, too. It's an equal-opportunity issue."

"I'll never live it down with my crew."

Logan chuckled and shook his head. "Jess, they're just relieved you're going to be okay. You'll earn a Purple Heart out of this for your personnel jacket."

She grimaced. "Has someone informed my parents?"

"Yes. They know you were wounded and that you're going to be okay."

"I'll call them once I get to Bagram. They're probably beside themselves with worry." She looked up, noticing it was almost dark. Logan was carrying his ruck, M4 rifle and her go-bag knapsack. Jess didn't like feeling helpless; it just wasn't in her DNA. "Can't I at least carry my go bag?" She watched him grin down at her.

"Not a chance. I need you to rest and relax. Okay?"

They walked out of the village proper, the mountains already dark, the sky fading to night. There were three Special Forces sergeants at the helo landing area, armed and on watch. Jess was relieved, although her gaze kept scouring those hills the Taliban had charged out of toward their position. The wind was cool and she shivered.

"It won't be long before the medevac arrives," Logan told her, wishing he could tuck Jess's shoulders beneath his arm and hold her close. He could already hear the chopping sounds of blades off in the distance, coming their way. The A-team men had already thrown green chem lights in a circle so the helo would know where to land. Medevacs would rather pick up wounded at night, giving them cover, very few of the Taliban having night-vision capability. It meant less chance of bullets or, worst-case scenario, an RPG hitting their Black Hawk Army helicopter.

Jess nodded, suddenly highly emotional for no reason at all. Was this how it always felt after being shot? Did everyone go through these kinds of feelings? Absorbing Logan's closeness, she was glad Brad Parker had allowed him to go along with her. Right now, she was feeling shaky, her knees weakening. Logan must have sensed it because he slid his arm around her waist, drawing her against him. His warmth was fortifying, and she sighed.

"How did you know?"

Logan looked down at her shadowed face. Her eyes were dull looking. "Because I care about you, Jess." Hell, he wanted to say that he was falling in love with her, but that wasn't a topic to be spoken about right now. She was battling her reactions to being wounded, emotionally vulnerable. Her soft mouth curved faintly, and he felt his heart swell. "You can lean on me any time you want, Babe."

His guttural words flowed through her, making her feel less vulnerable. As they approached the cleared area where the medevac would land, the three Army black ops soldiers were standing, backs to them, scanning the area through their NVGs and M4 scopes. She didn't have a pair of the goggles, but Logan drew his own set down over his eyes, flicking them on. She heard the Black Hawk coming, its heavy, puncturing beat disrupting the cooling night air. As she stood beneath Logan's arm, Jess felt protected. One of the soldiers threw another green chem light into the center of the circle as an additional bullseye for the pilot to zero in on. They weren't bright enough to be seen by the enemy, but a pilot wearing NVGs would see them standing out brightly in the darkness.

Logan knew that this was a three-line flight for the medevac. That meant that it, and the patient, were not critical. More than likely, there would be the two pilots, the air-crew chief and one medic on board. It was a relatively easy flight for them in the realm of their work-load responsibilities. And hopefully, no one would start shooting at them as they landed or took off. He saw Jess pull her left arm against her body, her lips thinning. She wasn't one to complain, and Logan knew he was going to have to read her body language, and the tone of her voice, to keep tabs on where her condition was at. Otherwise, she wasn't about to tell him she was in pain. He hoped the other surprise he had ready for her once they landed at Bagram would make her happy. He'd see.

Jess sat strapped in on one of the two jump seats in the rear of the cabin of the Black Hawk. The medic had checked her out once on board and declared her stable. He'd fashioned her a triangular sling to put her left arm in, easing the constant pain. Jess refused the Ibuprofen the medic wanted her to take. She'd only just recovered from a fogged brain, and didn't want to go back. Being the fragile-goods delivery, she was allowed to sit in the jump seat instead of on the deck like everyone else. Wearing a helmet, she was on the ICS, inter cabin system, and was able to hear the pilots talking to Ops and to the tower at Bagram. Logan sat on the deck, his back against one of the Black Hawk's sliding doors.

Tiredness leaked through her. How badly she wished she could be alone with Logan. Jess had stayed overnight at Bagram before and knew she would go to the women's barracks on the base and Logan would go to the men's barracks. They'd be separated. Right now, the way she felt, all she wanted to do was crawl into his arms, go to sleep with him and be held. But it wasn't going to happen. Once they landed, she'd first be taken over to the hospital Emergency Room and checked out. Then, she'd get a bus over to the women's barracks. Jess tried to fight the longing she felt for Logan. The cabin of the Black Hawk was utterly dark. Everyone but her wore NVGs. She closed her eyes, feeling the burn of tears beneath her eyelids, desperately choking down the need to cry.

Logan never left her side in the ER. It was a busy place, and he seemed to know it all too well. The nurse who took her to the cubical and, later, the red-haired woman doctor who checked her wound, both gave Logan long looks, but said nothing. Even though patients were supposed to be treated alone in the ER, SEALs were given leeway, Jess figured. And the look on his face as he leaned against the wall, his M4 hanging in its harness across his chest, probably detoured them away from saying anything, as well. She felt Logan's protectiveness, a silent embrace, and she hungrily absorbed it, more than glad he was with her. The doctor wrote her a script for antibiotics, a full container of them, and then the nurse gave her a set of orders to come back in six weeks for a final exam.

Leading Jess outside the doors of the ER, Logan guided her toward the bus stop not far away. It was chilly and he'd retrieved her jacket and helped her put it on. And then he rearranged the sling for her arm, which gave her much relief from the pain. At the bus stop, Jess turned to him. The base was most alive at night. There were two separate landing zones: an airstrip for fixed-wings, and many circular, concrete pads for helicopters. The roar of jets was nearly constant, the very air vibrating from the noise.

"How are you doing?" Logan asked, standing behind her to shield her from the wind. Jess was spiraling down. He'd seen it in the ER. The shock was really hitting her now.

"I'm whipped," she admitted, turning, looking up into his shadowed eyes. Jess could literally feel the heat rolling off his body, he was that close to her. And she didn't care who saw them. She knew fraternization wasn't allowed. And Logan didn't care either. But then, Jess knew SEALs more or less made up their own rules… and no one challenged them.

"I have a surprise for you." Logan saw her eyes widen. He smiled. "A good one," he amended.

"I could stand some good news," Jess uttered. "What is it?"

"When the bus comes," he said, watching her expression carefully, "we're going to tell the driver to drop us off at the conjugal unit building."

Her eyes widened enormously. Jess turned, staring up at him, her lips parting. "But… that's only for MARRIED men and women, Logan. We aren't married!"

Giving a nonchalant shrug, he murmured, "They don't know that. We walk in, you show your orders. We'll have a nice room with a bathroom and shower. What isn't there to like about that?" and he gave her a wolfish smile.

"But… they'll know."

Logan gave her a patient look. "Babe, you haven't been around Bagram enough to know how things work here. The clerk at that desk, once they see I'm a SEAL, they can't say anything except give me the key to the room. Okay? Unless, of course, you don't want me to hold you while you sleep with me?"

She scowled, considering the suddenly sprung stealth mission. "I'd love to be with you, Logan. You know that. But, I'm worried. If someone wants to see a marriage license, demands to see my wedding ring…"

"You're SUCH a worrywart," Logan accused gently, leaning over, kissing her brow. "Let me handle this. Okay?"

"Okay," Jess muttered, shaking her head. "We could get into a lot of trouble, though, Logan."

"We won't," he reassured her. "Here comes the bus...."

Jess felt suddenly shaky. But it wasn't from shock. It was from the hope that Logan could really pull this off. The look on his face, that unshakable confidence that was always there, gave her hope. After all, who was going to question a SEAL? They had a fierce reputation and, although she hadn't been around them much at all yet, their legends preceded them. One just did *not* screw with them. SEALs had their ways....

The Army clerk behind the registration desk at the conjugal unit didn't say a thing as Logan filled out the form and handed it back to her. Jess tried to look relaxed as if they did this sort of thing all the time. Inside, however, she was sweating bullets. Logan looked like the most relaxed person in the word. Jess kept looking at the clerk, to try and spot suspicion on her face, but there was none. When the clerk handed Logan the key and they were safely on their way to the elevators at the rear of the building, Jess finally let out a long breath.

"See?" Logan said, once they got into the elevator to go to the third floor.

"You're either the luckiest damned man in the world, or that SEAL uniform of yours really *did* do the trick," Jess accused, grinning over at him. There was no small amount of pride dancing in his eyes. The elevator stopped on the third floor. He gave her a boyish grin and led her out the doors and down the highly waxed hall.

"I'm lucky to have *you*," Logan rasped, kissing her lips lightly before turning the key and opening the door.

Ushering Jess into the large, nicely appointed room, Logan smiled and shut and locked the door behind them. He saw her look around with amazement in her expression.

"Like it?"

"Well, it's not the Marriott, but it's a *lot* better than I ever thought it could be."

"Far better than a hard-packed dirt floor and a sleeping bag, eh?" Logan threw the keys on the dresser. There were dark green drapes drawn across the windows. He turned, watching her reaction.

"I've always heard of places like this," Jess murmured, "but I never dreamed I'd be in one of them."

Logan stowed their gear in one corner. "We have a 2100 hour flight out of here tomorrow night. That means we can sleep in, catch a late breakfast at one of the chow halls, get over to Navy Supply, and then plenty of time left over to come back here." He gave her a feral look. "I hope you're ready to be sufficiently loved by me?"

Her whole body went white hot over the look Logan gave her. "More than ready," she promised, her voice low as she held his burning gaze.

Logan led her to the bathroom that had not only a large shower, but a *bath-tub*, a rarity indeed in the military world. The pink tiles gleamed. Everything was neat and clean. "Do you want some help getting out of your clothes?"

Jess nodded. "Yes."

"What's your arm doing?"

"Aching, but that's all. Nothing to write home about." Jess sat down on a small stool just outside the bathroom door. As she leaned down to start to untie her combat boots, Logan knelt down and did the job for her. "I can do that," she protested.

"Hush. Tonight, and tomorrow, Jess, I'm going to spoil you rotten. Let me help you. I know what a bullet in the arm does. And frankly," he growled, meeting her eyes, "I don't want you aggravating it. I want your focus on us, not it. Let me do the heavy lifting around here for now, okay?"

Her heart warmed and she watched his long fingers fly over the shoelaces, quickly opening the boot so she could pull her foot free. "Okay," she whispered, suddenly choked up by his fierce care of her. "I guess I'm so used to doing things for myself, I don't know how to be a team person." She saw his sensual mouth curve and it sent heat straight down to her womb.

"SEALs are nothing *but* teamwork." Logan patted her leg gently and moved to the other boot. "And you're a team player, Babe. I've seen you out there with your drilling rig. Your crew loves you."

In no time, Logan had her undressed, standing naked before him. He checked the waterproof bandage the nurse had placed around her arm to make sure it was properly sealed. Moving his hands lightly across her shoulders, he saw a number of bruises probably gotten when she'd hit the ground during the firefight. Jess was beautiful, and it took everything for Logan not to just pick her up, place her on the bed and love her. "Come on," he urged, leading her into the bathroom. He picked up a washcloth, opened a bar of soap and put it in the shower tray for her.

"Will you do me a favor?" Jess asked, feeling no embarrassment at being naked in front of him. She saw the desire burning in his eyes.

"Anything. What do you need?" Logan asked, gently pulling the rubber band off her ponytail, allowing the dusty strands to fall around her shoulders. He saw her gaze become warm.

"Shower with me? Wash my hair? I can't get this damn arm even above my shoulders."

He grinned. "Thought you'd never ask. Go ahead and start. I'll join you in a minute...."

The shower was steamy as Logan entered. Jess had wet her hair and it lay in thick, heavy strands across her neck and the tops of her shoulders. Logan saw the dark smudges appearing beneath her eyes, knew she was slowly crashing. Taking the shampoo, he gently and thoroughly washed her hair first.

Then, lathering the soap, he washed the rest of her. Logan saw how much her arm pained her, yet Jess said nothing. But the thinned line of her lips told him everything; she was not a whiner or complainer about pain. When he had finished with her, he washed himself. If it had been any other circumstance, Logan would have taken Jess right then and there, in the shower. But not now.

Shutting off the shower, he held her hand as she stepped out. Gathering a thick white towel, he drew it across her shoulders and guided her to the small, cushioned stool. Grabbing another towel, he dried her wet hair. With her direction, he dug into her go bag, finding her comb and brush. Logan wanted to tell her how satisfying it was to comb through her straight, thick hair. He thought he saw tears in her eyes but wasn't sure. Jess had bowed her head down and he couldn't see her expression as well as he wanted. He began to carefully pat dry her shoulders. It was then that he felt her quiver, as if she were holding herself back tightly.

Kneeling in front of her, he placed one finger beneath her chin and gently tilted her head up slightly. His heart contracted. Jess was trying to stop from crying. "Hey," he murmured, standing up, "stop fighting the tears, Jess. Come on…," and he slipped his arm beneath her knees and back.

"I-I'm sorry, Logan," she quavered unsteadily, pressing her face against his neck and jaw as he effortlessly unfolded up from a crouch, bringing her with him.

He kissed her hair, smelling the scent of vanilla in the strands. "No apologies, Babe. You've been through hell today. I'll take you to bed and just hold you. Okay?" and he walked into the darkened room, gently depositing her on the bedsheet. Logan saw the misery in her expression. He turned the light off in the bathroom, throwing the room into utter darkness. Hearing Jess sniff, his mouth compressed. Climbing into bed, Logan brought up the sheet and blanket. Jess crawled into his arms, her body against his, her wounded arm resting across his torso. She burrowed into his shoulder, and he could feel her warm, wet tears plopping onto his flesh. Sliding an arm around her, he held her close. Logan could feel the tension she carried, knew it was the shock working its way up and out of her. His heart bled with sympathy because Jess wasn't used to violence. Few people were. The SEALs lived and trained for it, so their reaction was much different from someone like Jess.

"It's okay, Babe, just let it go. Get it out of your system," he urged gruffly against her damp hair. Logan moved his palm down her shoulder, skimming her upper back, and heard the first real sob tear out of her. Closing his eyes, he gently held Jess. When a person's fabric of calm reality was ripped away from them, the terror of the violence behind it shredded them emotionally. Pressing small kisses to her hair, to her wet cheek, Logan absorbed her weeping.

CHAPTER 10

LOGAN FELT JESS finally fall asleep in his arms. She'd cried deeply, sometimes sobbing in jerky spasms. It wasn't a time to discuss how she was feeling, or to even talk at all. He understood women enough to know tears were an outlet, a release, for them and it was a good thing. Even SEALs cried, mostly when they lost one of their team members, but they did it alone and out of earshot of others. He lay there with her against him, her breath soft and shallow now across his upper chest. Grateful he could afford this type of protection for her; Logan knew it was going to help her get her feet back under herself more quickly as a result. Jess had to go back out to that valley. She had five wells to sink in five different villages. And she knew she and her crew were now at serious risk. Jumping straight back in the saddle was going to be more of a challenge for her than she currently realized.

Would this experience change her life even further, beyond the here and now? Logan had seen some SEALs' whole demeanor shift and change, when wounded. SEALs felt they were invincible until that first gunshot wound. Many plowed through the experience and went on to remain solid operators. Others, it shook their whole world loose. They weren't always as good as before. Every man was different. He slid his hand lightly down her forearm, her palm resting against his heart.

Worse, in many life-changing ways for his own proficiency as a warrior, Logan knew that what they shared was a helluva lot more than just good sex. Earlier, when Chris had sent out the radio warning to all of them that a Taliban attack was underway, all Logan could think about was protecting Jess. That, if something happened to her, it would cut through his world as nothing else ever had. From the moment he'd accidentally met her at Landstuhl, she had become a vital part of him, lodging deep in his heart. That was a blessing beyond imagining but could also be a curse for a warrior whose very role depended on them thinking only of their team.

Finally, Logan closed his eyes, willing himself to sleep because sleep was precious. A SEAL's world was never safe. Chaos of one sort or another ruled. And it was always different, on a daily basis. But, for now, he decided to stow his concerns for the future away. To have the woman he loved in his arms, even for just one night, was an exquisite gift and he savored Jess next to him, her curves soft, her skin warm against his.

Jess awoke slowly, feeling as if she'd overslept by twelve hours or more, her mind barely functioning. At first, she didn't know where she was until she sat up in bed and looked around. Her wounded arm protested loudly, and she grimaced, looking down at it. The dressing looked so glaringly white to her. The memories sluggishly came back to her. The room was empty. Logan wasn't here, and she saw that his clothes he'd hung over the chair were gone, too. She heard the landing and takeoff of jets and helicopters outside. The reverberations could be felt like subtle, invisible waves rippling constantly across Bagram. Missing Logan, she looked down at his pillow. As before, there was a note sitting on it. Picking it up, she saw that it read: *Jess, got up at 0700. Will be back by 0900. Got some things to do. Logan.*

Setting the note back on the pillow, Jess looked at the clock on the dresser. It was 0830. He'd be back in half an hour. That would give her the time to get dressed and ready for her day over at Navy supply. She found out quickly that, with a cranky arm, unable to lift it very high, even trivial tasks became excruciating exercises in planning. That was rapidly becoming really depressing to her. She was generally a patient person by nature, but hauling on her trousers with one hand, and then struggling with the button and zipper one-handed to boot, were teeth-grinding chores. And getting her combat boots laced up was a completely frustrating fiasco. The pain was so bad that Jess finally caved in and took the Ibuprofen the doctor had given her, plus her daily dose of antibiotics. Going to the bathroom and brushing her mussed, but blessedly clean, hair was another acrobatic chore. She couldn't even pull her hair into a ponytail at all. When she tried to force her wounded arm up higher, she almost fainted from the pain. It just *refused* to work. Frustration thrummed through Jess. She felt raw and vulnerable enough this morning, and then to not be able to even take care of herself properly, just added to that.

The door to their room opened and closed. Jess looked out the opened bathroom door, but couldn't see the entrance from that angle.

"Logan?"

"Yeah, it's me," he called.

She saw him stop at the bathroom door. He looked so handsome; his face dark with stubble. SEALs generally didn't shave every day, just the opposite out here, in fact. They grew beards and faded into the male Muslim population, not wanting to stand out. He was holding some sacks in his hand, mirroring their first morning together in Germany. Worry was in his eyes as he checked her over from head to toe.

"How are you feeling?"

"Rugged," Jess admitted. "And very frustrated." She held up the rubber band in her right hand. "I can't even get my hair into a ponytail." It came out more like a whine, and Jess hated sounding like that. It just wasn't her. She saw him nod and put the sacks on the dresser.

Logan took the rubber band from her finger and gently turned her away from him. "Is there a special way to do this ponytail thing of yours?" he teased. He luxuriated in sliding his fingers through her brushed, shining black hair as he gathered it between his hands.

"No," she said. "I feel so damned helpless, Logan. I hate this."

"The first week after getting shot is always roughest," he told her, quickly gathering up her thick hair and taming it into the ponytail she always wore. "There. Look okay?" and he smiled a little, trying to lighten the darkness he saw in the mirror's reflection of her green eyes. Logan saw her mouth twitch, almost smile-like, but she was grumpy, for sure. He took it in stride.

"Looks great. I wonder what I'll do when we're back at the village? It took me nearly thirty minutes to dress myself. Thirty minutes, Logan! I usually dress in five."

He turned her toward him, hands light upon her shoulders. "Give yourself some breathing room, Jess. It isn't every day you get shot. And yes, you're going to feel frustrated, angry, upset, irritable; all of the above. It all comes with the territory of getting wounded. Once we get back to the village, I can help you dress and undress, on the sly. You want me to get your sling? You're looking pale."

Nodding, she grumped, "Yes. Please? Hell, I can't even put my own sling on by myself."

He smiled a little, kissed her lips lightly and said, "Come on, I went over to the chow hall and got some breakfast food to go for us. I even have coffee." He saw her eyes light up over that last comment.

Logan had her sit down in one of the two wooden chairs. He placed the dark green sling on her left arm, seeing immediate relaxation in Jess's mouth, her pain lessening.

"Thanks," she said, meaning it. Logan brought over a cup of coffee, took off the lid, and handed it to her. It smelled wonderful. He laid out an egg-and-bacon sandwich for her as well. Her stomach growled.

Logan sat down, absorbing her sleepy features. "Did you sleep solid last night?"

"Yes, thanks to you." Jess gave him an apologetic look. "I wanted so badly to love you last night, Logan, but I had all these crazy emotions flying through me."

He sat back, eating his own egg sandwich, coffee in the other hand. "It's normal, Jess. You're thinking like that because you feel like you've been emotionally beat to hell, that it's not all right. But it is."

"I remember last night you telling me you'd been wounded?" She searched his blue eyes. She saw worry in them for her. Care. Jess wasn't sure how she'd have handled getting shot if Logan hadn't been there in the breech, someone who cared deeply for her, to be her guide.

"Once here," and he angled his jaw toward his left shoulder. "Six years ago. My first wound."

"How did it affect you?"

"Like it's affecting you right now," he told her wryly, finishing off the first of his three sandwiches.

"Did you cry?"

"Not in front of anyone," and he grinned a little. "But in private? Yeah, I had a few shakedowns with it. When the shock starts wearing off, Jess, that's when you go through that roller coaster emotional hell. I thought I was invincible. I was a *SEAL*. I could do anything. But there I was, in the Bagram hospital with a shoulder wound. Stuck. Couldn't go back to my platoon. Cut off from everyone I knew. And, like you, I was told it would take at least six weeks and a helluva lot of physical therapy before I would be released back into the field. I was NOT happy. In fact, I got really depressed. Waded through that shit for nearly three weeks. I was not a happy camper, believe me."

She nibbled at the sandwich, not sure about her stomach. "I feel... raw."

Logan nodded, giving her a sympathetic look. "You will for a while, Jess. It's just part of the healing journey you're going to take. What else are you feeling?"

She took in a ragged breath. "Honestly? Questioning what the hell am I doing out here? I've NEVER been attacked, or shot at, in my ten years as a Seabee. Oh, I know we're trained to shoot and defend ourselves, but I guess... I guess, it's been such a shock. First Dan being killed. And now me getting wounded."

"Your world has been shattered, Babe. It has changed forever because of it."

His words were softly spoken but Jess winced visibly over them. She stared at Logan; his face readable for her to search. "Did it shake your world *this much* when you got shot, Logan?"

"Yes. In every way. It's a process and a journey, Jess. It's one day at a time. Once I rejoined my platoon, it did a lot toward helping me through that emotional rough patch." He shook his head, looking out the window through the drawn-back curtains. "When I was stuck here at Bagram, I went through my own personal and emotional hell."

"I believe it. I just never thought of how getting wounded could affect a person."

"Deeply," he muttered. "What else is going on inside you?"

"Fear," she admitted. "Fear of dying. You know I took out my chicken plates on my Kevlar vest. It was just too heavy for me to wear all day long. I've been thinking long and hard about that. If that bullet hadn't hit my arm, it could have hit my body. I didn't have the protection on that I needed." She frowned, and looked away, her voice strained. "I could have died out there, Logan."

"Yeah," he murmured. He saw the tears in her eyes, and her lower lip quivered. Getting up, he took the mostly untouched sandwich from her hand and set it on the dresser. He came back, then crouched down in front of her, his hands resting on her knees, looking up into her haunted expression. "It's a rough trip for you, Jess. You see yourself and your crew as doing something good that's going to improve the lives of people. And you've had that reality up until very recently. You've been welcomed with open arms everywhere by villagers, until you got assigned to that particular valley, a Taliban area of heavy resistance."

Nodding, she placed a hand on his. "You're right. Ten years of feeling like the good guys, doing good things for people who have such a brutal, hard-scrabble life… and then to get shot for trying to improve their lives. To get told we aren't welcome even though what we're doing for them is peaceful. And good. It will give them more food, improve the health of their babies…"

"Yeah, but these bastards' reality is very different from yours. The real question, Babe, is will you adjust *your* reality or not? Some people, after they're shot, it shatters them in every way. They lose themselves. They might spend a long time trying to recobble their life back together." He turned his palm over, entangling his fingers with hers, gauging her reaction.

"Well," Jess whispered rawly, "it's sure spun me around, Logan. I guess the biggest thing for me is the fear of dying."

"Yes," he said, "and you don't know how the end effect will be yet. You're probably feeling unsure about even returning to the valley, about now?"

She nodded, avoiding his gaze. "I feel so ashamed about even thinking like that, Logan. I'm afraid… afraid to go back… it's so cowardly of me…."

"No," he said, "it's normal. I went through that same process after I got shot. When I first started patrolling, after I got back to my platoon, I was so damn scared. I wasn't sure I could do it anymore. I worried that, if I wasn't focused, I would let my team down. Because SEALs work as a team. We need to have each other's backs." He kissed her hand and watched her eyes change, grow warm, some of the fear in them dissolving.

"What did you do?"

"Gutted through it, Jess. And so will you. We live scared after that. It's the fear of dying. Fear of our life ending, when we have so much of it left that we don't want to leave or give up." Searching her dark green eyes, seeing the pain in them, Logan reached up, caressing her wan cheek. "I'll be here for you, Jess. You have me to go to on a bad day or night. I'll be your team member. I'll have your back while you flounder through this shit."

"I'm lucky and I know it," she admitted in a strained tone, her skin tightening where he kissed it. "It's just so—life changing…"

"I know it is." Logan patted her hand, giving it back to her. "You're going to be too hard on yourself. Try to be a little kinder? Let me help carry some of your load? I'm pretty good as a listener," and he slowly rose, kissing the top of her head. "Come on, you need to eat. I know your stomach is probably on the fritz, but you need food for energy," and he handed the egg sandwich back to her.

By mid-afternoon, Jess had gotten over to Navy supply and picked up the list of items that Lieutenant Parker had requested. Luckily, with Logan at her side, he could get the supplies into boxes and then take them over to the helicopter terminal and place them on the pallet that was going to be airlifted back to the unit. Jess knew she'd have had a hell of a time getting it all done with the way she felt. Even aside from compensating for her arm troubles, Logan knew the system at Bagram. She didn't. They had stopped around noon, and eaten at one of the many chow halls on base. Her weakness disappeared as she ate. She knew she had to force herself to eat whether she had an appetite to or not, just in order to keep going. Right now, it was as if food was the LAST thing on her mind. Logan explained it was the shock. And he kept passing her protein bars from time to time, watching her start to regain her energy and her old strength back.

Jess had called her parents again, reassuring them that she was fine. They sounded more than relieved. In the twenty years her parents had been Navy Seabees, they'd never been shot at once. Jess didn't share how she was really feeling because she knew they'd worry about her even more. She shrugged at the cocked eyebrow look Logan gave her after she finished the call.

"I don't want them to worry."

"I know. But I'm glad you're honest with *me*." Logan gazed into her green eyes, seeing some of the cloudiness was gone. Just getting back into a routine she knew and loved was helping her climb out of that dark shock. Jess gave him a look of gratefulness as they walked from the bus stop back toward the conjugal building.

"I'll never NOT be honest with you, Logan." Except that it was almost tearing out of her how much she was falling in love with him. They'd both had marriages that had failed. And they'd met under the worst of circumstances: in a war zone. What chance did she have of their love surviving? She'd just been shot. Who knew if there was another bullet waiting for her out there? It hurt to tuck away her feelings for Logan. Jess told herself she had to focus in on *right now*. Not the future. She saw Logan smile over at her, the now-familiar heat sheeting through her, holding her heart so gently. The other day, she'd seen him combat mode. It had been a startling difference from the Logan with her right now. More and more, Jess realized that when Logan was with her, he was truly himself: open, available, able to share with her. It made her body ache. It made her heart yearn for him. *Only him. Forever.*

Jess always felt a bit guilty when they passed the clerk's office inside the conjugal building. Logan placed his hand on the small of her back, as if sensing her discomfort, guiding her to the elevator. Here, touching was permitted. And she hungrily absorbed it like an emotion thief.

In their room, she put her baseball cap on top of the dresser alongside Logan's. She turned to him, sliding her good arm up and around his shoulder. "I want to make love with you," she whispered, placing her mouth against his, feeling his instant reaction, his arms sliding around her. Logan was being careful with her. Jess had never known how much one damned wounded arm could be such a pain in the ass. But it was, and Logan was even more aware of the situation than she was.

"Are you sure?" he asked, brushing her lips, feeling her heat, feeling her move her hips against his.

"Positive."

He lifted his head, studying her eyes. "You know that when we get back to the village, there will be times I can spend a night with you, Jess. I don't want you thinking, just because we're here, you have to make love to me. I need you to be really sure. Getting wounded does funny things to people. Most of all, they act out of character." He wanted her so damn bad. The look in her green eyes, the dappled gold in their depths, told him she was emotionally where she needed to be. For him, that was a huge relief. There was nothing more bonding, nothing emotionally stronger, than being able to love Jess.

"I'm positive, Logan." She gave him an amused look. "But you're going to have to help me undress." Logan's mouth curved faintly, and she saw that feral look of his leap to his eyes. There was no question: he wanted her. *Bad.*

"I like getting my hands on you," he rasped, leading her over to the chair. "Sit down. We'll start with your boots."

"I want to lose myself in you," she whispered, her fingers grazing his short hair as he knelt over her boots.

Lifting his head, Logan growled, "Fair warning, Babe. You're not leaving that bed with me until an hour before we have to get that flight tonight."

All her fears, her trepidation and depression, dissolved beneath his low, guttural tone. Nothing had ever felt so right as being with Logan in this minute. And, after he shed her clothes, always mindful of her cranky arm, it was an equal pleasure watching him undress before her. Jess's whole body began to vibrate inwardly with yearning, needing his touch, needing the pleasure she knew Logan would give her.

As she lay down on the bed, he knelt near her hip, pulling over another pillow, gently placing it beneath her left arm.

"This way," he explained, "you might not be able to use it, but it will be supported, and you can focus on what I'm going to do to you."

"I guess there will be no gymnastics this time?"

His mouth widened into a smile as he pushed the potentially entangling sheets and blankets safely toward the end of the bed. "No. I'm afraid it's the good ole missionary position for you right now, Babe." He saw her pout. Jess didn't realize how sexy she looked when she pushed that lower lip of hers out like that.

"But I want to please you too, Logan." It came out as almost a whine of frustration.

He laughed softly, laying down near her, propped up on one elbow, sliding his hand across her soft, rounded belly. "We'll have other times," he assured her. As he moved his fingers down across her left hip, across her curved, firm thigh, her eyes shuttered closed and he could feel her focused only on them. And that's right where Logan wanted her. The hours that were left to them would be about giving back to Jess, supporting her shredded emotional state, gently sewing her back together again by tenderly loving her. As he slid his hand between her legs, and she opened to him, he heard her moan in anticipation. But, unthinkingly, she had automatically lifted her left arm to curve it around his shoulder.

Instantly, Jess grimaced, her arm frozen midair.

Logan placed his hand beneath the left elbow and said, "Relax it, let me guide it to the pillow."

"I wasn't thinking," Jess muttered, shaking her head, giving him a look of apology.

He tucked the pillow back beneath her arm. "It happens, Jess. And it's okay. Don't be hard on yourself. Focus on me, okay?"

"That's so easy to do," she whispered, feeling foolish over having been so careless as to lift her arm. Now, it ached so much again that she was sure she couldn't, even if she'd wanted to. Logan seemed unfazed by the gaff, but it bothered the hell out of her. Before she could think of anything else, however, his mouth came down upon hers, hot, hungry, and her entire world anchored to a scalding halt. If she'd thought Logan was going to be tepid about loving her, she'd been wrong. And that thrilled Jess, being equally starved for him in every way.

CHAPTER 11

J ESS SLEPT AFTERWARD, exhausted. She awoke two hours later to Logan watching her. Giving him a sleepy smile, she whispered, "I must have died…"

"Bad pun," he murmured, brushing her cheek with his fingers, holding her green-and-gold gaze, her lashes barely open. "Let's just say it was the best sex ever?"

She melted beneath his lazy smile, seeing how satisfied he was. "It was…," she sighed. "Didn't you sleep?"

Logan shook his head. "With you in my arms? No way. There won't be all that many times like this ahead of us, for now. I want to remember this day," and Logan sifted the sleek black strands of her hair through his fingers, hearing her make a happy sound in her throat. Her cheeks were still flushed and there was new life in her eyes. Logan knew Jess well enough by now to see that she was not only utterly satisfied, but happy. And that meant more to him than anything. Jess had amazing resilience and maybe that was due to her growing up all around the world with her Seabee parents. He took a deep breath, fear moving through him. Not much scared him anymore, but what he was about to say, did. Logan was worried about Jess's reaction. Maybe, this wasn't the time to say it? He was unsure but took the plunge regardless.

"Look," he began, his voice low with feeling, "I like what we have, Jess. I wasn't looking for a relationship, to tell you the truth." His mouth quirked as he watched her gaze grow thoughtful. "But… I think about you all the time. The things you've shared with me. And I want to know everything about you." He moved his thumb across her smooth brow, watching her eyes change, grow warm at his touch. "I know we're in one helluva situation in that valley. And I'm going to be there for as long as you and your team are. I guess, I'm wanting to know if you feel similarly or not? About us? Maybe it's one sided?" He hoped not. No woman had ever gotten under his skin like she had. Not ever. But under it, Jess was. He couldn't think two thoughts without including her in them. Or wondering what she thought about something. She had an earthy, common-sensed intelligence that called to him. Searching her eyes, watching her brows move down, he felt the fear arc stronger through his heart. Had he read her wrong? Logan prided himself on reading people right the first time, but ever since he and Jess's fateful meeting, he felt his whole world had turned inside out. Was he losing perspective?

Jess slowly moved and, with Logan's help, sat up. Her hair fell around her shoulders. She brought her left arm in its sling against her torso. It caused her less pain in that position. There was such seriousness in Logan's voice and face. She realized this was an important talk. Logan sat back against the headboard and guided her up beside him. She came carefully, hating the arm wound, but not able to ignore it, either. Resting her head on his shoulder, she fitted herself against Logan. His arm came gently across her left shoulder, carefully avoiding that upper arm. "I guess we're sort of like two tops spinning around," she murmured sleepily, raising her chin to look up into his dark blue eyes. She saw such desire in them for her. The only times she hadn't seen that look in Logan's eyes was when he was on duty, or in combat mode. "I sure wasn't looking to a relationship, either," she admitted wryly.

"I sort of figured that out."

Nodding, Jess nestled her head more solidly against his shoulder, her brow resting against his jaw. "Logan, I like you a lot. And it scares the hell out of me. I wasn't looking for a man to complete my life. My life was just fine the way it was."

"So was mine."

"But there you were," and Jess smiled fondly, remembering that afternoon not so long ago. "You were filthy, covered with blood, dirt in your hair, on your face, mud on your boots. You looked rough, like such a fierce warrior to me. But I saw your eyes. I know we barely looked at one another when you came into the surgery lounge, but I saw YOU."

He grazed her hair, looking down at her. "What do you mean?" There was such openness and honesty in her expression.

"Your eyes were alive with grief and anxiety. You looked tough on the outside. Really hard. Invincible. But your eyes spoke of your humanity. Your heart." She saw the understanding in his gaze as he listened closely to her words.

"When I walked in there, I was an emotional mess inside, Jess. And then, I saw you." Logan shook his head, one corner of his mouth pulled upward. His hand stilled over Jess's hair, and he held her gaze. "Two impressions hit me about you in that split second when we barely glanced up at one another. One was I thought you were beautiful. Oh, I know you were dirty, like me. Your hair had dust in it. I saw the blood on your cammies and I knew you'd been in one helluva firefight." Logan stopped, working to put the words together. This was important. "I saw your beauty, but when I looked back and really absorbed what I had seen, I realized how vulnerable looking you were. You had something terrible happen to you, but you were open. You hadn't closed up like most people do, Jess."

"What did that say to you?" she wondered. There was a need for her to know how she impacted Logan. It was a key to him.

"My marriage," he said abruptly. "My wife was closed up. She never really trusted me... entrusted herself to me. I never knew, from one minute to the other, how she was really feeling. What she was thinking." He pulled a few black strands of her hair through his fingers, holding her upturned gaze. "With you, it's the exact opposite. I saw your grief, your hope, and your anxiety. And you didn't try to hide any of it when I walked in. I was a complete stranger to you, but you had the strength, the confidence, just to be yourself."

"And that's important to you?" Jess wanted so much to reach out with her left hand and caress his cheek, but that wasn't going to happen with her wounded arm.

Nodding, Logan said, "It was. I mean, when I got married, I was really too young. I was pretty damned immature. Maryann was beautiful, accomplished... the whole package."

"Except she wasn't open or available to you?"

"Not like I needed," Logan admitted. "I came out of a set of parents who talked to one another honestly, all the time. I was there when they had arguments, but they never screamed or got angry with one another. They always talked it out. It was a lifelong lesson, a blessing is the way I feel about it, in how to handle serious talk between two adults."

"So, there was trust between your parents? It does sound like they have that rare kind of relationship where both people are completely open and honest with one another, Logan."

Nodding, he placed a kiss on her brow, inhaling her fragrance. "We men aren't real good about putting what we feel into words," he admitted, giving her a sour smile.

"You're different from other men I meet. You sell yourself short."

"Oh?"

Jess gave him an affectionate look. "One of the many things that drew me to you Logan, was your openness. Not many men express themselves as well as you do. I think your parents rubbed off on you in the best of ways. I like the fact you're honest with me. I can see what you're feeling because you don't try and hide it from me. I really appreciate that about you."

Logan raised his eyebrows. "That's good, then."

"Very good," Jess agreed, watching some of the tension leave his face.

"What was the other thing you saw in me when you walked into that surgery lounge?"

"Well, that came later," he admitted. "After the surgeon came and told you that your chief hadn't made it through surgery, I felt horrible for you. I wanted to go over and just hold you because it was written all over your face." His mouth thinned. "But I didn't, Jess. I was so full of pain, exhausted, that I had nothing left to give to you even though I wanted to."

"But you wanted to?"

"Yes."

"What touched you about me, Logan?" and Jess searched his eyes, feeling some unknown worry in him that he wasn't telling her about.

"Actually, it was when you came over, after being told your friend didn't make it, and you had enough strength, maybe care or humanity is what I mean, enough *compassion* left in you to worry about someone other than yourself. You walked over and touched my shoulder and told me you hoped that my friend would make it out of surgery." Logan shook his head. "You have NO idea what that did for me, Jess. I felt the heat where you touched me on my shoulder. I felt my heart opening up, and I wanted to cry. You touched me so deeply with your care and kindness..." He studied her, grazing her temple and cheek, inches from her soft lips that were still slightly swollen from their hungry lovemaking earlier. "I just don't have the right words for what you did, Babe. You reached out beyond your own grief, pain and suffering and you extended yourself to me in those moments. I found that incredible. It was then that I knew I wanted to know you. I wanted to know who this woman was that wore her heart on her sleeve and, despite her own grieving, had compassion enough left over to try and make another terribly suffering human being feel better."

Sighing, Jess closed her eyes as he slid his fingers around her ear and then slowly down the length of her neck. "How could I not, Logan?"

Cupping her jaw, Logan angled her just enough to kiss her tenderly. "You are one extraordinary woman, Jess Courtland," and he moved his mouth tenderly across hers, feeling her warm response, unable to get enough of her. Not wanting to *ever* get enough. He heard that soft sound of satisfaction of hers in her throat, a sound he lived to hear. It was like music to him, uplifting him, giving him hope he'd never dared consider before. Sliding his hand across the back of her neck, he deepened their kiss. They were naked against one another and her breasts were pressed against his chest. Her nipples grew hard and he could feel them against his own tightening skin. Her breath was growing shallow and rapid as she eagerly matched his need for her.

Ever so slowly, Logan broke their kiss, tasting Jess, moving his tongue across her lower lip. She was to be slowly savored. Her eyes were closed, those thick black lashes stark against her flushed cheeks. He waited for her to open them as he slid his hand across her jaw. When she did, his heart contracted fiercely with love for her. Logan was such a goner. His mouth hovered near hers, their eyes locked. "Jess, I want to know if I have a real, long-term chance with you. I don't want to lose you going forward." Logan held his breath. He was laying all his cards on the table here. Searching her glimmering green eyes, seeing the natural ardor and care that was always in them, made him want her even more.

"It's going to be complicated, Logan," she whispered, regret clear in her voice, her brow wrinkling.

"I don't care, Jess. So that's a yes?" and he held his elation in check because he could see the concern in her gaze, could feel her thinking through so many things about and between them.

Jess dragged in a ragged breath, seeing the glint in his stormy eyes. She felt the fine tension running through him. His intensity tugged at her heart. "Logan… I don't know how… you're a SEAL. I'm a Seabee. We not only live in different worlds, but we would never even be at the same base together, either."

"SEALs are the best at workarounds, Jess." Logan patiently maintained his heading. "Just tell me if I have that chance with you? I'm serious about you. This isn't a casual fling. You have to know that by now, Jess. I want a chance to get to know you better, spend time with you, talk… Laugh. Make love. Go for a hike in the mountains of Wyoming. Fish in an ice-cold glacier stream in the Tetons." Logan had seen that Jess loved the outdoors, the very earth beneath her feet, just as much as he did and, from the wistful look in her eyes right now, he knew his instincts had been on target. *Please* he begged her silently, *just say yes….*

"It's my nature to look at reality," Jess told him gently.

"And that's fine. Like I told you before: Where you see obstacles, I see solutions, Jess."

The corners of her mouth curved softly upward. "The idealist and romantic in me tells me to say yes. And to have faith that, over time, it will work out. That we'll get to see one another, even after this assignment is done."

Logan waited. He couldn't force Jess into anything, nor did he want too. And he knew that getting shot was altering her view of the world already in large and small ways he might have no awareness of. At least, not yet. "I like both sides of you, Jess. Maybe that's what appeals to me so strongly about you. I like your common sense. But here, when we're together, that dissolves, and this incredible woman who enjoys sex with me so much is another part of our equation. We're good together, Jess."

"We are," she admitted. "But I see it as more than just sex, Logan. I know it's a guy thing," and she managed a sour smile. "See, when I'm with you, when I kiss you, for me, it's making love WITH you. It's more than about sex for me. My heart, all my emotions, are in the mix, as well," and she stared up at him, watching understanding coming to his eyes. "Maybe it's just my romantic side coming out again, Logan, but I see all this as so much more than just being in bed with you. I love that bit, don't get me wrong. But you touch my heart... my soul..."

Groaning, Logan kissed her, feeling her mouth move beneath his, felt her warm breath against his cheek. Sliding his fingers through her hair, feeling Jess melt trustingly against him was the greatest gift he could ever have. Slowly, he released her wet, smiling mouth, drowning in her eyes that were alive with love. Yes, *love*. Neither of them had gone there. He was dancing around that word as much as she was. And Logan couldn't blame Jess or himself. They hadn't known one another that long. They had to allow time for whatever it was they shared to gel. And the biggest step of all was here and now and was to be taken in his arms: Trying to coax Jess into committing to him whether *she* saw a solid way forward with him or not. Logan had never wanted anything more. He could taste it. In his heart, in his mind, he knew without a doubt that he was already in love with this woman of the earth. But did Jess love him? Logan honestly didn't know. Wouldn't go there. He had to get her to agree to a relationship, first.

Jess grimaced and forced her left arm to move slowly. Less pain that way, and it got her hand where she wanted it: right over Logan's heart. His chest was dusted with dark hair, giving him a powerful masculine quality. The look in his eyes was a mix of love for her, coupled with anxiety. "I don't know where we're going with one another, Logan," she began quietly, holding his stare. "I'm not a risk taker like you SEALs are. I guess... I guess I like things uncomplicated, straightforward."

"Life isn't like that," Logan told her, unable to not touch her and feel the warmth of her skin beneath his trailing fingers. He smiled a little. "I know drilling a well is like that, but human beings, Babe, are complicated animals at best. Nothing is easy when you meet someone that you are immediately drawn to."

Jess studied him from beneath her lashes, tangling her fingers through the soft silk of the hair across his chest. "When I wake up in the morning," she began softly, "I always wish I could turn over and you'd be there, Logan." Shrugging, she held his glimmering eyes, felt the invisible protection he afforded her. "I find myself during the day wishing you were beside me.

Something I wanted to ask you. Something I wanted to share with you…" Her voice grew low with undisguised feeling. "Honestly? I've been so scared of what's happened between us. And it's not you. It's me. I just can't see it working, but here we are. I don't want to lose you, Logan. But I can't see how what we have is ever going to work," and Jess swallowed, searching his darkening gaze. Logan brushed her cheek, and she felt a quiver go through her. His touch always made her super sensitive to him, wanting him in every way.

"Then," he told her, his voice thick, "why don't we agree that we have something special and not put a label or expectation on it? Something good, Jess? You let me figure out how we'll make it work? Like I said, SEALs are famous for workarounds and you're just going to have to trust me on that." Looking deeply into her eyes, Logan saw such yearning in them for him. His heart burst wide open in return with such powerful feelings for Jess that he almost blurted them out. But… he didn't dare use the word love. Not yet. Not until he could prove, over time, that they could make it work. He saw her lush mouth grow soft. Her eyes became luminous.

"Okay, Logan, I'll take this step with you. It's just… our schedules. The different branches we work in in the military… It's not you. I LIKE having you around. It's wonderful."

Hearing the quaver in her husky voice, he smiled a little. "Let me worry about logistics. All I need to hear from you is that you want the same thing I want, that's all."

Nodding, Jess licked her lower lip. "Logan, you were never the question in my life. I WANT you in it. And I know you keep reassuring me, but I still just can't see *how* we can make it work." She saw amusement come to his eyes. That chiseled mouth of his grew into a cocky, confident grin. Without words, that grin said: Logan would find a way. He'd already found one by showing up in her life again after Ramstein, after their parting at Bagram that followed that glorious first encounter. So why was she so hesitant? And then it hit Jess. Hard. Gently, she shifted her hand, moving it over his powerful, slow-beating heart, over that life-affirming pulse she could feel beneath her palm. "One more admittance, Logan."

"Okay."

"I don't give my heart easily. When my marriage collapsed, when I realized I hadn't seen Mark for who he really was, it devastated me. I've gone around, since then, blaming *myself* for my bad judgment about men." She frowned. "This is *my* issue, Logan, not yours."

"But it's still playing out between us, Jess. Maybe part of your hesitancy is that we haven't had enough time together yet for you to see how I impact you… how I might impact on your life?"

"Yes," she admitted, being brutally honest about it. "I fell for Mark. It was a whirlwind romance. Looking back on it, I should have taken a lot more time. I'm convinced now that, if I had, I'd have seen some of those other, negative sides to him. It would have red-flagged me and I wouldn't have married him."

"And you're worried about the same thing here?" This was something Logan could deal with. He saw the hurt and the worry in Jess's expression. Her experience wasn't something to whitewash. It was something to be understood and, hopefully, be used to help both of them get their burgeoning relationship on a more solid footing.

"Yes. I know it's not fair on you, Logan. I get that. It's just that... I'm afraid. I just need time, and that's the other wall I'm up against. I don't see HOW we'll ever get that kind of time together."

He smiled a little and guided her lifted head back down onto his shoulder. "I'll give you all the time you want, Jess. You're important to me. I'm not walking away from you. I'll hang in there with you for as long as you're willing to put up with me."

Closing her eyes, she felt a huge load lift off her shoulder. "I needed to know that, Logan. I know it's *so* not fair of me to paint you with the same brush as Mark. That's *my* issue. I just need some time..."

Logan pressed a kiss to her hair. "Take all the time you want, Babe. Like I promised, I'm not going anywhere. And if you don't know anything about SEALs, know this: when we have an objective, we get to it, no matter how much is standing in the way." He felt her relax, felt her release a deep breath. "I'm sorry to be the one to tell you this, but you're not getting rid of me, Jess."

Nuzzling against his shoulder, Jess grinned at his light-hearted turn of phrase, but inside, felt her world seriously shift and change. It was subtle, but it was there. The man holding her in his arms was warm, protective of her, cared about her as a person, and wanted a long-term relationship with her. All this, everything most people dream of, had come out of the blue. What were the chances? Jess had no experience with this kind of powerful draw to a man. It scared the hell out of her, but at the same time, she had never felt so right about anything. And Logan was confident about them. She was not. And it was all *her* garbage, her experience with Mark, standing in the way. More than anything, Jess wanted to clear that barrier, see Logan only, not kneejerk from past experience. He didn't deserve that. He'd been honest and up front with her from the beginning. If he only knew how much she was falling in love with him. *Time.* They had to have time. Would they get it? Jess didn't know. What she *did* know was that, right now, being beside Logan, his fingers moving slowly through her hair, as if to sooth and calm her worries, made her feel incredibly cherished and loved.

BRAD PARKER MET them after the Chinook landed at nightfall. The pallet with the supplies was quickly offloaded by the two crew chiefs and Jess's well-drilling team. It wasn't wise to do things like this in the daylight. But, even under cover of darkness, they always worked quickly. Jess had them take the supplies to a mud hut next to where Brad had his office. After the Chinook took off, she walked with Brad down the street. Her arm was still in its sling, and Brad took care not to walk too closely to that side of her. Logan was on her other side, his M4 in his hands. He wasn't going to allow her to go anywhere without an escort from now on, if he could help it. Once he dropped her off safely at Brad's office, he was going to speak with LT Anderson.

Since their serious talk, Jess seemed more settled. Happy even? Logan thought she was. She was more like her civil-engineer mother mind-wise than she realized, he thought. Engineers saw the world in terms of problems to be solved. Black and white. Maps, drawings and firm reality.

Logan lightly touched her shoulder to let her know he was leaving as Brad opened his office door. She turned her head, nodding silently. One thing had not changed: neither of them wanted anyone to know about their relationship. At least, not yet.

Logan continued down the bare village road, then stopped and knocked on the door of Lieutenant Sean Anderson's mud-and-stone hut, quietly speaking to let him know who it was. There was no window built into the rough-hewn wood door. Anderson opened it.

"Come in," he invited Logan. "How was Bagram?"

"Busy as always," Logan said, safing his M4 and hanging it on its harness. Inside, there were a couple of candles shedding light on Anderson's desk where he had a topo map laid out. "What have you come up with on this latest attack? Anything?" Logan saw the lieutenant move his fingers in a distracted motion through his short blond hair as the man sat down on a stool at the table.

"Not much," Anderson muttered. "Have a seat," and he gestured to the other stool on the opposite side of the briefing table. "No drone yet. That sucks."

Logan scowled. "You couldn't convince your people at Bagram?" A drone was considered a top-tier strategic asset, and Logan knew the CIA didn't easily relinquish their turf to military requests. There were two drone-holding entities. One was the DOD, the Department of Defense, run by the military. The other belonged to the CIA boys, who had their turf rigidly staked out and rarely wanted to work with the military. Each group had their given reasons to be stingy with their resources. None of them good, in Logan's opinion. They desperately needed a drone over this area.

"I convinced my colonel that this is serious," Anderson said, "but the drones available to them are all being used on what they consider more important areas of concentration."

"What about the spooks?"

Anderson grimaced. "I called them. They weren't interested. There was nothing in it for them." He glanced up. "You know how they are."

Cursing softly, Logan nodded. "Did you turn up anything else?"

Rubbing his bearded jaw, Anderson said, "Bits and pieces. I talked with Colonel Markham about our situation. Two attacks within two weeks of one another. Both times, involving Jess." He frowned. "You aren't going to like this, but Colonel Markham feels that Khogani is targeting Jess specifically."

Logan's gut clenched. He kept his face neutral. "Reasons?"

Shrugging, Anderson muttered, "They want to kidnap an American military woman. The Taliban could upload a video somewhere, make an example of her. Rape her? Beheading? The usual things. It's an open secret they want to get a woman. They've already, over the years, kidnapped twelve American military men. But their sought-after prize is to get a military woman." His voice went dark. "And, if that happens, you know the hell it's going to cause at every level of the military, not to mention how civilians are going to react to the shitstorm when the major internet and mainstream news media in the USA get ahold of the whole thing..."

Grimly, Logan nodded. "What's your plan to protect Jess, then?"

"Hell, I'd like to get her transferred out of here," Anderson growled. "But, see, I was on the horn to Commander Johnson, her C.O. I explained the situation. And he's looking at potentially removing Jess from this valley. I'm not sure he believes me that she's a specific target of the Taliban. He's buying it, up to a point. The problem is, if she fights the order, that causes a lot of shit for him to deal with, too... shit that he doesn't want on his plate right now."

"I don't think Jess would fight it," Logan said. If he *could* get her out of here, that would be the best-case scenario. Though, he sensed Jess would be pretty damned ambivalent about it. She wasn't a person who ran from a fight. But, at the same time, she'd been wounded and maybe that would make her think twice. Maybe it would be enough to make her relent, let this assignment go, move on to another, far safer, Third World country.

"You think so?" Anderson gave him a hard look.

"Yeah. She just got wounded. You know how a bullet can change your life."

Anderson nodded. "Got two to prove it."

"Me too."

The officer studied him in the building silence. "Do you think I could go to her, reasonably present what we've found, what we think's really going on? And she'd be open to it? Quietly let herself get reassigned somewhere else that's safer?"

Shrugging, Logan said, "I'd give it a try, Sean. You have nothing to lose."

"Yeah, but there's a connection between the two of you. If she bucks my reasons to get her reassigned, maybe you could make the difference?"

Logan gave the officer a steady look. He wondered if Anderson suspected their relationship. Of course, the officer *was* in black ops, so not much escaped him. He shouldn't be surprised. Most of all, Logan wanted to protect Jess's reputation and her career. There was nothing wrong in having a relationship with her. They were both enlisted and that much was allowed. What *wasn't* allowed was that kind of fraternization between military branches. He had to be careful with the LT. "Our connection is that we unexpectedly met at Ramstein. She was there for her chief, as you know. I was there for a buddy of mine who got wounded in a firefight." He saw the lieutenant nod, not giving anything away.

Anderson replied, "Look, I like Jess. I'm protective of her because she is a woman. I guess she wouldn't want to hear that, but right now, I can use all the help I can get. I don't think Jess will leave without a couple of us, who she trusts, giving her good reasons to do so, is all."

Logan nodded. "Well, keep me informed. You've worked with her longer than I have. And you seem persuasive. One thing I *am* going to do is: Chris and I are going to closely shadow her movements. I have to talk to her about this and get her cooperation. Whichever of us who isn't on overwatch on her drilling crew, will be boots on the ground wherever she's at and wherever she goes. I'm not about to let her drive out to that damned field alone again to troubleshoot some issue. She needs a 24-7 guard from this point on."

"Agreed," Anderson said. "I'm fine with that as long as you two are."

"I've got to talk to Chris. He's next on my to-do list," and Logan grinned a little. Although Anderson might suspect a deeper tie with Jess, he wasn't going there. That was a relief. Some officers could be a pain in the ass if there was fraternization going on. Others, if it was handled quietly and behind-the-scenes, ignored it. Logan had some fine lines to walk with keeping his and Jess's secret, but stealth was a SEAL's middle name. He would doggedly protect Jess, and never give Anderson a reason to intervene or cause further havoc in her life. She had enough of that, as is.

CHAPTER 12

A GOOD KIND of tiredness inhabited Jess tonight as she sat down on the wobbly stool in her mud house. They'd arrived back at the village two days earlier. Everything had gone well since, much to her relief. Eli had repaired the backhoe upon receiving its replacement hose, and good progress was being made on the ditch that would eventually carry the well water into the irrigation complex she had designed with the help and ideas from the villagers. While she'd been away in Bagram, Sean Anderson had had some of his men improve her hut's entryway security. Not only had a more secure door been fitted, but there were also new, much stronger hinges on it. And, although there was no lock on the replacement door, they had installed a security drop bar made of thick wood that ran horizontally between the two huge metal hinges when engaged. The door opened inward, so the bar across it would stop anyone from entering much better than a mere door lock ever could. As Jess untied her shoes with her one good hand, she thought about how much better she'd been sleeping at night with this added layer of security in place.

There was a knock at the currently open door. She looked up. The one candle she had on the table shed just enough light for her to recognize Logan's heavily shadowed presence standing in the doorway. "Come in," she said, smiling up at him. He pulled his NVGs up onto his forehead and stepped inside.

"Got a minute?" he asked. Anderson had told him about the reworking of her door, and he carefully checked out the new, heavy wooden bar. The LT's men had done a good job of making the door secure, including the new, heavier replacement hinges. He closed it, lowering the bar into place, satisfied that the hut's single-entry point was a helluva lot better secured than before.

"Sure, I always have a minute for you." She saw how serious Logan looked. What was the matter? Pushing her boots off, Jess pulled off her sweat-dampened socks as well, wriggling her toes, glad to let them breathe. "What's going on? You look worried."

Logan came over and put her combat boots down at the end of her sleeping bag for her. "How is your arm doing?" he asked. Jess looked like her old self. Logan knew that being back into her routine was helping her deal with the trauma. Tendrils of hair clung to her cheek, perspiration gleaming across her face. Her cammies were dusty. And he could see dust coating the strands of the ponytail between her shoulder blades.

"Oh," she muttered, "it's cranky. Nothing new."

"Have you been taking the Ibuprofen?"

"Yes, Doctor, I have," and she smiled because he was constantly on her like a broody old hen, making sure she was taking the antibiotics and Ibuprofen. He walked over and framed her face with his large palms. Logan was going to kiss her. How she'd yearned for exactly *that* all day long. But he'd been out of sight most of the day. She'd seen him working with Lieutenant Anderson and, later, talking with her boss, Brad. She knew he was concerned for her safety and was probably talking to the officers about just that. As his mouth slowly brushed her lips, she moaned softly, raising her right hand, sliding it around his neck, feeling his hunger against hers. This was exactly what she needed. Reluctantly, Logan broke their kiss, leaving both of them breathing unevenly. She knew he probably had an erection, although tough to tell through the cammies. *She* was certainly turned on, wanting more, an ache building within her.

Logan released her and brought the other stool around the table and sat next to her. He steeled himself for what he had to say. "I have been getting intel from LT Anderson about this last attack, Jess. The identification and maps we pulled off those two dead Taliban were carefully studied back at Special Forces HQ at Bagram, by their Intelligence section. They put the photos of the men's faces through their computer ID system." He picked up her good right hand, holding it between his own. "Both LT Anderson and Parker think that it's Qader Khogani's soldiers. He's the Hill Tribe leader. He's been active in this valley for over a year."

"Okay," Jess murmured. She saw something in Logan's eyes that bothered her. She tangled her fingers among his where he rested his hand against his long, hard thigh. "What does that all mean?"

"The CIA has been picking up a lot of cell-phone chatter at the Afghan-Pak border. They shared their intel with the Army." His mouth flattened and he held her gaze. "What they've found the last two weeks, that none of us knew about until now, was that Khogani had made a deal with a Pakistani warlord who was wanting an American woman as a sex slave. He's already put a quarter of the full bounty of a million US dollars into Khogani's bank account in Pakistan."

Frowning, Jess stared at him. "What does this have to do with me?" she asked, mostly as a way to delay the oncoming answer she dreaded to hear. She could already feel fear beginning to eat away at her. And she could see the seriousness in Logan's narrowing eyes.

"Everything," Logan uttered, watching the flare of dismay in her eyes. "You weren't mentioned by name, Jess. But the intercepted calls from Khogani to this warlord described you down to a tee. And the bastard pinpointed this village as to their target's whereabouts."

Her throat tightened as she considered his heavily spoken words. "Then... that's why the two attacks... so close together?"

"Yes. Both times, they were trying to kidnap you." Logan moved his thumb gently against the back of her workworn hand.

"Oh...God..." And Jess frowned, swallowing hard, looking around the hut. "Is that why the door is different? Stronger?"

"Kind of, yeah." Logan allowed the information to sink in. "All this has been suspected ever since the second attack, and precautions were initiated, but now the confirmation has come through officially. What you might not know is that there's always been an active slave trade in girls *and* boys between Afghanistan and the rest of the Middle East and Asia. Girls are stolen from their parents and sold into sex slavery. So are young boys."

"That's horrible, Logan! But," she stumbled, giving him a bewildered look, "I'm not young."

"You're an American military woman," Logan told her patiently. He saw the confusion in her expression, holding her hand a little more firmly. "Look, we in the black ops community were briefed on this scenario years ago. It goes something like this, Jess: The Taliban kidnaps an American military woman. They take her into Pakistan where the likelihood of her ever being found again is about zilch point zero. They would then take this woman and humiliate her in front of a video camera. Then, that video would be uploaded on major Al-Qaeda websites for the world to see. It would cause one hell of a reaction in the U.S., for starters. American citizens would see one of our women in a highly compromised position." He didn't want to have to say rape. Or stripping her naked in front of the camera. Or beheading her. Or all the above. Jess was looking at him as if he were an alien who had just landed in front of her. And he saw her connecting the dots: that she was just such a target of opportunity.

"This... this is a nightmare," Jess whispered, giving him a fearful look. Are you SURE, Logan?"

He nodded, seeing the anxiety in her eyes, hearing it in her voice. He knew that having been shot would just feed that terror. And it hurt him to see it. He loved Jess. He wanted her out of here. Safe. Not a kidnap target of one of those sick sonofabitches. "The CIA is cooperating with Army Special Forces at

Bagram on this very issue."

She pulled her hand free, touching her brow. "What should I do, Logan? They've come close twice already."

It hurt him to see the fear gripping her so solidly now. But maybe it would help to get her to listen to reason, too. "Look, Brad Parker is going to be receiving a set of orders tomorrow morning, Jess. Those orders are going to be for you." He saw her scowl. His voice deepened. "They will be orders removing you from this site. That's all I know. I don't know where they're going to send you, but it's going to be far away from this place."

Stunned, she stared at Logan. "Brad told you this?"

"Yeah, a little before we sat down to eat our MREs together earlier. They just called him." Logan shrugged. "I wanted to be the one to break the news to you, Jess, and alone, not in front of Chris. I asked him if I could at least let you know about all this. He's going to give you the full set of orders tomorrow morning. He'd like you at his office at 0800."

Shakily, she pushed her hair away from her temple. "But, if they shot me, I'm no good to them."

Logan grimaced. "They probably didn't intend to shoot you, Jess. It could have been a ricochet, or just bad aim. Things happen in a firefight. We're sure that they were coming to kidnap you and kill the other two men. I don't know if you noticed, but they had a saddled horse with no rider with them. Did you see that?"

She shook her head, biting down on her lower lip.

"The conjecture is that they were going to tie you on that horse and ride away and quickly disappear into the hills with you in tow."

Her gut clenched. "This is crazy!" she muttered.

"Crazy? Yeah. But it's as real as it gets, Jess. They're targeting you. And they aren't going to stop until they get you." Logan brushed her cheek, now gone pale, getting her attention, looking deep into her troubled eyes. "They aren't going to stop, Babe. That's what you have to understand about all of this."

"You seriously think they'll try again?"

Nodding, Logan growled, "Khogani needs the money from this transaction, Jess. This is how he feeds his men and horses and gets the bullets and AK-47s for his army. And there's that deposit on you, sitting in that Pakistan bank, as the clincher." He hated scaring her, but he could feel Jess's indecision, her reluctance to believe it because her team, her job, was here. And she wasn't a woman to be scared off easily. The stubborn set of her jaw told him volumes. "Khogani isn't going to walk away from this, Jess. He's already got his down payment. He's going to come after you again *and again* until he gets you."

Logan would make damn sure that would never happen, but felt he had to hammer the point home for Jess to look at the situation realistically. And, indeed, he saw the reality sinking a little deeper into her.

"But," she insisted, "*you're* here… with Chris. And there's that twelve-man A-team."

"And, even then, we haven't been able to stop him getting close to you," he warned her heavily. "They're opportunists, Jess. They saw the backhoe break down and waited like patient wolves to see if you would be going out there to check it out. And you did. None of us foresaw them planning something so carefully like that. They're constantly changing their tactics, getting slyer and smarter."

"It means they were watching me." Jess suddenly felt cold. And terrified.

"Yes."

"But… you have a satellite that passes overhead every day. Why can't you find them? Send an Apache helicopter after them? Drop JDAM bombs from a B-52 on them if they're hanging around like that?"

Logan's grimace was pained as he saw her becoming shaky and resistant. Her voice was low, quavering. Jess was starting to glance around like a trapped animal, not wanting to believe any of this. But this *was* as real as it got, he hadn't just been saying that to convince her. Sliding off his stool, he nudged her knees apart and stood between them, reaching his hands down and framing her face. "What we *need* is a drone over this position," he told her quietly, his thumbs brushing across her temples. "We can't get one, Jess. And without it, we're blind, deaf and dumb. I don't like admitting it, but we are. According to Anderson, this issue has gone all the way up to the DOD secretary. And he's the one who has issued the orders for you to leave here tomorrow. There's just too much evidence pointing toward you being kidnapped, Babe. And we don't have the high-tech stuff we need to keep tabs on Khogani. Hell, he and his men can hide in the hundreds of caves up in those mountains above us. They can hide behind hills and get damn close to this village. Don't you see? You HAVE to leave. It's the only thing that will keep you safe."

Making a frustrated sound, Jess leaned her brow against Logan's chest. She felt his arms come around her shoulders, making soothing motions across them, as if to take away some of the fear eating at her. "This… this just isn't right," she whispered, tears burning in her eyes. "I've been with my crew for five years now…"

"I know," Logan said softly, hearing the pain in her voice, kissing her hair, wanting so badly to lift this new shock and awareness off her slumped shoulders. "It's for the best, Jess."

She pulled up, looking up at his grim face. "Do you agree with them?"

"In a heartbeat. I don't even like having you spend one more night here. The only good thing about it is they have attacked twice in daylight hours and Anderson feels you're safe here, out of sight. That's why he reinforced the door for you. No one's going to be able to knock it open and grab you at night."

"I did wonder about the door when I first saw it," she whispered, still reeling from the sudden shift in her fortunes.

"And I'm staying with you tonight," Logan told her, seeing relief come to her gaze. "I'm not leaving you alone, door be damned." Logan saw a lessening of the fear in her eyes. That was good. "LT Parker will give you all the info tomorrow morning at 0800. We'll both know where they're going to send you next."

Her heart ached. They'd only just spoken about this; the hurdles in front of them to make their relationship work. "I'm just sick about this," Jess breathed, looking at him. She saw the anguish in Logan's eyes. He wasn't even trying to hide how he felt about losing her again so soon.

"I'm relieved," he admitted. Logan eased from between her legs. "We'll figure something out, Jess." She had enough to worry about without putting their burgeoning relationship on top of everything else. Kissing her brow, he said, "Let me pour some water into your bowl for you? To clean up?" Logan wanted to distract her. He saw Jess rally beneath his care.

"Yes... thank you..." and she slid off her stool, standing, frowning. The worst part, more than anything, was being torn away from Logan. The pain in her heart increased over its final acknowledgement of the fact. Jess would lose her crew, who were loyal to her, too. The men under her were all like younger brothers to Jess, and they worked so well together. Tears burned in her eyes, but she forced them back. Jess knew nothing in life was fair. But this truly sucked at the highest level. Her arm was aching. She'd better take her pills.

"All right," Qader muttered to his captain, Afir, "we will do it your way."

Afir sat just inside the opening to a cave, their small fire hidden from the outside by a low stone wall built for that very purpose, watching their meal for the evening cook in a black pot suspended from a metal tripod. His leader sat next to him, scowling heavily, unhappy. He felt like pointing out that he had been right, but Afir knew it wouldn't be wise to rub Khogani's nose in two failed attempts to capture the American woman.

"My lord," he said, keeping his voice subservient, "we tried our best." He gave an eloquent shrug. "There is no blame."

Qader nodded, mollified. "We'll wait until the messenger returns." Twenty of his men also sat in the alcove. The goat meat boiling in the pot, along with some onions and potatoes, smelled good. He worried over the American woman's wounding. Would the Pakistan warlord still want her? He'd wanted her unmarked. Qader mulled over what to do about it. She had an arm wound. Would the warlord not accept her because she was damaged merchandise? Or still buy her, but lower the purchase price he'd promised to pay?

Qader had already sent a rider north, with a message for the warlord about the situation. Cell towers weren't exactly numerous, but there were enough on the Pak border that, if one got within range, calls could be made. That soldier, a young fifteen-year-old boy named Shekaib, had been sent riding at high speed to that area. Qader *had* to know whether to move ahead with the plan or not. The rider was to return tonight sometime. Qader moved restlessly, wanting to know what happened. He flexed a fist, feeling angry. His men had been given strict orders to NOT shoot at the woman! But it had happened, anyway.

The sound of a horse trotting outside the cave got everyone's attention. Qader stood, realizing it was his messenger, Shekaib. His heart beat a little faster. The boy dismounted at the cave opening, pulling the tired, wet horse in with him. Qader headed him off, giving him a sharp gesture to leave the horse standing and walk with him out of earshot of his other soldiers.

"What news?" Qader demanded as they stood just outside the cave entrance where no one could hear them.

"My lord," Shekaib began in a low voice, "the warlord wants his money back. He said the agreement was that the American woman would be in perfect condition."

Qader cursed softly, glaring down at the thin fifteen-year-old boy, still barefaced, unable to grow a beard yet. "What else!"

"My lord, I contacted your commander in Pakistan. He called the Taliban leader in Peshawar. The Taliban will give you a hundred thousand American dollars for her." He smiled a little. "They do not care if she's been shot, so long as she does not die enroute to them. The commander told them it was an arm wound and that she was in good condition."

"Only a hundred thousand?" Qader ground out, his hands moving into fists. Rage flared within him. He wanted to put a bullet in each of the surviving men who'd ridden on that attack. They'd cost him *nine-hundred thousand* dollars! Money badly needed to keep his army together.

Shekaib winced. "I'm sorry, my lord. Yes, that is the amount they offer. They want her delivered over the border, to your usual meeting place. So long as she is alive, that's all they care about. They laughed and said all the better that she's been shot. And they said to tell you that they don't care if the merchandise is soiled or not. If she comes to them with bruises or cuts, they don't care. But they don't want her to have any broken bones. Nor do they want her raped. They will do worse things to her on the video."

That was a relief. He hated Americans. Especially the women. He relaxed his hands. "When do they want her?"

"As soon as possible."

"Is there a deadline?"

"Two weeks, my Lord."

Qader cursed to himself. That meant Afir's plan would have to be put in motion.

"Very well," he snapped. "Take care of your horse and then get something to eat."

"Yes, my lord," Shekaib murmured, trotting into the cave.

"I can't sleep," Jess muttered, pressed against Logan. They lay with their work shirts and cammies on. He didn't want them naked tonight because some kind of attack could come at any moment. Everyone military at the village was on high alert. His M4 was at hand between him and the wall of the hut.

Logan knew with his SEAL instinct that it was somewhere around 0200 in the morning. Jess had slept, but restlessly, often awakening and then falling back into a light doze. Gently, he brought her even firmer against him, her head resting on his shoulder. Her hair was clean, he'd helped her wash it earlier, and it smelled sweet as it tickled his nose. "I know," he murmured, sympathetic. Her arm was in its sling tonight, even during sleep, Logan wanting her to give it as much rest as possible. Jess moved her leg over his, snuggling as close as she could get to him. He smiled to himself, liking her boldness. Jess knew what she wanted. There was never any guesswork about her.

"My mind is going a million miles an hour, Logan. In five different directions. This situation is driving me CRAZY."

"What's the top one?" he asked, inhaling her scent, pressing his mouth to her wrinkled brow. He heard her make a soulful sound in her throat, sensed she was close to tears.

"You."

"What about me?" Logan felt her press her face against his neck. He tightened his arm just a bit, trying to give her the support she needed.

"I-I don't want to lose you, Logan. We've just found one another and I'm acting like a sniveling teenager."

The moon was full tonight and milky light spilled silently through the only window in the hovel. Easing Jess onto her back, propping himself up on one elbow, Logan laid a hand across her belly. Drowning in her shadowed face, her beautiful high cheekbones softened by the grayness of the light, he held her glistening eyes, sensing her sadness and anxiety. The sadness was over them parting. The anxiety was over her world coming apart under her again. It was a lot for anyone to deal with, Logan knew. He slipped a fingertip across her temple, watching the black strands it brushed aside glimmer in the moonlight. "Jess, I'm a rock in your life. Okay? You might leave here tomorrow, but we'll be in touch. I'll know where you're at. I'll figure out a way to see you." He saw huge tears form and then slip silently down her cheeks.

"My heart aches, Logan," she whispered.

He shared a tender smile with her. "So does mine."

"I-I just feel like my heart is absolutely being torn apart. I've NEVER felt like this before, Logan." Desperation came to her low voice. "It's a terrible feeling; as if I've lost everything… Silly, really. That's not logical."

He moved his finger down from her brow, removing the tears, and then kissed her damp cheek. "A lot has been piled on you, Jess. *Anyone* would be reeling from it, feeling like they were tearing loose inside themselves. All you have to do is hold on to me. To the fact that I want you in my life. That I'll make that happen one way or another. That's a promise."

The deep emotion in his voice calmed her. Logan meant every word of it. She saw it in the stubborn quality of his eyes, heard it in his thickened voice. His mouth moved into a slight smile as he dried off a cheek with his thumb.

"I want to share a dream I have for us," he rasped. "Maybe it will give you something to hold on to?"

She swallowed and nodded. "Please… tell me? I want something… anything, to hold on to Logan." Because her life, as she'd known it, was slipping away.

"Ever since you told me you kicked around the world, grew up a wild child, I've been harboring this dream inside of me: I want to take you home to Wyoming, take you to the Tetons, where I loved to go with my parents. We'd drive over them at least twice a month when I was on summer vacation. We'd hike, fish and just soak up the beautiful mountains around us." He followed the curve of her eyebrow with his finger, watching calm come to her eyes. "You and I are going up to a place about seven thousand feet in the Tetons. There's a glacial stream that rushes out of a nearby lake. It's filled with trout. I can see us pitching our tent there, laying out our sleeping bags, setting up a Coleman stove and getting out our fishing gear. We'll catch the trout, panfry them with butter, salt and pepper. There's nothing like fresh trout. And we'll go hiking. There's a lot of beautiful places I want to show you. Plenty of grizzly around, too, but I know what to look out for, and there's buffalo, pronghorn antelope, deer, elk and raptors: birds of prey. It's the Garden of Eden for me." Logan saw her expression soften, saw the hope burning in her eyes. "I want to share those happy times I had back then with you, Jess. You're of the earth. You'll find a piece of heaven there, I hope."

She closed her eyes. "It sounds wonderful, Logan."

"Thought it might." He kissed her lips gently, wanting to erase the anxiety he knew she wrestled with. Jess hadn't had the time to absorb the fact she'd been shot, much less process it fully. Now, she was being ordered out of her job, being sent somewhere, away, but not knowing where. And was being torn away from *him*. Logan understood he was central to her stability from the standpoint of someone to talk to, to let down with, and be able to cry in front of. He knew Jess had a lot of inner strength; that wasn't the issue. It was just about being there for her during this major stage of her crisis. And now, she was going to be ripped away, plopped somewhere new, alone and without friends or support. That was the military for you, and it sucked. But she knew the drill and would shore herself up accordingly and get through it. He was going to miss her. Because he loved her. Torn, Logan wondered if he should admit it, or not, right here and now, and then decided no. It was just piling more onto her already-full plate. There would be a quieter time when he could tell Jess and love her. A time to fully celebrate that glorious next step of togetherness.

CHAPTER 13

LOGAN LEFT AT 0400. Jess knew he didn't want anyone, other than Chris, to know the depth of their relationship. She promised him to put the wooden bar down on the door the moment he silently slipped out into the night, heading for his own hut. She couldn't sleep after that, felt depressed, and took her antibiotic. Logan had stressed she should keep the bottle on her person, so she put it into one of her jacket's pockets. She kept busy by finishing the packing of her duffle bag. Logan would come by later, after she'd had her meeting with Brad. Where were the new orders taking her?

Jess pushed back tears. She hated leaving her Seabee crew. They were tight. They worked together like a well-oiled machine. They were just damn good at what they did. And now, she wondered if the DOD orders would place her back at Port Hueneme Naval Mobile Construction Battalion in California. That would make perfect sense, being about as far out of harm's way as one could get. And that would be a career killer for her. Now that the DOD knew about her, knew she was on the Taliban's radar, Jess wondered if she'd be reassigned anywhere but a "safe" place ever again. Or, instead, placed in an endless series of backwater posts, on other continents where she wasn't a target. That meant a whole new crew each time, a new lieutenant to work under, and starting all over again. All that seemed too daunting to Jess to dwell on right now. She had to give herself a break from everything that was happening to her. She had the age and maturity to know that, sometimes, life became a ball of unraveling yarn. Right now, the best thing she could do is just have blind faith that it would all work out in the end for her.

Once she'd finished packing her duffle, which weighed a good eighty pounds by the time she was done, she pushed it back into its corner with the toe of her boot. Her heart ached for so many reasons. Peeking out the lone window, wincing only slightly as she did her ponytail, she saw it was dawn, around 0500. By 0600 her crew would have eaten and they would start their day of drilling. *Without her.*

She needed to empty out the bowl of dirty bathing water. Trying to manhandle the thick, heavy wooden bar open was always more work than it should be. Lifting it out of its brace, and then up out of the way of the door, would be easy with two hands. Impatient, she removed the sling. Her arm hurt, but not like before and she pursed her lips; a bit of good news. Her arm free, she took the opportunity to carefully shrug on her trusty old, tattered Levi jacket, as it would be cold outside. Then she wrangled the drop bar up and pushed the door open with her boot. With two hands, it was easy to carry the bowl of water outside.

The coolness of the night invaded her far warmer hut. The dawn light was grayish, and she could see the peaks of the Hindu Kush becoming illuminated as the sun marched closer to this corner of the world. As she carefully took the large bowl in her hands, not wanting to slop the water on her uniform, Jess heard a child crying nearby.

Frowning, she looked around as she emptied the water outside the hut. It was unusual for children to be up and about at this hour. The child's cry was coming from the stand of bushes across the way, down from her hut. What on earth was going on? Jess set the bowl down. The sound of a young child crying, somewhere behind the grove, tugged at her heart. Unable to see the child, she hurried toward the stand for a closer look. The village children played in this grove all the time. Usually hide and seek. Had one of the families in the village had a toddler sneak out their door? Thinking it was time to play hide and seek, then getting turned around in the bushes, lost? That would explain the child's piteous cry.

Mouth quirking, Jess hurried around the stand. She halted. Her heart slammed in her chest. Standing there, waiting for her, were three Taliban soldiers. All of them were near their horses, their AK-47s pointed at her. *Oh, God....*

Qader, nearest of the three to the American woman, glared at her. He saw her blanche, her face turning white. Instantly, he stepped forward, his AK-47 trained on her. He'd never seen her face up close before. Her left arm was not in a sling any longer, but he could see by her posture, the way she held it, that it troubled her. She was definitely the one they were after. Gripping her un-wounded upper arm, he yanked her forward, right up in his face. He pressed one finger against her lips, savagely shaking his head in the unmistakable meaning of: *you scream, you die.*

Afir came up, quickly taking the pistol out of the holster she wore. He quickly frisked her for any other weapons, finding none. He nodded to Qader, who led up the extra horse they'd brought with them.

Terror sizzled through Jess. She saw the hatred on these men's bearded faces. They were dressed like typical Afghan men. Except, they were heavily armed, and the looks they hurled silently at her were pure venom. She heard the child crying again and saw another soldier holding a little four-year-old girl who was terrified. They'd used the poor child as bait in the trap they'd set!

"Mount," Qader told her in thick English, shoving her roughly forward.

No! There was no danger greater than being taken! Jess drew in breath to scream for help.

Afir's fist exploded in her face.

Jess felt the pain roar through her left cheek. She was falling backward from the blow, the attempted scream never leaving her mouth. Instead, she merely grunted as she felt herself falling, her knees suddenly buckling beneath her. She hit the ground hard, the impact sending a shock through her entire frame, jarring loose something unnoticed by both her and the men from her jacket pocket to roll away.

Strong, hurting hands gripped her upper arms. She felt a cloth being pulled hard between her lips, tightened, so she could not make any sounds. Pain roared into her wounded arm as they jerked her wrists together in front of her. Harsh ropes were wrapped around them, tightened, another bolt of agony. She was hauled up to her feet, semiconscious from the blow to her face.

Qader made a jerking motion of *get the woman on the horse*! He had his other soldier roughly set the crying child down in the dirt. Quickly, they pushed the dazed American woman up into the saddle of the bay horse, the spare. She was wobbling in the saddle. Afir roped her bound hands to the saddle so she couldn't fall off. He held the reins of the nervous horse and, gripping them tightly, mounted his black gelding next to it. They had to get out of here *now*! Before they were discovered!

Jess felt her horse leap forward, trotting strongly. She lifted her head, her entire cheek throbbing with pain and swelling. The leader with his black beard and hate-filled brown eyes, rode at the head of the pack. Her horse's reins were in the hands of a second soldier riding ahead of Jess, and two other men rode behind her. Stunned by the blow, her left arm aching, Jess tried to pull free of the bonds that held her wrists to the saddle. Terror arced through her as, the moment they were clear of the village, the group whipped their horses into a hard gallop, heading for the taller, rockier hills just ahead of them. She wanted to scream. To alert the A-team, or anyone else who might be up at this hour. The gag cutting cruelly across her face made it impossible.

There was no commotion from the village, nor any sign of pursuit; The A-team soldiers who walked the village on patrol had not seen her being kidnapped! She closed her eyes, feeling the movement of the horse beneath her. The animal was moving at top speed, the cold morning wind tearing past her face, making tears leak from her eyes. She was in the worst trouble of her life. Stupidly, *carelessly*, she'd fallen for a trap set for her by the lead man, surely

Khogani, and his soldiers. What was going to happen next? Her mind spun but kept shorting out due to the blow to her cheek. *Logan!* He would come after her! Jess knew he would. But how long would it be before he even knew she was gone? Logan was coming to see her at 0600, *an hour from now.*

The brown hills loomed before them. Jess felt the rawness of the bonds abrading into her wrists. Her fingers were going numb through loss of circulation. They rounded the first big hill, galloping hard. Up ahead, she saw a trail that snaked up into the slopes of the Hindu Kush, up into the trees dotting down from where they abruptly ended far above, around ten thousand feet. A sinking, terrified feeling pervaded her adrenaline-charged body. What if Logan couldn't find her? They had no drone eyes. Only a satellite that passed overhead once a day. Her mind rocked with gnawing, gut-eating fear. These were Hill tribesmen, and they knew the mountains and their caves like few ever would. They could hide her. No one would see her. And then, she'd be taken across the Pak border, to be lost among the millions there, never to be seen again.

Logan was barely awake in the hut where he and Chris slept, when there was frantic pounding at their wooden door. *What the hell?* He quickly got up, opening it. A young mother, her head covered with a scarf, her eyes terrified, started speaking swiftly in Pashto to him. She was crying, her tears disappearing beneath the scarf across her nose and cheeks. The tone of her words was pleading, filled with fear.

Chris sat up. "What's going on?" he muttered, rubbing his face.

"I don't know," Logan said. He knew it was unusual for a woman to be coming alone to a male stranger. Muslim law forbade it. So, what the hell was going on? Logan pushed out of the door because the woman was pointing repeatedly at the grove down at the end of the village. He turned, seeing the woman's husband running toward him, his eyes also wide and filled with fear. Logan caught sight of one of the three A-team sergeants who patrolled the village throughout the night hours. He gestured for the man to come over. One good thing was that Special Forces teams always had one or more members who spoke the local language. In this case, Pashto.

The husband of the upset woman stood by her side, frantically looking around. He was fearful and he kept trying to speak to Logan, who didn't have a clue as to what he was saying. The sergeant, Lloyd Magaw, ambled over.

"'Morning," Magaw said, his hands resting across the weapon that hung around his neck.

"Hey," Logan greeted, "this woman came banging on our door. Can you find out what she's upset about?"

"Yeah," Magaw said. He focused on the husband and asked in Pashto why his wife was so upset. Why had she come to the SEALs' house?

Logan saw the Special Forces sergeant begin to scowl, and lifted his head, studying the grove. A bad feeling crawled through his gut.

"Hey," Magaw said, "go check on Jess? This guy said two Hill tribesmen broke into their home earlier this morning, took their four-year-old daughter. They warned them to stay in the house or they'd kill their child."

Scowling, Logan said, "Why would they do that?" He ducked back into the hut and quickly retrieved his M4 rifle.

Magaw shrugged. "They kidnap children, too, unfortunately. Come on, you check on Courtland. We need to set up a search, try to find their child."

Logan nodded, trotting down and across the dirt road toward Jess's hut. Something was wrong. Had Khogani and his men found her house secure? Unable to get in? Had they gone to this farmer's house and stolen a little girl instead? He didn't know, but his gut tightened with foreboding. *Shit*, his instincts were rarely wrong. As he broke from a trot into a run down the road, he heard Chris coming up behind him. He came abreast of Logan, his M4 at the ready in firing position.

"Those bastards could still be in the village," Chris huffed. "I just woke up LT Anderson, gave him the info. We're going on full alert."

Nodding, Logan neared Jess's house. They halted as they came around the corner. The door was wide open. Logan spotted the metal bowl on the ground nearby.

"Jess?" he called, heading for the door. "Jess!"

Logan shoved the partially opened door aside. Ducking his head in quickly, he didn't see her in the hut. What the hell? His heart stopped. There on the table was her sling for her wounded arm.

"Hey," Chris called, "come out here, Logan."

Logan emerged, scowling. And then he heard it. A child crying.

Chris was giving him a signal to move to the other end of the grove as he headed toward the nearest end of it. Quickly and silently, Logan made his way around the thicket. There, in the middle of the small clearing behind the grove, was a little girl sitting and wailing. He saw Chris come around the other side, weapon up. They both lowered their guns slightly and ran toward the terrified child.

Logan picked up the little girl. Huge tear tracks streaked down her dusty face, and she cried even more when he held her. Looking around, Logan saw no one else. What the hell was going on? Where was Jess?

The mother and father of the child ran up to him. Logan handed off the screaming child to them. She was in no condition to tell them anything. Magaw joined them, also looking around.

"Have you seen Jess?" Logan demanded of the sergeant.

"No. Why?"

"Because she's not in her hut," Logan growled. Holding up the sling up, he said, "This is her sling for her arm. She always wore it and it was in the hut." He began to look around at the prints on the dusty ground. And then, his heart tumbled. Down over the bank of the clearing, he saw something small, white and cylindrical. Sliding down the small slope, he recognized the object as Jess's antibiotics bottle. Picking it up, he felt as if the world had just been yanked out from beneath him. Lifting the pill bottle up, he saw Chris shake his head in angry frustration, recognizing it immediately.

"They've kidnapped Jess," Logan yelled. He jammed the toes of his boots into the loose yellow soil, pocketing the bottle of antibiotics, quickly making his way back up to the grove.

Chris got on the radio, informing Anderson and Parker. His face remained hard.

Magaw looked at the bottle as Logan showed it to him. "They set her up," he growled, pissed. "Stole the little girl, set her out here to start crying and, probably when Jess came out of her hut, she heard the ruckus, went and investigated it."

Logan wanted to scream, but he quickly shoved all his emotions deep down inside himself. He couldn't do Jess any good that way. He had to think. Following the muddy horse tracks, he knelt down near the end of the grove. His heart plummeted. There was Jess's boot imprint! She wore special construction boots that had steel lining in the sole, different from the standard combat boots everyone else wore. Chris leaned over him.

"It's her bootprint alright," he confirmed, his voice low.

"Yeah," Logan growled." He stood up, looking at the mix of horse prints trailing away from the village. "They've got her…"

Qader smiled to himself as he whipped his hard-working horse lunging and leaping upward through the trees and brush on the slope of the mountain. The sun was going to come over the peaks soon, and he wanted to be hidden in a cave by that time. Afir was behind him, leading the terrified-looking American woman. He was going to have to reward Afir for his subtle strategy of luring the woman out of the hut. A child would always get a woman's attention. And, just as Afir had predicted, the American woman had come to the grove to try and find the crying brat. And she'd walked right into their hands. It was a perfect trap, executed flawlessly.

He wasn't celebrating too much just yet though. Qader knew there were drones in the desert skies. He wasn't sure if there was one in the valley or not. But one thing he *was* sure of, once the American soldiers in the village discovered this woman missing, they would be sending Apache helicopters overhead with infrared tracking ability to try and pick up their body-heat signatures. And then, they'd either send truckloads lot of trouble after them, or just rain down hell then and there. Mouth thinning, he rubbed his beard and whipped his horse on the rump again, hearing the animal grunt as it lunged upward through the steep *wadi*, or ravine. If they didn't hide soon, the coming Apache's would locate them. And then, if they valued the woman enough to not just blow her away along with him and his men, Qader knew they would send those damned SEALs after them. SEALS were relentless. Looking up, he saw the large cave he was aiming for, mostly hidden by trees, about five hundred feet above them. At the top of the *wadi*, was the entrance. Their horses were laboring, sweaty, foam covering their necks and haunches.

Jess could no longer feel her hands at all. They were a bloodless white, the tight bonds shutting off her circulation. Her left arm screamed unremittingly. Luckily, she could not feel any blood running down inside the sleeve of her jacket. It was cold and she shivered, unprepared for this kind of temperature drop. Surrounded by woods and brush, the horses kept pushing up the steep and rocky *wadi*. Up ahead, she saw the black maw of a cave mostly hidden by trees. She had no idea how long they'd ridden, only that her bruised legs ached, being as completely unused to riding a horse as she was. Her cheek was throbbing. Thirsty, she longed for a drink of water. What were these men going to do to her? Jess tried to think. She'd never taken the SERE course, the grueling two-week escape-and-evasion course given to men and women who fought in danger zones, and could potentially be captured in battle, or caught behind enemy lines. No one put Seabees through SERE; the likelihood of them getting captured was too low. She knew next to nothing about how to escape! But she had to do *something*. She wasn't going to be taken to Pakistan. *No friggin' way.*

Looking up, reading the now-medium-blue sky and the angle of the sun's rays on the white clouds drifting over the summit far above, she knew Logan would know by now that she had been kidnapped. He'd do something. He'd put things into motion. Could they find her in time? Her horse scrambled up out of the *wadi* and, in moments, Jess found herself riding into a vast, wide cave that was at least ten feet high and forty feet long. For the most part, it was hidden from the outside world.

The man holding the reins of her horse turned in a tight circle and rode up alongside her. He glared at her as he pulled her horse to a stop. Jess saw the rest of the men dismounting, encircling her. Her mouth went dry with terror. The leader, with his black beard and brown, wool rolled cap, stood with his hands on his hips. He looked her up and down, as if she were a piece of meat.

A knotted feeling made her stomach ache.

"Get her down!" Qader ordered Afir.

Jess saw the soldier with a dark blue turban, the one who had the reins to her horse, walk over to her. He untied her hands from the saddle. And then, he snarled something at her, grabbed her left arm, jerking her off the horse and throwing her to the ground.

A gagged cry tore out of Jess, pain arcing up her wounded arm. She slammed into the dirt with an *omhph*. Jess tried to scramble up out of her vulnerable prone position, but her legs had no strength after the punishing ride. The man grabbed her by her ponytail, jerking her upright. Jess bit back another cry, pain radiating all over her scalp. He slammed her up against the sweaty, hard-breathing horse. The smile on his face filled her with even more terror as he held her put by her hair while the other man in the rolled cap sauntered over, smiling at her.

Qader didn't like the fact the American woman was taller than any of them. She was like a giant, and he hated her even more. Her cheek was swollen where Afir had struck her earlier, and he could see that it was turning purple. The fear in her eyes made him smile more broadly. *Good.* She *should* be afraid. He remembered her wound. Had it reopened from the rough treatment and ride? Keeping in mind the Taliban wanted her alive, he growled to Afir, "Take her to the rear of the cave. Check that her wound hasn't torn open. I don't want her dying on us before we deliver her."

Grunting, Afir said, "Yes, my lord." He released her hair and shoved her forward, past the horses.

"Make sure she is fed and watered," Qader called. He saw Afir raise a hand without looking back, acknowledging his order. Turning, he snapped at his men to take their horses down another tunnel, to a deeper cave with a pool of water in it. There, the horses could drink their fill. Turning, he couldn't help but feel hugely pleased about having the American woman in his grasp. Soon enough, he knew, the Apache helicopters would be flying overhead, searching for them. And they would never find them in this cave. He chuckled to himself, already counting in his mind the hundred thousand dollars the Taliban would give him for this bitch.

He saw Afir shove her down to the cave floor, pushing her back against the rough wall. She was properly terrified. As Qader approached, he saw her long, spare hands were fish-belly white, with blood crusting around her wrists.

"Afir, tie a rope around one of her ankles. Release her hands. She's harmless and I don't want her hands looking like that. It is better she arrives in better condition, not worse. I may be able to get more money for her."

"Yes, my lord," Afir muttered. He took his knife from its sheath, expertly cutting her bonds.

Jess gave a little cry, feeling the blood rush back into her hands, the pain of it pulsing and throbbing. She sat there, feeling hatred radiating off the soldier as he stalked away. She was free of bonds. But the man with the rolled cap stood in front of her, his arms across his narrow chest, intently studying her.

"Do you know who I am?" he asked her in halting English. He saw her eyes widen enormously as he spoke in her language. What? She thought the Taliban were stupid and illiterate! His smile deepened as she stared in shock up at him.

"I don't know who you are," she lied, trying to sound less frightened than she really was. What was he going to do with her? His black eyes were close set over a thin, fine nose. His black beard was long, dirty, and she could see bits of food tangled between the strands. The smell around him was that of sour male sweat. Jess swallowed hard, not knowing what he was going to do next with her.

"Qader Khogani," he said. His smile dissolved. "Now that I've introduced myself. You must do the same."

Her heart leaped in her chest. The Hill Tribe chieftain had lost his smile, becoming serious as he watched her like a bug under a microscope. Jess knew she didn't dare make this man angry. Her military training kicked in; certain Geneva Convention protocols had to be followed. "I'm Petty Officer First Class Courtland, US Navy."

He waved his hand. "Do not repeat your military serial number to me. What is your first name, woman?"

"Jessica." She saw him smile, pleased that she'd cooperated.

"Very good. So, you are Jessica Courtland." He saw Afir stalking back with a length of rope in his hand. "Well, you are my prisoner, woman. Afir is going to tie that rope around one of your ankles. I would just break it instead, but I can't have you with broken bones, or have you die on me, before I take you to a certain Taliban warlord waiting for you in Pakistan. So, we will give you water, food and take care of your wound. Do not try my patience. If you try to escape, you will pay a very heavy price." Qader smiled a little, watching Afir tighten the rope around her ankle. He then tied the other end of the ten-foot rope around a jagged outcropping of rock.

"Please," Jess begged, "let me go?"

Qader laughed. "For a woman without a set of balls, you are outspoken." His scowled. "You can say goodbye to the life you knew," he snarled. "I own you now. And you will do exactly as I say, or you will be sorry."

Afir didn't know English, nor did any of the rest of his men. All the Khogani male children who were in line to lead the Hill Tribe, were forced to learn English. Afir let the foreign babble wash over him as he quickly set to work, jerking at her jacket, needing to take it off her so he could get at her left arm.

Jess gasped as the man grabbed the front of her jacket. Automatically, she threw up her arms, jerking away from him. Was he going to rape her? Adrenaline soared into her bloodstream as Jess pushed back with her heels, away from his hand. He snarled something she couldn't understand. His hand whipped out like a snake striking, grabbing her by the neck, yanking her back toward him.

"Afir," Qader cautioned in their native tongue, "be gentle. She doesn't know what you want her to do. Let me tell her, so she doesn't think you're going to rape her, as she undoubtedly does," and he chuckled.

"Jessica," Qader said, "sit still. Afir only wants to get you out of the jacket so he can check your arm."

Breathing raggedly, frozen, Jessica felt Afir's hatred to her bones. His brown eyes were fixed on her with loathing as he crouched over her. Qader looked entertained. Giving a jerky nod, she realized she had no choice but to trust him at his word, worthless as it probably was. She gestured, hands moving to her jacket front, to indicate that she would take care of it herself. Afir stood up, snarling at her, waiting for her to get it off. With shaking hands, Jess sat up and unbuttoned her jacket with trembling fingers. Beneath it, she wore only a dark green t-shirt. She hadn't even put a bra on yet, and more terror flowed through her at that realization as she worked to pull the jacket off.

Qader smiled as he watched the woman disrobe. Afir grabbed the jacket, kicking it aside, dust rising into the air, and jerked his finger to the ground, indicated she had to sit down. He hated the American woman. But most interesting were her full breasts against the tight fabric of her t-shirt. He saw pleasing terror in her eyes as he focused on those breasts. He crouched down, his Russian-made medical kit open at his feet.

Qader walked over, assessing her wound. It had not ripped open and seemed to be healing. He again felt rage. One of his stupid soldiers had shot her. If that hadn't happened, he'd be sitting on a million-dollar captive right now.

"Are you thirsty?" Qader asked her as Afir cleaned around her wound for good measure and wrapped it.

Jess nodded, feeling pain radiating through her bicep but was relieved it was not bleeding. Afir was not gentle. He wanted to make her feel more pain than was necessary. He wrapped the cleaned wound expertly, to her amazement. Almost immediately the ache in her arm receded. To her relief, he got up, grabbing the medical kit, getting as far away from her as he could.

"Stand up! Get your jacket back on," Qader ordered. There was relief in the woman's eyes as she struggled to her feet and to get her jacket on to hide her breasts. He turned to Afir.

"Bring water and some food." He saw his soldier's deep scowl. If Afir were running this kidnapping, he'd probably beat the woman to death. There was no leniency in his captain's face. An American drone strike had killed his entire family, his wife and four children. Afir had good reason to hate Americans. But Qader needed this woman alive and ready to go to a much worse fate. What the Taliban did with her after he handed her over, Qader didn't care. He would have a hundred thousand dollars in his bank account. That's all he wanted out of this trade.

More than anything, Jess was thirsty. She had no appetite. When Afir brought back a goatskin bag containing water, she gulped down the muddy-tasting liquid. In the back of her mind, she knew the water wasn't purified, and that so many Afghans carried worms and other parasites in their gut. She didn't care, her throat dry and her thirst overwhelming. Afir crouched nearby, watching her, a perpetual sneer on his thin lips. He pushed half a loaf of dried bread into her hands.

Jess took it, chewing on it, knowing that, if she was going to try and escape, she needed to stay hydrated and fed. Otherwise, her body would never carry her anywhere. Choking down the dry bread, she watched Afir rise. He turned, barking an echoing order across the large cave. She saw another, younger soldier come running. Qader was standing back, watching and saying nothing. He seemed interested in her and that scared Jess. He'd seen she wore no bra; seen her breasts visible beneath her t-shirt. She wanted to die of embarrassment, but the look in his eyes had terrified her as he'd studied her breasts openly, without apology. Were they going to rape her? The word sent more spasms of adrenaline through her.

Her mind and pounding heart turned to Logan. Surely, he knew by now something had happened to her? When none of them could find her in the village, he would know Khogani had kidnapped her. What could Logan do, though? Who would send help with him to locate her, and how much? More than anything, Jess knew Logan would turn hell on its ear to find her. And that's what gave her hope. Just knowing Logan was out there, somewhere, made Jess hyperaware for a chance, any chance, at escape. The rope tied to her ankle left her hands free. And her hands were aching like fire itself, now that the blood was refilling their veins, the gnawing pain making her want to groan. She saw sunlight, bright and clean now, flooding the area in front of the cave. The sun had cleared the mountain range. What was Logan doing? Would he be able to find her?

CHAPTER 14

LOGAN STOOD WITH the officers in Anderson's hut. The radios were squawking nonstop. He had a map open of the terrain of the hills and mountains near the village. An hour had passed, and he was gearing up to leave to track Jess. Tension was running high. Anderson was in touch with Bagram HQ for the Army. Chris was in touch with FOB Bravo, with the Master Chief of their platoon. The chief was in touch with SEAL HQ at Bagram. Two Apache helicopters had been sprung loose from Bravo and were on their way over the Hindu Kush mountains right now. They would use infrared to see if they could pick up any heat signatures of humans or mounts on this side of the mountains. SEAL HQ was asking the CIA unit at Bagram to give them a drone over the range. Everything was moving at light speed.

Logan stilled his frustration. If the CIA had stopped playing favorites, stopped their damned fight with DOD, and had just given them a drone when they'd first requested one, this kidnapping would never have happened. Now, they were playing catch up.

"All right," Anderson said tightly, glancing at the two SEALs standing on the other side of his desk, "Lowrey, you're staying here to coordinate with Randall as he tracks Jess and her kidnappers."

Chris nodded, his voice grim. "We'll have our radios. We both have sat phones, which are going to be even more important. I'll be coordinating between Logan and the rest of you. I'll be the hub to the comms wheel."

Rubbing his beard, Anderson nodded. Three senior sergeants were with him as well, the hut seeming small with all the big, muscular men crowded into it. "Okay, your Master Chief Carter is going to handle the CIA end of this deal, and their drone."

Chris had out a notepad and pen and was scribbling down the info. "Roger."

"And *we'll* work with the Apache's and any other aircraft assets that we can call into this search," Anderson said, glancing off to his right at his communications Sergeant Terry Henderson.

Henderson, Logan's height, sporting a red beard and floppy cammo cap, nodded. "Roger that, sir."

"Then, that's it," Anderson said, straightening, on edge. He looked over at Logan. "You got that ruck ready to go?"

Logan nodded. "Yes. I'll hitch a ride to the hills. There's an old man who lives up there that's a horse trader. I'll pay him for a horse and then pick up their tracks. If we're lucky, maybe he even saw something this morning."

"Good," Anderson murmured. "Let's roll. Sergeant Henderson? Drive Randall to the base of the hills."

Logan was more than glad to get out of the stuffy hut. He'd laid out all his gear right outside it. Henderson went to pull the Humvee around from the rear of the hut. Logan's adrenaline was flowing strongly, his heart clamoring, but he had to stuff it down. He would be no good to Jess if he let his emotions run wild; worry about her being beaten, raped or worse. All of those were possibilities. He felt his gut knot painfully, hefting his seventy-pound ruck as the Humvee rolled around to a stop in front of him, and throwing it in the vehicle. The two other sergeants helped put the rest of his gear in the rear seat.

Chris approached, searching Logan's eyes. "Stay safe out there. SEAL HQ says there's the possibility that two hundred odd of Khogani's soldiers are already located in this area."

Logan nodded, hauling on his forty-pound Level 4 Kevlar vest. "I'll be careful," he promised. Reaching out, Logan shook his friend's hand. He and Chris had gone through BUDs together. He was his swim buddy. That gave them a powerful and unspoken connection.

"Just keep those damned radios active," Chris muttered, stepping back as Logan settled into the passenger side of the Humvee. "You have extra batteries. Right?"

"Absolutely. Don't worry," Logan said. He lifted his hand in farewell and shut the heavy door, giving Henderson the nod to take off. Logan had two radios on him. There was a short-range one, and then there was the satellite phone, which could bounce signals anywhere in the world. Normally, Logan would have two other backup radios on him, but he couldn't be carrying that much gear on this outing. Henderson was the comms sergeant for the Special Forces team, an expert in his field. Chris, although not comms, would keep the SEALs in the mix by being point man while Logan tracked Jess. The urgency to get something done was eating away at Logan's normally massive patience. The sun has just crested the Hindu Kush mountains, spreading warm rays into the chilly valley below.

Henderson drove him to the mud-and-rock hut of an old Afghan called Qaseem. Logan was out of the Humvee before it rolled to a stop. There were two corrals with several Afghan ponies in them. Qaseem, stooped over with age, with white hair and beard, and wearing a black turban and brown wool clothing, came out of his hut. He had dark, shining eyes. As he approached him, Logan said nothing, knowing he'd have to rely on Henderson's Pashto to speak to the old man.

Henderson came up and gave the Muslim greeting and salutation, launching quickly into the need to buy the strongest, best gelding in the lot for Logan, explaining that the horse would need to be able to carry nearly four hundred pounds of man and equipment.

Logan saw the man's eyes light up. And then he started jabbering excitedly, pointing again and again toward the mountain in the distance. Logan saw Henderson's face take on a surprised expression. The sergeant turned to him.

"We've caught a break," he told Logan. "The old guy saw four Hill tribesman gallop by with a woman in tow. He said the woman had black hair and looked military. Her hands were tied to the saddle of the horse she rode."

Logan stilled his sudden hope. Any strong emotions were a detriment. "Did he see her? Was she all right?"

Henderson nodded. "They passed within two hundred feet of his house when he was out feeding the horses early this morning." Henderson looked at his watch. "This was one and a half hours ago." He turned, pointing up at the slope of the mountain. "You'll probably pick up the horse tracks leading somewhere up there."

Hope bled through Logan, despite his best efforts. Qaseem folded his long, arthritic hands together, gazing up critically at Logan, as if sizing him up for a horse he had in mind. He turned and spoke quickly to Henderson.

"Okay," the sergeant said, gesturing for Logan to follow him, "the old dude says he has a black gelding that's half Arabian breeding, and is a little taller than the other horses. He thinks it's the best choice for you and the weight you're carrying. The horse has staying power."

"Okay," Logan said, following the old man around the house. There were at least six horses in the two corrals. And only one black one. It was probably about six inches taller than the other Afghan ponies. None of them were tall as American horses, having been bred with the harsh region's rugged terrain and sparsity of food and water in mind. They were all short backed and sturdy. "What's he want for it?" and he pointed toward the animal, busy eating dried grass that had been thrown into the corral earlier.

Henderson spoke to Qaseem. The old man babbled excitedly, throwing his hands into the air.

Logan knew horse traders were wily salesmen. It wasn't lost on the Afghan that they were in dire need of a good horse. Qaseem would make them pay through the nose because he knew they were in a helluva hurry to track the Hill

Tribe soldiers. He heard Henderson bickering back and forth for the animal. There was a bridle hanging off one post and Logan grabbed it, slipping between the rails, heading for the steed. Let Henderson squabble with Qaseem.

The black gelding was powerful looking, his hind quarters thick and well developed. Logan knew plenty about horses, having been raised on them in Wyoming. Putting the bridle on the animal, he quickly ran his hands down each of the horse's front and back legs, looking for problems. There were none. Afghan horses generally went barefoot; never shoed, horseshoes being just far too expensive for desert folk. Logan picked up each leg, thoroughly checking the hooves, making sure there were no stones lodged in the frog, the vital rubbery cushion of the hoof, or in any cracks. The black looked like a good choice, indeed, and Logan led him over to the wooden gate.

"Tell this guy I only want the bridle," Logan said. "I don't want a saddle." He saw Henderson grin.

"What? No wooden Afghan saddle with rusty nails to stick in your ass as you ride?" and the sergeant chuckled.

Logan opened the gate, pulling the horse out of the corral. "Got that right." From time to time, on some assignments, Logan had had to ride with a damned Afghan saddle. The things were put together with nothing but nails. The nails would work loose and, sooner or later, stick in the rider's butt. There was no way, with the kind of climbing Logan was going to do with this horse, that he wanted a lousy Afghan saddle to deal with. He'd grown up riding bareback, and he was going to do the same right now.

Henderson pulled out some US dollars and put them into Qaseem's open hands. The Afghan was grinning, most of his front teeth missing. "Okay, stud, you got yourself a horse. This old dude just made himself a hundred freakin' US dollars for that beast," and he shook his head.

Qaseem smiled, nodded and bowed to them.

"He gave us intel," Logan said, walking the horse around the house to the Humvee. "That's worth any amount of money."

Henderson agreed and helped him by opening the Humvee door and holding the black gelding while Logan shifted his heavy ruck over his shoulders, belted it up, and settled his black baseball cap on his head above the wraparound sunglasses he had on to shade his eyes from the day's mounting glare. Logan threw a leg up and over the animal's sleek black back. The sergeant brought over his M4.

"Okay," Henderson said, "you're ready to roll." He patted the horse's rump. "Stay safe out there?"

Logan nodded. Clamping his long thighs around the horse's barrel, he muttered, "I will," and clapped his heels to the horse's flanks. The black leaped forward.

Logan easily picked up the tribesmen's mounts' tracks about two hundred yards from the horse trader's hut. The black horse was frisky, eager, but Logan held him tightly in check, wanting him to conserve his strength. Soon enough, Logan knew as he followed the trail at a loose trot, they'd be climbing the damn steep, rocky mountain rising up in front of him. He wanted to hurry more, but he also had to remain aware that Khogani and his men could have set up an ambush for anyone trying to track them.

The slope of the mountain consisted of loose rocks, brush and a few spindly trees. Over the course of years, Afghan wood cutters had scoured the lower mountain slopes, cutting every worthwhile tree down to sell as firewood to the villages. They knew nothing about ecology or the long-term wisdom of not clearing a slope bare of trees, Logan thought, as he continued to follow the tracks. There were traces of the tribesmen's passage in leaf debris and brush that had been ridden over, branches newly broken and easily followed. Looking up, the mountain towered thirteen thousand feet tall above him. From nine thousand feet upward, it was coated with thick early-September snow. There were two *wadi*, ravines, that Logan spotted. Which one had Khogani taken? *Wadi* were easier to traverse than the raw, cutting rocks of the slope. They were also filled with brush and trees, making them easier to hide in.

The radio piece in his ear crackled to life. It was a woman Apache pilot calling in to Lowrey. Logan could hear the faint beat of the combat-assault helo's blades cutting through the thin air at fifteen thousand feet. Pulling his horse up, he listened closely to the conversation. He took out his radio, keying the mic close to his mouth, giving his code sign. What Logan *didn't* want is to have the approaching Apache's spot *his* body heat and send auto cannon rounds into him and his horse. They had to know where he was located so they'd mark him as a friendly and take him off the enemy combatant list. He gave his GPS coordinates to the copilot of the Apache.

Taking a drink of water from his CamelBak, Logan sized up the steep slope above them. His horse was now breathing harder, sweat starting to make his black fur look shiny beneath the sunlight streaming down from overhead. The temperature on the mountain was much lower than in the valley. Logan was glad to have his heavy H-gear jacket on. Another issue was going to be finding his horse a water source. That was going to prove tough. Logan knew some of the limestone caves he saw dotted along the snowline of the mountain would have pools in them. And the snow melt at that height would leave puddles here and there. But that was all still a long climb away.

As he rode higher, following the tracks into the second of the two *wadi* running thousands of feet upward, Logan heard even better news over his earpiece. The CIA had *finally* released a drone, and it was heading their way. The punctuating beat of two Apache's was much closer now. He spotted them through the thickening woods that surrounded the *wadi*. Calling in again, he gave his new GPS position, seeing the helos flying a thousand feet above the mountain's slope. He hoped against hope they would spot Khogani riding with Jess in tow. But he knew the Taliban and Hill soldiers weren't stupid. They hid in caves during the day when they spotted the Apache's around, only leaving their safety and moving on after the helos had left. Generally, Logan knew, the Taliban didn't travel at night because they didn't have the night-vision capability the Americans did. For now, though, the air cover would force Khogani to stop and make camp somewhere underground. And that's where Logan figured he could intersect the group. And rescue Jess. IF she was alive. He tried to push the thought away as he urged his hard-breathing horse up the *wadi*. He wished he could send her a telepathic message that he was coming for her. That he would find her. His heart ached with fear. Over losing Jess. If only… if only the Apache's, now slowly flying the slope half a mile away, would pick up on the group. If only….

JESS HEARD THE familiar thunking of Apache helicopters blades. She was sitting behind a rock wall, barely able to look around it to see the huge cave opening. The arrival of the helicopters had put fear into the faces of Khogani and his men. She watched as they all slunk to the rear of the cave. A young Hill tribesman, a teen, was in charge of watching over her. He had no beard yet, being still so young, but the AK-47 he held in his arms as he stood nearby, watching her, kept Jess sitting quietly.

She'd eaten the dried bread, drunk more water, and was relieved to see Afir did not come over to her anymore. He hated her. She could feel his rage cutting straight through her. Lifting her hand, she touched her aching cheek. It was hot and swollen now. The young teen soldier watching her became nervous, looking anxiously toward the opening as one Apache helicopter flew by just above their cave. The heavy beat of the blades reverberated punctured invisible pressure waves throughout the hollowness where they hid. Jess wanted to slip her ankle binding, run out, scream and throw her hands up, hoping the pilots would see her. If she tried, though, she knew she'd be killed long before she ever reached the lip of the cave.

Khogani was crouched with two of his soldiers, scowling. The Apache's put the fear of God into them. And well they should. But fearsome as they were, they couldn't look into caves with their instruments and see the Taliban hiding there. Jess kept her eyes down, trying not to stare at any of the men. She didn't want to invite their attention any more than necessary. The heavy echoing of the Apache continued shuddering through the cave like boxing gloves pummeling all of them. Jess could feel the thumping ripples moving through her body; they were that powerful. The horses were not there to panic; they were kept elsewhere. What would Khogani do? Was he staying here? Were they moving out? Jess felt the constant leak of adrenaline into her bloodstream. Within minutes, the Apache was past the area, moving on. Jess saw relief in the faces of all the soldiers.

As she moved a little to stand up, her ankle tied to the rock, the young soldier lifted his AK-47 in her direction. She held up her hands slowly, trying to signal that she needed to stand for a while. He looked wary. Right about now, Jess wished she had that heavy armored vest on that she'd been cursing only days before. She had to go to the bathroom. Not knowing Pashto, she felt fearful, scared to try and talk to the kid.

"What do you want?" Khogani demanded, walking up to her.

Relieved, Jess said, "I have to go to the bathroom." She saw Qader shrug.

"Go where you stand."

Humiliation sheeted through Jess. "But…"

Qader grinned over her discomfort. He told Shekaib, the beardless welp, to turn around and not look. The woman's face melted with relief. Shaking his head, he turned away, stalking back to his soldiers. There was planning to undertake before they left the cave.

Jess, feeling vulnerable, found a packet of tissues in her cargo pants' pocket. Shekaib turned his back to her. For the moment, she was alone in the cave, all the soldiers having disappeared down one tunnel. She looked around again, confirming that it was just her and the teenager. She wondered if she could overpower him. He had an AK-47. She wished she had the training, any training, to know how to attack the kid and grab the rifle out of his hand. Jess wasn't even sure she could bring herself to kill him, if it came to that. It tore at her. As quickly as she could, she went to the bathroom, pulled up her cargo pants and zipped them up. As she pushed the packet of tissues back into her right-thigh pocket, her fingers struck something else. Her heart picked up in beat for a moment. Moving her fingers into the corner of the pocket, she realized it was her Swiss Army knife! They'd patted her down briefly upon capture, but either hadn't found the rounded, compact tool, or hadn't thought it a weapon. And the blade, when extended, was two inches long. Plus, it was sharp and would be able to cut through the rope around her ankle in a split second.

Hesitating, Jess's mind whirled with options. She was alone with Shekaib.

The boy still had his back to her. If she could jump him? Overpower him? He was thin, and two inches shorter than she was. Her heart was pounding now. Adrenaline was surging through her as her fingers wrapped more surely around the hidden knife.

Suddenly, Jess heard male voices. Her head snapped to the left. Khogani was stalking out of the tunnel. She pulled her hand out of her pocket, seeing the boy turn around, scowl at her and then gesture for her to sit back down. The moment was gone. Jess felt terror mixed with desperation. She should have acted sooner! She'd had the opening. Why hadn't she taken it? Sitting down, she pulled her knees up toward her body, resting her head on them, one arm around her shins. Her emotions were roiling. She didn't want to kill anyone. It wasn't in her. Who had she been kidding? Even though she was a prisoner, she knew she couldn't find it in herself to kill a child. Okay, so he was in his teens, but he was someone's son. He had a mother and father. Probably sisters and brothers. Her mouth was dry, and Jess swallowed hard against her tightening throat. She hadn't joined the military to kill. She'd joined following in her parent's footsteps to help those who had so little. Tears burned behind her tightly shut eyes and Jess felt like crying. She couldn't. She didn't dare show these bastards any weakness.

Her heart turned to Logan. Inwardly, Jess knew he was out there looking for her. The Apache's were proof of that. He was a sniper, and he knew how to track. Could he find the hoofprints of Khogani's men? Follow them? Jess didn't know, her heart lurching first with terror and then hope, and then back to terror. As she felt through her fear, Jess tried to assess her options. That left only one choice open to her: escape. Somehow, she was going to have to wait for an opening and then run. In doing that, Jess knew without a doubt, that if they caught her, they'd kill her.

She heard the rumble of thunder. Lifting her head, she saw the sunlight was gone. Outside the cave entrance, it had darkened and suddenly began to rain heavily. Jess knew the mountain weather was in a constant state of flux. The fresh, clean scent of the rain entered the dry cave, and she inhaled it deeply. As she watched the veil of rain thicken, almost blotting out everything outside the cave entrance, Jess wondered if she'd ever see it rain again.

Logan was in touch with the lead Apache pilot. They'd carefully, in a grid pattern, moved across the slope of the mountain where Khogani was assumed to be hiding. They'd turned up some deer, a fox, but that was all. He wiped his brow, settling the baseball cap on his head once again. Right now, he was stopped to give his mount a momentary breather. The sky was turning stormy. In the mountains, it would rain or snow without any warning. Mountains made their own weather. Logan knew that better than most. And, without a doubt, any rain would wash away the prints he was following.

Cursing, he dismounted and continued to look for clues in the form of bent blades of grass or small, freshly broken sticks. He was still two thousand feet below the top of the *wadi*. The prints were disappearing as the plops of raindrops began to descend over the area. He tugged on his horse, leading it over to a small group of evergreens. The sudden downpour was heavy, covering the area with a veil and Logan was unable to see anything, even his hand in front of his face.

A bolt of lightning struck down the slope. His horse jerked and jumped. Logan spoke quietly to the frightened animal, settling a hand on its neck, feeling it quiver with terror. Where was Jess? His mind rolled over the possibilities. Was she safe? Had they beaten her up? Grimly, Logan didn't want to think about rape. He hoped like hell that they'd leave her alone. Sex slaves' prices dropped if they became damaged goods. If Khogani followed that maxim, then he'd keep his hands off Jess.

How was she doing? He wanted desperately to find her. Hold her in his arms. He couldn't begin to imagine where she was at emotionally. She'd been reeling from so much already; losing Dan, being shot, becoming a marked target. *Now this new horror.* But Logan knew she was internally strong. And he relied on that, hoping that if she could escape, she would. The risk of doing so would be high. If she did, then Khogani would go after her. Shaking his head, the water dripping down his neck, leaking in beneath his jacket and vest, Logan took off his dark glasses, pushing them into a pocket. The gray mist, the wind and the thunder now moving away from the area told him that, shortly, the downpour would cease.

Worse, the tracks he had been following would be wiped out. Looking upward, he could barely see two hundred feet higher in the *wadi*. Water was beginning to wash down through it, soaking his boots. Logan knew he had to move because there could be thousands of gallons of water starting to plunge down the ravine. And just like in the southwest of the US, a flash flood could be the result. And it could be large enough, violent enough, to wash him and his horse away in it. Having no choice, Logan hunched over, water dripping off the bill of his baseball cap as he led the nervous horse up the steep, rocky bank. If he didn't get out of the *wadi* shortly, they could both be found dead thousands of feet below, killed by the rush of water, pounded to death by the sharp rocks that comprised it.

As he climbed, slipping and grabbing on to thin pieces of brush growing on the sides of the slope, Logan worried about Jess. He couldn't help himself. Their conversations, their loving one another, the laughter they'd shared, sank deeply into his aching heart. So many things could go wrong. And most of them, to Jess. All *he* had to worry about was an ambush or being spotted by Khogani's men. Logan's mouth thinned, the water running down in rivulets across his hardened face. The horse was grunting, scrambling, falling once to its knees on the muddy, slippery slope.

Above him, Logan could hear the roar of water coming. *Shit!* It was a wall of water rushing down, unseen, toward them! He clucked to the horse, grabbing rocks sticking up out of the earth with his gloved hands. The roar got louder and louder. It was going to be close! Making a lunge as his horse leaped and scrambled up beside him, Logan grabbed for its thick, long mane. He wrapped his fist into it. The horse was wild eyed, wanting to get out of the *wadi* before the wall of water hit and killed them. His back legs were like huge, pumping pistons, rocks and mud flying in all directions beneath his sharp hooves. Logan allowed the horse's forward momentum and eight hundred pounds of muscle to drag him faster up the steep slope. He jerked a look back across his shoulder, seeing a ten-foot wall of water rushing downward, filled with soil, rock and trees, all being torn and ripped out of the *wadi* as it crashed thunderously down the mountainside. The air shook around them from the power of the runaway and violent wall of water.

The horse snorted, lifted his front legs, digging in with his rear. He was pulling not only Logan's two hundred pounds, but the sixty pound ruck he wore. And that was enough to pull the horse off balance. It struggled, snorted again, made a jerky hop and then a larger jump forward. Logan felt the strain, the burning in his shoulder joint as the gelding made that last life-saving leap. Jerked upward by six feet from the horse's staggering efforts, the rush of the water roared past them. Clucking to the horse, Logan was dragged up and over the wall of the *wadi*. The horse's front legs collapsed beneath him, his muzzle hitting the mud and rocks, exhausted by his struggle to not die in the flash flood. Logan released the horse's wet, slippery mane and pushed himself to his hands and knees. *Damn, that had been too friggin' close!*

Staggering to his feet, Logan held on to the gelding's reins. The horse was snorting, his sides heaving in and out like giant bellows. Calling to him above the roar and noise, Logan saw the horse respond, shoving shakily to its feet. The black shook himself, his body gleaming and rain soaked. Logan went over, patting the heroic animal. Looking down, he saw the horse had badly scraped both his front knees. Examining them closer, Logan saw a deep, bleeding cut on the inside of one knee. That wasn't good. Now, the question that hit him was if his horse was now lame. He wouldn't know until after the storm passed over them. They stood between four tall evergreens, somewhat protected, but not by much. The wind whipped through the area, howling at seventy and eighty miles an hour. The horse turned his butt toward the wind. Logan did the same, turning his back against the angry weather, and hung his head, waiting it out.

CHAPTER 15

S HIVERING, JESS WAS led into yet another cavemouth. Khogani had moved them shortly after the initial thunderstorm and they'd been slipping in and out of caves the rest of the day. More thunderstorms had cropped up in the afternoon and she'd gotten soaked. The group remained around the snow level, sometimes dipping down from it. Either way, it was damned cold at this altitude, especially now, at night. Her teeth were chattering, and she could see nothing, not even realizing she was in another cave until the echo of sounds around her changed. They had been heading north all day long; that she knew. And there had been no more overflights of Apaches, either.

Heart sinking, Jess wondered if the military had sent up a drone. Where was Logan in this mix? She knew he wouldn't let her be kidnapped and not try to find her. She couldn't imagine how *he* felt. *Her* emotions were raw, and she was scared. All day, they had kept her ankles tied beneath the horse. As before, Afir held the reins to the animal, making escape impossible. Every once in a while, her hands being free, she'd tear off a small piece from the raggedy elbows of her denim jacket and let it drop to the ground. It was the old breadcrumb method, probably not practical outside of children's stories, or even *in* them now that she thought about it, but Jess had to do *something* to indicate where she was at. There was constant terror over getting caught doing it.

Once in the cave, one of her ankles was untied and she was jerked off the horse by the angry Afir. Her legs were raw and sore from riding all day on the uneven, steep mountain trails. She heard men talking in low tones as she stood by her weary horse. It was utterly dark. So, when someone grabbed her by her good arm and pulled her along, she marveled at how they could see when she could not.

Jess felt from the reverberating sounds that she was led to near the opening of the cave, where another soldier grabbed her arm instead. She sensed it was Shekaib because he did not treat her as roughly as Afir had, and they were the only two so far who had touched her. Pushed down, she was given a goatskin of water to drink. More than thirsty, her throat raw and dry, Jess didn't hesitate to gulp down nearly all of it. And then, another hard loaf of bread was jammed into her hands. She heard Shekaib walk away. Had the soldier tied her remaining bound ankle to another rock? How far away was he from her? Was he standing nearby with his AK-47, guarding her? Jess didn't know, wanting badly to dig the Swiss Army knife out of her pocket, slice the rope around her ankle and run off. She finished off the water, filling up. Tonight, if the men all slept, she might be able to make a break for it, but Jess would have to wait and see. God, if only she had a set of NVGs!

Logan listened to Chris as he transmitted the drone feed to him. Once the drone had arrived on station, it had finally caught Khogani and his group, including Jess, weaving in and out of the high mountain slope. Logan sat hidden within a grove of trees; his weary horse tied to a limb as he leaned back against a trunk. With his Toughbook laptop open and the drone's night-vision feed coming in over it in grainy black-and-white images, he saw Jess for the first time. His heart damn near burst out of his chest. It was the only time Logan had consciously allowed himself to feel anything. He zoomed the camera in on her. Her cheek was swollen, one eye nearly shut, and she appeared exhausted. He could see her ankles were tied beneath the belly of the horse she was on. A Taliban solider rode ahead of her, with her mount's reins in his hand.

Wiping his mouth, Logan narrowed his eyes, watching as they pulled into another cave. He took notice of the GPS coordinates on the screen, and the current time. It appeared the group was most likely holing up for the next few hours of total dark. Taliban normally did not travel at night, precisely because they couldn't see where the hell they were going. Usually, they quit at dusk, took tea, and then slept, getting up just before dawn to push on. He watched the screen as the drone's viewpoint flew by at a steep angle. His eyes narrowed coldly. Jess had a rope around her ankle and was being led by a soldier near the opening to the cave's maw and forced to sit down. She was given water and food. That was good. At least she was hydrated and fed. He saw the soldier wrap the rope around a boulder so that if she tried to get up and go anywhere, she couldn't. The soldier then walked back into the cave and Logan lost sight of him.

Punching in the coordinates into his hand-held GPS, Logan cut the feed and shut his laptop down. He had only so much battery left in it. Right now, according to his GPS device, he was two miles away from that cave. He shoved the laptop into his ruck, pulled out a protein bar and ate it. Then, he opened the side pocket on his ruck and brought out the satellite phone. It too was powered by batteries. Everything hinged on batteries, so Logan didn't use it unless he had to.

Logan called Chris, who quickly came through on and said, "There's fifty Taliban to the west of your position," and gave the coordinates.

"Khogani's men?" Logan demanded in hushed tones.

"Probably, but unsure. The drone has also picked up another thirty men of unknown affiliation waiting east of Khogani's present position. Anderson and I think he's headed there to meet up with them."

Mouth tightening, Logan muttered, "That won't be good."

"No. What's your plan?"

"Get as close as I can to that cave where they have Jess held. I don't know if they're going to keep her where she's presently at in there, near the entrance, or not. I'll just have to wait and see."

"If you can get her, now's the time to do it."

"Roger that. I'll be in touch. Out." Logan shut the phone off and put it away. His SEAL radio was getting on the edge of losing transmission with Chris. The further north he went, the worse it got, and Logan knew he'd be out of range shortly. And then, he only had the sat phone. It wasn't an ideal situation, but then, in the field, pretty much nothing ever went smoothly. He was glad he'd put some spare new batteries in his ruck for the sat phone before he left. The old SEAL saying, *one is none and two is one*, applied well in this situation. He got up, pulling his NVGs down and flicking them on. His horse was resting and, fortunately, the cut on his knee wasn't hampering him. All Logan needed right now was a lame horse. He'd have to abandon the animal and continue on foot, which he would still do, if necessary.

Now, he had to ride close enough to get eyes on that cave. That was going to be tenuous at best. Logan knew horses had extraordinary hearing and could see in the dark better than a human. If he rode his horse too close to the cave, the other horses would hear it and then, worst-case scenario, start whinnying. That would wake up the sleeping soldiers for damn sure. He'd have to tie the horse at least half a mile from the cave and go on foot to get to it. And even then, Logan knew horses: if they were posted too close to the opening, they would still hear or smell him. Then, it became a question of whether they would spook, whinny, or just watch and do neither. Animals were far more attuned to the darkness and movement in the night than any human. Even with his sure feet, he'd have to do his damndest to be a ghost or awaken the soldiers and then he'd be screwed.

Jess waited, her heart doing a slow pound. She had been left near the cave opening. The horses had been taken toward the rear of the cave, but she couldn't see where. Shekaib had come back, taken the other end of the rope, and tied it around his own ankle. He was lying down, nearby, perhaps five feet away, if she could trust her hearing. What gave her hope was that, by the full moon risen over the mountain, she could see gray and shadowed stands of trees outside. The cave opened onto a rocky slope, with about fifty feet of open ground between herself and the trees.

Jess slowly turned and sat up. She could hear the snores or the soldiers deep within the cave. Some of the horses, from what she could now discern in the deep shadows, were lying down. Others were standing. As Jess's eyes adjusted even more to the dim moonlight spilling in, she saw that all had hobbles on to prevent them from running away and were unsaddled. Their heads were hanging.

Looking at Shekaib, the boy slept with his arm beneath his head, his other hand over the AK-47 at his side. There was indeed about five feet between them. Jess felt shaky and scared as she slowly pulled the Swiss Army knife out of her pocket. The rope they'd tied her with was thick and rough. Trying to ease open the knots they'd used, as tightly drawn as they were, would surely awaken Shekaib. Pulling out the largest blade, Jess began to saw through the one-inch rope, breath held. Even the sawing was making a rasping noise, loud to her overly nervous ear. Would it make a horse suddenly alert? Whinny? Move around? If it did, any one of the soldiers could awaken. If they found her trying to escape, Jess had no idea what they would do to her. It wouldn't be good. That she knew.

By the time the rope fell off her ankle, Jess's hand was trembling. She slowly moved, only enough to put the knife back into her pocket without a sound. Adrenaline was surging through her bloodstream, and she felt shaky, as she slowly made an unrushed, silent, rolling motion, ending outside the cave. Rocks and gravel bit at her hands and knees. If she moved too fast, the horses would spook. Then, they would awaken the soldiers and she'd be caught. Everything had to be done in torturous slow motion. Her gaze flicked from the sleeping Shekaib to the men and horses at the rear of the cave. Her mind whirled with what to do. Which way to go? Jess knew if she could reach the tree line, she had a slim chance. But she didn't dare stumble, fall, or step on any fallen twig. Any of those could awaken her captors or, at the very least, alert the horses. Just let her get to the tree line without being discovered!

Jess was coated with mud by the time she had carefully, ever so carefully made it to the tree line. It was freezing out here, her breath white vapor rolling out of her mouth, open wide to allow as silent breathing as possible. Giving the cave one last look, Jess slowly stood up fully, for the first time since cutting the rope. She knew the horses could see her. Standing still, she waited. Wanting to run and not daring to do it yet, she remained tense, listening. *Nothing*. Relief shattered through her for a moment. Looking down, her boots caked with mud, she took her first step past a tree, watching carefully where she placed the toe. If she made ANY sound, they would awaken.

Jess felt as if her life was hanging by one slender thread. Her heart ached for need of Logan. Now, she stood on a slope of a mountain in the Hindu Kush, at nine thousand feet, in the middle of the night, with sure death dogging her every step. And she knew she had to go down the mountain and head east to get into the valley she was kidnapped from. Could she do it? She had no water or food on her. It was daunting, but Jess would rather risk dying than be in the hands of the Hill Tribe. She took another step. The floor of the grove was littered with sticks and rocks, very little soft, bare soil. Slipping and sliding, she held out her arms, as best she could, to keep her balance as she slowly walked deeper into the grove. Her wounded arm ached, but she ignored it. Jess was sure they had trackers among Khogani's men. And, once they discovered her gone, they would do their best to hunt her down.

Time pushed her, and she continued down the steep, rocky slope. Sometimes she would grip the trunk of a tree with her good, right hand to stop from falling or slipping. Jess heard an owl hooting in the distance. Otherwise, all she heard was the near-constant rush of wind through the upper trees and her heartbeat pounding in her ears like a drum. Swallowing hard, she kept her eyes riveted on the ground, never wanting to make a sound. Her left arm ached and throbbed, using it as she was when she knew she shouldn't be. Right now, though, pain was not a deterrent, it helped keep her wide awake, along with the adrenaline roaring nonstop through her.

Jess had no idea how long she traveled, but her knees were getting wobbly from the steep, continuous downhill grade. She wished to hell she was in better shape. The insides of her thighs were already rubbed raw by the wooden saddle she'd had to sit on, and now they were screaming with every step. The air was cold and clean smelling. Her boots slipped and slid from time to time. The grove opened up maybe half an hour later, the trees more widespread here. Jess could see open areas, flatter areas, where there weren't so many rocks sticking up out of the soil. Easier to traverse quickly but, at the same time, if she went across them, her muddy boot tracks would be easier for the Taliban to follow. Grimly, she chose the rocks, skirting the meadow-like areas. Pressure to live, to escape, kept pushing her. Jess wanted to run, but her knees were shaking from the stress of now perhaps an hour's worth of downhill challenges. But she was aware that, in terms of actual distance, she hadn't really gone all that far. If she fell, it could still awaken them.

Jess had just moved into another thicker area of trees when a hand suddenly curved around from behind her. She screamed. The noise went nowhere beneath the large hand.

"Jess!" Logan hissed against her ear. "It's me!"

She gave a little cry of relief. Jess felt Logan's tall, powerful body come up against her back, his arm snaking around her waist, and him slowly releasing his other hand from her mouth. Twisting around, Jess choked back a sob. She saw his deeply shadowed face. Logan had his NVGs hanging around his neck. She couldn't even hug him because of the bulky H-gear he wore around his torso, magazines sticking out across it. She saw him put a finger to his lips.

Quivering, she nodded, hot tears rushing to her eyes. He held her shoulder, steadying her. Logan had found her! She didn't know how, but the relief was so sharp that she slowly fell to her knees, pressing her hands to her face. She felt Logan crouch next to her, his hand never leaving her shaking shoulder. Noise could get them killed and Jess fought to not cry, swallowing repeatedly, trying to get a handle of her wildly escaping emotions.

Logan looked around, listening. Nothing out of the ordinary. Not yet. He saw the terror in Jess's face, saw the relief in her huge, shadowed eyes. There was swelling along her cheek, one eye partly swollen shut. Controlling his rage, he could feel her shaking. He took the radio and clicked it twice, not knowing if he was out of range or not. Clicks were used when near enemies who might hear speech. Logan had agreed with Chris that if he found Jess, if she was in his possession, he would give two clicks. He knew that the drone would then be brought above them, becoming their eyes in the sky, to help them avoid the enemy groups to both the east and west of them. Not to mention, Khogani and his men were less than a mile above them in that cave.

"Jess," he said in a low tone, "listen to me. Just nod your head yes or no. Are you still ambulatory?"

She choked, and nodded, looking up into his glittering, narrowed eyes. Now she was seeing Logan as the warrior he was. He was constantly looking around, alert, listening.

"Are you thirsty?"

She nodded. Logan turned slightly, leaning his shoulder in her direction and she pulled the tube to his CamelBak to her mouth. She drank thirstily, not muddy-tasting muck like the Taliban had given her. More relief pumped through her. She gulped as much of the delicious water as she could. Logan was wearing a huge, heavy ruck on his shoulders. His mouth was a thin line, his gaze never stilling as he continued to scan the area. She shut the water off and nodded.

Logan straightened up. "Are you hungry?"

Jess shook her head. Right now, her stomach was knotted and hurt. Food might be wanted by her body, but all *she* wanted to do was run and escape.

"When I stand, I want you to hold on to my belt at my waist. Left side of it, with your right hand, so you can move without tripping on my feet. Then, we'll head toward my horse. He's nearby."

Jess nodded. Her knees felt weak, and she was grateful when Logan rose and then placed his hand beneath her arm, helping her to rise. For a moment, she leaned against him to get her feet properly under her. Jess could see the sheen of sweat across Logan's brow, his face hard and unreadable. She felt anything *but* hard, tears still burning in her eyes. *Come on, Courtland,* Logan didn't need her falling apart on him. They were in absolute danger. He was one SEAL against Khogani and all his men. They could be found and killed. She knew they were nowhere near safe at all.

She slid her fingers into the web belt around his waist, and he nodded, flipping down his NVGs and moving silently in an easterly direction across the slope. Jess forced herself to watch where she was putting her feet. Logan seemed to glide like a silent wraith through the sparse woods. She felt clumsy, and as if she was holding him back from his normal stride.

Jess had no real idea how long they traveled. Only when they entered a very thick, brushy grove, did Logan slow down. Ahead, by the milky light filtering down through the trees, Jess saw a black horse tied to a tree branch. It had no saddle. Logan pulled her hand free of his belt and turned toward her.

"We can talk quietly here," he told her. "We're two miles away and east of the cave." Smiling a little, he reached up, caressing her cheek. "I love you, Jess. I should have told you that a long time ago," and Logan leaned down, gently caressing her mouth with his. He felt her sob beneath his kiss, her trembling hands moving to his chest, across his H-gear. Lifting his lips from hers, he smiled into her tear-filled eyes. "I'm going to get you out of here. Okay? Are you all right? Hungry? Thirsty again?"

Wiping the tears from her eyes, not proud of the fact she was shaking like a scared rabbit, Jess managed, "I-I'm okay. Bruised, battered, but fine. I'm not hungry... thirsty... just scared out of my mind, Logan."

He caressed her hair. "I know you are," he soothed. "Go ahead and sit down to rest. I need to make a sat phone call to Chris." He pulled out a protein bar from one of his harness pockets and handed it to her. "You need to eat. Keep up your strength."

Jess sat and took it and shakily opened the wrapper, not tasting it at all, but knowing Logan was right. She saw him shrug out of his ruck and sit it carefully on the ground. The sat phone was in an outer pocket. As she ate, he talked quietly to Chris at the other end. They talked in military lingo. Most of it she didn't recognize. Black ops speak, she thought. Finishing the bar off, Jess rubbed her filthy hands down her damp trouser legs.

She couldn't tell how Logan was feeling, only catching one end of the conversation, his end: professional, cold, blunt. But the slant of his mouth gave him away. It was thinned. Then his voice changed slightly. Her heart started to pound. Something was wrong. Terribly wrong. Logan slowly unwound and put the sat phone away. His eyes glittered like obsidian in the moonlight. Jess stood up, pushing the empty wrapper into her pocket, wanting to leave no evidence behind that they'd been here.

Logan untied the reins to the gelding and turned to Jess. "There's a drone up above us, watching the area," he told her quietly. "Khogani has just discovered you escaped."

Her heart leaped into her tightening throat. Jess gave him a panicked look.

Logan reached out, caressing her cheek. "They can't find you easily because it's dark. But they do have moonlight, and the trackers are out following your boot prints."

Her heart plunged to her feet. "Oh, no...."

"It's all right," he murmured, settling his hand on her shoulder. "There's two miles between us."

Jess wanted to run. She wanted to cry. Scream. Get out of here. Anxiously, she watched Logan's face, seeing him thinking, strategizing. She felt his hand become firmer on her shoulder.

"We're surrounded on three sides by enemies," he told her, watching her inner fear mirror itself in her widening eyes. "To the east and west of us, there are groups. Khogani's north of us. I'm fairly sure the bands east of us are his soldiers. The ones west: some kind of rendezvous party. And he's probably in radio contact with them right now. The only place we can go is down to the south."

"H-how far are we from the valley? From help?"

Logan said, "Fifty miles east of the valley."

"But... can't we get help? A helicopter come in and pick us up?"

"No. These Taliban have RPGs among them. Maybe a Stinger missile. We just don't know, Jess. I have to get us far enough away for a possible helicopter rescue. Right now, it's impossible. We're in heavy woods. They'd have to hover. They'd be sitting ducks, shot down in an instant, so we're on our own for right now."

Her heart sank. *Oh, God....* Jess still felt shaky with adrenaline, crashing from it, feeling her knees weakening. She had to be strong for Logan. For herself. He looked so calm. So unperturbed by their dilemma.

"What we have going for us are the night hours. Trackers will have a hell of a time finding your boot prints. And, even when they do, it will be very slow work. What Khogani will do is most likely order his east and west bands to wake up, mount up and ride toward him in a pincer-like movement, hoping to snare you in the process."

Gulping, Jess nodded. "W-what can we do, Logan?"

"Go down the slope." His mouth quirked. "But it's not that easy. There's a cliff about a hundred feet from where we're standing. I'm going to have to backtrack us to the east to get around it. That will bring us closer to that band that's probably already on the move. Like I said, the darkness is going to slow them down a lot. I believe we can dodge them." It was going to be close, but Logan didn't tell her that. Jess was scared out of her mind as it was. There was no need to tell her anything more. "We're just going to have to be quiet and slip through their lines."

"O-okay. What can I do?"

Logan brushed her mussed and tangled hair with his hand. "I'm going to mount the horse. Then, I'll pull you up in front of me."

Gulping, Jess nodded. She watched Logan effortlessly put the reins over the head of the black gelding and then leap up onto its sleek, bare back. He pushed himself toward the rump of the horse, holding his gloved hand down to her. She took it, worried that she couldn't mount. Surprisingly, he hauled her upward, as if she weighed nothing, and she found herself lifting her right leg up and over the horse's withers. Settling down on the horse's back, Jess grabbed hunks of the horse's mane between her cold, numb fingers.

"Good," Logan praised quietly, moving his arms either side of her. In one hand, he had the reins. The other, he slid around her waist. She was tensed and hunched over. "Relax, Jess. Sit up straight. I won't let you fall off."

Her heart was pounding in her throat. Her fingers were whitening as she clung to the mane. Slowly, she did as Logan asked, feeling safer with his strong arm around her waist. She gulped as he pulled her solidly against the front of him. Logan turned the horse around, aiming him down and around the trunks of the trees. Just being finally, solidly on the move helped Jess steady her wildly fluctuating emotions. Logan rode easily, as if part of the horse. And then, she remembered he'd been born in Wyoming. He'd been a wrangler, around horses since birth, and that made her feel even better. The horse was moving slowly, at a walk, and she closed her eyes for a moment, leaning against Logan, some of her terror abating.

The horse stumbled.

Jess gasped, thrown forward. Instantly, she felt Logan's arm cut like a vise across her waist, hauling her back up against him.

The horse steadied itself and moved on.

"Okay?" Logan rasped against her ear.

She nodded, wildly gripping the mane. She felt Logan's warm breath by her ear and his calm voice took some of the resurging terror out of her.

"I've got you, Jess. I won't let go of you...."

CHAPTER 16

L OGAN'S GUT WAS in chaos as they slowly rode around the top of the cliff's drop. With two-dimensional NVGs on, everything looked flat. A rock sticking up didn't look like it was sticking up at all. The intense concentration he had to use, plus keep his hearing keyed for any out-of-the-ordinary noises that could mean Hill or Taliban were nearby, kept him laser focused. The relief at having Jess riding in front of him, an arm around her waist, keeping her solidly on the horse, would have overwhelmed him, had he allowed it to. She was frightened, tense, and he couldn't blame her at all.

Logan didn't dare go to his heart. He loved her, and they were in so much deep trouble that he wasn't sure he could get them out of it alive. And that is what kept trying to tear at him the most; the one thing he couldn't protect himself against was his love for this brave, courageous woman. The way Jess soldiered on, despite her obvious fear, spoke volumes about her true grit, honed by military discipline.

As they passed the point where the cliff rejoined the surrounding slope and ceased being a threat, Logan halted. He slid off their mount, pulling his NVGs up onto his forehead, asking Jess to hold the reins and keep the horse still while he shrugged out of his ruck. Taking out the sat phone, the regular radio still being out of range, he placed a call to Chris. He gave his partner their current GPS coordinates, plus the status on Jess, and they discussed the latest drone update on where all the Taliban players were located. By his watch, it was 0300. They had until 0500 before the first light of dawn would crack the night, leaving them vulnerable to the eyes of the Taliban. He shielded a tiny penlight in one hand as he opened a map, spreading it on the ground, going over with Chris any cave locations within a two-hour ride. They came up with several possibilities and Logan wrote them down. He finished off the call, saying he'd check in once they'd reached a cave where they could hide for the day.

Jess was shivering in the cold. The back of the horse was warm, and it felt good, but the strong gusts of wind that rocked the area, coming down off the fourteen-thousand-foot snow-covered peaks, were causing the air temperature to plummet. She didn't want to say anything, knowing Logan had his focus on getting them out of this alive. Jess was seeing him in SEAL mode; his face expressionless, but his eyes alive, aware, his gaze constantly moving around the area. He took nothing for granted. And it kept her on an adrenaline high, understanding, even as a Seabee, the oppressive threat of being surrounded on three sides by the enemy. Looking up at the stars overhead between the fragmented clouds, Jess figured two hours until dawn. And when that light came, the Taliban could not only track her boot tracks easier but could spot her and Logan outright if they got close enough.

Logan folded up the map, tucking it inside his cammie jacket. He then slipped the sat phone into an outer pocket of the ruck and came over to Jess. Placing a gloved hand on her thigh, he could see her deeply shadowed face even without his NVGs in place. The terror in Jess's eyes tried to tug powerfully at his heart. He shut that down fast, squeezing her thigh to lend her comfort and gain her concentration. "We're going to continue down the slope at an angle," he told her. Knowledge would take some of the fear he saw out of her. "We'll ride two hours, and Chris has a couple of caves that we can check out."

"Caves?"

"Yeah, we're going to have to hole up for the daylight hours and hide from the Taliban."

Jess licked her lower lip, her brows moving down. "Then, we only move at night?"

Logan heard the strain in Jess's husky voice and gently rubbed her thigh to try and ease some of the tension out of her. "Yes."

"But… they know the caves. Won't they find us in one?" Logan's hand felt comforting, and she ached to be in his arms right now. He always gave her such a sense of safety.

Logan shrugged. "There're hundreds of caves around here, Jess. They don't have that many men to search every single one."

"What about our tracks?"

"I swept out your tracks before I mounted up back there. What they'll find, eventually, is only horse prints. Whether they put it together that it's you or not, I don't know. They think you're on foot, so they're going to be looking for boot prints, not horse tracks."

"Are there horses wandering around loose in these mountains?"

He smiled a little, holding her dark gaze. Jess was smart. "Yeah, some get loose. There's Afghan horse traders who travel through these areas, too, bringing strings of them."

"You think they'll not know you were here with a horse?"

Shrugging, Logan said, "That's what I'm hoping. If we manage to fool them, it means confusion in Khogani's ranks. He won't be able to tell his army in the east and west where to go to hunt for us." He patted her thigh, seeing some of the tension in her face dissolve. "How are YOU doing?" he demanded, searching her eyes.

"I'm cold."

"Yeah, it's a bitch at this altitude," Logan muttered. He was plenty warm because of the H-gear harness he wore around his torso, but he needed to keep that on *him* for the ammo. "We're heading down. I'm hoping in two hours we'll reach those caves, and they're a lot warmer than the outside air, as you probably noticed." He leaped up behind her, settling his ruck so that it rested on the rump of the horse even though he kept it on his back. It took some of the strain off his shoulder muscles.

Jess closed her eyes for a moment as Logan wrapped his arm around her waist. He was so tall and broad that he became a windbreak for her, and she wasn't nearly as cold as before. Except that her hands were freezing to the point where she could no longer feel them. A small price to pay, she thought, for getting away from Khogani. Logan nudged the horse forward and the gelding slowly picked his way down the littered slope of rocks, fallen limbs, and brush. She kept her fingers wrapped firmly in the mane, worrying that the horse might trip again, and fall for real this time. She kept Logan's words replaying in her head; that he had her, that he wouldn't let her fall. Jess wanted to tell him how much it meant to her that he'd come for her. But she continued to respect his need for focus. All that would all have to wait.

THE DAWN WAS just crawling up to challenge the night sky when Logan found one of the caves that Chris had identified for him. Jess remained on the horse, reins in hand, while he shoved his ruck near the cave entrance and went in with his M4 rifle, checking it out, clearing it for any potential enemy within. The wind had calmed and there was a muted silence around them. The cave was up an escarpment of smooth rock, so there would be no hoofprints to be found by the Taliban trackers. It had a small entrance, tall and narrow, reminding Jess of an opening to an Indian teepee. It was about eight feet high and five feet wide. She had no idea how big it was inside, or if it was a dry or wet cave. It stood on a dolomite skirt of white-and-gray rock, overlooking the evergreen forest below.

Logan silently reappeared, scaring her. Jess placed her hand against her heart as it banged away in her throat. The horse just lifted his ears toward Logan. He walked over to her, placing a hand on her leg.

"It's clear. Chris picked a good one. Come on, I'll help you down," and he placed his hands around Jess's waist and easily lifted her up and off the horse. Jess kept the reins in her hand, fearful the horse might run away, and they'd have nothing to ride. Her knees nearly buckled when her boots touched the ground. Logan kept his arm around her waist, standing solid, allowing her to get her feet under her.

"I'm not used to riding," Jess muttered, gripping his arms. "My knees…" She saw him smile a little.

"Yeah, it's rough on the butt, the thighs and knees. You're doing good, Jess." He saw her rally beneath his low words of praise. Her hands on his arms felt good and he wanted to kiss her. That would come later once they were inside, well hidden, and the horse taken care of.

"Thanks," Jess muttered, shaking her head. "I'm okay now."

Logan didn't let go of her hand. He took the reins to the horse and said, "We got lucky. There're openings in the cave roof. They're going to give us light inside. Otherwise, we'd be blind as bats because NVGs don't work in caves for the most part. Follow the horse and me? I think you'll like your new digs," and he grinned.

The moment Logan's face broke into a boyish smile, Jess's heart melted. He was incredibly handsome, confident, and she was so grateful he was at her side. She slowly followed the horse into the cave. Looking around, Jess saw ragged holes up above, perhaps twenty feet from where she stood, light from the soft pink dawn sky outside already falling inside the cave. The cave got warmer the more they walked toward the rear of it. To her surprise, she saw a tunnel to the left and Logan took it. It was sheer rock, and the floor was nubby with sharp-pointed stalagmites about one inch tall. The horse was carefully picking his way in and around them, just like she was. Jess would not want to fall on any of them, thinking that the sharp points would impale her.

The holes above in the cave ceiling were large and small. They reminded her of the many holes found in Swiss cheese. In some places, as Jess walked in the tunnel, she saw where bits of dirt, rocks, or pieces of plant had fallen through the holes onto its floor. The warmth continued and she finally felt her fingers begin to thaw.

They walked almost a quarter of a mile before the tunnel opened up in an amazing chamber that took Jess's breath away. It was an oval cave, and a quarter of the ceiling had a long, narrow opening. She could again see the night being chased away by the coming dawn through it. Hearing water, she saw Logan leading the horse over to a small pool. Amazed that there was water, Jess saw it was dripping down from the roof, over a wall of rocks and collecting in the pool at the bottom. The horse pushed forward, thrusting his muzzle eagerly into it, gulping noisily, drinking deeply. Logan stood to one side, turning and watching her progress.

"Home away from home," he murmured, holding out his hand toward her.

Jess slid her fingers into his gloved hand, feeling his warmth. "Won't our voices carry?"

"As long as we talk in a low voice and not a whisper, those carry further, we'll be fine." Logan handed her the reins to the horse. "I need to wipe out any evidence we're here. If Taliban happen by, they'll be looking for tracks. When they find none, they'll move on." He saw the fear come to Jess's eyes. "We'll be okay in here," he reassured her. "I'll be back in about thirty minutes. Got to go down off the escarpment and erase the horse prints for a ways down there, too."

"What do I do with the horse?"

Logan pointed to a rock sticking out of the wall. "Once he's done drinking, take him over there and tie the reins around the rock. He's tired. All he wants to do is stand and rest."

She grimaced. "Like us."

He grinned. "Yeah. When I get back, I'll take care of you, Jess."

Her heart throbbed with need of Logan. Ordinarily, Jess didn't need reassurance, but, being thrown into this situation, she wanted Logan near. Be in his arms. Holding him. "Be careful?"

He nodded. "Always. I'll be back..."

Jess had sat down near where the horse stood with one of its hind legs cocked in a resting position. She lost track of time, apart from the sky through the slit in the roof showing the night was nearly gone. It *was* warm in the cave, and, for that, she was more than grateful. Logan had left his ruck, and she'd opened it up and found a gallon of fresh water. She drank plenty, knowing she had to remain hydrated. The fact there was a pool where the two plastic one-gallon containers could be refilled, made Jess feel better. She found a stash of protein bars and ate one, stopping the growling of her stomach.

Logan appeared like a ghost out of the tunnel, scaring her again. Jess gasped, her hand flying to her throat.

"Sorry," Logan murmured, walking over and placing his rifle against the wall nearby. He shrugged out of his heavy H-gear, setting it near the rifle. "How are you doing?" and his gaze went to her upper-left sleeve with all its dried blood stains.

"Better," Jess murmured, watching him shuck out of his gear and his cammie jacket. Logan was sweating, the gleam across his brow. There were dark spots beneath the arms of his jacket. "I drank some of your water and ate another protein bar."

He nodded and pulled out his medical kit from the ruck. "Good. I need to look at your arm. Here's your antibiotics back. You dropped them where you were captured." He walked around and knelt on her left side.

"Thanks. I noticed that missing." Wryly, Jess elaborated, "I had two things in my pockets: the antibiotics and a Swiss Army knife. Good thing it was just the pills that fell out. I used the knife to cut the rope they had around my ankle to escape."

"Never leave home without a knife on you," Logan agreed, opening up the medical kit. He pulled on a pair of latex gloves. "Let me help you get off your jacket so I can look at your gunshot wound?"

Jess unbuttoned it and, together, they eased the sleeve off her left arm. She looked at it. The dressing the hateful Taliban soldier had applied was intact and relatively clean. "I guess I'd better take my pills, now that I have them back," she muttered, picking up the plastic gallon jug. It hurt to use the arm, but Jess tried to ignore it. She popped the drugs into her mouth and took a swig of water, setting the jug down beside her. Logan reached across and took it from her hand. He wet a washcloth, unbinding the dressing, and began to scrub the area around the wound.

"This is going to hurt," he warned her. Logan could smell Jess's scent, and he dragged it deeply into his lungs. Her hair was mud streaked here and there, her hands, and the arms of her jacket sleeves, dirty and soiled. "Did you roll out of that cave?" he wondered, cleaning the wound.

"Yes. I thought if I tried to stand up, the horses would snort or jerk around, waking up Khogani and his men."

He gave her a look of pride. "You're one smart lady. You know that?"

His praise was warmth flowing through Jess. "Thanks. I was just so scared, Logan." Her voice trembled a little. She saw him lose his game face. Instead, Jess saw sympathy come to his eyes.

"I can't even imagine how you were feeling. I knew you had to be scared out of your mind." Logan frowned. "Did they hurt you at all?" His breath hitched. He knew how much the Taliban hated American women.

"Just clipped my cheek with a fist was all," she said. "They didn't touch me otherwise, thank God."

He released his breath and kept cleaning the wound. "Good. How's your cheek feeling?"

She managed a half smile, beginning to relax. Being with Logan made her feel safe. "Swollen. A couple of my lower molars are loose, but that's all."

"I can see the swelling and purple coloring," he murmured. Logan quickly added antiseptic to the upper arm wound, wrapped it, and placed a waterproof dressing over it. Helping Jess on with her jacket, he saw the tension in her eyes and face was just about gone. That was good. Logan understood the power of touch, of care of one human being to another. "You up for a breakfast MRE? I got some in my ruck." He gave her a teasing look. "This isn't a Denver Omelet with all the trimmings, but we need to get some serious food into you." He slowly rose, his joints stiff.

"I'd love an MRE," Jess said. Logan had his ruck very neatly packed. Everything in it had a place, and every place had a thing. He pulled off the latex gloves and shoved them and the old dressing into a plastic bag, tying it up and tucking it back into the ruck. They couldn't afford to leave anything behind, or the Taliban would know they had been here. Even the off chance that they found it in time for that to make a difference was still a risk to be avoided.

"What I'd give for a strong cup of black coffee," Logan said, handing her an MRE and sitting down near her boots, facing her. He pulled his open. She did the same.

Groaning softly, Jess said, "That sounds *so* wonderful." She opened up her MRE, its magnesium heating tab having done its work, and started to pick delicately at it. Indeed, a Denver Omelet it was *not*. But it was heavy in protein and carbohydrates, necessary fuel for her body. And Jess knew they had a ways to go.

Logan ate voraciously. He had purposely packed twice the amount of MREs he would have ordinarily, assuming he'd find and rescue Jess. It had increased his carbohydrate load, but watching her hungrily eat, he was glad he'd thought ahead. "Would you like to clean up?" He pointed to the pool. "It'll be colder than hell, but I have unscented soap and a washcloth and a towel. Interested?"

Was she ever! "That sounds absolutely wonderful." Jess wrinkled her nose, looking over her dirty... well, *everything*, except her hands which she had washed before the meal. "Are you going to wash up?"

"Any chance I get," Logan assured her. "This Afghan desert sand rubs my body raw. It gets into every crack, fold and crevice. But I'll let you go first. That pool has a runoff and is always being fed fresh water from above. The horse has had his fill and I'll top off the jugs, with some purification tablets throw in, and then we can bathe."

"Luxuries," Jess murmured, shaking her head. "We're so spoiled, aren't we? I shouldn't joke, though. For real, Afghan villagers have no plumbing, no running water, no shower or bathtub."

"No, they survive on very little," Logan agreed, sadness in his tone. Jess was relaxing and he could see the exhaustion shadowing her eyes. "As soon as we get done eating, we'll wash up, and then I'll spread the sleeping bag out on the floor, and we'll sleep together." He saw her expression become soft. Yeah, he sure as hell wanted Jess at his side, in his arms, where she belonged. "Sound good?"

"Does it ever," Jess quavered, giving Logan a teary-eyed look. The heat in his eyes told her how he felt about her. Jess wanted nothing more than Logan at her side. He loved her. *He'd said it!* And she was desperate to feel just a little bit safe in this constantly hostile environment.

"Comfy?" Logan rasped against Jess's temple as he brought her fully against him. He'd opened up his sleeping bag and brought the top of it over her. There wasn't enough for him, but he was more concerned she be kept warm because she was clearly in shock, on top of her recent exposure to the harsh mountain cold. With her freshly washed hair damp against his jaw and shoulder, he heard Jess make a happy sound in her throat, her arm sliding across his torso, snuggled up against him.

Logan couldn't make love with her, although that's exactly what he wanted to do. If they were compromised or needed to get out of here in a helluva hurry, they couldn't be naked, that was for sure. He had his M4 lying next to him so, if he needed it, it was a hand's length away.

Jess inhaled Logan's fresh, male fragrance, and placed her lips against the strong column of his neck, feeling the coolness of his flesh. She trembled as he slid his arm beneath her neck and brought his other arm across her, one hand resting comfortingly against her hip; keeping her as close as they could get to one another without... *no, best not to go there.* Logan tensed as she kissed his neck and nuzzled. His mouth slid across her temple as she moved her hips languidly against his. She felt his hard erection beneath his trousers. It was enough to inflame her, and she felt an ache centering low in her body.

"You smell so good," Logan rasped, controlling himself. The last thing they should be doing is loving one another. He understood Jess was in shock and she'd thought she was going to die. And when people went through that kind of experience, they often wanted to prove life over death. Survivor sex was one helluva way to confirm life. And they'd already experienced that at Landstuhl. He felt Jess press against him, and he desperately wanted to follow through with what she wanted from him. Tactically, it was the stupidest move he could make under the circumstances. Somehow, Logan had to get through to Jess that it couldn't happen. Not here. Not now.

Raising up on one elbow, Logan eased Jess onto her back, caressing her cheek, looking deep into her half-closed eyes. Logan saw desperation, anxiety, fear, and desire all tangled up within them, confirming what he already knew: survivor sex was pushing Jess. He couldn't fault her. She still wasn't herself and he knew it. "Listen," he whispered across her mouth, "I want that as much as you do, but now's not the time, Babe." He felt her deflate. It was nothing obvious. No sound of disappointment, no body language. Just a sense. He lifted his mouth away, lightly touching her brow, watching her anxiety abate. Touch meant everything, on a basic human level. Logan knew this well, and saw the effects of his grazing contact. "You're in shock, Jess. When we're like that, we aren't thinking straight…," and he saw the apology come to her expression. And then he saw tears. Now, he felt rotten.

"You're right," Jess said in a watery voice. She sniffed and wiped her eyes, embarrassed as Logan watched her with sympathy in his own. There was a tender smile across his mouth, and she felt a lump forming in her throat. Turning into his arms, hugging him close, Jess buried her face against Logan's chest, the hot tears streaming freely out of her eyes.

"I'm sorry," Logan rasped, feeling like shit that he'd caused Jess to cry. He knew it was the shock, but he felt as if he'd contributed to the damage. He hadn't handled it very well, either and that was on him, not Jess. He loved her, and tunneled his fingers through her drying hair, feeling her shake with sobs as he held her. This was for the best, Logan told himself. He was sure Jess hadn't cried since being kidnapped. She'd been on high adrenaline, unsure if she'd even survive, already struck by one of them, roughed up. He was damned thankful they hadn't raped her. Kissing her hair, whispering her name, Logan skimmed her shoulders and back, trying to sooth Jess. Slowly, she stopped weeping, moving into a series of hiccups and then, finally, she lay quiet in his arms, his undershirt damp with her spent tears.

Jess absorbed Logan's arms, comforting around her as if he knew she was feeling horribly vulnerable, stripped of civilization, thrown back into a time and place of ongoing, nonstop savagery. Her throat ached from crying so much and she kept her eyes closed, starved, but devouring Logan's warm, hard length against hers. He made her feel safe. Protected. And she loved him fiercely, so afraid of losing him. Jess felt him loosen his grip, and he pressed her down on the sleeping bag, worry in his expression, laid her back against one arm enough to look into her face.

"Don't look at me," she muttered thickly, "I look awful…"

Logan's mouth curved faintly. "You look beautiful to me, Jess. Feel better now?" and he nudged a few strands of hair away from her wet cheek. His whole lower body was on fire. Logan wanted nothing more than to bury himself deep within her beautiful, welcoming body. What they shared sexually was the best he'd ever had. And it was because Jess was herself, a woman of the earth, sensual and incredibly trusting.

She wrinkled her nose. "I feel ripped up, Logan."

"I know you do."

"And I feel ashamed."

"Why?" He gazed into her eyes that still glistened with unshed tears. There was humiliation in Jess's expression.

"B-because I got suckered into a trap." She sniffed and wiped her eyes, her voice hollow with anguish. "I got up an hour after you left. I got dressed and I went outside to empty that damn bowl of water." She frowned. "And then, I heard a little child crying over at the grove. I-I didn't think, Logan. I just ran over there thinking one of the toddlers from the village got out of their house and had come down there to play hide 'n seek and got lost or something. Only," and Jess's mouth thinned, "it was too early."

"The Hill and Taliban soldiers aren't stupid," he told her gravely, cupping her cheek, making Jess hold his gaze. Logan could see how embarrassed and sorry she was that she'd fallen for the trick. "They studied you, watched you, figured out what they could use, after two aborted attempts, to kidnap you the third time. Someone in Khogani's group had the answer, Jess, children. They probably saw you at the village picking up kids and hugging them all the time."

"Or giving them candy," she mumbled.

Logan smiled a little more. "That, too. You spoiled them rotten, Jess. And they all love you for it. There's a hidden mother in you," and he kissed the tip of her nose, wanting to make her feel better, not wanting her to take the blame for her kidnapping.

Shrugging, Jess said, "Children are innocent. It's the adults that suck."

Laughing quietly, Logan nodded. "Got that right."

"When I went running around that grove, I about died, Logan. There were three Taliban standing there, waiting for me." She swallowed hard and closed her eyes. "I didn't *think!*"

"Hey," he chided, placing a finger beneath her chin, forcing her to look at him, "don't go there. We're all human. You're not black ops, Jess. You're used to working in safe places where people love you and are glad to see you. All your experience was in that direction. This is the first time you've been in Afghanistan. It's just a horse of a different color, is all, Babe. You can't blame yourself for what happened. They were very cagey and smart as to how they tricked you, was all." Logan saw Jess give him an unsure look. "Tell me what happened after that?"

Jess closed her eyes. When she told him about being struck, he automatically pulled her a little tighter against him. She could feel Logan's rage, but he never said a thing. When she finished, she wearily looked up at him. His face was set and hard, eyes burning with anger. His emotions were palpable, but he remained silent. "I'm tired now," she whispered. "Can I just curl up against you and sleep?" Instantly, Jess saw Logan change. She saw the man behind the SEAL persona come back to her again. His eyes grew gentle, and he kissed her mouth with such tenderness that Jess swore she felt on the edge of orgasm. Logan had that kind of hot, sensual effect on her body because he held her heart in those large, scarred hands of his.

"Come on," Logan urged, laying down beside her, pulling her against him and then bringing the warm cover of the sleeping bag tighter across her shoulders. "Sleep all you want, Jess. We can't move until after dark."

Already, Jess could see the sky getting lighter. She thought she heard a bird singing somewhere near that slit in the ceiling. "I'm just glad you're here, Logan." Jess closed her eyes, face pressed to his shoulder, brow against his jaw. She inhaled deeply, absorbing his masculine scent, feeling his arm slide around her waist and capture her hips. For now, she was safe.

CHAPTER 17

JESS AWOKE WITH a start. She sat up, confused, unsure of where she was at. She heard the horse munching quietly nearby. It was grayish in the cave. The drip, drip, drip of water from the pool caught her attention as she sat up. Grimacing as pain throbbed through her arm, Jess suddenly felt scared. Where was Logan? She hadn't felt him get up and leave. What was the horse eating? She slowly got to her feet, rubbing her face, trying to come awake, her heart starting to pound in dread.

Just then, Logan silently returned to the cave. This time, Jess had seen him coming down the tunnel, so she didn't start. He had his M4 and he was back in his battle garb. The sat phone was in his left hand. When he saw her, she saw his game face dissolve, soften momentarily, then returned to being unreadable. Jess could tell he had something difficult to tell her and, as he walked over to her, she asked quietly, "Is everything all right?"

Logan shook his head and safed the M4, placing it against the wall. He was wearing his H-gear, the tops of magazines sticking out of its pockets across his chest. "I just finished talking with Chris," he said guiding her over to the sleeping bag. "Khogani is actively hunting for you. And, somehow, it looks like they've tracked us to this general area. He's called in his east and west troops and now, they are surrounding this slope."

Her heart sped up and she stared in fear at his grim, shadowed features. "What can we do?"

Logan tried to keep his voice emotionless, seeing the fear in Jess's eyes. "They're spread out partway around us. Khogani's figured out that you'll try to escape to the valley, so he's got his men in a rough semicircle about a mile below where we're at, like a bowl for us to drop into."

Her heart rate kicked up and she nervously licked her lower lip. "What do we do?"

"We're on the slope of the mountain range. It means going up and over the mountain spine and down the other side. The nearest forward operating base to where we're at presently is Bravo, where I'm stationed. It's roughly fifty miles on the other side of this mountain." He saw Jess's eyes widen with the implications.

"But… that means we aren't getting picked up?" She saw the set of his face, the lack of expression. How could Logan be taking this so calmly? She felt shaky inside. Terrorized that Khogani would find them.

Logan reached out, smoothing some of her hair back into place. "We're at nine thousand feet. To the east of us is a pass that the Taliban uses to go back and forth across this mountain range, Jess. The place is crawling with enemy. There's a village on the other side of this mountain. Goat herds are out during the day below the nine-thousand-foot level. We wouldn't be able to tell friend from foe, Jess. We can't just bring in Apaches and shoot people we suspect are Taliban. And Chinook helicopters don't do twelve-thousand feet too well. What we'll do is go north, climb up to the snow level where Khogani won't suspect us of going. His whole focus and army is in the south. Then, we'll travel east toward that pass. We'll cross it at night when everyone is sleeping. There's a lot of goat trails and ratlines, paths that Taliban take to carry fertilizer and weapons on, that we can choose from once we get down off that pass. Our main focus is to get into the valley below. It will be warmer, but it also means we're more exposed to Taliban eyes."

Jess pulled her arms around herself, staring up at him. "This sounds almost impossible to do, Logan."

He shrugged. "Under the circumstances, it's our best strategy, Jess. It's not going to be easy. Will it be dangerous? Yes." He caressed her cheek, watching his touch calm her. "We can do it. I've patrolled these mountains off and on for years. We just need to keep avoiding Taliban on horseback, is all."

She felt abandoned in a way, by the military. All this technology and little of it could be used to help them escape Khogani. She knew it wasn't Logan's fault. Or anyone else's. "I guess, I'm just scared witless, Logan. I want this to be over with…," Jess admitted, giving him an apologetic look.

"I know," he rasped, leaning down and kissing her wrinkled brow. "Just trust me and we'll get out of this alive."

"What can I do to help?" Jess wasn't going to whine. That would just be one more pressure on Logan. He saw her give him a faint smile.

"Oh, don't go there," he teased, brushing his mouth against hers. He felt Jess respond, stepping toward him, her good arm sliding up around his neck. The H-gear prevented her from really getting as close to him as he wanted. Her lips were soft, welcoming, warm beneath his. It was a helluva invitation. One that neither could indulge in right now. Logan eased his mouth from hers, seeing the need for him reflected in her eyes. "You can just keep being strong for me, Jess. I know it's tough to ride on a horse and you're not used to it. Focus on staying loose and easy on the horse's back. Don't fight the mount's natural rhythm."

"I'll try that," she said, stepping away, her mouth tingling with the power of Logan's kiss. "What else?"

"Just keep your eyes and ears open. Any sounds that are out of the ordinary, let me know? The horse is a damned good guard dog. He'll hear and see things long before we do. And," he kissed the tip of her nose, "just have faith in me. We'll get to Bravo in one piece and alive. There's a lot of cold weather out there. You're not equipped to handle it." And that worried Logan. He had a plan but wasn't going to let Jess in on it yet. She was frightened enough. No sense in scaring her more.

"Let's do it," Jess told him grimly. "I don't like the alternative."

Logan nodded. "Neither do I. As long as I have that sat phone, we're in good with Chris and everyone knows what's happening. He's already contacted the CO at FOB Bravo and he knows we're going to head his direction. He'll have Marine patrols out in the valley looking for us or, at least, providing us some cover. Or maybe causing distraction with the Taliban in the area, making it easier for us to slip by them, unnoticed." Jess's hair was mussed around her face and needed a comb. He had one in his ruck and walked over, pulling it out for her.

"Let's eat. We can't move until it's completely dark. I've been cutting grass for the horse for a couple of hours, so he has some fuel to work with."

"Thanks," she murmured, gratefully taking the comb. "Are the Taliban closing in on the cave?"

Logan shook his head. "No. Chris and I both think that Khogani's lost your track somewhere in this general vicinity and they're confused. Like I mentioned, it looks like he's forming a fishnet of sorts so we can't get through it to reach the valley. It looks like he's putting all his eggs in one basket. If that holds? That's good news for us because it means all his people power is south, and we're going north. It will be much safer for us, as a result."

She pulled the comb quickly through her hair and then Logan tied it back into a ponytail for her with a rubber band. "Does that mean they haven't put together that you came in on a horse to rescue me?"

Nodding, Logan leaned down and rolled the sleeping bag up and placed it with ties on top of his ruck. "Yeah, that's what I think it means. We did a good enough job of wiping our prints here and there that they haven't figured it out." *Yet.* Logan knew the Hill people and the Taliban were not stupid. They knew SEALs, Rangers, Delta Force and Special Forces had snipers in the mountains watching for them. And they also knew that there would be a huge effort to find Jess. "The Taliban knows that US forces will be looking for you, too, so they know they aren't out here operating with impunity."

"They have to be wary of drones. Flyovers? Apache helicopters?" Jess asked, as he handed her a breakfast MRE to eat.

"Exactly," Logan murmured. He invited her to sit down near the horse, who was hungrily nibbling up the last scraps of the grass Logan had provided him earlier. "Khogani knows we aren't *not* going to search for you. He has to be scared of SEAL teams coming up from the valley and interdicting with his men as they lay their trap on the lower southern slopes for you."

She smiled a little. "It's a huge chess game."

Grimacing, Logan said, "Yes, it is."

"Do my parents know I'm okay?"

"They know you're in US hands. We can't tell them anything more. It's top secret. They know you're safe." *For now.* But Logan didn't add that to the mix, seeing her eyes fill with relief. Logan knew how many things could go wrong. Murphy's Law, *if it could go wrong, it would,* was alive and well in SEAL ranks. There wasn't one mission he'd been on where something hadn't gone sideways. No matter how much attention SEALs paid to every little detail, the great unknown of the enemy was the chaos sitting out there, lurking to mix things up.

"My poor mom and dad, what they must be going through," and Jess felt badly for her parents. Who wanted to know their child had been kidnapped and had been in Hill soldiers' hands? The nightmares, the anxiety it had to be causing them. "My mother, once this is over, is probably going to chew my ear off about getting out of the Seabees to become a civilian and work with their company." Her mouth quirked as she looked over at Logan quickly eating his MRE, "At least I'd be safe."

"Yes, and that's important," Logan agreed. He could see Jess considering the nature of her military work. This situation had shaken her world view, no question. And, selfishly, he'd like to see Jess out of the Navy, safe in San Diego, working in her parents' multi-million-dollar construction company. And, yeah, that was a selfish desire. He was willing to admit that to himself, but he didn't care. He loved her. And never mind her possible future assignments, Logan wasn't even sure if they were going to get out of *this* situation.

"Look," he told her, "I want you to wear my Kevlar vest." He saw Jess lift her head, shock in her eyes. "You're sitting up in front of me," he explained. "If we suddenly run into Taliban, and they fire at us, you're the target, not me." He hated saying it, but it was true. And Jess frowned, mouth tightening, and then she nodded.

"You're right."

"You know the drill: it's forty pounds of weight with the chicken plate in it," he told her. It wasn't going to be easy to ride a horse properly with that heavy vest on her upper body, overbalancing her.

"I'll manage it. Don't worry."

Now he was seeing her grit. And she was going to need every ounce of it. Logan knew no one else was trained to the high degree the black ops community was. Jess had no drilled-in muscle memory or reflexes to know what to do in a firefight. Yes, the military had taught her how to fire an M-16 rifle, and a .45 pistol, and hit the target. But this kind of situation wasn't in her purview of experience, at all. That placed the weight of responsibility on him. He wished he could be the one riding up front on the horse, but his H-gear, massive around his torso, plus wearing the sixty-pound ruck on his back, wouldn't allow it.

After they finished their MREs and tucked the leftover foil away in his ruck, Logan shed his H-gear and pulled off his Kevlar vest. Jess came over and he helped her into it. It hung on her frame. She was five inches shorter than he was, and half his muscle and bone mass.

Turning around, she smiled faintly. "Well, not exactly the height of fashion, Randall, but it will do."

He grinned back and pulled the Velcro closed down her front, and then took off his gloves and told her to wear them. He took out the yellow-and-green-checked *shemagh* of hers that he had brought along, wrapped it around her head like a loose scarf, and then snugged it around her neck and shoulders. Jess knew the unique tribal colors of the *shemagh* shouted of its tribal lineage. Each tribe had its own colors and design. These were the color of the Shinwari tribe, prevalent where they were going. The Afghan tribesmen would recognize it, and see them as friendly, not Taliban. It was an easy way to identify a stranger and what tribe they were from. "How's that *shemagh* feel on you?"

"Warm," she murmured, "thanks."

Logan nodded. "Now, you look more like a Shinwari tribesman. If the Taliban sees you, they might mistake you as one. Let's get ready to leave." Logan wished to hell they could go *hajii*, meaning to wear full Afghan male clothing that would camouflage them completely. Normally, SEALs on sniper missions or long patrols, would go *hajii*, blending into the fabric of the Afghan desert and its people.

Jess glanced up at the slit in the ceiling. She could see dark grayness above in the sky. Feeling her adrenaline kick up as Logan led her over to the horse, she said, "I'm not walking out?"

"Not necessary. Gotta save your strength." He cupped his hands together so she could slide her boot into his palms. "Grab the mane and I'll boost you up."

Jess found that, with sixty-five extra pounds, she was awkward and gawky as he easily hefted her up and over onto the back of the horse. Grabbing the mane, she saw Logan pull the NVGs down on his helmet rail and settle them across his eyes. He picked up the horse's reins and led the gelding toward the tunnel. The horse's back was warm. Jess worried if Logan would be warm enough. She knew he was trying to keep her from going hypothermic even as things were. And that pass they were heading for, was at *eighty-five hundred feet.* The winds blew down off the slopes of the Hindu Kush at night at up to a hundred miles an hour, in savage gusts, the temperature plunging thirty or forty degrees below freezing.

They left the tunnel, coming back out into the entrance chamber. Jess's heart rate amped up as Logan cautiously looked around, leaving her and the horse at the back of the cave. He had crouched, M4 ready to fire, and disappeared into the night. She could see a few stars here and there through the cave entrance. And the wind was rising and falling outside. Already, she was grateful for the warmer vest he'd given her. She waited tensely, and Logan came back about ten minutes later, appearing at her side and scaring the hell out of her yet again. She had not heard him coming. *The man was like a damn ghost.* But the horse had pricked up his ears a moment earlier, looking pointedly in a particular direction. Jess realized she needed to pay a lot more attention to the animal. She felt Logan's hand on her thigh. It made her feel a little safer.

"All clear," he told her in a low voice. "Take my rifle for a minute. I'm climbing on board."

Jess held his rifle, and Logan mounted the horse's back behind her. It wasn't easy, but he was so athletic that he made it look that way. The horse shifted. The animal was now carrying not only their combined body weight, but also a hundred and twenty pounds of gear. It was enough that the horse anchored itself on its four spindly legs to rebalance. Jess didn't know how the tough Afghan pony was able to carry them at all. But he had already, after all.

Earlier, while Jess had been sleeping, Logan had carefully run his hands down every leg of the horse to ensure he was still sound. The deep cut on one knee was obviously still bothering the horse but, apart from cleaning it and applying some antiseptic, there wasn't much else that Logan could do about it. He'd also cleaned out the frogs at the bottom of each hoof, picking out tiny stones or other debris that might cause the horse to go lame. Satisfied, he'd patted the stalwart gelding, tough as nails. The horse had gotten a good amount of food and water, too. And he'd been able to rest for twelve hours, often lying on the ground near the pool of water, dozing. He thought that all in all, the three of them were in the best possible shape they could be, under the harsh circumstances.

Logan took his rifle back, snapping its harness across his chest, slid his arm around Jess's waist, and took the reins. He clucked softly to the horse, and the animal walked out of the cave. Logan guided it to the left, around the escarpment. As they traversed the steep hill, he watched the land right in front of their laboring mount through his NVGs. If it tripped, they could go down in a heartbeat.

"Listen," he told Jess, near her ear, "if this horse goes down, I need you to tuck and roll. Can you do that for me?" He didn't want to scare her, but he also didn't want her not knowing what to do if it happened.

"Yes," she said in a low voice, "I've got it." Jess didn't want to sound scared or unsure. Logan needed her confident. He had enough to worry about. She didn't want to add to his load. Jess felt him give her a gentle squeeze and warmth fled through her. He was a hero in her eyes and heart. She knew she was a liability of the worse kind in a situation like this. She was never trained for escape and evasion. Logan had been. She was the weaker of the two of them strength-wise. But he knew what he was doing, and she had a fierce confidence in his knowledge. All the while, Jess fought the fear of something happening to Logan, of being spotted by the Hill soldiers or the Taliban. The wind roared by them and it was cold and cutting as they climbed higher and higher. Jess burrowed into the warmth of the *shemagh*, pulling it up across her nose so only a slit across her eyes went unprotected from the freezing, savage gusts.

Logan looked down at his watch. It was 0300. They'd been traveling nonstop at a lumbering walk across the rugged landscape for hours. At nine-thousand feet, there were ample trees to keep them from being spotted. The horse was tired, tripping regularly now, and he knew they had to halt and give the gelding a breather. He could feel Jess leaning against him, adapting fast to the mount's gait, though the tension never fully left her body. But she was warmer than before, and wasn't shivering, and that was good. Logan was comfortable, except that he could no longer feel the fingers of his now gloveless hands. They did not speak. Voices carried. For all he knew, there were Taliban nearby, hunkered down, sleeping. Their horses, however, would hear. And if they whinnied, it would alert the Taliban and they'd awaken and start firing their AK-47s indiscriminately into the blackness of the night, hoping to kill them.

The chances of any alerted Taliban actively chasing them were pretty much nil, and Logan knew it. They weren't going to risk running their horses over unknown terrain they couldn't see. They'd just scattershot the bullets, spray-and-pray. But Logan didn't want to risk even that. He saw a thick grove of woods ahead and pulled the horse to a stop. Sliding off, he helped Jess to the ground. The horse groaned. Logan patted its neck and handed the reins to Jess.

"I'm going to scout around. See if I can find some water for the horse. Stay here and don't leave this area."

Jess nodded. She could see around her with the moon full in the sky. The horse was sweaty, and she felt sorry for the gelding, patting him gently on one damp shoulder, speaking softly to him. Roughly, Jess figured the horse was carrying around four hundred- and seventy-pounds total. No wonder the poor animal was weary. She heard the wind blowing through the trees. But the *shemagh* was keeping her head, neck and shoulders protected. She wasn't shaking or shivering as before. Jess saw Logan melt out of the woods, M4 in hand.

He said near her ear, "There's a pool of water about two hundred feet down this hill. Come on...."

The horse plunged its muzzle into the water, gulping it noisily. Logan stood with Jess nearby. He pushed the NVGs up on the helmet rail. His ears were freezing, and he wished he'd thought to stash a second *shemagh* into his ruck. They were handwoven by Afghan women out of wool and were damned warm and protective. Sliding his arm around her, he brought Jess as close as he could, kissing her hair. He felt her arm come around his waist, squeezing him. Jess never complained.

Logan searched her eyes and saw love shining in them for him. He smiled down at her, thinking how beautiful she looked. There was so much he wanted to talk with her about. A future. The two of them. Even through this whole mess, the thought of finding the right time and place to have proper downtime together was an ongoing priority for him, a brightness at the end of this dark tunnel. Something to aim for. Logan refused to bend to the fact of the military always playing havoc on love and families. They were secondary to his mission. Somehow, he was going to make Jess the priority in his life. Logan didn't know how yet, but he'd figure out a workaround. This was the woman he wanted in his life forever. The only question left to answer was if Jess felt the same way about him. He'd said those three, irretrievable words, *I love you*, she hadn't. But he was going to hold out hope that Jess felt like he did and wanted something permanent and lasting between them.

After half an hour, they mounted up. Jess knew that the pass was nearby, above them. The stars glittered overhead, sometimes hidden by thick clouds rolling across the pass, hanging on the summits of the Hindu Kush. It was at those times, when the clouds embraced them, that she could feel Logan tensing. It was nothing obvious, but he pulled the horse down to a very slow walk, the clouds like thick fog; they couldn't see even a foot in front of them. And where the horse placed his feet, that was imperative to their safety. When the clouds descended around them, it made Jess shiver. Dampness surrounded them and everything became muffled.

They were heading down a steep hill, coming out of the woods, inching toward the pass that Logan could see a thousand feet up in front of them. The ground was now nothing but rocks with very little brush and trees. He was looking around, seeing if he could spot any movement, when the horse suddenly grunted.

In an instant, Logan felt the gelding's knees collapse, the one with the deep cut giving out first.

Jess was yanked forward. He gripped her waist hard, throwing her back up against him to stop her from tumbling over the animal's head.

Everything became a blur. Logan released the reins, grabbing Jess's shoulder as the horse fell hard. One moment they were on the horse, the next, they were tumbling through the air. He heard Jess give a cry. Damn! They were going to land on nothing but rocks! Logan twisted his body midair, hauling Jess up, above and in front of him.

And then Logan crashed into the rocks, his ruck taking the full, brutal impact. He grunted as Jess's weight slammed down upon him. Logan instantly released her after she hit the front of his body. He hoped she'd roll free, rather than have his bulk roll over on top of her. The impact was so hard that his head smashed secondarily into the rocks, momentarily stunning him, even through his Kevlar helmet. And then, Logan was thrown up, spinning, into the air again. He tucked, keeping his head bowed against his body, his hands and feet tight against himself. Hitting the rocks again, he heard the horse nearby, and hoped like hell its flailing legs wouldn't strike him. If they did, Logan knew a hoof in his face could kill him outright.

He bounced along, gritting his teeth every time he hit the unforgiving rocks. Finally, his ruck jammed between two larger rocks, stopping his rolling. Grunting softly, Logan blinked. He quickly assessed himself, feeling bruises, but nothing more. Jerking upward and to his feet, he frantically searched for Jess. She was up above him, slowly sitting up, holding her head. Below them, the horse lay sprawled out, unmoving. *Shit!*

Scrambling silently over the rocks, Logan reached Jess. He flipped the NVGs off his eyes, able to see her face in the moonlight. Her eyes looked cloudy with confusion, and she was holding her brow.

"Where are you hurt?" he asked, crouching in front of her, breathing hard.

"I hit my head," Jess muttered dully. "Are you all right?"

"Bruised is all. Hold still," he ordered, gently gripping her hand and easing it away from the side of her head. Logan saw a thin trickle of blood down the side of her jaw. "Look at me," he commanded. He knew the signs of brain injury. When Jess lifted her face to his, he anxiously scanned her eyes. Both pupils were equal size, and he breathed a sigh of relief. No head injury. "Any dizziness?"

She shook her head. "No… just a little rattled is all. Give me a minute?" She felt Logan's hands moving from her neck, across her shoulders and down her arms, swiftly examining her for any other injuries. Jess looked up and groaned.

"Our horse…."

"Yeah, probably broke a leg or his neck. I'll check on him next. Any other injuries?"

Jess shook her head. "I'm okay." She saw Logan give her a wry look.

"Now you sound like a SEAL."

Touching her scalp, Jess felt the blood. "We're sitting ducks out here on this rock slope, Logan."

Nodding, he got up, squeezed her shoulder and murmured, "Don't move. I'll be right back."

Jess watched him scramble effortlessly down the rocky slope. He knelt at the horse, who remained unmoving. She saw the grimness in Logan's features as he patted the animal's neck and rose. He had been right, the horse had broken its neck in the fall. She knew if Logan hadn't done what he had, she might not be alive right now, either. Her heart bled for the valiant horse.

Logan leaned down. "Broken neck. He didn't feel a thing. It's a good way to die."

Grimacing, Jess shook her head. "I feel so bad…"

"I know. So do I. He was a good horse. But there's nothing we can do but move on." Logan searched her sad face. "Do you feel like testing your legs? We need to get off this slope as soon as possible."

Nodding, she held out her hand and Logan gripped it, standing and drawing her upward. For a moment, she was dizzy, but then it passed. "Okay," Jess told him. "Just don't let go of my hand?"

Logan placed her hand on his belt. "This is even better. Just like before. I'll take it slow, but if it's still too fast for you, Jess, speak up?"

Nodding she swallowed hard, tears in her eyes. *The poor horse.* She gripped his belt and followed awkwardly, around rocks large and medium, and stumbling over small. Some were sharp, others rounded. Jess felt her heart thundering in her chest and she worried if someone was watching them. Logan had said a drone had been following their movement, but that it couldn't go over the summit of the mountains. Clear air turbulence, caused by the high mountains, would tear the drone apart. He'd said another drone from FOB Bravo would be put into place as soon as they were down off the pass. The only consolation Jess had was the fact that, as they got off the slope and Logan began a slow trot down a wide dirt path between the huge mountains, he was alert with rifle in hand.

Sometimes, dizziness would strike her, and she'd tug on Logan's belt, asking him to stop. Jess felt nakedly vulnerable out on the trail. There was nowhere to hide. The feeling was wretched, and she tried not to slow him down, but she knew she was doing precisely that. If Logan minded it, he never gave a hint. He would take her hand, slow his pace, pull her close, and they'd do a long, fast walk with one another, instead. At other times through the one-mile pass, he would stop, offer her the tube to his CamelBak and insist she drink water. Jess felt incredibly protected by Logan regardless of them being two stark shadows, walking the dirt path, that could be seen from any direction in the moonlight.

Finally, they blended back into the tree line and Logan guided her off the well-used path. Jess knew he was angling toward another cave that was somewhere around seventy-five hundred feet. Chris had given him its GPS coordinates. He was taking them deeper into the quiet, dark forest. Jess felt relieved to be hidden by the trees once more. She tried to calculate what kind of time it would take now that they were on foot. It would slow their pace down a lot. Four legs were always better than two.

Logan located the cave. It was mostly hidden by thick brush across the front of it. He went in, clearing it first, and then gestured for Jess to join him. It was near dawn, and she could just barely make out the oval interior of the cave. The ceiling was barely eight feet tall. Logan picked up her hand, guiding her to the rear of it. Off to the right, there was a tunnel. It was much smaller than the previous; a horse would never have gotten through. The tunnel was short and narrow, leading into another chamber about the same size as the first. Jess heard water dripping somewhere, and hoped there was a pool nearby. She was sweaty, dirty, and longed to get clean. Above, she saw a jagged zigzag opening in the ceiling. The clouds were coming across the area again and she saw no stars, only murky thick fog and grayness.

Leading Jess to the pool near a rock wall with water leaking down it, Logan urged her to rest. Shrugging out of his pack, he knelt next to it, opening the outer pocket to retrieve the sat phone. He scowled, pulling it out in two pieces.

"Oh, no," Jess whispered, her hand flying to her mouth. She stared in shock over at Logan's dark expression. "The sat phone... It's broken."

Mentally cursing, Logan looked over the unit, trying to determine if he could fix it. But quickly saw there was no chance. *Dammit!* Without the sat phone, he had no direct line of communication to Chris or anyone else. He'd heard the terror in Jess's voice. Shoving the useless phone back into the pocket, he searched the front of his H-gear, digging into the pocket where his

SEAL radio was kept. It too, had been smashed as he'd tumbled down the rocky slope. Logan remembered hitting the front of the gear across his chest on a huge rock during the fall from the horse.

Jess stared in disbelief as he held the shattered radio in the palm of his hand. They had no radio. *Nothing.* Suddenly, they were abandoned without technology to aid their escape. She gulped, feeling panic. Without a radio, no one knew where they were. Worse, would Chris and the CO at Bravo think they were dead? Captured by the Taliban? *Oh, God....*

CHAPTER 18

"WHAT ARE WE going to do?" Jess asked Logan in a low voice. She saw his mouth had tightened. Fear rose in her. With no radio, they were completely vulnerable.

Logan shook his head. "Do it the old fashion way," he told her wryly, looking at her, seeing the apprehension clear in her widening eyes.

"But what will Chris think?" Her voice was strained as Jess searched Logan's shadowed face.

Shrugging, Logan said, "He has options. He'll know my SEAL radio is out of radius, and he'll think the batteries in the sat phone died."

"And he won't think we've been captured?" Because that's what she would think.

"Probably not," Logan told her, opening the ruck and handing her an MRE. "Batteries fail out in the battlefield all the time. Also, there can be satellite issues, and interference with the signal. He'll check that angle to make sure." He saw the nervousness in her expression, understanding Jess was, once again, thrown into shock. It was adding up like layers on her. He could see the distress building in her face. Logan knew to keep things low key with Jess, act as if nothing had happened, and that they would be fine without a radio. They probably wouldn't be, but he wasn't going there with her.

Jess felt her stomach tightening. She didn't feel like eating but knew she had to keep up her strength. "How are you doing, Logan?" She saw his mouth twitch. Amazed at how calm he appeared after discovering the radios were broken, she didn't know what to think about his reaction. Maybe SEALs were used to this sort of thing, but she wasn't.

"Bruises and bumps," he told her mildly, sitting down opposite her with his own MRE.

"That was a horrible fall," she said, shaking her head. "I feel so sorry for that poor horse. He was so strong and steady for us." Tears jammed in her eyes and she swallowed several times, pushing her emotions deep down inside her once more.

"*We* survived it. That's the important thing," he replied gently, giving her a sympathetic look.

She ate and said nothing, her mind in a state of panic. "Do you know where we are?" Because she didn't.

"Yes. We've got forty miles to cover. It's ten miles to get off this mountain, twenty across that valley, and ten more miles to reach FOB Bravo."

"If Chris can't get in touch with you, what will he do?"

"He'll be in touch with the CO at Bravo and tell him we're no longer in sat phone contact. What Chris will hope is that, as we get closer to Bravo, we might run into a Marine squad on duty, looking for Taliban trying to sneak across the valley."

"But if that doesn't happen?"

"Then Chris may think the other radio is either destroyed or the batteries are dead in it."

"Or that we've been captured?"

He saw Jess thinking and felt her mounting panic. "But we aren't captured, Jess. And don't forget: Chris has drone eyes up there. He'll eventually have the drone operator fly this side of the mountain at a lower altitude where it can't be torn up by clear air turbulence. And he'll locate us with its infrared capability. He'll know something is wrong with the radios, but that we aren't captured." Logan reached out, squeezing her ankle. "It's okay to look at our situation realistically, but you're almost in panic mode over it. We aren't there, Jess. I need you to just keep the faith. I'll get us out of this."

Logan sounded so casual and confident! Jess felt chastised. "I guess it's my engineer brain," she confessed, shrugging. "My mind is set up to look at issues and, if there's a breakdown, how to fix it."

Logan grinned a little. "SEALs do the same thing. We call them workarounds. We're a creative group when it comes to thinking outside the box." He patted her ankle again, knowing his touch helped calm her. "Come on, I need you to eat and then we can get cleaned up."

"And then sleep?"

"Yes. Night travel only." Logan would hold Jess close. He could see her slowly unraveling beneath the stresses and demands stacking up on her. She wasn't trained to handle this kind of continued, massive stress. And anyone, outside a black-ops-trained person, would be feeling vulnerable and in danger right now. "The CO at Camp Bravo will be looking for us. They'll send out a Marine patrol, Jess. *Our* job is to make it across that valley. And we will."

JESS AWOKE SUDDENLY. She sat up, gasping. Groggy, not sure what time it was, she didn't see Logan anywhere. There was grayness though the ceiling tear above, and she looked at her watch. It was nearly sunset. She'd slept long and hard. Now, as she moved, she was stiff and sore. Looking around, she saw Logan had left his ruck. Where had he gone this time? Probably out scouting around again? She wiped her face, feeling scared. Her mind went to the darkest possible place. What if the Taliban had captured Logan, or...?

Just then, Logan appeared at the opening to the second cave chamber. Her heart leaped with relief. His face was glistening with sweat, his eyes intense and focused. When he saw her awake, she saw him drop his game face. He relaxed and shrugged his shoulders, as if rolling off the tension held in them.

Logan knelt next to Jess. He placed his M4 against the rock wall. "How are you doing?" he asked, grazing her hair. The strands were tangled, and he ached to slide his fingers through them and then make love to Jess. It wasn't going to happen, but Logan thought she looked beautiful despite the situation. He saw her green eyes were still drowsy with sleep. At least her eye on the side that had taken the punch from that Hill soldier days earlier, was open and the swelling almost gone. She must have just awakened.

"Better," Jess murmured, absorbing his brief touch. "Are you okay?"

He smiled a little. "Fine. I left about an hour ago and did some reconnoitering around the area."

"And?"

"No activity so far. It's quiet." He saw relief in her eyes. "Our objective for tonight is to reach that valley. That's ten miles. I figure thirty-minute miles, so we should easily make it."

Jess slowly stood up, moving her hands down her cammies, smoothing them out. "No Taliban?"

"They're around," he said, opening his ruck. He pulled out two MREs and set them on the sleeping bag. "We just have to move quiet and avoid them, is all."

She walked over to the dripping water and cupped her hands, splashing it on her face to wake up. Logan had hung a dark green towel on a nearby rock and she picked it up, wiping her face dry. Walking back, she sat down near him.

"I can't get over how calm you are about all of this," she admitted, taking the offered MRE from his hand.

"It's training, Jess. I've been at this for ten years now. It's like breathing to me at this point."

"Have you ever been in a situation like this before?" She opened the MRE, watching him.

"Where we've had dead radio batteries? Yeah, more times than I can count. Batteries are always our worst issue. Some guys forget to carry fresh spares. And sometimes, even when they do, they don't last or work for as long as we wanted." He smiled over at her, thinking Jess looked damn nice with her hair mussed. It was that wild child coming out in her again. "We have a mission with our OIC, officer in charge. Our master chief runs the mission, so even if we suddenly go out of radio contact, he's figuring it was due to the batteries."

"Not getting captured by the Taliban?"

"No, not that." Logan didn't want to tell her about a SEAL team who had been dropped into a Taliban hot spot. The radio had been working back at camp, but the one out in the field hadn't been. And, no matter what the comms SEAL did to try and get it to work, it wouldn't. It had left them vulnerable. The officer with the group had ended up having to use his personal cellphone and, luckily, he'd gotten through to HQ. Touch-and-go saves like that came through for teams all the time, and sometimes…they didn't. Logan couldn't go there with Jess, not with her this close to the edge. He had a cell phone on him but it wasn't even worth checking; the Camp Bravo area had no cell towers to even pick up a call. Jess had a terrier mind, he was discovering. Going over and over an issue, trying to come up with a fix, rather than accepting the reality of it and figuring a workaround, instead.

"Any extra thoughts on where your new orders will take you?" Logan asked, deciding to focus her on something more positive.

Jess hesitated. "I don't know. Still probably Port Hueneme, back to my old Naval battalion." She frowned. "I'm not sure what I'll do in the long run if we get out of this, Logan."

"Oh?" He saw Jess frown.

"I've gotten ten years into the Navy. I was hoping to make twenty."

"No reason you can't," he said, wanting to stay positive for her, pushing down his selfish desire for her to retire.

"I—I don't know now." Jess shrugged and gave him a look of consternation. "I've met you, Logan. I don't want to be sent half a world away from you. I wish… I wish we could have to some serious time together but," and she looked around the cave, "our lives are in chaos right now."

"Keep the faith, Babe." Logan finished off his MRE. "We'll get out of this, Jess. You'll find out what your orders say and we'll take it from there."

"It's a larger issue than that, Logan."

He saw the starkness in her gaze. "What else?" he probed.

"This… this whole incident, the kidnapping, is forcing me to look at everything."

His heart squeezed with trepidation. "Even us?" God, he hoped not. Jess's whole world had blown up in her face. And Logan knew she was roiling in shock. She'd had no time to absorb what had happened to her, or work out the emotions that came with it. Logan knew it screwed with people's thinking, that it distorted reality for them. When the corners of her mouth lifted, he felt less worried.

"No, you're the only constant in my life right now," Jess admitted, her voice emotional. "If anything, this experience forced me to admit what I already knew, Logan. That I loved you."

He tucked the MRE packets away in his ruck and moved over to her, their hips meeting. Reaching out, he eased his fingers through her hair, holding her gaze. "Hold on to that, Babe. I love you, too. We'll work this out. We'll get out of this. In a few days," Logan teased, "we'll be sitting and looking back on this experience and laugh about it."

"I don't know about laugh, but I know I'll be so glad it's over," Jess admitted, her scalp prickling with pleasure as he framed her face. She saw the narrowing of his eyes, the heat and desire in them, as he leaned forward, his mouth finding hers. For just a moment, Jess sank into a cauldron of heat, of wanting Logan so badly, despite their circumstances. His mouth was gentle, and she opened to him, wanting to taste Logan, feel his strength, feel how he cherished her. For just a moment, Jess languished in the heat of his kiss, his mouth slowly, deliciously, exploring hers.

As Logan reluctantly broke their kiss, he smiled into her softened green eyes. "That's what we have to look forward to, Jess. Just hold on to what we have...."

The wind was gusting as Jess held on to Logan's belt and they made their way down through the woods toward the valley floor. The valley was wide and almost completely flat. Through the branches of the trees, they silently walked in and around, she sometimes caught sight of the land far below. The air was cold, and she was grateful for the wool *shemagh* of hers that Logan had brought along. She wore his gloves, and worried about him being cold, but he told her not to bother herself about it.

They had walked for nearly an hour when they entered a craggy area where the trees thinned out. Rock outcroppings were everywhere. Jess had learned to walk differently, moving her boots parallel to the ground. That way, if the toe hit something, she could adjust, instead of stumbling. They came upon a narrow trail below a rock cliff. Logan hesitated. In the thin moonlight, Jess could see the trail curved around yet another huge boulder.

Suddenly, Logan swept his arm back, nearly taking her off her feet. Jess squelched a gasp, scrambling to crouch down behind the rocks.

Logan made a sharp hand signal for her to stay right where she was.

What was going on? Her adrenaline shot up. Tense, Jess gripped the rocks, somewhat protected by them. Logan crouched, his M4 up to his shoulder, the barrel pointed at the curve in the path.

Two men on horseback rode around it into view.

Jess wanted to scream. She saw they had NVGs on, and that they were armed Taliban. And, exposed as he was, they were going to see Logan! Her fingers dug into the roughened rocks. Everything started slowing down as a cry lurched into her throat.

The lead soldier was the first of the pair to spot Logan, lifting his AK-47 to fire at him.

Logan fired first, his M4 barking a single blast. The man cried out, flung out of his saddle, his AK-47 flipping up end over end into the air.

The second man fired.

The booming echo was massive. Jess hunkered down, bullets spraying past her. She saw Logan, unmoving, calmly aiming his M4 up at the soldier. He fired one shot.

A gasp tore from her as she saw the second man unseated, toppling off his horse.

Jess watched as Logan walked swiftly to the two, gun still trained on them, the nervous horses dancing around the motionless soldiers slumped on the dirt path. Seeing the two men unmoving, he quickly grabbed the animals' loose reins. Then, unholstering his SIG pistol, keeping it at the ready, he walked over to each soldier in turn. Gulping, Jess shakily stood up, her heart hammering wildly in her chest. She watched Logan carefully check each soldier. He signaled back to her that they were dead. Unsure of what to do, she remained where he'd gestured for her not to move from, her arms wrapped around herself. Clouds were sliding by again and hid the moon, making everything darker. Now, she could barely make out Logan leading the horses.

He walked back over to Jess. With his NVGs on, he could see her stark, frightened expression. "You all right?" he asked her quietly.

Jess gave a jerky nod. "They're… Dead?"

"Yes." Logan thrust the reins of the horses into her hands. "Our transportation. Wait here. I need to strip them of their outer clothing. We're going *hajii*. And I'm taking their NVGs and giving you a pair to wear." Jess watched as he did so, then saw him rolling the stripped bodies off the path toward the edge of a steep cliff a short way below it. It was gruesome work to Jess's eye, and she looked away, stomach tightening, to spare herself the sight of the men's bodies, white in the returning moonlight, tumbling from the cliff edge.

She could never do the work that Logan did. It made her appreciate him even more, realizing that, if they'd stepped around that corner unawares, the soldiers would have seen them first. They would have gotten the drop on them. And one, or maybe both, of them could have been captured, wounded, or killed. Jess swallowed against a dry throat, petting the tense horses. They were shaken by the gunfire just as much as she was.

Logan heard the men's bodies tumbling off the escarpment as they fell, before landing with twin thuds quite some distance below. He was sure that, within twenty-four hours, the bodies would be seen either by other Taliban soldiers or Afghans herding their sheep and goats through the area. He quickly went through the stripped clothes, looking for identification, maps or any other information they contained. Jess saw him tuck some papers into one of his cammie pockets. He then took up the dead men's hats, vests, trousers and shirts from the ground.

Logan returned to Jess, hands filled with clothes. "Watch what I do, Jess, and then I'll hold the horses and let you climb into the other set of clothes."

Within minutes, Logan transformed himself from looking like a SEAL into looking like an Afghan. He took the man's *shemagh* and pulled it over his helmet so it couldn't be seen and then wrapped it around his nose and lower face, covering them. If Jess didn't know better, Logan would totally pass as an Afghan to her eye. The pants were too short for him, his combat boots showing, but overall, and certainly from a distance, he no longer looked like an American soldier.

Logan took both sets of reins from her hand. He saw Jess's fingers tremble as she quietly pulled on the bulky brown trousers. Looking around, he worried about other Taliban on the trail tonight. These two had been riding alone, which was unusual. Normally, they traveled in groups. The clothes were expensive, compared to the type of clothing an Afghan farmer would wear. Maybe these two had been officers? Going somewhere to meet someone? Logan's mind spun with possibilities. Along with the papers, he'd found a radio in each soldier's clothes and had tucked them into another cammie pocket. Although he and Jess wouldn't be able to use them, the CIA would surely like to get their hands on them, because of the end-to-end encryption applications used by the modern Taliban. They could then turn them on and, hopefully listen in and pick up intel without the Taliban knowing they were in American hands.

Shortly, Jess was dressed. The clothes were warm and bulky on her. She pulled the man's rolled cap over her hair, not thinking too hard on where it had just come from, tucking her ponytail up under it. Logan told her to wrap the Taliban soldier's *shemagh* around her nose and lower face as he had, so she couldn't be identified as a woman. He knew what was going on in her mind: that she was wearing a dead man's clothes. It couldn't be helped. It was the best way to continue toward Bravo. Even through binoculars, Logan knew if

Taliban saw them, they could pass as brethren. That was a huge piece of luck that had just unexpectedly turned their way.

Jess mounted the bay horse, the wooden saddle feeling rough and awkward beneath her. Logan mounted the black horse and gestured for her to follow behind him. He'd used the leather rifle sheath on his horse to place his M4 in, taking the AK-47 and slinging it across his back. If the Taliban saw the M4, they would know they were Americans. Logan had placed the other AK-47 over across Jess's back, settling it into place the way a Taliban soldier would wear it. He'd taken the extra AK-47 ammo, and they split it between them. Extra firepower was always an advantage.

Logan had no idea where the trail led, but it was going down, the way they wanted to go, and that's all he cared about. Worried that the sound of gunfire would draw Taliban who were hunkered down for the night, he trotted the horse, wanting to put distance between the firefight zone and themselves. Overall, though, he considered the probability of Taliban mounting up to follow them as low. He'd given Jess the other pair of NVGs and, now, she could see as well as he did.

Jess rode tensely. She didn't really know how to steer the horse, except for the quick lessons Logan had given her. But the gelding seemed content to keep his nose near the lead horse's tail and just follow, and so she began to relax slightly. The wooden saddle she rode creaked. She'd placed as much as possible of the wool vest that hung to her knees beneath her butt to protect it from the uncomfortable saddle. Once in a while, her horse would stumble and it would rattle her, making her afraid the horse would go down like their other one had. But it didn't. It seemed to stumble a lot, though, which kept her nerves raw. Up ahead of her, Logan rode like a pro; slouched in the saddle, his hips moving with the sway of his Afghan pony. He looked like a Taliban soldier. She wasn't sure she did. There was some comfort in having the AK-47 against her back. Logan had briefly shown her how to use it, clicking the selector to semi-automatic in case she needed it. Jess had never used this type of weapon and hoped she didn't have to.

The wind was sharp and fierce as they rode down toward the valley. Logan knew thousand-year-old paths crisscrossed the slope, along with newly made rat lines. The rat lines had been created to carry fertilizer for bomb making material, as well as weapons, into Afghanistan. He couldn't tell the difference between the newer and older trails. Logan knew that the rat lines were active at night. This smuggling branch of the Taliban usually carried the supplies in on donkeys and double-humped Bactrian camels under cover of darkness, hoping to avoid detection. Even then, if a drone were around, Apache's, or even B-52s or jets, would be called in to destroy them.

As he rode, he wondered if there was a drone above them or not. They had been at a high altitude and the possibility that there wasn't one, was real. Logan's mind moved over their situation. The drone might be brought in at around five thousand feet, and he and Jess were still heading down to that altitude, probably currently at around seven thousand feet. When the drone came online, all Chris might see, if it were still nighttime, was two Taliban soldiers on horses. Unless Chris looked very closely at them, that is. The cameras on the drone were good, and Logan hoped Chris caught sight of his American combat boots. If he did, he'd know that they were alive, not captured. And that they'd gone *hajii* to avoid detection by the enemy. But all that was conjecture. He didn't want to tell Jess that Chris might also assume they'd been captured by the Taliban. They'd still look for them but wouldn't find anything. It left them in a vacuum of sorts, and Logan kept that info to himself. By riding *hajii*, it meant US forces would see them as the enemy. Logan knew he was dancing them on the edge of a sword that could cut them either way, but he had no choice, not without constant backup intel from Chris. And that was impossible, now, leaving them open to attack from either side.

Halting an hour later, Logan checked his watch. It was now close to 0300. The clouds were drifting across the slope, causing fog-like conditions once again. This time, however, the dampness was deflected by the thick, warm wool clothing they wore. He gestured to Jess to ride up beside him where he halted at the crossroads of three different paths. Standing up in the saddle, he rubbed his butt.

Jess kicked her horse, and it reluctantly moved up alongside Logan's. She followed suit and stood in the stirrups, rubbing her aching butt, too.

"Couldn't we get rid of these awful saddles?" she complained.

"No. Part of the camouflage," Logan told her, sitting back down after pulling as much cloth beneath his butt as he could. "Taliban don't ride bareback. We'd be spotted in a heartbeat."

Grumpily, Jess muttered, "I can't believe it. My butt is numb!" She heard him chuckle.

"Yeah, well, American asses aren't like Afghan ones. We're wider and bigger."

Snorting, Jess managed a sour grin. "How far do you think we've come?"

Logan looked around. He didn't like being even slightly exposed like this, but at least they were in decent enough rock cover here, even with the trees thinned out and far between. "About seven miles. We're making good progress. How are you holding up?"

Jess shrugged. "Okay."

"This will probably make you never want to ride a horse again," and his smile widened.

"Got that right," and Jess shared the smile with him. He looked like a knight on his steed, sitting straight and tall, shoulders thrown back, as if he owned this land. It was that amazing SEAL confidence.

Logan gestured to the paths' intersection. "I'm taking the path that goes down. I want to reach the valley floor before dawn. We should make it easily, but we need to look for a cave somewhere down there as well. Any port in a storm."

Frowning, Jess nodded. Chris was no longer available to give them terrain information.

Logan urged his horse down the path. Jess's horse obediently followed.

She saw the slopes ahead were absolutely cleared of brush and trees. Only rocks stuck out here and there. She worried that any Taliban nearby would spot them. Logan was constantly looking around. She did too, but she didn't know what to look for, except a human or horse in plain, obvious sight, and that was unlikely, she knew.

In another hour, Jess saw the path becoming less steep, more level. She saw patchworks of fields, bordered by two- or three-foot-high rock walls to demarcate each owner's land. Logan turned to the right, taking another path that led toward a rare grove of trees in the distance. The mountains were now clothed in clouds, their peaks hidden. The wind was less in the valley. She spotted a massive outcrop of rocks jutting out, reminding her of a huge ship's bow. Logan slowed down and guided his horse up toward it.

In a few minutes, Jess saw why. There was a series of caves along one side of it. She watched Logan halt his horse and dismount. He pulled the M4 from the horse's rifle sheath and unsafed it. Bringing the reins of his horse to her, he said, "Stay here. I have to clear this cave. I'll be right back."

Nodding, Jess gripped the animal's reins, watching him trot silently up around the rocks and then disappear from sight. Through hard-won experience, she knew firsthand how often the Taliban used caves at night. What would happen if Logan ran into a group sleeping in one?

CHAPTER 19

J ESS TENSED AS Logan silently came back. He halted at her horse.
"Taliban in the caves."

Her heart slammed with fear. She felt Logan's hand grip her thigh a little more, as if to reassure her.

"We ride. Follow me."

The sky was lightening by the minute as they left the grove. Logan found a path continuing down from the fields and dry, yellow hills above. They couldn't talk, and she rode drenched in terror. What if the Taliban woke up and saw them? They were now trotting their horses and, as the light got better, they would be easily spotted. Her heart pounded relentlessly in her chest.

Logan continued to keep watch as he pushed his horse to remain at a steady trot. The animals had had no water. He knew they were tiring. Now, they were in the gauntlet between the Marines he knew patrolled the valley below Bravo, sitting high on the opposite side, and the Taliban behind them. He saw farmers starting to come out to their fields with their implements here and there. Any of them could be Taliban sympathizers. They could well have a radio on them and call in to the enemy. He felt adrenaline continually leaking into his bloodstream as he rode.

Up ahead, Logan saw a road that was used by all vehicles, including military ones. How many IEDs had been planted last night along it? Taliban sympathizers did their work after dark, hoping an American Humvee would roll over it the next day. Logan opted not to use the road unless he had to. His horse could step on one of those unseen IEDs and they'd die in an instant. Better to use a footpath along the fields, instead, because that is where the farmers walked, and they would be loath to blow up one of their neighbors. Glancing over his shoulder, he saw Jess keeping up. She was learning to ride the horse, whether she wanted to or not, and a fierce love for her welled up in his chest. She had grit.

They rode for nearly fifteen miles, getting close to the halfway point of the valley, when Logan spotted a pool of water off to the side of the path. He brought his horse to a stop and loosened its reins so the animal could drink.

Jess rode up and did the same thing. They sat together, their legs touching one another, as their horses eagerly gulped down the water.

He could only see her eyes through the drawn-up *shemagh*. "How are you doing?"

"Okay," Jess said. "Scared. My butt's never going to be the same again." She saw Logan nod, his eyes crinkling, indicating he was smiling beneath the *shemagh* wrapped around his own lower face. "How far to go?"

"See that dirt road off to our left?"

"Yes."

"That's the main road through the valley. The Marines would use it with their Humvees and trucks when they patrol this area. It's probably got IEDs planted on it."

"And we're staying on this path?"

Nodding, Logan respected her intelligence. Jess very quickly caught on to any situation. "Right. We have another five miles to go and then we can start climbing the hills you see ahead. Camp Bravo is on the other side of them, sitting at eighty-five hundred feet up the mountains."

"Will there be a Marine patrol through here?" Jess asked, rubbing her numb butt.

"Don't know." Logan scowled. "Once we make it to the hills, we're going to get rid of our Afghan disguises."

"Because the Marines might mistake us as Taliban?"

"Yeah."

Jess looked up at the cloudy sky, the sun already riding high, somewhere above. It looked like it might rain. She saw a wide scattering of many men and younger boys out in the fields, tending the rows of crops. Sometimes, they would look up and watch them. It always sent terror through her. Her and Logan both drank deeply. Her now-familiar problem was back, stomach knotted so tight she didn't want to eat. Logan casually ate a protein bar. They were getting close to being safe. Inwardly, Jess wanted nothing more than to just be with Logan, out of danger, and not constantly worried about being attacked by the Taliban.

"Let's go," Logan told her, stuffing the bar's wrapper in his pocket. He wanted to reach out, touch her, but, with the eyes of Afghan farmers on them, he didn't want to raise suspicion.

Jess had learned how to ride at a trot by watching Logan. They trotted the horses along the path. Every mile that went by made the tension wind tighter within her. Sometimes, she would look over her shoulder to see if they were being followed. So far, so good.

Logan took a path that led up between two brown, rocky hills. Jess began to breathe a little sigh of relief as the horses, sweaty and tiring, moved through the notch between them. Logan veered to the right, off the path and pulled to a halt. She rode up to him. He was looking around, and then dismounted.

"Climb down," he told her. "We're getting rid of our *hajii* gear."

Jess was grateful when Logan walked around her horse, offering his hand to help her dismount. She groaned softly, never so stiff and sore. Logan squeezed her hand and released it once she had both feet on the ground.

"Okay, let's get rid of these in a hurry."

Jess quickly shucked out of the clothes. Logan gathered them up and threw them behind some rocks so they wouldn't easily be discovered.

"Give me your AK."

"Okay... Why?"

He smiled a little. "I don't want anything on us that might create suspicion or confusion with the Marines at Bravo. We're only five miles from the FOB."

The sun peeked out for a moment between the gray, low-hanging clouds. The wind was inconstant. And the temperature had rapidly climbed from below freezing to around eighty degrees Fahrenheit in the valley. Jess nodded and hauled the AK-47 off her back and handed it to Logan. He placed it behind the rocks with the clothing. He came back and hauled his M4 out of the leather sheath on his horse's flank, clipping it back on its harness across his chest.

Logan walked around her horse and slid his hand along Jess's jaw, looking deeply into her eyes. "We're almost home, Jess. Hang in there with me?"

She closed her eyes for a moment, savoring this unexpected moment of Logan's care. His hand was roughened with callouses. She gave a jerking nod, her throat dry. When his mouth slid against hers, she moaned, stepping closer to him, kissing him with everything she had. Feeling Logan go tense against her as she leaned into his strong, tall body, only enflamed her need of him. His mouth was gentle, and she craved his closeness. Gradually, Logan eased from her mouth, and she opened her eyes, drowning in his hooded gaze.

"I love you," he rasped, his thumb moving across her cheek, her skin soft velvet beneath it. "I'll get you home, Jess..."

They mounted up. Jess felt less encumbered without the heavy wool clothing she'd been sweating in for hours. Logan told her to put her own baseball cap on, as he settled his black one on his head. He slid on his wraparound sunglasses, and then gestured for her to follow him up a narrow trail that would take them higher. The horses labored, stumbling and tired. When the forward operating base came into view, Jess almost cried with relief. It sat on a flat-topped mountain, looking like a huge castle surrounded by concertina wire. She could see the road that led up to the gate. Logan kicked his horse into a trot and the animal sluggishly responded.

As they rode up, Jess saw two Marines with M-16s manning the gate. Logan dismounted and so did she. Her heart was hammering again, but this time with relief. She stood by him as he explained to the guards who they were. Instantly, the gate was opened, and they were allowed into the heavily guarded facility.

Logan was met by SEAL Chief Evans, head of Charlie Platoon. This had been his home off and on over the years and never had it looked this good to him. There was a large SEAL contingent at the CIA base. Another SEAL, one Logan didn't know, came and took their horses from them. They would be well cared for, watered, fed some grain and as much dried grass as they wanted to eat. Logan shook Evans's hand.

"Welcome home," Evans said, nodding toward Jess. "We got worried about you two."

Logan nodded. He placed his hand around Jess's arm and brought her forward. "Our horse fell and broke his neck. My sat phone as well as my radio were broken." Evans was six foot tall, his face darkly tanned, wearing cammies and a black baseball cap.

"We figured something happened. Most likely dead batteries, but we're glad to have you back, Logan. Helluva welcome home, eh?" and he gave him a lopsided grin.

"Can you call my partner, Chris? Let him know we're safe?" Logan asked as he followed the chief back toward their SEAL compound.

"Yes, I'll get on it. Are you two hungry? Need a shower?"

Logan grinned. "Yes, to both." It was good to be home with his SEAL friends at this compound, and he looked fondly at the one-story, gray-block building. It had no windows. They walked through its entry door and into a hall.

Evans stopped in the passageway. He pointed to a nameplate up above a doorway.

"Ma'am?" he said, "This is Sarah's room. She was an Army medevac pilot who was stationed here a while back. Married one of our SEALs in this building. The guys built this room for her so she could be with us, instead of the doggy Army," and he grinned. "It's comfy. You take it? I'll get one of our SEALs to rustle you up a towel, washcloth and soap. Someone will escort you to the FOB's women's shower unit area in a bit."

Jess nodded, more than grateful. "Thank you, Chief."

"Randall, you come with me to my office," the Chief ordered.

Jess saw Logan give him a nod. An irrational fear hit her vulnerable mind: *was he suddenly going to walk out of her life again?* He must have seen the look on her face.

"I'll be right back," Logan reassured her.

Inside Sarah's room was a twin bed, and the air conditioning was on, both seeming heavenly to Jess. A shower would complete the perfection. She turned slowly around as she entered and saw a small desk and chair, as well as another chair to sit in and relax. The room was a pale pink and there was a dresser with a mirror as well. Stumbling over her own boots, Jess grimaced, feeling the grit of the desert's ever-intrusive sand chaffing against her sensitive skin beneath her cammies. There was a knock on the door, and she turned.

A SEAL with black hair and brown eyes smiled and handed her the towel and other promised items for her shower. She thanked him.

Logan came back and retrieved her twenty minutes later. Jess walked with him toward some two-story blockhouses that comprised the shower area. She heard the whine of Apache helicopters spooling up for takeoff at the busy airport within the massive, busy FOB. This was a large place. She saw row upon row of desert-colored tents. It was a veritable city; needed to be to house the one-thousand-odd black ops personnel that manned it.

"How are you holding up?" Logan asked, keeping his stride short for her sake. Jess looked exhausted. He walked close to her but didn't touch her. They were behind the wire, and both were as aware as always of the military's hard stance on fraternization.

"Like I'm stuck in peanut butter," she admitted, casting him a wry glance.

Logan stopped at the showers. "Maybe some good, hot food will help, after we take our showers." He drowned in her shadowed green eyes. How brave and courageous Jess had been. "I asked the chief to put a call in through channels to your parents so they would know you're safe, now."

Relief surged through her. "Thanks, I'm sure they're dying of worry."

Nodding, Logan said, "We're going to get showered first, eat at our main chow hall, and then we're taking a late-evening CH-47 transport jet flight back to Bagram. Chris said that LT Parker was going to have your orders sent over there."

Her heart crashed. "I won't get to see my team? To say goodbye to them, first?"

Hearing the raw emotion in her voice, Logan said gently, "No. They can't risk it, Jess. You're a wanted woman by the Taliban. If you showed up at that village again, Khogani could be lying in wait." He saw tears come to her eyes, saw her fight them back. "I'm sorry."

Swallowing hard, Jess whispered, "No... I understand."

"Look, get cleaned up," Logan urged. "I'll meet you here in thirty minutes and then take you over to the chow hall to eat."

JESS SAT WITH Logan in the busy chow hall. It was early evening and there were about fifty people eating. Most of them, she assumed, were going on duty shortly. She saw some women in desert-colored flight suits sitting together, Apache pilots, Logan had told her. She'd learned there was an Apache squadron here, as well as a medevac squadron. Logan had chosen the last table, sitting with his back to the wall. Sitting opposite him, she hungrily ate fried chicken, peas and mashed potatoes with gravy. Food had never tasted so good. Logan had piled his own aluminum tray with so much chow that Jess didn't see how he was going to eat all of it. A number of Logan's SEAL friends came up to welcome him back, but they didn't stay long, allowing him some precious time with Jess.

"What now?" Jess asked between bites. Logan was clean, his short hair still damp from his recent shower. He hadn't shaved, and it gave him a dark, lethal look.

Logan heard the trepidation in Jess's voice. "For us?"

She nodded. "Yes."

"I'll be going back to the village where you were working because that was an ordered assignment, whether you are there or not. I was on the sat phone with Chris earlier and he said our orders hadn't changed. I filled him in with what the master chief told me that we're to stay until the well-drilling unit permanently left the area. Then I'll be coming back with Chris to Bravo for the duration of our time here." He saw the grief in Jess's eyes. "Remember when we met at Landstuhl?"

"I'll never forget it," she whispered, forcing herself to eat. For all Jess knew, she was going to lose Logan, *all over again*, tonight when they arrived at Bagram air base. "Why?"

"Hold on to that meeting, Babe." Logan searched her exhausted features, knowing she needed a good night's sleep. "I've got two more months before my platoon returns to Coronado. Then, I'll be home for eighteen months on U.S. soil." His voice lowered. "And, providing you're Stateside, I want to spend my sixty days of leave with you."

That sounded so good to Jess. She saw the burning quality in Logan's eyes. The love she felt for him nearly overwhelmed her. "I want the same thing. But I don't know about my orders, where they'll send me. I could be another foreign country…"

"Let's take it a step at a time," Logan soothed. He could see her getting anxious; he knew Jess hated not knowing. She was an orderly person and did best when she knew the lay of the land. Unlike SEALs, who worked in chaos all the time. There was no regime or rhythm to their lives and they dealt with it. Jess did not. In that way, they were exact opposites.

"I lease a condo on Coronado Island from a SEAL," Logan told her. "It's a good place to be, Jess."

"And my parents live in San Diego, right across the bay from the island," she agreed, sipping the hot coffee, relishing it.

Logan gave her a warm look. "Then, you have to come home if you get orders stateside, Babe. I'll be there and so will your parents."

"You could meet them, Logan."

Nodding, he said, "I want to."

Despite all the reassuring talk, Jess felt her world collapsing in on her. She needed to cry. She needed to be alone with Logan. He must have read her expression because he cocked his head, giving her a dark look.

"We'll stay in the conjugal unit at Bagram, like we did before."

Rolling her eyes, she said, "Two times in a row? Aren't you pushing your luck?"

He grinned. "Nope. Wait and see…. Tonight," and his voice grew rough with promise, "we'll be together."

By the time the CH-47 landed at Bagram, it was close to ten p.m. Jess had gotten a few hours' sleep in Sarah's room at the SEAL compound on Bravo. The nurse at the dispensary at the base had cleaned her wound, changed the bandages, and said there was no infection. That was good news. Surprisingly, her arm wasn't as achy as it had been, and the nurse had told her the muscle was rebuilding what was lost by the bullet wound, and Jess was relieved. As they walked down the plane's ramp into the dark of the night, she felt Logan grip her hand. She couldn't see anything. Again, he was the one wearing the NVGs. Logan guided her into Ops and out the doors to an awaiting Humvee. He gave the driver the address of where he wanted them to be dropped off. As Jess sat in the back of the Humvee, she was too tired to even look around. It seemed all the shock was still rolling through her and she felt beyond exhaustion. More than anything, Jess wanted to sleep in Logan's arms.

When they pulled up to the three-story building, Logan led her up the now-familiar steps. Inside, he gave the clerk, the same one as before, the set of orders. In no time, Logan had the key and led Jess to the elevator at the rear of the building. Once inside it, he slipped his arm around her, giving her a gentle squeeze.

"Almost there," he told her, kissing her temple.

"Did you lie to the person on the desk, again?"

He grinned. "Not this time. Master Chief Evans made a phone call for us," was all Logan would tell her. "He knows we're in a relationship."

Gasping, she whispered, "You told him?"

Grinning, Logan said, "Master Chief's run the universe. They are mind readers, and they have a sixth sense like a wolf. He figured it out and I told him that we were serious with one another."

Eyes widening, she gulped and whispered, "And you won't be in trouble?"

"Nah," he said, his smile widening. They stepped out into the highly waxed hall, and he led her down to their room and opened the door. "Go in," he invited, barely able to keep from smiling more broadly. Master Chiefs ruled the SEAL universe. And Evans had done him a big favor. SEALs stuck together.

Jess walked in, unable to still her surprise. The room was *huge*, with not only a king-sized bed, a dresser and sofa, but an even larger bathroom! The door closed behind her. She turned on her boot heel and stared up at Logan. He looked like a little boy who had been caught with his hand in the cookie jar.

"I'm not even going to ask how your Master Chief, managed this."

"Naw, it wouldn't do any good, Jess. That's top-secret intel." Logan walked over, settling his hands on her shoulders. "Your orders will be sent over here, and you can pick them up tomorrow morning at the clerk's desk downstairs. Until then, you and I have this place, and each other." He looked around. "Not bad. I've never been in this section of the conjugal unit before, but I've heard some other unmarried SEALs say it rocked. And it does."

Jess shook her head. "You guys are impossible," and she added a slight smile.

"Does that shower look good to you?" Logan saw that there was a clean set of cammies for Jess laying on top of the dresser. And a set for him, as well. The Master Chief planned every detail to perfection.

"Yes," she uttered.

"You're about ready to collapse," Logan said, kissing her hair. "I think, right now, you need a shower and then bed."

"I'll be with *you* in that bed," she murmured, looking longingly over at him. "That's all I want."

He guided her to the bathroom. "Go get clean. I'll be next."

CHAPTER 20

THE NEXT MORNING, Logan brought up coffee and rolls to the conjugal unit at Bagram from below, along with the orders Jess had been anxiously waiting for. He had climbed into his cammies and work shirt, and pulled on his combat boots, before going downstairs. Jess was dressed in a white terrycloth robe, sitting on the bed she'd made in his brief absence. She was still drowsy looking, and Logan felt his heart expand with love for her. He suddenly and powerfully wanted her, but he stilled his own needs, seeing the clear anxiety in Jess's green eyes. Right now, her life was up in the air. She didn't know where she was going to land.

"Figured some coffee might help," he offered, placing the tray down on the bed. He pulled the orders out of his pocket and handed them to Jess.

"Thanks," she whispered, taking them. "And thanks for the coffee and rolls." His thoughtfulness touched her deeply. Logan nodded and sat down on the edge of the mattress, picking up his paper cup filled with steaming coffee. Her heart was beating hard in her chest. And it didn't help that her fingers trembled as she opened the envelope.

Logan watched Jess's face carefully as he sipped his coffee while she read her orders. He watched her fine black brows knit. "CONUS?" he asked. That meant orders back to the United States.

"Yes," and she shrugged, handing them to him. "They're reassigning me as an instructor at the school. Port Hueneme, Oxnard, California."

Rapidly scanning the papers, Logan felt immense relief. He glanced up at her. "Unhappy about it?"

"Only because I can't say goodbye to my crew I've known for five years. We've dug a lot of wells together." Her voice softened. "We've helped a lot of people."

Logan sat the orders down on the bed and handed Jess her coffee. "Come on, drink up."

Rallying, Jess nodded, their fingertips touching. She felt warmth flood her hand and she drowned in his alert gaze. "How do you feel about it then?" What Logan thought was important to her. She saw him hitch a shoulder.

"You're safe, Jess. That's all I care about." He saw her stare down at her coffee cup. Logan knew it was a bitter pill for her to swallow. He tried putting himself in her place. What if he'd been ripped unceremoniously out of his platoon, never to return to the same brothers he'd fought with for so many years? It would be gut wrenching, tearing him out of the fabric of a life he'd known for nearly a decade. Reaching out, he trailed his fingers down her lower arm. "One good thing about it?"

Jess swallowed. She heard the grit in Logan's voice and looked up into his caring blue eyes. "What?"

"When I get back to Coronado, it's only a three-hour drive between us. You're stationed above Los Angeles and I'm in San Diego. That's close." He saw her regroup a bit.

"I hadn't thought about that," Jess admitted. "But that's nice to know." For many reasons.

She looked so damned sad. Logan took the coffee cup from her hand and got off the bed. He picked up the tray and set it on the dresser. The suffering in Jess's eyes tore at him. It was going to take weeks, maybe months, for her to work through everything that had happened to her. Climbing back on the bed, he punched up some pillows and placed them up against the headboard, settling his back against them.

Holding out his hand, he said, "Come here?"

Jess pulled up the ends of her robe and moved up beside Logan. The moment his arm went around her, hauling her against him, she nestled her head against his neck and jaw. Pulling up her knees, the robe slipped off, revealing her bruised thigh. Logan gently brought the robe across it once more. Right now, Jess just wanted to be held. Closing her eyes, she sighed and slid an arm around his waist.

"You've been through a lot," Logan told her quietly, caressing her hair. "And it's going to take a while for you to sort it all out, Jess."

"I feel like I'm in freefall."

"Yes," Logan murmured, hearing the strain in her husky voice. "You are. It's not a pleasant place to be."

Jess slid her hand across his work shirt, feeling his muscles respond to her grazing touch. "I need to quit sulking and get on with it."

Laughing quietly, Logan gazed down at her, amusement in his voice. "I've never seen you sulk, Jess. You aren't the type, Babe. Sorry, but you're just not a prima donna or a high-maintenance kind of woman." She was a woman of the earth; sensual, real and hot-blooded.

She felt bathed in the sunlight in Logan's voice and smile, seeing merriment dancing in his eyes. "Instead of bitching about it, I should be grateful I survived the kidnapping. I really need to get my priorities straight. We could have died out there."

"Well," Logan hedged, "in all fairness to you, Jess, you got hit with a lot, one major event right after the other. You're reeling emotionally, and that's normal. I'm just glad we can talk about it and that I can hold you."

Closing her eyes, Jess wondered how many men would be this sensitive to her predicament, much less understand the pressures upon her. Her ex-husband certainly would not have. She could feel the slow, heavy beat of Logan's heart beneath her palm. "I don't want to lose you, Logan. I just found you. I know we're both probably feeling extruded through a straw right now." Jess heard and felt him chuckle.

"That's putting it mildly, but I'm not fazed, Jess. And I promise, I'll be very careful the two months remaining on my deployment. I want to be three short hours away from you," and he kissed her hairline.

"Will we be able to stay in touch?" and she pulled back enough to look up into his eyes. "You're black ops. Do you disappear?" His boyish smile made her feel better.

"I'll give you my platoon email address. Sometimes, when I'm lucky, I can get on Zoom. But that won't be often. Emails are probably going to be it mostly."

"When do you have to leave, Logan?" Jess pulled out of his arms, sitting up, crossing her legs and pulling the robe over them.

"I have a flight to catch at 1300, one p.m." He saw sadness come to her eyes. He felt equally glum. Reaching out, he took her hand. "I wish we had more time, but the military isn't interested in our personal lives, or even approving of them. Except for in the Master Chief's universe. He understands human nature and that we are in a serious relationship with one another."

"He's been very kind toward us," she agreed quietly. "You SEALs really *do* have your own universe, and it doesn't necessarily jibe with the one I have to live in."

He nodded and frowned. "When do you have to depart Bagram?"

"I have orders to leave at 1400 today. We'll be going different ways." She had to catch a C-5 flight from Bagram to Rota, Spain. Then roughly forty-eight hours of flying on different military transports to finally land at Point Magu, the Naval Air Station attached to Port Hueneme on the Southern California West Coast.

"Do you think you can get some leave when I get back to Coronado?" Logan knew SEALs were the only ones to get sixty days after deployment to be with their families. They were gone so much that this chunk of time was the important glue that held families together. The military usually only gave out thirty-day leaves. He searched her eyes.

"Yes, I'll make it happen."

"You can spend your thirty days with me at my condo."

That sounded wonderful. "And if I did that, you could meet my parents."

"They have to be special people to have you as a daughter," he said, meaning it. Logan saw a faint blush come to her cheeks. He liked that Jess was easily readable. She never tried to hide who she was or how she felt.

"Once I get back to my battalion," she said, "I'll put in for leave for that timeframe, first thing."

"Good, because I intend to spend a lot of time alone with you. And not just in bed."

She felt him teasing her, trying to make her feel better. "Bed sounds awfully good, too. But I'll be happy no matter where we are, Logan. I just want the time to be around you, kick back, relax, go do silly things together."

"Would you like to learn how to scuba dive?" he hinted broadly, moving his fingers down her arm.

She felt the darkness leaving, felt a shift that she couldn't explain, but it moved her out of her depression. "I'd like that. I've always loved the water. My folks are the same. That's why they wanted to settle in San Diego. To be near the ocean."

"How about... roasting hot dogs and marshmallows out on the beach?"

"Mmmm, now I can really sink my teeth into that one."

He chuckled. "Take you to The Prado Restaurant over in Balboa Park some evening? They have great food and even better wine."

"I love Balboa Park," she sighed.

"Then, we'll pack a picnic basket, a blanket, and go over to the park, sit under one of those big, white-barked Eucalyptus trees, and eat."

Jess gazed up at him, feeling a strong flow of happiness chasing away her glum outlook. "I think thirty days is a gift we've earned with one another, no matter what we do or don't do."

Logan smiled into her green eyes, seeing the flecks of gold in their depths shining with especially intense love and life right now. Her hair was soft and shining, blue highlights layered. "Tell you what. You put together your wish list of San Diego things you like to do and email it to me. We'll build an itinerary from it, with a decent amount of do-nothing-much time built in?"

Jess felt endlessly grateful for his support and insight. She knew what Logan was trying to do. Trying to lift her spirits, get her to have something to look forward to. With him. She squeezed him and murmured, "I'd love to do that...."

So many emotions welled up through Jess as she kissed Logan goodbye.

They did so in the privacy of their room, away from the prying eyes of the military. Jess felt complete trust, an almost sacred sense of refuge. As never before, she *knew* what Logan did as a SEAL. She'd been a part of his world. His ingenuity, alertness and intelligence, as well as his vast experience in hostile territories, had gotten them safely through. As they ended their kiss, Logan studied her in the silence.

"You're not going to worry, are you?" he teased, caressing her cheek, seeing the anxiety in her green eyes.

"No, I won't." It was an outright lie. "I want you focused on your work, not worrying about me worrying about you." Jess saw a wry grin tugging at his mouth. A mouth she'd never get tired of kissing.

"Sure?"

"Hundred percent sure."

"And I'm not going to have to worry about you, Babe. You'll be safe and sound in Oxnard."

Nodding, Jess put on her game face and voice. As a leader and manager of people, she knew how to do it. "I will be boringly safe."

"Not looking forward to being an instructor?" Logan knew by now that Jess liked getting her hands into the soil, being outdoors, and savoring every minute of it. She'd never be an indoor, or office pogue, kind of person. Of course, he was built the same way. Logan could never see himself in a button-down, nine-to-five job, either. He smoothed her hair, watching her eyes change, knowing she was absorbing every touch he gave her.

"Not really." Jess frowned and said, "I've got a lot of decisions to make, Logan. More than anything, I want us together as much as we can manage it."

His grin increased. "Send me your end of the to-do list? I'll put mine together, too. They're going to be a lot of adventure, maybe laughter, and comparing." It would give him more information about Jess and that was important to Logan. He saw her eyes dance with happiness.

"I promise, I will. It's something to look forward to." She saw his grin dissolve and sensed a serious change in him.

"Look," Logan said, his voice thick with emotion, "there's one more thing we need to discuss, Jess." He drew his thumb against her flushed cheek, skin like satin. "And I need to tell you about this. I'm going to change the status in my personnel jacket to being engaged to you. I want to put your name down as the first person to be contacted in case I'm injured or dead."

Her heart plummeted over the word 'dead'. Jess knew, all too well now, how dangerous a life Logan led. She saw him struggling with a lot of unspoken feelings as he gently smoothed his hands across her shoulders.

"All right," she whispered, understanding as never before how deeply he loved her. So much had happened in such a compressed time, but their hearts knew their connection to one another was solid.

"I don't think anything is going to happen to me," he added quickly. "I just don't want you outside the loop, is all. As it stands, my parents in Wyoming would be contacted, but I want you on that priority list, too." Logan searched her eyes, seeing the fear deep in them. Seeing Jess wrestling with it. "It's my commitment to you," he said. "We might not have a lot of time on our side knowing one another yet, Jess, but I can't imagine my life without you in it." He saw tears form and then she swallowed a couple of times. "I never expected to fall in love," Logan admitted. "You just slammed into my life in the most unexpected and wonderful of ways, Jess."

"I wasn't looking for anyone either," she admitted. Reaching up, she drew a few short, stray strands of his dark hair off his brow. Logan looked so damned confident and sure of himself. Little rocked his world, but Jess realized that *she had*, and it made her heart expand with even more love for him. He had the courage to tell her and that meant everything to her. "I guess I was always pulling my punch with you, Logan. I felt like we collided into one another and something... magic maybe... just took ahold of both of us. Being with you in Landstuhl was... well... wonderful. I've never felt more alive. Happier. Despite the reason I was there... losing Dan." She searched his expression, seeing how much her emotional words were impacting Logan. The corners of his mouth were drawn in, his hands a little firmer around her shoulders, as if he didn't want to let her go. Jess didn't want to let him go, either.

"Same here." Logan held her luminous gaze, wanting to always remember her unique fragrance as a woman. Wanting to feel her special strength, that husky voice of hers, that laughter, and the look of love resting in her eyes right now, for him. "I need to go, Babe..."

It tore at Jess's heart as he released her and went over to pick up his gear and rifle. Already, she could begin to see Logan's game face coming back into place. "Stay safe," she choked, trying to look strong for him.

Logan smiled down at Jess, swept her into his arm, crushing her against him. He tasted the sweetness and softness of her mouth beneath his, inhaled her scent, absorbed her passionate response. Reluctantly, Logan broke their kiss, staring hard into her eyes. "I love you, Jess. I'll see you in two months, Babe..."

CHAPTER 21

November, 2020, California, USA

LOGAN PUSHED HIS need for sleep aside as he stepped out of his Chevy pickup. It was eight a.m., the late November sun shining brightly across Oxnard, California. Dressed in a clean set of civilian clothes, Levi's and a black t-shirt, settling his black baseball cap on his head, he looked around the quiet suburban street. Jess didn't know he had come home two days earlier than he'd told her he would. It had been a lucky fluke, Logan having been able to take advantage of the flight schedules out of Rota, Spain. In just the same way he'd shown Jess on their flight out of Landstuhl, what seemed now a lifetime ago, he slept in a hammock between the huge cargo containers strapped to the deck of the C-5 heading for Joint Base Andrews near Washington, D.C. It hadn't been the best sleep, but it was better than none. He'd been in transit for seventy-two hours, with only ten hours sleep the whole while.

He could have called Jess once he landed, his cell phone now able to connect once again, but instead, Logan wanted to surprise her. His heart swelled with love for her. In his pocket was their thirty-day schedule. It had been something to look forward to, receiving emails from Jess, and planning their busy, but not too busy, itinerary. If anything, Logan's love for her had deepened over the past two months they'd been apart. He pulled the bouquet of red roses he'd picked up on the way over from the seat of his truck, his palms damp with excitement. Jess had sent some jpeg photos of where she taught on base, some of the flowers she'd planted outside the house she rented, and other scattered minutia of her new life, but none of her.

Logan walked up the concrete path toward the one-story yellow house with white shutters around the windows. There was a white wooden rail enclosing the front porch. Red and yellow Hibiscus bushes were in profuse bloom on either side of the wide concrete steps up to the porch. It was cooler on the porch, with a soft ocean breeze he pulled into his being. There was a rocking chair, and a small table with a white tablecloth, at one end. Logan wondered if Jess came out here on weekends to have a cup of coffee and just watch the world go by in the morning. Would she be home? It was a Sunday morning. The cul-de-sac was lined on both sides with houses similar to the one she lived in. A dog was barking somewhere but, otherwise, it was quiet as if the families who lived here were still sleeping in.

He knocked on the white door with its four small windows in the upper part. His heart began bounding; he wanted Jess in his arms, wanted to see how she was. Logan hoped he didn't shock the hell out of her by showing up unannounced. He knocked again, louder this time.

No one answered.

He saw her green Toyota Prius beside the house, recognizing it from photos, so he knew she was home. Maybe still sleeping in, herself? Wandering back down the steps, Logan walked around the car in the concrete driveway to a white wooden fence, about six feet tall. He peered over at it, his heart taking off. Jess was down on her hands and knees with a trowel, digging around some of her flowers. A smile tugged at his mouth. Her black hair was plaited into a single braid hanging over her left shoulder. She wore jeans, sensible tennis shoes and a light pink sleeveless tee. Jess was focused on her digging. Logan saw a pile of weeds she'd already pulled, sitting nearby. She was deeply tanned, looking winsome and so much a part of the earth she loved so much. Logan spotted an empty coffee cup tipped jauntily in the dirt nearby. The flower garden was profuse, multi-layered, and Logan wondered if Jess had landscaped the place herself. He wouldn't be surprised.

Quietly opening the gate, Logan stepped through, turned, and closed it. He didn't want to scare her to death, so he remained near the gate.

"Hey, Jess," he called quietly, "do you think you can plant these?" and he held up the bouquet toward her. She glanced up. A gasp broke from her and her green eyes got huge.

"Logan!" she cried, scrambling to her feet. Jess brushed off her hands as she rushed toward him.

Logan opened his arms, meeting her halfway. Jess threw herself into his arms and he groaned, taking a step back, laughing. He could smell her sweet scent as she hugged him tightly, her sun-warmed body pressed fully against him. "You are so beautiful," he growled, kissing her hair and, as she turned her face toward him, he swept his mouth down across her smiling one. Jess was damp with perspiration, and he tasted the salt on her lips, heard her moan, her arms tightening around his neck as she hungrily returned his kiss. She was like a wriggling puppy in his arms, kissing him, running her fingers through his short hair, her eyes wild with happiness.

"Logan!" she whispered, choking up, "why didn't you let me know you were coming home early?" Jess saw the gleam in his eyes, melted beneath his boyish smile.

"I wanted to surprise you."

Her brow wrinkled and she groaned. "But look at me! I'm dirty. I have my gardening clothes on—"

"And I love the way you look right now," he rasped, cupping her cheek, taking her mouth again, feeling her strength, soft beneath his. She moaned and hungrily returned the kiss. Logan felt himself go hard, wanting her. Wanting all of her. She smelled of sunlight and fresh ocean air, and the loose tendrils of hair around her temples only emphasized the naturalness of the outdoors woman that she was.

Jess released him and he handed her the bouquet.

"For you," he said, watching her eyes go soft with joy as she carefully enclosed the two dozen red roses in her arms. "I figured, with all the emailing me about planting flowers in your backyard, you might like these." It made him feel good to see her cheeks flush, the warmth in her eyes, as she lifted the roses to her nose and inhaled deeply.

"Ohhh, these are so fresh and fragrant," she murmured, giving him a look of thanks. Jess saw smudges of darkness beneath Logan's blue eyes. "You look thinner," she said, worried, reaching out, tangling her fingers between his.

"Part of patrol work," he said, shrugging it off. "You happen to have some coffee in that house of yours? I could use a cup."

"You bet I do. Come on in…," and Jess eagerly led him in the back door of the craftsman-style house. She wiped her shoes on the mat and then gestured for him to follow her down the hall. The light oak-wood floor gleamed with morning sunlight.

Logan moved behind her, watching the way her hips swayed. Jess had such long, beautiful legs. He wanted her so damn bad. That long black braid swung easily between her proud shoulders as she led him into the airy, bright pale-yellow kitchen. It was an open-concept layout, and, in one spacious corner, he saw two wooden rockers and a couch. Everywhere he looked, there was wood or natural stone. There was a small fireplace made of red brick and white mortar. This home suited Jess. It seemed to be all about inviting nature in.

"Sit down," Jess murmured, motioning toward the large, round oak table that sat on thick, curved wooden legs spreading from its center.

"Nice place," Logan murmured, pulling out a straight-backed chair at the table when she gestured for him to sit. There were two, a dark green cushion on the seat of each. He sat and looked around, seeing four pots on the bright windowsill. Herbs, he would imagine. He watched Jess pull a large glass vase from beneath the sink.

"How did you get home two days early?" she asked, filling the vase with water.

Logan relaxed, arms on the table, absorbing Jess hungrily. Every motion she made was pure grace. He wanted those hands on the vase on *him*. All *over* him.

"Lucky fluke," he said. "There was a C-5 ready to leave Rota about an hour after I arrived. I made it through Ops, found out they had one space available, and grabbed it. Otherwise, like a lot of my team, I'd have to have stayed there until the next morning. And that would've also added an extra day wait at D.C. for the next connection. That one fluke let me daisy-chain flights straight through." He watched her cut the end of each stem and gently place it in the vase. Pretty soon, the full two dozen roses were in it. Jess walked through and placed it in the living room, on a wooden coffee table in front of the sofa.

"You look whipped," she observed, moving back into the kitchen. Jess pulled down two clean coffee cups and filled them. Carrying them to the table, she sat down at Logan's right elbow. "Are you hungry?"

"I dropped my gear at my condo and then stopped at McDonald's," he said. She looked gorgeous, wearing no makeup, her hair gleaming with blue highlights. The love in her eyes for him made Logan ache. Two months apart from Jess had been a special hell.

Jess stared over at him, her hands around her cup. "It's *so good* to see you sitting here."

Nodding, Logan sipped his coffee. "I've never looked forward to coming home as much as this time, Jess," and he held her luminous eyes. He went hot as her full lips curved.

"I was counting the days," she admitted softly.

"You never said much about your job as instructor," Logan said. "How's it going?" He saw Jess frown a little. Something was up; he could sense it.

"Well," she hedged, moving the cup slowly around between her hands, "I've been hiding something from you, Logan." She licked her lower lip, giving him an apologetic look.

"Hiding? As in?"

Shrugging, she said, "My enlistment is up in a month. I'd always thought I was a lifer, figuring I'd put my twenty years into the Navy and then get out, like my parents did."

Logan stilled inwardly. This was serious stuff. He could tell by the unsureness in Jess's gaze. "But?"

She sat up, rolling her shoulders. "But my experience over in Afghanistan shook me to my soul, Logan. It's colored my outlook on whether I wanted to remain in the Navy or not."

Nodding, he murmured, "It would anyone, Jess. You're not alone."

"I know, I know. My poor parents," and she rolled her eyes. "I never realized just how much my being kidnapped impacted them until I got home and saw the results. It was pure hell on them. Torture."

"I imagine they were deeply shaken," Logan said. He saw the stress on Jess's face, the small wrinkles gathering on her broad brow. She was grappling with a lot of emotions.

"They were struggling, but so was I, Logan." Jess gave him a long look. "I'm still ramping down from the shock of it all. I still wake up some nights, screaming, seeing Khogani, the hatred of his men toward me. It's left me shaken in a way I've never been before. I feel like I'm still putting myself back together again."

"We all get those nightmares, Jess," and Logan reached out, sliding his hand along her slumped shoulders, seeing the misplaced shame in her eyes. "And it's going to take you probably a good year or more to work through what's happened to you."

"You get nightmares, too?"

"Yeah. I don't know of anyone in our business who doesn't. You're dealing with life-and-death situations, Jess. We're human. We have feelings. I know most SEALs don't talk about this stuff, but it's there."

"That's one of the many things I love about you, Logan. You're fearless when it comes to owning up to your emotions."

He grinned a little. "It's easy to do around you, Jess." Because he loved her. Logan wanted no secrets between them. He saw her perk up a bit, but she was still chewing on the reenlistment question. "So, what are you going to do? Re-up? Or not?"

She sighed and shook her head. "I'm so torn, Logan. My parents are pleading with me to quit and come work for their construction company. I see the damage my kidnapping did to my mom every time I drop by for a visit." Jess searched his eyes. "How do you feel about it?"

"There's no guesswork for me," Logan told her quietly. "I want you safe, Jess. If that means you quitting the Seabees, I'm fine with it. But it's your decision, not mine. And I'll love you whatever you decide to do."

Rubbing her chin, she sighed and nodded. "Logan, I cannot tell you how much I needed to hear that! And thanks for the feedback. It's important. I want to be safe, too."

"Look," Logan murmured, "you're a woman in a man's world, Jess. It is what it is. The problem I see in the future is that the Navy is going to send you to other hotspots around the world. Most of the places that need wells drilled are Third World countries. There's a lot of fanatical Muslims in many of those. Look at Africa. And you may be put on a different continent, with some group there that might not be called the 'Taliban', but it'll still be one that's just as dangerous and just as willing to either kidnap or kill you only because you're an American woman. And, Jess, you're 'the one that got away'. You're famous in Taliban ranks now. That means glory-seeking fanatics all over the world know your name and want you as a special prize." He didn't want to put it so harshly, but that was the reality. He could see her evaluating his words.

Finally, Jess pushed her coffee out in front of her, folding her arms on the table. "I was never so scared as when Khogani took me, Logan. I tried to be brave. I thought I'd never see you again. Or my parents. Or my way of life…"

"Those things had to run through your mind, Jess."

She turned and laid her fingers across his lower arm. "I didn't want to lose you, Logan. I know we crashed into one another at Landstuhl, but what I felt in my heart for you was so deep, so special and wonderful, I grieved that I'd lost you for the rest of my life." Jess closed her eyes for a moment, struggling with her emotions. Opening them, she held his narrowed gaze. "I love you, Logan. I want a life with you. I don't want to worry about being a target, or possibly being kidnapped again. And I know it could happen. You're right: lesser-developed countries *are* the well-diggers' stomping ground."

He took her hand into his, squeezing it gently. "I'd like it if you never went overseas on assignment again, Jess. It's purely selfish on my part. I think going to work at your parents' company would be perfect for you. But it's your life, Babe. I want you happy, whatever you decide to do." Logan studied her anguished-looking gaze.

"I've never run from a challenge before, Logan."

"Jess, this was more than a challenge. It's men who want you dead or want you as a victim to be sold. That's a jarring reality."

"I feel like I should stand up and fight it, Logan. Go back to Afghanistan and face my fear."

"It's not something you can do by yourself," he counseled. "Look at it from another perspective, Jess. If you get kidnapped again, you're putting other operators at risk who will try to save you. These men have families, too. They have people who love them. I don't think you'd willingly do that. Do you?"

Grimacing, Jess shook her head. "No… I wouldn't want to do that to them. Even after I got kidnapped by Khogani, I kept worrying about you and Chris. I was afraid for your lives. As much as I wanted you to come rescue me, there was another part of me that didn't want you to die trying. Precisely because of what you said: you have families who love you, too. I don't want to put anyone else at risk, Logan."

"Have you discussed this with your parents?"

Nodding, Jess said, "Yes. They want me to quit the Navy."

"You wouldn't be quitting without a very good reason, Jess. Sometimes, we all come up against something so big that we can't possibly scale it. And, when we hit those times, then we need to look around for other ways to live our life and make the adjustments."

"Have you ever hit one?" Jess asked.

"Yes." And then he shrugged. "My marriage. There was nothing I could do to change my ex-wife's mind. I had to be gone a lot. She didn't accept it. So, there was no way around it, Jess."

Frowning, she whispered, "I can relate to that one. My ex-husband didn't want to respect me as an equal. He didn't want to change for me, and I sure as hell wasn't going to be subservient to him."

"See?" Logan said, smiling a little. "We all hit those brick walls, Jess. You're up against one right now. Best thing you can do is follow your heart. It really is your compass. How you feel in there is how you should make your decision." Because he loved Jess, he wanted to sway her, but Logan knew, from long experience, that didn't work in a relationship. If he swayed her, and she later regretted it, she'd blame him. Not a wise move to make.

"Enough of me," she muttered, sipping more of her coffee. "What do you need?" And, as soon as she asked, she saw his eyes glint with that predator-like look he gave her when what he wanted was *her*. "I mean," she stumbled, and then laughed with him. "Slip of the tongue."

"I like your tongue."

Her whole lower body went hot. "I always know where you stand, Logan."

"No guesswork," he agreed, giving her a warm look.

"Aren't you tired?"

"Not anymore."

She gave a ladylike snort. "You look absolutely whipped. You need a shower."

"You think?" and he chuckled. "Two days flying transports and no shower. And I didn't even stop to get one when I hit my condo, just threw my gear into it, got a change of clothes and then jumped in my truck."

"That says a lot." She stood and gripped his hand. "Come on, I'll show you where the bathroom is."

Logan almost suggested Jess come in with him, but he was damned tired. There would be other times, so he bit his tongue on that matter, following her down another hall. "I like your house."

"Thanks. Is it me?" and Jess turned her head, giving him a smile over her shoulder.

"Very," Logan agreed. "All organic and natural. Wait 'til you see my condo."

"What? It looks like a fishbowl. You have a huge aquarium in it, sailor?"

He liked her teasing. He'd missed Jess. "SEALs *parachute*, you know, and we work on *land*, too," he teased.

Jess stopped at a cabinet in the hall and pulled out a thick, blue terrycloth towel and washcloth. She handed them to Logan. "I would say, from what I know, hmmm… you were born in Wyoming, so, even though you're in the Navy, I bet your condo has a Western flavor to it."

"We'll see," he said, giving her a teasing look.

"I'll be out in the kitchen if you need me. I think I'd better get serious about making us dinner tonight?"

"No way," Logan growled. I'd like to take you out, to your favorite place?"

"Oh, then that means La Jolla, my favorite oceanside retreat. I love going to the Crab Catcher Restaurant. Best seafood on the West Coast."

Logan was far too tired to drive through Los Angeles, all the way back down to La Jolla in San Diego, but he sensed Jess was joking about that anyway. "Let's eat in, then. And I suppose you have teaching duties tomorrow?"

"Yes. My leave doesn't start for two days," and she leaned up, giving him a quick kiss on the mouth. "So, you either stay here for two days with me until that happens, or pine away for me in your condo?"

"I'm staying," Logan told her. "And you're going to have to be lucky to get out of bed to leave to go teach tomorrow morning." He saw her eyes grow amused. At the same time, her cheeks flushed. Yeah, he was going to love the hell out of Jess. Two months had been way too long without her at his side.

Jess had been out in the kitchen for nearly an hour when she had heard the bathroom door open. Frowning, she wondered where Logan had wandered off to when he didn't reappear. In the hall, she saw the bathroom was empty. Turning, she went to her bedroom. Her heart turned over. Logan had dried off, pulled on his Levi's and t-shirt and laid down. He was sprawled out on his belly, sound asleep. Jess knew he was super sensitive to sound, and she didn't want to wake him. Backing up quietly, she turned with a smile on her mouth and padded toward the kitchen.

She busied herself with making them a pot roast with carrots, potatoes and celery. She knew Logan had probably not slept for at least forty-eight hours. And he was suffering global jet lag on top of that. And who knew what other stressors had been on him before he and his team had even left Afghanistan? Jess knew she would never be able to push for that length of time without caving in to the need for sleep. He was a SEAL, and he was used to brutally pushing his body physically when necessary. Jess knew how badly he'd wanted to get home to see her. A new warmth flooded her as she peeled the potatoes.

Luckily, she lived on a very quiet street, with older couples. The bedroom was at the rear of the house, so Logan should be able to sleep without getting awakened by any sharp noises or other sounds. The urge to go in there and slip beside him was real, but Jess knew she'd wake him up. And he desperately needed some sleep.

In her musings, Jess revisited their earlier conversation about her reenlistment. Logan was completely unlike her ex-husband, the all-too-macho Mark Willard, who would have just *told* her what to do. Instead, Logan's sensitivity, his understanding and respect of her boundaries, was completely different and refreshing.

She pressed her hands on the countertop, closing her eyes, feeling torn over leaving the Navy or staying. Life wasn't simple. She'd already put Logan and her parents through a special hell, not to mention, herself. And she was still paying the price for the kidnapping. If someone approached her from behind, and she didn't hear them, it scared her out of her skin. She was jumpy. And then there were the nightmares. The guilt that Logan had killed men to get her to safety. They had families, too. Jess had cried more often in the last two months than she had in the whole rest of her life. Everything would suddenly hit her, out of nowhere, and she would begin sobbing.

Logan understood what was happening to her. Probably because he'd gone through some of it himself. She was sure *he* felt no guilt about killing those two men. It was his job. His responsibility had been to get her to safety. And Jess knew those two Taliban soldiers would have killed them in a heartbeat. She wouldn't be standing at her kitchen counter contemplating this if Logan hadn't done what he did.

Shaking her head, Jess continued to peel the rest of the potatoes for the pot roast. She hadn't anticipated Logan being here for two nights yet, and her fridge was mostly empty. The least she could do for him was make nice meals for the both of them, as a welcome home. And she was a good cook. Drying her hands on a nearby towel, Jess sat down at the kitchen table and wrote out a list of things she'd need for dinner tonight and tomorrow night. Logan was going to get absolutely spoiled.

CHAPTER 22

A T FIVE P.M., Jess was putting the final touches on a salad for the evening meal when Logan silently appeared, scaring the hell out of her as usual. That was becoming a regular skit of theirs, it seemed. She jumped and gasped as he came around the corner. His hair was tousled, eyes drowsy, his feet bare.

"Sorry," he mumbled, wiping his face.

Heart pounding, Jess stared at him. "Can't you make some noise, Logan?" He was heartbreakingly boyish looking. She remembered his game face as he extricated her from the Hill soldiers. Now, his eyes cloudy from a long sleep, he stood, relaxed, staring at her. The contrast was as of night and day.

"How about if I put a bell on me?" and he gave her a cockeyed grin, coming over and taking the knife out of her hand, laying it on the drain board. Sliding his arms around her shoulders, he drew her against him, inhaling the spicy scent of her hair. "I need to work on making some noise," he agreed gruffly, kissing her hair. "I don't want to make you jump." He felt Jess relax into his arms, a soft sigh issuing from between her lips.

"Thank you. My heart's pounding in terror, Logan. I get hit with flashbacks…"

"Yeah," he murmured, kissing her temple and cheek. "I can feel it against my chest." Her reaction was much more than from just a usual fright and Logan knew it had to do with the kidnapping trauma. Whether Jess knew it or not, she had PTSD. Logan felt her melting into him and he leaned his hips against the counter, taking her full weight. "Why did you let me sleep so long?"

She kissed his neck, his unshaven jaw, and then pulled away to drown in the burning, hooded look he gave her. "Because you needed it? Basic common sense?" She watched one corner of that beautiful male mouth curve upward.

"You're such a feisty little thing."

"I'm hardly little, Randall, so don't go there."

"Hmmm," he growled, moving his hands across her back, encasing her hips and drawing her tightly against him. "I like a woman with some meat on her bones and, Babe, you are the real deal. Don't change a thing. I like you just the way you are."

Her lower body felt scalded. But it was down to sex or eating. And she'd worked all day preparing a major meal for two and wasn't about to let her pot roast burn in the oven. Gripping his upper arms, she stepped out of his embrace. "Food first," she told him firmly.

"Hey, a guy can try."

"Yes, but you need to eat, Logan."

"You're right." He sniffed the air. "Smells good. What is it?"

"Pot roast."

"Are you making gravy?"

"Yes," she said, pointing toward the kitchen table. "There's coffee. So, if you want, pour yourself some while I make it. We're going to eat in twenty minutes."

Running his fingers through his hair, he yawned and then padded toward the opposite counter. "I slept hard."

"Like I said, you needed it," Jess murmured, pouring milk into the pan. "You must have crashed after you took a shower?"

Logan watched Jess work over the stove. Damn, she looked good in an apron. Who knew she had such a house-frau side? "I did. The bed sucked me in and I told myself 'Just ten minutes', dammit," he muttered, still waking up. His lower body sure as hell was online, but the rest of him was jet lagged, still half a globe away. He needed some decent food in him, having lived off MREs the last couple of days inbound to the States. "I had such good intentions, after taking the shower," he said, smiling a little, hand looped around the cup. "Quick nap, and then I had every intention of coming out here and carrying you back off to bed with me."

"You can do that tonight."

"Promise?"

Jess tossed him a look over her shoulder while stirring the gravy. "Promise. In spades, Randall. You spoiled me and I want more of what you have."

"Let's just skip dessert?"

He gave her a very heated look. And her body responded, clenching with need. Jess sighed. "No, now, I made a special dessert for you tonight. Besides me, that is."

"Yeah?" He sipped his coffee. Logan thought the best dessert possible was Jess, naked, in his arms. In his bed. *Forever.*

"My mom's favorite: butterscotch pudding with pecans. Oh, and I have a can of whipped cream if you like it on your pudding."

"I can think of a lot of things to do with that can of whipped cream."

Jess laughed fully. "Is that ALL that's on your mind, Logan?"

He gave her an amused look. "Babe, I'm *made* out of testosterone. Yes, I think of you in my bed. Making love with you. Waking up in the morning and kissing you. All kinds of sexy things. Oh, and it's not limited to the bedroom, either. I'm an equal opportunist, so you should be warned."

Jess feigned a dark look his way. "Are you this way all the time?"

"No." Logan opened his hands. "It's been two months, Jess. You can't tell me you aren't a little hungry, too?" He watched her lips twitch, merriment in her eyes. Logan liked her fearlessness. And he'd seen her real courage under fire.

"Oh, I am," Jess murmured coyly. "But I think we need some fuel first."

Logan ate like he was half starved to death. Jess sat there watching him gulp down half the roast, three potatoes, a huge pile of carrots, gravy smothering everything, and then he ate half the massive bowl of pudding she'd made as well! Topped with huge mounds of whipped cream, as if the pudding helping, alone, wouldn't have choked a hippo. He had a satisfied look on his face as he helped her take the dirty dishes into the kitchen.

"I'm surprised you can even walk. Don't you have a stomachache?"

Logan gave her a one-eyebrow-raised look as he took the rinsed-off dishes from Jess and placed them in the dishwasher. "It's easy for a SEAL to consume up to twelve thousand calories a day, Jess. And your dinner was incredible. That gravy was to die for."

"Good thing I can cook. I'd hate to see a restaurant bill for you," she teased, wiping her hands off.

Logan shut the door to the dishwasher, turning it on. "You're just one surprise after another, Ms. Courtland."

Logan took her into his arms, kissing her long and sweetly, feeling Jess sink against him. He broke the kiss reluctantly and tucked her shoulders under his arm. "Come on in the living room? Sit with me? We need to talk."

It sounded serious. She nodded. "I need to sit and digest the meal, anyway," she admitted.

Settling Jess against him as he sat down in the corner of the couch, the way she tucked her legs beneath her made Logan smile to himself. He felt her lips against his neck, kissing him. Logan smoothed a hand across her hip, keeping her close. "I've had two of the longest, most godawful months of suffering away from you, Jess." He rested his chin against her hair, feeling her relax totally against him.

"The suffering was mutual," she assured him wryly, resting her hand against his shoulder.

"That's what got me."

"What? The suffering?"

"Well, the quality of the suffering," Logan specified.

Jess frowned. "I don't follow."

Logan didn't expect her to. He eased her back just enough so that their eyes could meet as she rested her head against his shoulder. "You do realize that we met under the worst possible circumstances?" He saw her eyes darken at the memory of losing her friend, Chief Dan Callahan, a man she'd worked with for years. "See? That's my point."

"I... don't understand where this is going, Logan?"

"Yeah, well I didn't either for a good month after you left," he grouched, holding her confused-looking gaze. "We fell in love, right there, in Landstuhl, with one another. I lost one of my best friends and so did you. It shouldn't have worked."

Jess sat up, turning and staring into his serious features. "What are you talking about, Logan? You've LOST me."

He reached out, grazing her cheek. Her skin was like satin. "We met under the worst circumstances, Jess. Okay, so we had a night in bed. It shouldn't have gone beyond that. A need to feel alive, to grieve, to feel good in someone's arms who wanted you, all that eased our grief." He saw her eyes widen. "We had less than twenty-four hours with one another and yes," Logan shook his head, looking away for a moment, and then locking his gaze back on her, "by rights, we should have walked away from one another. Right?"

Jess opened her mouth and then closed it. She stared at him, nonplussed. "WHAT are you trying to say, Logan?" He was so serious. He was almost as focused as when there'd been Hill soldiers nearby and hunting for them.

"Jess, we met, we made love, and we separated, going our different ways."

"Well... yes, we did. So what?"

"Something happened, Babe." Logan smoothed his fingers down her forearm. "I couldn't get you out of my mind, my heart, or my body. Something happened that night. Something important. Real."

"Yes, it did." Jess tilted her head, frowning. "Why are you looking like that, Logan? I know we met under terrible conditions. But what happened for me, with you, was... well... life changing. I didn't know it at the time, but I sure did after we split at Bagram. I felt," and she lifted her hand, pressing it against her heart as she drowned in his hooded blue gaze, "as if I'd been completed in a way, with you, that I never knew existed. Until that night. Until you walked into my life." Jess swallowed hard, tears threatening to spill. She saw Logan's face turn emotional, to an extent she'd never seen before.

"That's what I'm trying to say, Jess. It's crazy. It shouldn't have worked between us. But it does."

"Have you been trying to explain me out of your life? That we don't have time in grade, and it shouldn't work? That what we share isn't serious?"

His mouth quirked. Logan heard the strain in Jess's voice, and he winced. "No, Babe, I wasn't. I was trying to figure out how love could hit me over the head with a sledgehammer like it did." His eyes glinted with amusement. "There was never a moment since we've been separated in those two months that I didn't need you, want to hear your voice, hear what you thought, Jess. You complete me in a way that amazes me. I think I'm still in shock over it," and Logan searched her shadowed green eyes. He could see her thinking, putting it all together from his perspective. Obviously, not her reality. But she was trying to understand HIS reality. His love grew even more for her. Jess wasn't the kind of person to impose her life standards on another person. She had a bonafide live-and-let-live attitude toward everyone. Even him. Logan rolled away from her, pulling something out of his pocket.

"It seems our relationship is not based on length of time spent together," he told her. "We've both been married. We're more mature now, we know what it takes to make a relationship work or not." Logan took her hand and placed a plastic zip-lock bag into her palm. "Jess, two months ago I emailed my mother. I told her I was ready to use my great-grandmother's wedding rings. She sent them over to me." He gave her an apologetic look. "This isn't fancy, and you deserve better, but my great-grandmother, in her will, said that my mother's first-born son would get them. She had a fifty-year marriage to her husband, my great-grandfather John." He covered the small plastic bag in her palm with his, and held it there, looking into her shimmering eyes. "I don't care," he rasped, "how long or short the time is we've had between us, Jess. I fell in love with you, I think, from the moment I saw you. And, when you loved me, your heart was so wide open that I couldn't believe it. You were fearless. You trusted me with yourself completely. It just blew me away, Babe. And then, to see you under fire, under that kind of relentless, ongoing pressure after you escaped Khogani, made me so much more aware of what you're made of."

Logan closed his fingers over hers, seeing the tears flow silently down her cheeks. His voice grew thick. "Jess, you are the most courageous woman I've ever met. And, dammit, I want to marry you whenever you say the word. If you need one or two years to think about it, that's fine with me. I don't care how long it takes; I'm committed to you. I saw more of you in those days running from Khogani than I probably would in a lifetime, with anyone. Never once did you whine or cry or say you couldn't do something, Jess. You just gutted it out and you did the very best you could." Logan smiled a little. "I gotta tell you, I would NEVER want to be put in that position again, with any other woman, civilian *or* military. Nobody could ever measure up to how well *you* did. You were a champ. And you stole my heart, Jess."

With a sob, Jess tried to wipe the tears from her eyes as she stared down at the gold wedding band and diamond solitaire engagement ring in the zip-lock plastic bag in her palm. "Oh, Logan…"

He picked up the bag and carefully opened it, placing the two rings back in her palm for real. "My great-grandmother, Sarah, was a woman of the land, Jess. Our ranch has been in our family for over a hundred years. She was born in Ohio and came west with her husband, John. They created the ranch that my mother and father work to this day. She really was a woman of the earth. I was ten when she passed, but I remember her vividly. She was always on her hands and knees, digging in the ground. Hands in the earth." Logan looked into Jess's tear-filled eyes. "You remind me so much of her. I guess I was destined to find a woman of the earth to fill out the rest of my life."

Gently, Jess touched the wedding bands. They were very old, by the cut of the diamond and design. It made them just that much more special to her. With her fumbling fingers, she kept on trying to wipe away her tears, absorbing the comfort of Logan's arm around her waist, holding her gently, silently supporting her. "I-I never expected this, Logan…"

"We've done everything else fast," he murmured, catching that green gaze of hers that made his heart swell with love. "I don't care what your decision is about staying in the Navy or not, Jess." Logan picked up the solitaire engagement ring. "No matter what you decide, I want you to wear this. You're mine. And I'm yours. That's all I need from you, Babe," and he held her lustrous gaze.

Logan had thought he knew what love was the first time he'd married. Looking back on that, over the last two months, he'd realized that he'd been too young, too selfish and self-centered, to make it work. He'd never taken the other person into consideration. But years and hellish experiences had honed and shaped him, matured him. And now, he knew he loved Jess with every fiber of his being. There would never be another woman for him but her. She'd gone through hell with him. Her courage under fire had been remarkable. And he wanted her as his mate for the rest of his life.

"You're in the military like I am," he went on. "There's a word that fits us well, Jess: countermeasure."

"Employing a device or strategy that has the objective to impair the operational effectiveness of the enemy," she said.

"Exactly. When you were kidnapped. You escaped. I found you, and then we escaped Khogani's search for us, *together*. We kept thwarting his attempts to find us."

"We both used our skills and experience to stop him from finding and capturing us again," she agreed. "We employed a lot of countermeasures, Logan.

Mostly yours, though, because you knew how to use your experience in Afghanistan to keep us under his radar, even the trick of wearing Afghan clothes to look like Taliban."

"But you had the guts to use your Swiss Army Knife to cut the rope and you escaped out of the cave, rolling, never standing, keeping your head. That was your countermeasure."

"Good point," she murmured, touching the rings.

"Do you need time to think about this?" Logan asked her quietly.

Jess made a soft sound in her throat, shaking her head.

"No… no, I don't, Logan." Jess closed her eyes and took in a deep breath and released it. She pressed her brow against his. "I've done a lot of thinking and feeling these past two months, too. About myself. About us. What is important in my life." Jess lifted her brow away from his, absorbing the cool, slight weight of the rings in her hand. "My heart always had the answer, Logan. My head got in the way so many times. I couldn't explain why I had fallen so deeply in love with you, so quickly. I still can't. All I know is that you fulfill me. We're a good team together. I saw that when we were escaping from Khogani. If we can get along under such a horrible, stressful circumstance, I'm sure we could make a marriage work. Don't you?" She saw Logan give her a faint smile.

"We'll make it work, Jess. That's my promise to you." Logan picked up her left hand and slid the diamond engagement ring on it. "Now," he said thickly, "I'm going to pick you up, carry you down the hall to our bed. And I'm going to love you, Jess…"

Never had Logan wanted to love a woman with all his body, his heart and soul, as he did Jess. He laid her on the bed and saw the longing in her eyes matching his desire. Standing before her, Logan pulled off his t-shirt and shoes, got rid of his Levi's, and his boxer shorts. His eyes never left Jess as she quickly removed her clothes. There was a palpable, sizzling, aching connection between them and, as she knelt on the bed, pulled him toward her, she was an equal partner in every way.

Jess smiled into Logan's dark, glittering eyes. His large, calloused hands slid around her smooth shoulders, and she whispered, "No condom, Logan. I want to feel you. All of you, tonight." She saw him hesitate, his brows dipping momentarily. "I just had my period less than a week ago. We're in a safe time." She placed a kiss against his powerful chest. "Please?"

There was such a difference between using a condom and not using one. Logan had wanted to take Jess that way, but time hadn't been on their side. Easing his fingers through her loose black hair, he framed her face, leaned down, sliding his mouth against hers. "Anything you want, Babe," he rasped, feeling her lips open hungrily. Her fingers enclosed his biceps and Logan felt himself drowning in the splendor and heat of her mouth. Groaning, he eased her back on the bed, settling beside her, wanting her mouth once more.

Nothing existed anymore for Logan, but Jess. She moaned as his tongue glided across her lower lip, her breath growing uneven. Rolling on her side, she met and moved against his erection, pulling a growl out of him. More than anything, Logan loved her boldness as a bed partner. She wasn't limp or tepid in his arms, shy or unsure, wanting him to lead the way. Her lips were eager, hungry and glided against his, her fingers sliding through his short hair, holding him, her tongue dancing sensuously against his.

Only Jess existed. Her scent, the silk of her hair against his jaw, her little moans catching in her throat as he grazed the curve of her breast, his thumb moving languidly across that tight, hardening nipple. Pressing soft, lingering kisses against her eyelids, her cheek and finally, seeking the scalding heat of her mouth, she writhed in his arms as they held her captive. Releasing her mouth, Logan next sought and found that nipple just begging to be further seduced. As his lips settled over it, he heard Jess cry out, her back arching, pressing herself solidly against his erection. Heat rolled up through him and he felt himself tremble as her warmth, her satiny skin, moved against his flesh.

The power of her love for him broke him in a way that shattered his heart, sending such a powerful tidal wave of emotion through his chest that Logan lifted his lips from her nipple and simply wrapped her in his strong embrace, holding Jess, absorbing her in every possible way. There was such a driving need in him to couple with her, make her his forever, brand his essence deep within her loving, inviting body. He felt as if she sensed and understood why he held her so tightly, his head bowed against hers, their breaths ragged and uneven, and it was true: Jess did.

As Logan pressed gentle kisses against her hair, trailing them to her cheek, he encountered her salty, warm tears. It was as if they were in touch with one another on a completely different, incredible level. She wasn't crying because she was sad or grieving. No, as he lifted his head away from hers, drowning in the dark green and gold of her luminous eyes, Logan understood they were tears of celebration and happiness. That Jess was once more in his arms, wanting him within her, moving in sync like they always had. As she slipped her hand down across his lean ribcage, sliding it between the two of them, enclosing his erection, he shut his eyes tightly and tensed. A low, animal groan rose in Logan's chest as she moved her fingers deliciously around him, so close to losing control over her exploring touch. Logan felt so busted open beneath her hands, her lips opening to his, meeting him fiercely, their hunger for one another nearly overwhelming.

He felt her release him, tearing her mouth from his, her eyes narrowed, filled with arousal.

"I want to ride you, Logan...."

Those were the sweetest words he could ever hear, and he gave her only a dark, hungry look in response. Without speaking, he rolled onto his back, picking Jess up effortlessly with casual strength, helping her settle her satiny, curved thighs against his narrow hips. The languor, the starvation for her, made his erection throb with need at the settling of her wet, hot core against him. He saw the huntress gleaming in her eyes, her black hair thick and loose across her shoulders as she smiled down at him. Settling his hands against her hips, he guided down upon him, closing his eyes, anticipating...

Her long fingers skated across his darkly haired chest as she slowly, torturously eased herself back. Instantly, Logan groaned, thrusting his hips upward to meet and hold her over his aching erection. She slid like such warm, drizzling honey down across him that he gritted his teeth, afraid again that he could no longer control himself. Jess leaned down, her teeth taking small nips along his corded neck, then licking his flesh and then kissing each area. Her hands were ever roaming, softly moving to his nipples, squeezing them teasingly, making his back arch, pressing him more powerfully against her core. She was such a tease that his fingers dug more deeply into her sinuously moving hips, the fire enveloping him. If she kept up this burning form of sexual torture, he'd never last. The gleam in her eyes was of a woman not only pleasuring herself against him but holding a luminous love with every touch she shared with him, whether by her mouth, her hands or that incredible, sweet core.

"Babe," he groaned, lifting his hands, framing her face, making her look at him, "I'm not going to make it if I don't get inside you..." Logan watched her full lips curve.

"I was wondering when enough was enough," she laughed huskily, leaning down, dragging her breasts across his chest as she slowly took his mouth.

He was burning beneath her stunning, feverish desire for him. Logan felt her lift and then make one scalding downward movement that brought a hiss from between his clenched teeth. In that one fluid motion, she moved him to her entrance and, without hesitation, sheathed down upon him fully. His body buckled. He growled out her name, gripping her hips, unable to think any longer. And when Jess began to establish a hard, pressing rhythm, all Logan could do was match it. He felt her muscled walls collapse inward, felt her stiffen, throw her head back and cry out. Her orgasm flooded around him and she was paralyzed on top of him, her eyes tightly shut, her lips parted. Logan thrust deeply into her, holding her hips, keeping her angled to milk her every sensation. And then, just as she had a second, crashing orgasm, he felt heat slam down his own spine, roaring through him, flooding into her with his essence.

Neither could move, frozen against one another, trapped in heated ecstasy. Logan heard Jess sobbing his name, her fingers frantically digging into his chest wall, her entire body quivering as she was deluged with intense, ongoing pleasure. It felt so incredibly good to be inside her, feel the power of her as a woman, and then to empty himself within her, claiming her. Making Jess his.

CHAPTER 23

JESS LAY ON top of Logan, feeling his roughened hands moving slowly up and down her curved, damp back in the aftermath. His touch was incredibly tender, loving, and she never wanted to move again. Having him within her, feeling his inherent strength, her cheek against his sweaty shoulder, their breathing torn and jagged, made her feel a profound, soul-filling contentment, and she closed her eyes. Her heart swelled with such intense love for him. Her throat tightened from all the many beautiful emotions she held *only* for him. As he slid his fingers through her tangled hair, smoothing it, pulling it aside so he could lean over and press a kiss to her cheek, she sighed. How could she ever show Logan with words how much he meant to her? Moving her fingers up across his chest, outlining his collar bone, feeling his muscles leap beneath her exploring fingertips, Jess smiled.

"I don't want this to ever end," Logan whispered against her ear, tendrils of her hair tickling his nose and mouth.

"Me either," she whispered unsteadily, moving her hand to his stubbled jaw, tracing his chiseled mouth, that mouth that gave her such incredible pleasure. "Can we just stay like this forever?" and Jess laughed softly. She heard and felt a matching chuckle rumble up through Logan's chest.

"It sure as hell feels better without a condom," he told her, easing thick black strands off her shoulder, laying them across her back.

"Mmmm, it's the best dessert in the world, Logan…" and it was. She'd come so swiftly, so easily, that it had rocked her soul. They weren't just *good* together, they were *mind-blowingly* good together. They suited, fitted, each other perfectly. Logan slowly arched his hips, drawing a moan out of her from how thick and powerful he still felt within her. And, when he enclosed her with his arms, kissing her temple, inhaling her fragrance, nothing had ever felt more right in Jess's world.

"You're not leaving this bed," Logan warned, lifting his hips, feeling himself hardening once more, feeling her body constrict and grip him.

"Neither are you," Jess laughed quietly. She eased herself up, from laying prone against his torso into a sitting position, closing her eyes, feeling him still deep within her, the fiery signals starting all over again. As he cupped her taut breasts, his thumbs brushing those ripe nipples, she sank into his open palms, a small cry of pleasure trapped in her exposed throat. And as she became limp in his hands, Jess felt him move slowly onto his side, easing out of her. She moaned his loss as he gently guided her down upon her back, rising above her, his knee nudging open her thighs. Jess saw that hunter look was back, burning in his gaze. Jess watched him settle between her thighs, his dark, sunburned hands coming to rest upon her white hips. This time, he laid across her, pressing against her wet entrance, his hands framing her head, staring deep into her eyes, watching her, watching how she reacted as he began to tease her, moving slowly in and out, languishing that knot of swollen nerves just by her entrance.

"Now," he growled, "my turn to tease the hell out of you." His smile turned predatory. "Not that you don't have this coming, woman…"

Oh! Logan knew how to precisely pleasure her mercilessly, the fire licking and laving up through her.

Logan could feel Jess coming close to orgasm. He held her head and lay heavily against her, almost completely preventing her from moving with his superior weight. But the way he curved his mouth against hers, his tongue tangling, dancing with hers, emulating what she wanted so badly below with him, drove her into a mewling state of frustration. And then, he entered her again, teasing that hungry knot that throbbed and ached so badly.

"…Logan," she gasped, her voice low, "…. please, I need you."

He lay still within her, watching her, kissing her wet, warm mouth. "Like I did you? All's fair in love and war, Babe," and his smile went deep into her turbulent, aroused eyes. He finally saw the surrender in those eyes, saw the stark, raging hunger for him again. Yeah, they were sure as hell good for one another. In every possible way. Sex had never been more fulfilling, more powerful and satisfying, than with Jess. Logan twisted his hips just enough to feel her arch beneath him, her eyes shuttering close as he gave her the pleasure she was pleading for. He would never deny her. Not ever. Well… not for long, anyway. Logan set about giving her exactly what she wanted because it filled him with a happiness that nothing could ever buy. Because he loved Jess with a savageness that was so damned primal and animal-like, Logan would never be able to give it words.

But he could show her, play with her, tease her and love her with a necessity that did not *need* words. He felt her thrust her hips upward, seeking even more pleasure from him. Releasing Jess, he shifted a lot of his weight from her, sliding one hand beneath her hips to give her that favored angle that would send her into keening with ecstasy. Her entire body bowed against him, her fingers digging deeply into his shoulders, as Logan felt her grip him and that flush of wet, hot heat shatter through her. To hear Jess cry out his name, to feel her silky heat enclose him, her flesh damp, sliding against his, lost him in his five boiling senses, absorbing Jess into his body, his heart and his soul.

Jess made a muffled sound against Logan's neck. It was dark as she drowsily awoke. She felt Logan's arm around her shoulder tighten, as if to guard her, to keep her safe. It was an overwhelming sense of protection, and Jess smiled softly, stretching her hand across his powerful chest. Her body simmered with such satisfaction that she could barely move. She was a thirsty sponge, satiated in the pleasure still simmering through every cell in her glowing body.

Logan had awakened instantly when Jess made that soft sound in the back of her throat. The languor within his body made him relax when realized he was in a bedroom with her in his arms, her warm, soft curves against him. Her moist breath flowed across his upper chest, slow and deep. Logan had never felt such peace, such laziness, but a laziness he savored. Because it came from loving Jess. He moved his head just enough to press a kiss into her hair.

"You okay?" he asked, his voice thick with sleep.

Jess smoothed her hand across Logan's chest. "More than okay. Still floating... You are incredible, Logan..."

Her words made him feel good, feel worthy of her as a man. He slid his fingers across her upper arm, feeling the goosepimples it raised as he traced her velvet flesh. "We must have drifted off," he mumbled, lifting his wrist, looking at his watch. "It's 0300."

"I want the world to go away," Jess muttered. "I wish I could call in sick and just be with you all day today..."

Grimacing, Logan squeezed her shoulders. "It's going to happen soon enough."

Jess slowly eased away from him. She pushed her tangled hair off her face as she sat up. The light out in the hall spilled just enough into the bedroom that she could see his drowsy, satisfied expression. Even in repose, Logan reminded her of a lion who might look tame, but was not. She propped herself up on one elbow, lacing her fingers through the dark hair across his chest, absorbing his expression. Logan's hair was mussed, his beard darkening his lower face, again reminding her of his primal side that was in such scalding, satisfying parallel with her own.

"When I go in this morning, I'm going to the Personnel Office, Logan." Her voice lowered with emotion. "I'm going to tell them I'm not reenlisting." Her hand settled over his heart, its beat slow and powerful beneath her palm. "When we drive down to Coronado, to your condo, I intend to stay there and live with you. Not just drop by for a visit." She searched his shadowed blue eyes, so intense upon her. "Are you all right with that?"

"More than all right, Babe," he rasped, cupping her cheek, drawing her down. He met her soft, warm lips and slid his mouth strongly against them. His heart did flipflops of unparalleled joy. Never had Logan wanted a woman more than Jess. She had just told him she was walking into his life, *settling* into it. He felt her smile softly beneath his mouth and he eased away, seeing the radiance in her gaze.

"You're really okay with it? All of it?" Jess saw his mouth begin to curve up, and heat flooded her from her head to her toes. The look Logan gave her was of a man claiming his woman. *Forever.*

Logan eased himself up into a sitting position. He stood the pillows behind him and rested against them on the headboard, pulling Jess back into his arms. He saw the tension, the unsureness and worry, in her eyes. He'd heard it in her low, sultry voice. Sliding his hand against her cheek, guiding her gaze up to his, voice thick with feeling, he rasped, "Jess, I was committed to you the first afternoon I met you. Nothing's changed. Nothing is ever going to change. I want you happy, Babe. I always want you to go where your heart tells you."

His words were balm for her soul. Jess leaned upward, her lips brushing his. "My heart has *always* been in your hands, Logan." She closed her eyes feeling the tenderness as his mouth took hers with such exquisite gentleness, as if she were some priceless, fragile being that could break at a moment's notice. But it was more than that, as Logan drank deeply of her mouth, tasting Jess, sharing their breath. It was his loving of her in equal measure. It brought tears of joy to her eyes, warm tears, meeting and melding between their mouths. They were one, coming together, becoming whole. And together, they had unlimited strength and grace to give and share with one another.

As Jess slowly separated from Logan's mouth, his breath ragged, his eyes glittering with need of her once more, she felt as if a heavy pressure had dissolved from her shoulders. Logan searched her face, memorizing it, embracing her silently with the love he held for her. Jess knew she'd made the right decision.

"I want to marry you, Jess, but there will be a lot of away time from you."

"I want us together whenever it can happen," she assured him. "Besides, I'll have my job at my parent's construction company. When you're gone on training or deployment, Logan, I'll be plenty occupied."

Logan nodded, seeing the flush in her cheeks, the happiness shining in her green eyes. "You'll worry a lot, Jess. I know you will."

Shaking her head, she said wryly, "Not as much as you think, Logan. Remember? I was with you in the Hindu Kush? Running for our lives? I saw you in action. Any question I had about you being in over your head, has been answered. I know your work is always dangerous. And will I *not* worry? Nooo… But I'll be worrying a *lot* less. Does that help?" and Jess smiled warmly into his eyes.

"That helps a lot," he growled, thinking how fragile and beautiful Jess really was. Logan still found it impossible to comprehend where her hidden strength to gut through that escape with him had sprung from. Maybe it was because she was a woman of the earth; grounded and strong in ways hidden until they were needed. His great-grandmother Sarah, had been a tough frontier woman, helping carve their present-day ranch out of the earth, out of the very mountains, and Jess had been cast from the same mold.

"I want you happy, Babe."

"I am. And I know my parents are going to breath a huge sigh of relief knowing I'm no longer in the Navy. They're so fearful I'll get ordered overseas into a dangerous area again."

"I know," Logan murmured, sliding his hand down her shoulder, watching her eyes go warm, then grow aroused. Jess was so easily moved. Willful. Fearless. *His.* "This means we're going to have *sixty* days together. Think you can handle that?"

She grinned. "In a heartbeat, sailor."

Yeah, she was a fierce warrior woman, no question. Logan met her smile with one of his own. "How about, at some point, we take a week, and we fly back to Wyoming? To meet my parents? I can teach you how to ride a horse even better. We have good saddles that don't put nails in your butt."

Laughter bubbled up out of her throat. "I NEVER want to be on another horse again, Logan Randall! I'll watch YOU ride. I'll bet your mother is great at canning, and I would love to trade recipes with her. Canning is something I love to do every Fall. I like eating organic."

Nodding, he gathered Jess back into his arms and she gladly came, snuggling and nuzzling happily against him. "My mother is a canner. But she also rides horses, herds cattle, and is a wrangler."

"I think I'll stick to the canning."

"Well," Logan warned her with a grin, "be prepared. My mother has been ragging on me for years to get remarried. She wants *grandkids.*"

Smothering a laugh, Jess said, "Who knows? By then, I just might be pregnant?" and she gave him a wistful look.

Shock, but a good kind of shock, rolled through Logan. He saw the yearning in Jess's eyes and heard it in her low voice. "You want a family?"

"Of course."

"We had a discussion about it once."

"I remember."

"I'm okay with it, Jess. But you have to seriously think through it because, as a SEAL, I'm gone three-fourths of every year. I won't be around much to change diapers or be a father."

Nodding, Jess said, "I already figured that out. We can wait, Logan. I'm all right with that, too. A child needs a mother *and* a father."

He took in a deep breath and his mouth became thinned. "That *would* be the sensible thing to do, but...the truth is, Jess..." Holding her tender gaze, he admitted, "I've got a lot of years in as a SEAL and honestly? My knees aren't going to take it much more. I've had two operations. I've had a lot of injuries to them, off and on over the years. It's rough, hard physical work, Jess."

"So," she said, sympathetic, "are you thinking of quitting at some time in the future?" She saw his eyes grow dark, knowing how much he loved being a SEAL. And he was the best at it, as far as she was concerned. For her to beg Logan to quit being a SEAL, she knew would not work in their favor, over the long run.

"Yeah, I was seriously thinking about it." Logan gave her a tender look. "My enlistment is up in sixteen months. That means I could continue being Stateside forever if I quit being a SEAL."

And out of danger. Jess kept the words to herself. Her heart beat a little harder. Excitement thrummed through her. Logan would be safe! She'd lied that she wouldn't worry much, not wanting to stand in the way of his love of being a SEAL; their careers were always on the front lines and, deep within her, was the terror that a bullet would find him, snuff out his precious life. She cleared her throat, giving him a hopeful look. "Then? We could be married sooner? Your parents and mine could be present for it? Maybe, if all this happens, we could think about me getting pregnant sooner?"

Nodding, Logan moved his hand across her rounded belly. Jess had wide hips. She'd easily carry a baby. And he knew how good a mother she would be, just from seeing her with the Afghan village kids. "That's kind of where I was going with all of this, but I needed to know how you felt about it, Jess. My parents have been wanting me to come home, to start taking over the ranch, getting married, having kids. You know how parents are?"

She raised an eyebrow, her lips curving. "Yes." She saw him grow concerned. "What's bothering you, Logan?"

Shrugging, "If I got out, I'd like to go home to Wyoming, Jess. But I don't know how you'd feel about that. My skills are being a wrangler. I grew up on a ranch. It's something I know well. I could start taking over the ranch duties from my parents so they could retire someday in the future. You and I, and our children, would then run it and own it. We could build my parents a retirement house on the property. I know they'd like that. My mother would love our children and babysit them if you had an outside job."

It was her turn to shrug. "You know what? I could get a job in construction anywhere I wanted, Logan. My parents might be sad about me leaving San Diego for Wyoming, but I'm okay with it. We could invite them to come up for visits whenever they wanted." She tilted her head, her voice low. "I love you. I want you happy, too." Because she knew Logan would always be an outdoorsman. A man of nature. Like she was a woman of nature. And then she gave him a mischievous grin. "Just don't you dare ask me to ride a horse."

A huge weight dissolved from Logan's shoulders. "I don't care if you never throw a leg over a horse again, Babe. I just want you happy, too."

"Logan, I would love to have your parents nearby. I'm sure, if we start having children at some point, they would love to play the doting grandparents. I like the idea of them being close."

He groaned. "My mother would be in heaven if she heard you saying these things."

She eased a hand across his chest. "Then, we sort of have a general roadmap we've made for ourselves. Something that makes us both happy?"

Logan couldn't believe how easily his future dreams for their lives was unfolding. Above everything, he wanted Jess happy. And the glow he saw in her face when speaking about children gripped his heart as nothing ever would. "We'll both be happy," he promised her, caressing her cheek, drowning in her radiant expression. "I think we need each of us to call our parents and give them the news. You okay with that?"

"Absolutely," she whispered. "More than okay with it. My parents wanted grandchildren, too. This is going to make them all happy."

"Then? Let's go take a shower together, get dressed, and go out to the living room and write down the plan, the dates when my enlistment is up, a date for when we'd like to get married. Since I'll remain Stateside to finish out my enlistment? We can get married a lot sooner, and that's what I want. Would you jump on board for that?"

She grinned. "In a heartbeat."

"Because of my seniority," Logan said, "there's a good chance they'll send me to San Diego, to Coronado to train recruits, or maybe to be an instructor there."

Her eyes widened. "Oh! That would be wonderful!" she said, joy flooding her. "My parents would love that, Logan. I know they'll love you from the moment they set eyes on you. You getting to know them is so important to me…," and she reached out, caressing his stubbly jaw, lost in the love she saw shining in his eyes for her alone.

"And maybe? This coming Christmas? We could fly my parents out from Wyoming, to stay with us in San Diego, and they'd get to meet your parents? How do you feel about that plan?"

"A dream come true," she whispered, kissing him on his mouth.

He slid his hand around her slender neck, holding her lips against his. "Then? Let's make this a reality, shall we, Babe? Having a life with you is way more important to me than being a SEAL. Life has given us something we probably *both* thought was impossible. There aren't many people who actually have their dreams come true." He kissed her long and deep.

As he left her soft, willing lips, drowning in her loving gaze, he rasped, "YOU are my dream come true. And I'm looking forward to our lives together. Forever."

THE END

Available from
Lindsay McKenna

Blue Turtle Publishing

SHADOW TEAM SERIES
Last Stand
Collateral Damage
No Quarter
Unforgettable
Hostile Territory
Shadow Target
Countermeasure

NON-SERIES BOOKS
Down Range (Reprint)
Dangerous Prey (Reprint)
Love Me Before Dawn (Reprint)
Point of Departure (Reprint)
Touch the Heavens (Reprint)

WOMEN OF GLORY SERIES
No Quarter Given (Reprint)
The Gauntlet (Reprint)
Under Fire (Reprint)

LOVE & GLORY SERIES
A Question of Honor, Book 1 (Reprint)
No Surrender, Book 2 (Reprint)
Return of a Hero, Book 3 (Reprint)
Dawn of Valor, Book 4 (Reprint)

LOVE & DANGER SERIES
Morgan's Son, Book 5 (Reprint)
Morgan's Wife, Book 6 (Reprint)
Morgan's Rescue, Book 7 (Reprint)
Morgan's Marriage, Book 8 (Reprint)

WARRIORS FOR THE LIGHT

Unforgiven, Book 1 (Reprint)
Dark Truth, Book 2 (Reprint)
The Quest, Book 3 (Reprint)
Reunion, Book 4 (Reprint)
The Adversary, Book 5 (Reprint)
Guardian, Book 6 (Reprint)

DELOS

Last Chance, prologue novella to Nowhere to Hide
Nowhere to Hide, Book 1
Tangled Pursuit, Book 2
Forged in Fire, Book 3
Broken Dreams, Book 4
Blind Sided, BN2
Secret Dream, B1B novella, epilogue to Nowhere to Hide
Hold On, Book 5
Hold Me, 5B1, sequel to Hold On
Unbound Pursuit, 2B1 novella, epilogue to Tangled Pursuit
Secrets, 2B2 novella, sequel to Unbound Pursuit, 2B1
Snowflake's Gift, Book 6
Never Enough, 3B1, novella, sequel to Forged in Fire
Dream of Me, 4B1, novella, sequel to Broken Dreams
Trapped, Book 7
Taking a Chance 7B1, novella, sequel to Trapped
The Hidden Heart, 7B2, novella, sequel to Taking A Chance
Boxcar Christmas, Book 8
Sanctuary, Book 9
Dangerous, Book 10
Redemption, 10B1, novella, sequel to Dangerous

Harlequin/HQN/Harlequin Romantic Suspense

SHADOW WARRIORS

Danger Close
Down Range
Risk Taker
Degree of Risk
Breaking Point
Never Surrender

Zone of Fire
Taking Fire
On Fire
Running Fire

THE WYOMING SERIES
Shadows From The Past
Deadly Identity
Deadly Silence
The Last Cowboy
The Wrangler
The Defender
The Loner
High Country Rebel
Wolf Haven
Night Hawk
Out Rider

Kensington

SILVER CREEK SERIES
Silver Creek Fire
Courage Under Fire

WIND RIVER VALLEY SERIES
Wind River Wrangler
Wind River Rancher
Wind River Cowboy
Christmas with my Cowboy
Wrangler's Challenge
Lone Rider
Wind River Lawman
Kassie's Cowboy
Home to Wind River
Western Weddings: Wind River Wedding
Wind River Protector
Wind River Undercover

Everything Lindsay McKenna

My website is dedicated to all my series. There are articles on characters, my publishing schedule, and information about each book written by me. You can also learn more about my newsletter, which covers my upcoming books, publishing schedule, giveaways, exclusive cover peeks and more.

lindsaymckenna.com

www.ingramcontent.com/pod-product-compliance
Lightning Source LLC
Chambersburg PA
CBHW071502170626
46811CB00007B/2682